THE LIONESS IN BLOOM

VOICES FROM ASIA

THE LIONESS
IN BLOOM

MODERN THAI
FICTION ABOUT WOMEN

TRANSLATED, EDITED,
AND WITH AN INTRODUCTION
BY SUSAN FULOP KEPNER

University of California Press
Berkeley · Los Angeles · London

University of California Press
Berkeley and Los Angeles, California

University of California Press, Ltd.
London, England

© 1996 by The Regents of the University of California

Library of Congress Cataloging-in-Publication Data

The Lioness in bloom : modern Thai fiction about women / translated,
    edited, and with an introduction by Susan Fulop Kepner.
        p.   cm. — (Voices from Asia ; 9)
    Includes bibliographical references and index.
    ISBN 0-520-08902-2 (alk. paper). — ISBN 0-520-08903-0 (pbk. :
alk. paper)
        1. Short stories, Thai—Translations into English.   2. Thai
fiction—20th century—Translations into English.   3. Women in
literature.   I. Kepner, Susan Fulop, 1941-   .   II. Series.
PL4208.L56   1996
895.9'130 108352042—dc20   95-52953
                                                                                        CIP

Printed in the United States of America

9 8 7 6 5 4 3 2 1

The paper used in this publication meets the minimum
requirements of American National Standard for Information Sciences—Permanence of Paper for Printed Library
Materials, ANSI Z39.48-1984.

To
Herbert P. Phillips
Professor Emeritus of Anthropology
University of California, Berkeley

What is like to be Thai women?

Contents

Preface

This anthology focuses on the lives of Thai women during the twentieth century as they are reflected in short stories and novels. In the main, it is intended for the nonspecialist, although I hope that readers with an interest in Thai literature will be glad to find translations of works they may not have had the time or opportunity to read before.

The most important consideration in making the selections has been *range;* for no single representative Thai woman may be assembled from fragments of fiction. There are only individuals, in life as in literature, and it is a diverse procession of fictional women indeed that walks through these pages: young, middle-aged, and old; urban, suburban, and rural; wealthy, middle class, and desperately poor; joyous, resigned, or despairing. In the short stories and excerpts that follow, each woman has a distinct personality and a history; she is not a type or a stock character.

Not every writer whose work is included here is famous, and some well-known and highly respected authors do not appear for reasons that have nothing to do with their importance in Thai literature or the quality of their work. In some cases I have decided not to include a short story or novel excerpt because of its similarity to an even more interesting work on the same subject. I have included two short stories by one author, Sri Dao Ruang, because they differ so much and because each is important. One, "Sai-roong's Dream of Love," uses humor to explore the generally taboo subject of women's sexual fantasies; the other, "Matsii," is an urban tragedy in which Buddhist beliefs are alluded to in a revisionist manner that has caused controversy.

I have reluctantly set aside some fine stories because I thought they could just as well have been set in another country while simultaneously attempting, with what success the reader may decide, to elude the dread beasts of essentialism and exoticism, those banes of the translator who works with an Asian language.

Another feature of the selection process concerned literary quality.

If a selection includes a portrayal of a woman's life that is interesting in terms of sheer information but is, in my opinion, poorly written, awkwardly structured, or unconvincing, I set it aside. Upon what criteria could I, a foreigner and non-native speaker, make such judgments? First, I sought the opinions of many Thai readers, including critics and other people who are active in the literary community. These generous people made a first cut, providing me with dozens of stories and suggestions about novels. I read them all, and then I made the second cut. The eventual, final step was to discover how each of the potentially final selections, in translation, would appear to non-Thai educated readers who are not Thai specialists. Would they find a particular story or novel excerpt well conceived, well told, and compelling? The eventual result of all this is the body of work included here: sixteen works written over a period of sixty years, including eleven short stories and excerpts from five novels.

Originally, I planned to limit the anthology to works written by women; however, it soon became apparent that such a limitation would be counterproductive. For example, it would mean the loss of the male writer Wat Wanlayankul's poignant short story "Deep in the Heart of a Mother." I was reminded, as I read it, of Florida Scott Maxwell's wistful words, "No matter how old a mother is she watches her middle-aged children for signs of improvement."[1] It is difficult to imagine a reader feeling anything but gratitude for the privilege of getting to know Wat's heroine, a remarkable old woman whose children have turned out disappointments, but whom she loves no less for that, deep in her heart. If any selection in this anthology can be said to be universal and still distinctly Thai in terms of its setting and cultural references, it is this one.

The selections were also made with an eye to the balance between differing points of view among Thai writers about the realities of women's lives in the twentieth century. Writers tend to be idealists, and Thai writers are no exception; and those who paint the most dismal pictures are not infrequently the most idealistic of all. It would be a simple task to assemble a collection of works depicting a culture apparently dominated by political and moral corruption, prostitution, the loss of religious values, adoption of the worst of the West, and gen-

---

1. Florida Scott Maxwell, *The Measure of My Days* (New York: Alfred A. Knopf, 1968), 16.

eralized hopelessness. In fact, if Thailand is not really the land of smiles, as it has sometimes been called, nor is it the land of sorrows. Therefore, I have sought not only selections that explore the darker side of Thai society, including problems that affect women in particular (such as domestic abuse), but also selections that realistically portray contented people, and even a few that illustrate the Thai sense of literary humor, which makes exquisite use of irony, absurdity, and, occasionally, an engaging silliness.

After I have made this point, it may seem contradictory to state that, after all, the balance of selections in this anthology does tip somewhat toward the negative. To do otherwise would be to misrepresent the truth, which is that most of the finest novels and short stories written in Thailand during the twentieth century focus on what their creators have considered wrong, undesirable, or simply disappointing about Thai society and the people who shape it, attempt to conform to it, or simply endure it. This focus has naturally encompassed the fictional depiction of the lives of Thai women.

The decision to make range the guiding principle of this anthology—fiction representing women of many ages, in many locations, and in all social classes, over a period of seven decades—has one clearly negative result: the impossibility of assembling the selections in any truly satisfactory order.

Originally, I planned to organize them on the basis of works about mothers, wives and lovers, daughters, friends, and something I vaguely thought of as women at work. This organization seemed reasonable until I started reading and discovered the problem of overlap. A story about a mother necessarily involves a daughter or son; and a story about a wife might well include her mother. After an unsatisfactory experiment with chronological order, I settled on something close to my original vision: the stories and novel excerpts are placed in sections labeled "Mothers," "Wives and Lovers," and "Daughters." Overlap remains.

Because the selections vary so much—from the rather formal literature of the 1930s to the comparatively casual, conversational tone of contemporary short stories, and from high comedy to real tragedy —a brief line or two precedes each selection, so that the reader will have a fair idea of what to expect. Following each selection is a biographical sketch of the author, the length and nature of which depends upon what is known about the individual, and the extent and importance of his or her writings. This is followed by an explanation of the rationale for including this particular work in the anthology. Although I am aware that some readers will feel that this kind of information belongs in an introduction, I feel that it makes more sense for the reader to encounter it directly after each short story or excerpt, when characters, events, and ideas—the "world of the tale"—are still fresh in his or her mind.

Acknowledgments

I am thankful for the many colleagues and friends whose assistance, advice, and enthusiasm enabled me to turn a cherished idea into a book. I wish to express my particular gratitude to Anchalee Vivathanachai (Anchan), Anong Lertrakskun, Chamaiporn Sangkrajang (Pailin Rungrat), Chatsumarn Kabilsingh, Chetana Nagavajara, Duangmon Chitchamnong, Nitaya Masavisut, Pariyachat Bear, Somporn Varnado, Sukanya Cholasueks (Krisna Asoksin), Supa Sirising (Botan), Wanna Sawadsee (Sri Dao Ruang), Vinita Dithiiyon (V. Vinicchayakul), and Wibha Kongkanan.

For their encouragement and above all their patience, I wish to thank Sheila Levine, Erika Búky, and Rachel Berchten at The University of California Press, my agent and friend Martha Casselman, and Betsey Scheiner. I also wish to thank friends who read, criticized, and made suggestions about the selections, especially Jane Timberlake and Marjorie Fletcher. Finally, I should like to thank my husband, Chuck Kepner, careful reader and kind editor.

Notes on Transliteration

Spoken Thai is a member of the Sino-Tibetan group of languages. The ancestors of most of the people who now live in Thailand migrated from southern China during the seventh and eighth centuries B.E. (Buddhist era), along with other Tai peoples, including the Lao (whose language remains very similar to Thai). Written Thai was developed during the thirteenth century, C.E., and is one of many offshoots of the Devanagari writing system, which originated in India. The modern Thai alphabet contains forty consonants and twenty-four vowels, and the spoken language uses five tones (middle, high, low, rising, and falling).[1] This means that two or more words may be spelled the same but have entirely different meanings because they are pronounced with different tones. For example, the word *maa* means "to come" when it is pronounced with a level tone, but it means "horse" when pronounced with a high tone, *máa;* and it means "dog" when pronounced with a rising tone, *mǎa*. The non-Thai-speaking reader may be pleased to learn that these interesting facts are of no consequence at all in terms of reading and understanding the selections in this anthology.

TRANSLITERATION

The representation of Thai words in English presents several problems. First, no system of transliteration is fully adequate to convey actual pronunciation. Second, the systems of transliteration used by linguists are seldom comprehensible to the general reader of fiction, for example, the representation of the vowel sound "a" as in *hat* using the symbol ε, or the vowel sound "aw" as in *lawn* using the symbol $\jmath$. I have tried to achieve an acceptable compromise by using in the selections an accessible transliteration of Thai words for the nonlinguistically oriented, and in the introduction, footnotes, and biograph-

---

1.   This describes the central Thai dialect, which is taught in schools throughout the nation; there are regional tonal variations.

ical sketches—where its use seems warranted—a transliteration based upon the system developed by Mary Haas and refined by J. Marvin Brown, for example, "the poetic epic *Khun Chang Khun Phaen*, or *Khun Cháang Khun Phɛɛn*." Where the latter, phonetic system of transliteration is used, pronunciation follows these rules:

Transliterated Thai Vowel	Approximate Pronunciation
a / aa	ah / aaaah
i / ii	hit / heat
u / uu	put / pool
ʉ / ʉʉ	no corresponding vowel in English; it is similar to German *ü* and has a short and long version, like the other simple Thai vowels
e / ee	hay / longer version of same vowel sound
ə / əə	her / longer version of same vowel sound
ɛ / ɛɛ	hat / longer version of same vowel sound
o / oo	rope / longer version of same vowel sound
ɔ / ɔɔ	lawn / longer version of same vowel sound

Dipthongs

ua	truant
ia	idea
ʉa	combines *ʉ* (see above) with *a*

Transliterated Thai Consonant	
b	*b* as in *bat*
p	*pb* as in *top boy*
ph	*p* as in *pen*
k	hard *g* as in *go*
kh	*k* as in *keep*
d	*d* as in *door*
t	*td* as in *hot dog*
th	*t* as in *top*
ng	*ng* as in *sing* (*ng* is also used as an initial consonant, as in the word *nguu*, "snake")

Consonants that do not appear above (*m, n, s,* and so on) may be assumed to have the same pronunciation in Thai that they have in English.

Thai script is included in the bibliography for the convenience of those who read Thai and will find it helpful in tracking down a particular book or article. The English spellings of authors' names reflect their own preference if it is known; otherwise, I have used the spelling that seems most reasonable to me.

Introduction

Regally mounted upon her own war elephant, the proud queen
rides forward into battle beside her king.
　　　　　　　　　　　　　　　　　　　　　—Traiphumikkatha

TRADITIONAL PERCEPTIONS
OF THE THAI WOMAN

This early depiction of the ideal Thai woman is from the *Traiphu-mikkatha*, a masterpiece of Thai Buddhist literature composed during the reign of King Thammaracha Lithai, in the early Sukhothai period (1239–1377). Another description of an admirable woman from the same work shows her to be more than proud and courageous: "She is neither tall nor short . . . dear and precious to everyone. . . . Her skin is as soft as cotton which has been fluffed a hundred times and moistened in the clear oil from the joint of a yak. When [the King's] body is cool, her body will be warm; when his body is hot, hers will be cool. . . . Whenever she speaks or laughs, her breath is scented, like blooming lotuses."[1]

Four centuries later, during the Ayuthya period (1350–1767), the ideal woman, far from mounting a war elephant of her own, was compared to the elephant's hind legs, indispensable but obviously created to follow.

These perceptions of woman—brave and courageous, yet fragrant and lovely; intelligent, yet willingly subordinate and biddable—are reflected in Thai literature to this day, often quite consciously. In "A Pot That Scouring Will Not Save," a 1985 short story by Anchan that is included in this anthology, a woman recalls her mother's advice: "'The woman must be like the hind legs of the elephant . . . the husband like the front legs, which, though they must always lead, cannot move the elephant by themselves.' And: 'A woman must be like a reed, my daughter. In the dark of night, it may be whipped by the

---

1. National Identity Board, *Women in Thai Literature: Book 1* (Bangkok: Office of the Prime Minister, 1987), 19–29 (hereafter cited as *WTL*). The *Traiphumikkatha* is more fully described in Klaus Wenk, *Thai Literature: An Introduction* (Bangkok: White Lotus, 1995).

fiercest storm, yet we always find it the next morning, swaying in the breeze, glistening with dew drops, its gentle strength a miracle.'"

During the Ayuthya period, Thai society was divided by a rigid class system that extended to gender: inferiors served superiors; women served parents, husbands, and children; sisters served brothers.[2] But the practice of corvée labor effected a contradiction in this hierarchical system, for when men were away from home for months at a time, working on construction projects or participating in military campaigns, women became the de facto heads of households. Then, as now, most Thai women were responsible for handling family finances, a responsibility that extended to the management of family-run businesses and sometimes to work outside the home.

Today, many Thai women attain the same educational levels as their brothers, although preference is usually given to sons if a choice must be made for economic reasons. Middle- and upper-class women practice law, own and manage banks and businesses, and serve at high levels of government. For decades the percentage of Thai physicians who are women has been higher than in the United States. One of the nation's largest universities, Silpakorn, is led by a woman as of this writing, Chaisri Sri-arun. Women are at least as numerous as men in nearly all university faculties and frequently serve as department heads. Government scholarships and grants for study abroad are awarded strictly on the basis of merit, regardless of gender. I have noticed over the years that Thai women who have gone abroad on government scholarships tend to continue their relationships with other women who have had this experience. Decades later, they still are meeting for lunch, going on trips, and so on; there is no question that this "old girl" network is socially and also professionally beneficial.

Despite these significant legal, social, and professional gains, Thai women must contend with the ideal image of the dutiful daughter, the lovely, chaste and loyal wife, and the self-sacrificing and devoted mother. For women who work outside the home, personal time is nonexistent. Doing things for other people is so important a value in Thai life, especially for women, that any time left over is immediately reassigned to such activities as visits to elderly relatives or attendance

---

2. For the sake of convenience, the word *Thai* will be generally used, although the name of the country was officially changed from Siam to Thailand only in 1939.

at funeral rites, which are of great importance.[3] The "superwoman" problem that is written about in the West is magnified in Thai society. Moreover, the emphasis on physical beauty and on beautiful behavior is unabating, continuing to reflect the words of Khunying Kirati, the heroine of a 1937 novel who declared that "women are born to decorate the earth."[4] In recent years, the standards of beauty have become ever more difficult to achieve. Craig J. Reynolds writes: "The marketing of female Thai beauty in the global consumer culture has led to a new ideal of beauty, a paragon of regional and global personhood. Contestants in the beauty pageants often undergo cosmetic surgery to appear more Eurasian, and the Eurasian face is popular on Thai television. Advertisements in the glossy magazines show a distinct preference for male and female models who are light-skinned with Eurasian features, a kind of pan-Asian model of beauty that suits the exporters of Thai products to Asian markets."[5]

One has only to glance at the covers of Thai women's magazines to verify Reynolds's observation. I believe that the most important, although not the only, reason for the "whiter is better" criterion for beauty, is that while poor women toil in the fields and are dark, wealthy women are protected from the sun and therefore are pale by comparison. In addition, there is no question that the "Eurasian" ideal of beauty (never "Amerasian," which connotes the GI babies of the 1960s and 1970s) is a legacy of the years between approximately 1850 and 1925, when Thailand was struggling to avoid colonization by either England or France. The Thai kings who reigned during these years and their advisers worked hard to identify themselves and their nation with the European conquerers rather than with their own vanquished neighbors.[6] It is important to remember that in Thailand, the Victorian era is now recalled as an exciting time during which Siamese aristocrats traveled to Europe, met the members of European royal families *as equals,* studied in universities, and brought back things that

---

3. Depending upon the social class of the individual who has died, many funeral rites may take place before the actual cremation, which may occur months or even a year or more after death.

4. An excerpt of this novel, Sri Burapha's *Behind the Painting,* is included in this work.

5. Craig J. Reynolds, "Predicaments of Modern Thai History," *South East Asian Research* 2, no. 1 (March 1994): 75.

6. This is one of the major contentions of Thongchai Winichakul's *Siam Mapped: A History of the Geo-Body of a Nation* (Honolulu: University of Hawaii Press, 1994).

appealed to them, such as Victorian furniture, art, fashions, and ideas about literature. The typical photograph of a Thai noblewoman at the turn of the century shows her proudly dressed in a linen blouse with leg-of-mutton sleeves, her luxuriant dark hair stylishly poufed. Gone are the two-inch-long thatch of hair, the betel-blackened polished teeth, and the turmeric-yellowed skin that were perceived as beautiful during the previous several reigns.

During the past few years, admiration of King Chulalongkorn (Rama V, r. 1868–1910) and his reign in general has grown to such an extent that his photograph now hangs on the wall of nearly every store, bank, and noodle shop in the kingdom. Portraits and photographs of Queen Saovapha and of the two sons who succeeded him on the throne, Vachiravudh (Rama VI) and Prachatipok (Rama VII), also are popular.[7]

At the end of the twentieth century, the Eurasian/Victorian (and Edwardian) look is very popular for cover illustrations of books about Thai women, including two works published by the Office of the Prime Minister, in English: *Women in Thai Literature: Book 1* and *Thai Women*, a handsome book commemorating the 1992 Fifth Cycle Birthday of Queen Sirikit.[8] The overall objective of the latter book, aside from celebrating the queen's birthday and the major events of her life, is to celebrate the Thai woman, her qualities and her achievements, and especially her role in the life of the Thai nation. The illustration on the cover is a pastel rendering of a pale young woman in a modified nineteenth-century costume. But aside from her dark hair and something about the eyes that vaguely suggests Asian origins, she could be European.[9]

7.   See appendix, "Kings of the Chakri Dynasty." In accordance with general practice, the first three kings of the Chakri dynasty, which was founded in 1782, will be referred to as Rama I, Rama II, and Rama III; the subsequent six kings will be identified by parts of their names: King Mongkut, King Chulalongkorn, King Vachiravudh, King Prachatipok, King Ananda Mahidol, and King Phumipol Adulyadej. King Vachiravudh (Rama VI, r. 1910–25) instituted the use of the "Rama" titles, because he believed that the lengthy Siamese names were too difficult for Western foreigners. The next king, his brother Prachatipok, refused to be known as "Rama VII"; but the practice continued, no doubt because it was useful.

8.   A cycle consists of twelve years. The fifth cycle birthday, celebrating sixty years of life, has traditionally been an important celebration since in the past few people lived to celebrate the sixth cycle at seventy-two.

9.   An interesting, relevant discussion of the significance of cover art appears in Indira Karamcheti's "Cover Stories," *The Women's Review of Books*, vol. 12, no. 4 (January 1994): 20–21.

The male is head of the household.

Such contradictory perceptions and expectations of Thai women are at the heart of this anthology and are reflected in its title. While I was translating the selections and wondering what sort of title could reflect so vast a range of short stories and novel excerpts, I asked a number of Thai women to complete the sentence, "A woman should be . . ." By far, the most common answer was "like a flower," even if the respondent's opinion of such a depiction was decidedly negative. "On the other hand," one young woman said, "there is also the image of the lioness stalking the land, protecting her family. This is a dilemma, for some of us. Can one woman be both a *lioness*, who is active and strong, and a *flower*, which doesn't go anywhere and is simply beautiful? Can a woman be a flower that roars or a lioness that blooms?"

WOMEN IN CLASSICAL THAI LITERATURE: TWENTIETH-CENTURY REFLECTIONS

Although much has been written by Thais and by foreign observers and scholars about the subordinate status of women during the Ayuthya period, female characters in poetic epics of that era are at least as complex and as interesting as women in modern and contemporary fiction. Indeed, female characters in early Thai literature are almost sybaritic by comparison with their twentieth-century counterparts. Until recently, women in Thai short stories and novels have had to live up to the Victorian conventions upon which modern Thai fiction was built; and to be accurate, it is only the more daring writers who have attempted to challenge the status quo. In the famous Ayuthya era epic poem *Lilit Phra Law*, or *Lĭlĭt Phrá Lɔɔ* (A poem about Phra Law), two princesses fall in love with the same young king, beguile him with their charms, and cheerfully share his favors until disaster strikes them all.[10] According to the authors of *Women in Thai Literature*, in *Lilit Phra Law* the reader sees "how the high-born ladies use their feminine guiles to get the man of their desire without jeopardizing the behavioural standards expected of women of their status." The perceived strength of women also is displayed in this story

---

10.   The titles of *Lĭlĭt Phrá Lɔɔ* and other well-known Thai literary works are given their most frequently used English spellings, followed by phonetic spellings consistent with references to other Thai titles in this work.

through the "demonstrat[ion of] royal valour and the determination of the two princesses who stand beside the man they love until death . . . which is the climax of the romance."[11]

Phra Law also has a loyal and uncomplaining wife with whom he shares a tender scene before leaving her for the amorous princesses:

216

"Fevered and sad to part with my love,
Wrong may I be to leave love for love.
Should I remain, flames would consume my heart,
Leave you I must but shall soon return."

217

"If you go hence and consort with the two?
Would you ever come back to me?
Think not, hope not that they would set you free,
For they will imprison you in their embrace."

218

"Not from hate do I forsake you.
No distance can sever our love.
A lotus leaves a gossamer thread when plucked,
Fret not for I ne'er will forget my dear beloved."[12]

Each female character in this famous and beloved poem—whether wife, lover, or mother—is portrayed as a complex individual with plausible motives. In the 1960s, the woman writer Suwanee Sukhontha created female characters who are strikingly reminiscent of the princesses of *Lilit Phra Law*—led by their sexual desires, knowingly heading for disaster, and willing to take their chances. But Thai critics and readers do not typically look for such echoes of their own literary tradition when considering contemporary fiction, and so Suwanee's writing has either been compared with Western models or dismissed as "autobiographical." An interesting project would be an examination of Suwanee's work in the light of classical Thai works, with which this well-educated author was certainly familiar.

The epic poem *Khun Chang Khun Phaen,* or *Khun Cháang Khun Phɛɛn,*

---

11. National Identity Board, *WTL,* 63.
12. Ibid., 71.

had its origin sometime during the Ayuthya period but was substantially revised and polished during the first two reigns of the Chakri dynasty by the poet Sunthon Phu (1786–1855). In this poem, two men, Khun Chang and Khun Phaen, are rivals in love, both desirous of the lovely Wanthong. Although Khun Chang is wealthy, he is homely, bald, uncouth, and fat, while Khun Phaen, who was born poor, has become a glorious military hero who also is handsome, knowledgeable about women, and versed in the magic arts. Wanthong is never able to make a clear and final choice between these two men; she desires Khun Phaen, but she is fond of Khun Chang and pities him: "How miserable it is to have been born a woman! . . . I have been punished with . . . sufferings because I was in no control of my wavering heart. It is a pity that such a fickle heart should be housed in so lovely a body. Blessed with unsurpassed beauty and womanly skills, how could I sink so low?"[13]

Finally, Wanthong is forced to make a choice: "Khun Chang appealed to the King who commanded Wanthong to choose who [*sic*] she would like to live with: Khun Phaen, Khun Chang or Chamuen Wai, her son. She was reluctant to choose and evaded the issue by asking the King to decide for her. Enraged by her seemingly insatiable promiscuity, the King ordered her executed."[14]

Several elements of Wanthong's tragic life and death are routinely reflected in Thai novels, short stories, films, and television dramas focused on women's lives. Three of these elements are: (1) a woman's consciousness of the misery she experiences and feels as the natural and inescapable result of being born female; (2) her desire to please everyone she loves, often to her own detriment; and (3) her frank acceptance of her own beauty and of its negative effects on her life.

Phra Aphaimani, or *Phrá Aphaymanii,* is an eighteenth-century masterpiece composed by Sunthon Phu. Although Phra Aphaimani is the hero and leading character, practically all of the female characters are stronger and more resourceful than he is. He is abducted by a sea ogress, rescued by a mermaid, and loves a woman who not only refuses him but also runs away to become a nun. He relies entirely upon the advice of his female counselor and finally becomes king, whereupon his queen gives orders and leads soldiers into battle.

13. Ibid., 140.
14. Ibid., 147.

Despite all, he remains the hero of the story and is desired by women for his grace and beauty.

One of the many interesting women in *Phra Aphaimani* is the brilliant Nang Wali, who has been damned with faint praise as "the first woman in public service." "There was a thirty-four year old spinster named Wali who had a swarthy complexion. She was so ugly that not a man bothered to look at her. . . . She said to the king, 'I have not a bit of doubt about my ugly appearance, but knowledge, like an unblemished diamond, is my spiritual beauty. Among your host of beautiful concubines, you can never find as learned a one as I.'"[15]

Nang Wali is the prototype of what I shall call the "authentic nonideal" female character in Thai literature. She is not and can never be an ideal (beautiful, subservient, graceful) Thai woman, but she is a kind of woman whom every woman either knows or is. Some of the best examples of such characters in modern fiction are found in the work of the author and educator M. L. Boonlua Kunchon Thepyasuwan (1911–82), who wrote fiction under her first name, "Boonlua."[16]

The authentic non-ideal woman in Boonlua's work is often the heroine's best friend: a well-bred, intelligent, educated, outspoken person who is a bit sharp-tongued and very good-hearted. She also is plain and unlikely to marry. One such character is Adcharaa, in the short story "*Sanay jawak*," or "Sanàay jàwàk."[17] The virtually untranslatable title, which literally means "[the] charm [of the] ladle," refers to the housekeeping and cooking ability of the ideal Thai woman. The main female character in the story, a bride named Phachongchid, is a traditionally raised woman who is frustrated because of her inability to please her foreign-educated husband. She has been taught never to argue with a man and to do everything possible to provide a gracious, beautiful home, the center of which is the exquisitely set dinner table laden with perfectly prepared food. Her new husband is bored with these limitations. If Phachongchid is the ideal Thai woman, her friend Adcharaa falls sadly short. Herbert P. Phillips writes, "[Adcharaa is a] character who exists only as an occasional verbal allusion. . . . She

15.   Ibid., 127–28.
16.   "M. L." is the abbreviation of *mɔ̀ɔm lǔang*, a title indicating that one is the great-grandchild of a king; Boonlua was her given name, Kunchon her family name, and Thepyasuwan her married name.
17.   The original Thai version of this short story is included in a collection of Boonlua's short stories entitled *Chàak nɨ̀ng nay chiiwít* (approximately, "act one in life"; the stories are about problems encountered by young adults).

is an unmarried, physically unattractive, old classmate of the heroine [and] is going overseas for an advanced degree." Although her role in the story is small, I would say that Adcharaa is far more than "an occasional verbal allusion." She is a woman very like M. L. Boonlua, who went abroad to earn a master's degree at forty and was nearly fifty when she married. That the ghost of Nang Wali is alive and well between the covers of Boonlua's books is particularly fitting, for Boonlua was not only an important modern fiction writer but also a scholar and teacher of classical Thai literature who was well acquainted with Sunthon Phu, *Phra Aphaimani,* and Nang Wali.

PRE–TWENTIETH-CENTURY WOMEN WRITERS

Intriguing female characters abound in classical Thai literature, but there are few records of women writing before the twentieth century. Nevertheless, the fact that the contributions of a few woman writers are not only acknowledged but also respected suggests that there may well have been other women who wrote, but whose contributions were not recorded. Since the revision of dramas performed at court was a continual process and since women performed all the parts within the inner precincts of the palace, it is almost certain that they had a hand in these revisions. Two daughters of King Borommakot (r. 1733–58), Chao Faa Kunthon and Chao Faa Mongkut, were recorded as contributing excellent verses to the drama *Inao,* but nothing else is known of them.

Another pair of sisters, Khun Phum and Khun Suwan, ladies at court during the final years of the reign of King Rama III (1824–51) and the early years of the reign of King Mongkut (Rama IV, 1851–68), may fairly be considered the first important Thai women authors. Khun Phum was a competent poet, but Khun Suwan was truly brilliant. During the reign of King Chulalongkorn, Prince Damrong Rajanupap, a great scholar who was the king's brother and chief adviser, wrote an essay in which he asserts that Khun Suwan was insane, an opinion accepted until the middle of the twentieth century when literary scholars took another look and found not insanity but true genius.

According to Wibha Kongkanan, professor of Thai literature at Silpakorn University, in Nakhon Pathom, Khun Suwan's psychological insights about life at court, her subtle use of imagery, and her sheer mastery of poetic forms place her not only among her male contemporaries but far ahead of most. Khun Suwan's most important works are two unfinished, satirical poetic dramas entitled *Phra Malethethai*,[18] or *Phrá Malĕethĕethǎy* (Prince Malethethai) and *Unarut roi ruang*, or *Unarút rɔ́ɔy rûang* (literally, "the hundred tales of Unarut").[19] The character Phra Malethethai was invented by Khun Suwan; "Unarut" is the name of a famous hero in Thai literature. The obvious purpose of both works is to entertain, and many Thais love to sing excerpts from them, as Western opera enthusiasts sing favorite arias. These dramatic works were not written to be staged but to be recited in a private setting.

In *Phra Malethethai*, the prince, on a forest tour, awakens in the night to find a beautiful woman lying asleep at his side. He admires her body, awakens her, woos her, and finds her willing, and they make love. Neither of them knows that the god Indra has taken the woman from her bedchamber and put her by the prince's side. Although the story, theme, plot, and characters are conventional, the concept of a woman being spirited away in her sleep to meet a man, to love and be loved, is anything but conventional. *Phra Malethethai* is a female fantasy of sexual adventure and escape from repression; the intervention of the god Indra absolves her of responsibility. The name of this heroine, "Talaeng-gaeng," or *Talɛɛngkɛɛng*, can be literally translated as "the place where the prisoner is to be executed," by which Khun Suwan suggests that a woman's safe, chaste bedchamber is a prison.

The other famous work by Khun Suwan, *Unarut roi ruang*, is important for somewhat different reasons. First, it makes plain the fact that Khun Suwan had read widely, in a society in which no public education existed. Whatever knowledge she had of literature must have been gained in her home or at court. *Unarot roi ruang* reflects a profound knowledge of the classical dramas, preserving several works of Thai imaginative literature while developing a new style, the medley. The tale is filled with characters from Thai masterpieces and several minor works in the poetic tradition, but these charac-

18.   *Phra* means "monk," and is also used as a prefix for many religious and royal proper names.
19.   Wibha Kongkanan, letter to author, October 1, 1995.

ters are amusingly re-created. It is a challenge to the reader to identify not only the characters but also the linguistic tricks Khun Suwan uses, tricks grounded in the Pali and Sanskrit elements of Thai grammar. In addition, she invented an unconventional system for use within the *klon*, or *klɔɔn*, verse form she used, in which each line contains seven to nine syllables. A combination of meaningful and meaningless words might share a given line, or a whole line of meaningful words might be followed by a line that appears completely nonsensical. Careful readings by scholars have untangled this puzzle of words to find a phenomenal cleverness with poetic language.

Because sexual desire was considered to be a delicate subject and because Khun Suwan was determined to write about it anyway, she devised elaborate linguistic and stylistic strategies. It is possible that she encouraged the idea that she was insane to protect herself, for a work composed by a madwoman could be overlooked and her position at court preserved. Wibha suggests that the complexity of *Unarut roi ruang* may explain why it has been so steadfastly ignored by scholars, even though it has been available since Khun Suwan wrote it: "Some of the male scholars probably know that their knowledge about Thai literature is limited, and is clearly inferior to a woman writer of the old days."[20]

In his 1995 book *Thai Literature: An Introduction*, Klaus Wenk makes no mention at all of the prolific and innovative Khun Suwan but notes that her sister Khun Phum was "the first Thai poetess. . . . [She] appears to have been a person with a positive attitude towards life and moral values. . . . Nevertheless, she [indicates that she] regrets 'being a woman' and in the life to come she would like to be 'a handsome man.' It follows that this resolute lady Khun Phum does not stand for the ideas and aims of the feminist movement."[21] On the other hand, perhaps Khun Phum's expressed desires to return in a future life as "a handsome man" suggests something of her notorious sister's caustic style and stealthy ways.

When the new campus of Silpakorn University opened in Nakhon Pathom in 1968, Khun Suwan was chosen as one of four Thai authors to be studied by all freshmen majoring in liberal arts. The other three

---

20. Wibha Kongkanan, conversation with author, July 15, 1995.
21. Wenk, *Thai Literature*, 64.

authors were modern: two men, M. R. Kukrit Pramoj and Ajin Banjapan, and the contemporary woman novelist Krisna Asoksin. Studying these authors together represented a significant and controversial
departure from customary ways of teaching Thai literature. In general,
the word *wannakodi* denotes classical poetry and drama, and is distinct
from *wannakaam,* which denotes modern, Western-style short stories
and novels.[22] When students in Silpakorn's new program were encouraged to compare Khun Suwan's crafty court ladies of the nineteenth
century with the scheming society matrons of Krisna's mid-twentieth-
century popular novels, not all faculty members were pleased.

In view of the fact that most of Khun Suwan's work was considered incomprehensible during her lifetime, proof of insanity until less
than thirty years ago, and cause for contention when it finally was
taught in a university in the late 1960s, it is ironic that her work is now
cited to exemplify Thai women writers' opportunities, as in this remark by Mattani Rutnin: "[Khun Suwan's] satire on lesbianism [at]
court . . . is evidence of Thai women's freedom of expression and critical minds which have led to their continuing success in the world of
Thai literature from the early history of Siam to the present."[23]

FICTION

The Early Modern Period

The first recognizably modern Thai short stories and novels were written during the late nineteenth and early twentieth centuries by men
who had been sent to Europe for a university education, and who returned to Siam eager to apply Western literary forms to Siamese subjects. It is generally agreed that the first complete Thai novel is a much-
altered version of an English novel by Marie Corelli, *Vendetta! or, the
Story of One Forgotten.*[24] Phraya Surintharacha, a Thai aristocrat studying in England, was so taken with Corelli's book that he wrote a

---

22.   According to Wibha, a contemporary poetic drama would be classified as *wannakodi,* not *wannakaam,* if it strictly follows a traditional form and contains characters
and content considered by literary scholars to meet classical requirements and standards.

23.   Mattani Rutnin, *Modern Thai Literature: The Process of Modernization and the
Transformation of Values* (Bangkok: Thammasat University Press, 1988), 12.

24.   Reprint, London: Methuen, 1979.

Siamized version of it entitled *Khwaam phayabaat*, or *Khwaam phàyàbàat* (Revenge).[25] In the story, a grief-stricken man recounts his tragedy: after killing his faithless wife and her presumed lover, he was forced to flee—in Corelli's novel, to South America; in Phraya Surintharacha's, to Siam. *Khwaam phayabaat* was serialized in the magazine *Lak witaya* in 1902, and subsequently published as a book. The great success of the work prompted a cheerful parody entitled *Khwaam may phayabaat*, or *Khwaam mây phayabàat* (*No* revenge), by Khru Liam.

The practice of translating or creating versions of Western novels continued until the middle of the 1920s; favorite authors included O. Henry, H. Rider Haggard, and Sir Arthur Conan Doyle. It should be noted that translations of Western (and Chinese) works have continued to be popular to the present day, and that translations tend to be loose, reflecting the translators' beliefs about what Thai readers will or will not like. Translations of literature from other languages into Thai also reflect common standards of decency; for example, sexually explicit passages are almost always missing from the Thai version. When I have asked translators how they justify these expurgations, the usual response is that such passages are "not necessary" or "might be read by young people."

King Vachiravudh (Rama VI, r. 1910–25), who was educated in England and graduated from Sandhurst, was an accomplished and prolific author whose works—including essays, plays, and short stories—number in the hundreds. His influence on the advance of modern Thai literature is incalculable. A great number of magazines rose and fell during his reign, 128 intended for men and five for women. The first woman's magazine, *Narirom*, or *Naariirom*,[26] was published in 1919. Everything in the magazine, including advertising, was composed in the then-popular *klon* verse form. Not only was the publisher-editor identified as a woman (Nai Soop, or Nai Sùup), but women's contributions were also enthusiastically solicited. Moreover, a prize of four bahts, now worth less than a dollar but then a substantial amount of

25. An accurate, complete Thai translation of Corelli's original *Vendetta!* by the novelist V. Vinicchayakul (pen name of Vinita Dithiiyon, chair of the Department of Thai Literature at Silpakorn University) was published by Dok Yaa, Bangkok, in 1987.

26. *Naarii* is a polite word for "woman; lady," which usually appears in compounds; *rom* means "charming; beautiful." Information on this magazine is taken from pages 2 and 3 of *Phûuyïng bon nâa kradàat* (Woman on paper), a special publication honoring one hundred years of women's magazines that was distributed at a conference in February 1991.

money, was offered for the best literary work submitted within the year. Many submissions were received. Eventually it was discovered that the editor of *Narirom* was the king's uncle, Prince Damrong, and the first individual to receive the literary prize was King Vachiravudh, for a *klon* work entitled *Khon say ta san*, or *Khon săay taa sân* (A nearsighted person).

Before the overthrow of the absolute monarchy in 1932, several women's magazines were published that advocated progressive political and social ideas. Among these were *Siam yupadii*, or *Sayăam yúpadii* (Young Siamese girl) and *Ying thai*, or *Yĭng thay* (Thai woman), both of which contained strongly worded essays in favor of women's suffrage and other subjects of interest to feminists. Neither contained the love poems in *klon* form that had been the mainstay of *Narirom* and its successors; and both were shut down after a few issues.

In 1924, the first issue of *Thai kasem* was published. This magazine soon became very influential and published the work of every important writer of the 1930s, including Dok Mai Sot, a woman whose novels are still read today.

Very few women were sent abroad to be educated before the 1940s, which makes all the more impressive the fact that women wrote many of the successful early novels. All of these writers came from aristocratic, progressive families that had sent them to convent schools founded by European or American missionaries; some studied with English or French governesses as well. While their brothers were studying in Europe during the 1920s, M. L. Bubpha and M. L. Boonlua were following in the footsteps of other sisters who had lived and written before them: Chao Faa Kunthon and Chao Faa Mongkut, the daughters of King Borommakot, and Khun Phum and Khun Suwan, the court ladies who had created such a stir a century before, and whose talents had not yet been re-evaluated.[27]

Bubpha and Boonlua, born in 1905 and 1911, respectively, busily devoured English and French novels while studying at St. Joseph's Convent School in Bangkok.[28] They were certain that they could write

27. In 1968, when she founded the Faculty of Arts at the new campus of Silpakorn University, M. L. Boonlua made the decision that Khun Suwan's work would be studied by all students of that faculty during their freshman year.

28. M. L. Boonlua was educated in convent schools in both Bangkok and Penang during the 1920s, graduated from Chulalongkorn University during the 1930s, and earned a master of arts degree in education from the University of Minnesota in 1952.

stories just as good, with Thai characters in Thai settings. I have already referred to the work of Boonlua above; as for her sister, Bubpha, she became even more famous as "Dok Mai Sot." During its first year, the magazine *Thai kasem* published her first work, a one-act play, and in 1929, it published her first novel, *Satru khong jao lawn,* or *Sàtrùu khɔ̌ɔng câw lɔɔn* (Her enemy).[29] An excerpt from one of her later novels, *Phu dii,* or *phûu dii* (People of quality),[30] generally considered her best work, is included in this anthology.

In 1932, the absolute monarchy was overthrown in a relatively bloodless coup d'état carried out by a mainly civilian, middle-class group of men who had been educated in England, Germany, and France.[31] Thereafter, at least in Bangkok, new ideas about equality and opportunity for women as well as for men were widely discussed, yet the perception of the ideal woman's identifying characteristics changed remarkably little. Wimon, the heroine of *People of Quality,* may be considered an ideal Thai woman of the 1930s: educated and resolute, she is also beautiful and ever mindful of her first duty, which is to serve and protect her family. The reader is led to believe, as the novel ends, that Wimon, having acted quickly and shrewdly to save the family fortune following the unexpected death of her heavily indebted father, may now marry and permanently devote herself to being an ideal wife and mother.

Another woman writer who succeeded during the early period was Ko Surangkanang (the pen name of Kanha Kiangsiri), whose first novel, *Malini,* was serialized in the *Daily Mail* in 1929 when she was only eighteen years old. In 1937 she produced her masterpiece, *Ying khon chua,* or *Yǐng khon chûa* (An evil woman), a novel about a woman who becomes a prostitute not because she is intrinsically bad (the conventional wisdom) but as the result of the injustices and inequities of society.[32] Word got around that the author had spent some time ob-

---

29.   A translation by Ted Strehlow of this novel, titled *A Secret Past,* was published by Southeast Asia Publications, Cornell University, Ithaca, New York, in 1992.

30.   The Thai title, *Phûu dii,* is virtually untranslatable; *phûu* means "person; people," and *dii* means "good." A literal translation would be "good person" or "good people." In fact, the term signifies good character but also connotes wealth, especially old wealth.

31.   A concise account of events before, during, and after the overthrow of the absolute monarchy is given in Benjamin A. Batson, *The End of the Absolute Monarchy in Siam* (Singapore: Oxford University Press, 1984).

32.   This novel has been translated into English by David Smyth under the title *The Prostitute* (Singapore: Oxford University Press, 1994).

serving and talking to women in brothels, which added to the great success of the book. In the words of Nitaya Masavisut and Kwandee Attavavutichai, Ko Surangkanang wrote "to reveal the truth in an attempt to seek sympathy for . . . suffering humanity" and "let her characters be beaten by misfortune and the injustice of life and society."[33] This author's work became increasingly conservative in outlook and subject matter over the years, but her popular novels never failed to support the cause of the just against the wiles of the greedy and the cruel. In 1987, Ko Surangkanang was declared a National Living Artist.

During the 1930s, Thai women, by comparison with women in neighboring nations and for that matter in European nations, were granted an impressive array of rights, privileges, and opportunities. The promoters of the overthrow of the absolute monarchy did not succeed a colonial regime, and few of them had connections to the royal family. As they had developed their political and social agenda during the process of being educated abroad, they were greatly influenced by the socialist discourse of the Europe of the 1920s. As a result, Siamese women could not only vote during the 1930s, but those whose families could afford to educate them, and were willing to do so, also began to study law, medicine, or education. A ready-made agenda of the "rights and responsibilities of women" had been provided—by men. From the beginning, a complex set of expectations underlay this agenda: the "new" Thai woman was to enjoy the selected, wholesome fruits of Western egalitarianism, including rights for women, but she was to make this transition without sacrificing traditional Thai feminine qualities, attitudes, or behaviors.

POST–WORLD WAR II:
"ART FOR LIFE" AND "ART FOR ART'S SAKE"

After World War II, women in Thai fiction tended to reflect the ideologies of two major factions of writers. Writers in the first faction looked to socialism, and a few to Soviet or later to Chinese communism, for what seemed to them a truer expression of egalitarianism

---

33. Nitaya Masavisut and Kwandee Attavavutichai, "The Development of the Thai Novel," an unpublished and undated paper written during the 1980s under the auspices of International P.E.N. Thailand Centre.

than democracy as they had experienced it since 1932. They believed in "art for life," a literature of social justice and social conscience. In their view, fiction ought to reflect "real" (mainly, workers') lives; and it should be instructive, pointing out not only the inequities in society but also a better political and social path for the future. Except during a brief revival of interest during the early 1970s, another period characterized by a strong belief in social justice as not only *a* but *the* proper subject of literature, most of these works have long been unavailable; none has been translated.

The fictional women in literary works reflecting art for life express socially progressive ideas; they work for the good of the many and struggle to keep their ideals. In these novels and stories, nearly all written by men, it is men who drive the vehicles of progress, and women who help keep them in repair and occasionally fall beneath the wheels. The most famous example is the novel *Khwam rak khong Walya,* or *Khwaam rák khɔ̌ɔng Walyaa* (Walaya's love), written by the male writer Seni Saowapong.[34] Male critics have called *Walaya's Love* "a consciously feminist work," yet the book was never popular with women. (In the few novels concerning politics and political affairs that have been written by women, the story tends to revolve around the effects on a woman of her husband's political career. The most outstanding example is Boonlua's *Tutiya wiset,* or *Thútíyá wísèt,*[35] a novel loosely based on the life of the wife of a prime minister of the 1930s and 1940s.) Walaya says, "Love that is only a matter of individual happiness or desire, or at best a matter of such feelings between two individuals, is a narrow love. Our love should be wider: it should expand, to reach other lives—to reach the people! Only then will our lives have true value and meaning, and prove that we have not been born in vain."[36]

Walaya is an idealistic young socialist with impeccable morals. And yet, what is it that Walaya does best? She *sacrifices:* her ambitions for the greater good of society, her individual desire for love to the

---

34. This is the pen name of Sakdichai Bamrungpong, who wrote from a socialist perspective. His novel *Phĭi sàat* (Ghosts) is considered the great socialist novel of the 1940s. *Khwaam rák khɔ̌ɔng Walyaa* was published in 1952, just as the literature of social justice was being abandoned in deference to political realities; it epitomizes the idealism and also the didacticism of this genre.

35. Bangkok: Prae Pittaya, 1968. *Thútíyá wísèt* is the name of a decoration given to wives of politically prominent men; it is occasionally given to a woman for her own contributions to society.

36. Translated by Chamaiporn Sangkrajang, letter to author, August 27, 1990.

"wider" and worthier ideal of love for all mankind. She is, when all is said and done, one more ideal Thai woman—who happens to be more or less a socialist. In an essay that includes a discussion of the presentation of women in Thai literature, Chetana Nagavajara writes: "I have heard a critic say this about Walaya: 'When I read the novel for the first time, I was a young man . . . and I thought to myself, if I were to meet a woman like Walaya I would simply run away, or, at best, put her on a pedestal. Twenty years have passed and I have had a chance to reconsider. If I met a woman like this, I would ask her to marry me.'"[37] This remark is interesting in light of an important theme in the short stories and novels of Boonlua and other women whose work bridged the gap between this era and the more realistic fiction that began to appear in the late 1960s: the importance of education in women's lives.

Men in Boonlua's stories often make plain their boredom with uneducated women; in turn, these women feel inadequate in the eyes of their bored partners and resentful of other women who because of their higher level of education are considered more interesting by men. There is curiously little emphasis in all of this on the uses to which a woman could or should put her education, despite the fact that Boonlua and most of her female writing colleagues worked full-time, mainly as secondary school teachers, university professors, and civil servants in other government positions (all teachers in Thai public schools, colleges, and universities are by definition civil servants). In fiction, women's education has generally been treated as a quality of being rather than as a prerequisite to doing valuable work in the world. For example, when Kaew, the heroine of Boonlua's *Dr. Luuk Thung,* or *Dɔɔkthâɔ Lûuk Thûng* (Dr. "Up-country") meets her future husband, Krit, in New Zealand, he has a Ph.D. from the United States and is involved in agroeconomic research, while she, a university graduate, is acting as secretary to an older man who is a friend of the family. Once Krit has returned to Thailand, Kaew loses whatever interest in the job she may have had and prepares to go home. Quite a few female characters in mid-twentieth-century Thai fiction are reminiscent of the Victorian women who were daring enough to take sec-

---

37. Chetana Nagavajara, "Unsex Me Here: An Oriental's Plea for Gender Reconciliation," *Literary Studies, East and West / Gender and Culture in Literature and Film, East and West: Issues of Perception and Interpretation* (1994): xxxii.

retarial courses so that they could go out and work in the world until the right man came along.

The other major literary faction turned its collective back on politics
and on social issues with a political cast, fixing its gaze upon pre-1932
Siam in search of those values that the nation and its people ought to
cherish. For its members, King, Religion, and Country were paramount, and the graciousness of pre-1932 Siamese life (or, at least, their
version of it) was held up as the model for all that modern Thai life
might hope to reinvent. The heroines in literary works produced by
the "art for art's sake" faction are beautiful and good. They, too, can
be brave, but their bravery differs from that of their art-for-life sisters;
it is an elegant, even spiritual bravery, and it is always tied to family
matters. These heroines cannot be imagined entering a voting booth,
much less toiling among the masses. They create lovely, serene envi-
ronments for their husbands, children, relatives, and friends. The epitome of such a heroine is Ploy, in M. R. Kukrit Pramoj's great modern
historical novel, *Four Reigns*, which was written in 1953.[38]

Ploy is born into an aristocratic family in the 1880s, during the reign
of King Chulalongkorn, and dies on the same day as King Ananda
(Rama VIII, r. 1935–46). The beauty of her woman's heart is proved
by such acts as her acceptance of her husband's baby son, whose ex-
istence she discovers some weeks after their marriage. Her courage
is displayed in her insistence upon bearing a third child, when she
has been told that she will certainly die if she does. The daughter
whose birth nearly kills her grows up to exemplify the worst of modern womanhood: she falls in love with a greedy, shallow Chinese op-
portunist, blithely announces her intention to use birth control (which
nearly causes Ploy to faint away), and apparently possesses not a scintilla of gratitude, modesty, or grace. An aspect of Ploy's character that
has struck many readers as complex and fascinating, in an otherwise
relentlessly goody-goody portrayal, is her attitude toward her hus-

---

38. M. R. Kukrit Pramoj (1911–95) was one of the most influential Thais of the century. Educated in England from an early age, he graduated from Oxford and returned
to Thailand to work as a banker, an author, the editor in chief of *Siam rath* (the nation's
leading newspaper), an actor, and a consultant on classical Thai drama. His sporadic,
tumultuous political career finally led to a term as prime minister during the 1970s.
Many editions of *Four Reigns* have been published in Thai; a two-volume English translation by Tulachandra was published in Bangkok by Duang Kamol in 1987.

band, Khun Prem. He is weak in many ways and dependent upon Ploy, although neither of them would ever admit it. The respect she never fails to show him could be interpreted as little more than evidence of her habitual self-abnegation and submissiveness. After all, it is made plain to the reader that she understands him and knows his limitations all too well. Moreover, the only romantic love of her life had been a young man whom she knew before she ever met Khun Prem, and who broke her heart when he married another woman. Yet she perseveres to the end, and her dying thoughts are of her husband. Whatever Thai readers may find to criticize in Ploy, they cannot help but love her.

In the pages of *Four Reigns,* it is made clear that everything admirable, lovely, and worthy of praise in Siamese culture was present on the eve of the overthrow of the absolute monarchy in 1932; and that most of what has transpired since has been tainted with vulgarity and sadness. The enormous popularity of this novel and of the several television miniseries that followed provides irrefutable evidence that M. R. Kukrit's portrayal of Thai people and Thai values is one that a great many of his countrymen and -women continue to cherish.

FROM 1950 TO 1965: ROMANCE AND ADVENTURE

Because of internal and external political events, in the late 1950s a strong anticommunist campaign was launched, and art for life, or the literature of social justice, swiftly sank from public view. In 1957, Field Marshal Sarit Thanarat staged a nearly bloodless coup d'état, dissolved Parliament, and revoked the constitution, replacing it with the Interim Constitution of Thailand, which contained the infamous Article 17, giving Field Marshal Sarit Thanarat not only virtual control over the nation but also specific control over all literary products. Thereafter, political subjects could not be alluded to in any way. Intellectuals, artists, and all their works were suspect. Many writers were depressed, and few were willing to take risks that were likely to change nothing. Male writers responded to the new restrictions by turning out adventure stories and tales of tough guys who frequented bars and brothels, and got into trouble. For women writers and a few men writing under women's names, this was the heyday of the romantic novel. A typical heroine of the time was a lovely girl who had been born into a wealthy family but through some accident had been separated from them and was now living, poor and despised, unaware of the fact that she would inherit millions if she ever discovered her true origins.[39] These novels are populated by vapid heroines and magnificent villains—or, more usually, villainesses: rich, mean prospective mothers-in-law or rich, mean, jealous cousins—characters that continue to be the mainstay of most Thai romance novels and all television soap operas. However, when women writers finally decided to deconstruct their own elaborate fantasies of marriage, motherhood, and woman's role in society, fiction about life as it might be became the springboard for fiction about life as it really is.

FROM 1965 TO THE PRESENT

During the 1960s and 1970s, the course of Thai literature changed significantly. Male writers began taking courageous risks, writing fiction and poetry focusing on political and social problems. Some female writers took different but equally courageous risks by exploring their own lives and confronting new or newly realized women's issues. From the mid-1960s until today, Thai women writers have been developing distinctive voices, and some have dared to innovate in ways that have not been welcomed by all critics or all readers.

Throughout the 1960s the government continued to frown upon leftist literature, which was understood to include anything that challenged or criticized the political or social status quo. However, the nation's leaders apparently felt secure enough to allow writers considerable latitude. Two major themes of fiction and poetry in the 1960s and 1970s, particularly in men's writing, were the negative effects of foreign influences (i.e., the effects of Thai collaboration with the United States during the war in Southeast Asia) and, more important, the effects of decades of military dictatorship and governmental corruption on Thai society, both urban and rural, at all levels.

---

39. A common plot device in these earlier romance novels is the discovery of a birthmark proving the true identity of an upper-class heiress who was somehow lost or abandoned by her family. In Sri Dao Ruang's short story "Tosakan and Sita," she writes of a couple who "had become a veritable model of husband and wife, a couple to whom their neighbors invariably referred when they spoke of honesty, endurance, hard work, thrift, and high principles. Both of them came from poor families. No jewels had they, nor a single revealing birthmark." This story was originally published in the magazine *Lôok nǎngsǔu* (Book world) in 1984. The translation is included in my work in progress, "Married to the Demon King," an examination of Sri Dao Ruang's life and work.

Although more male than female writers were concerned with overtly political themes, one political event of the early 1970s was so important that its effects on writers of both sexes cannot be overestimated. The words *sip-see dulaa* literally mean "October fourteenth." On that day in 1973, government tolerance of the frankly left-wing pro-democracy movement came to a bloody end, and troops were ordered to attack thousands of students and other demonstrators as they protested in the streets of downtown Bangkok, demanding an end to military dictatorship and to controls on popular participation in the political process. Although subsequent repressive government actions have taken place since then, notably in October 1976 and in May 1992, each resulting in a greater loss of human life, *sip-see dulaa* remains the paramount symbol of political oppression and the violation of human rights in Thailand.[40]

The events of October 1973 have been widely reported and photographed. They were interpreted in depth and at length both within Thailand and abroad. The most hated military leaders were forced to flee the country, and a highly respected civilian was asked to serve as prime minister. Never before had writers, artists, and political activists enjoyed such a vindication of their liberal ideals and goals, not only in the eyes of their own nation's political majority but also in the eyes of the foreign press. The three years that followed, before the military crackdown of 1976 that would seem inevitable in retrospect, were heady years indeed. Male writers finally freed from the necessity of self-censorship could expand and elaborate upon the themes of rural suffering, governmental corruption, and official greed that they had been stressing since well before October 1973. Women's fiction proceeded in a somewhat different direction.

The differing responses of Thai men and women writers to the events of the 1973–76 period may be compared in certain respects to the responses of American men and women writers to the war in

40. Three useful English-language works that address the effects of this political era on Thai literature are Benedict R. O'G. Anderson and Ruchira Mendiones, eds. and trans., *In the Mirror: Literature and Politics in Siam in the Modern Era* (Bangkok: Editions Duang Kamol, 1985); Herbert P. Phillips, *Modern Thai Literature: An Ethnographic Interpretation* (Honolulu: University of Hawaii Press, 1987); and Katherine A. Bowie, ed. and trans., *Voices from the Thai Countryside: The Short Stories of Samruam Singh* (Madison: Center for Southeast Asian Studies, University of Wisconsin, 1991).

For political and historical information on the 1973–76 period, see David Morell and Chai-anan Samudavanija, *Political Conflict in Thailand: Reform, Reaction, Revolution* (Cambridge, Mass.: Oelgeschlager, Gunn and Hain, 1981).

Vietnam, Laos, and Cambodia, and to the antiwar movement at home. Fiction by women involved directly in the war, such as military nurses, has been negligible. As for the antiwar movement at home, quite a few American women writers have recalled it as an era in which men made the speeches and women made the sandwiches. The resurgence of the women's movement in the United States during the 1970s cannot be separated from the experience of political activism—and marginalization—during the late 1960s and early 1970s, and the gradual, depressing realization that not only had the roles allocated to them by men failed to render their daily life appreciably different from that of their mothers, but also that politics both within and outside of the establishment remained primarily the business of men.

Thai women's experiences were comparable in regard to the violent, tragic, sometimes glorious days of the 1973–76 period. A Thai woman who was a member of the committee to draft a new constitution in 1974 told me, "Given the nature of the times, they had to have one woman on the committee, and although we all got along well, I was always conscious of being that one woman." With a few exceptions, men's fiction of the time was about social injustice, and men acting to correct it. Women in these works tend to be either supporting characters or tragic examples, as in the short stories "Greenie" and "A Mote of Dust on the Face of the Earth," both included in this anthology.

The most gifted Thai women writers of this period set off in a new direction, creating fiction in which women pondered their place in the world and their relationships with others, especially men. Their works are distinctly political, but in a different way from works by men. For example, when Sri Dao Ruang wrote about factory workers, her stories reflected her own experiences as a factory worker, and her characters were based upon individuals who had been her friends; they were not simply bearers of a political message.

Another woman whose writing is far more personal and revealing than traditional women's fiction—and also highly political if less overtly ideological than the work of most of her male contemporaries —was Suwanee Sukhontha (the pen name of Suwanee Sukhonthiang), who ignored the formulas most of the time. One of her short stories is included in this anthology. Suwanee's unabashedly autobiographical writing, highly personal and unsparing of herself or anyone else— including children, friends, and lovers past and present—is lively,

Tailand was lucky because they never became a colony.

skillful, and full of strong visual images. Her writing was frequently ribald and funny, and her ear for everyday speech was flawless. She addressed social problems in some of her work, expressing particular dismay over the negative effects of urban super-growth in Bangkok on people's behavior, and over the widening gap between rich and poor throughout the country. She boldly deplored the greed, vulgarity, and immoral behavior of men in power and extolled the courage and honesty of those who dared to challenge the system. Her prizewinning novel, *Khao chu Kan,* or *Khǎw chûu Kaan* (His name is Kaan), relates the tragedy of a physician who strives to serve his upcountry clients despite political corruption. He also must contend with lack of support from his selfish wife, the spoiled child of a wealthy Bangkok family. While Suwanee and the other women writers of her generation were politically active and aware, their fiction invariably focuses upon the relationships between unique human beings, not upon interchangeable human units assembled upon a stage to display political opinions, as is often true of men's fiction of the time.

Until recently, there has been a general expectation among both critics and readers that women's writing ought to be elevating or at least conclude with a wholesome message; additionally, there has been a tacit understanding that ugly subjects such as violence, abuse, and exploitation in male-female relationships are not suitable subjects for fiction. In the 1980s, when some women writers began to examine problems in the relations between men and women with an unprecedented, sometimes "ugly" frankness, some male critics declared that this kind of writing did not deserve to be called literature.

Anchan (the pen name of Anchalee Vivathanachai), whose disturbing story of Nien, the abused wife in "A Pot That Scouring Will Not Save," is included in this anthology, is a leading writer who insists upon challenging the tacit prohibition against so-called ugly writing. This controversial story was published in the collection *Anmanii haeng chiwit,* or *Anmanii hɛ̀ɛng chiiwít* (Jewels of life), which received the SEAWrite award in 1990. The critical reactions to her work are discussed in the commentary that follows the selection. When a Thai woman professor of literature discovered that I had not only translated this story but was also planning to talk about it at a conference (and, worse yet, include it in this anthology), she politely expressed her disapproval. When I said that I did not really understand her concern, since domestic violence occurs everywhere in the world, she asked, "Are there any American women like Nien?" My assurance that unfortunately there were many did not change her opinion that I should instead include a "nice" story by Anchan in my anthology—perhaps, the one about a little boy who dreams of his beloved mother, after her death.[41] It was not the first time I have heard this story cited as evidence that Anchan can write acceptable fiction about women "if she want[s] to." In fact, in this story about a bereaved little boy, there is no living woman at all—only a dead, idealized one.

Other important contemporary female writers whose work is based in feminist concerns include Botan (the pen name of Supa Sirising) and Sri Dao Ruang (the pen name of Wanna Sawadsee). Information about these women's lives and careers follow selections from their work. It must be said that most Thais who react negatively to expressions such as "feminist concerns" (whether using the Thai term *satri niyom* or the Thai transliteration *feminit,* from English) respond to specific feminist objectives including equality of opportunity in the marketplace, parity of income, equitable divorce settlements, and child care as legitimate goals for women to pursue and achieve.

POETRY

Poetry has always been considered the preeminent form of oral expression and written literature in Thailand, and is still considered superior to prose. With few exceptions, it has been a male-dominated genre. Jiranan Pitpreecha, a woman poet who won the 1989 SEAWrite award for her collection *Bay may thii hay pay,* or *Bay máy thîi hǎy pay* (Lost leaves),[42] is an exception in two ways: she is a woman who writes poetry, and she writes about political subjects. The style of her political poetry is very like that of male poets, as demonstrated in the poem "The First Rain," written following the violent incidents of government repression in May 1992, and published privately in a collection

---

41. The story is "Mêε khráp" (approximately, "mother dear"), included in the SEA-Write award-winning short story collection *Anmanii hὲεng chiiwít* (Jewels of life) (Bangkok: Khom Bang Press, 1990).

42. Bangkok: Saeng Daw, 1990.

of writers' essays and poems. This excerpt from an unpublished translation is by Chetana Nagavajara:

The first rainfall of May
Streamed down in red,
A torrent of steely rain
That pierced human bodies,
flooding the streets with blood,
With a river of deathly stench.
How many stars did fall?
How many hearts did break?
The wound on this native soil,
When will it heal over?
Whose base power
Dared slay the people?

Other respected women poets include Thappani Nakhonthap and Nantha Khunpagdee, who is a professor of Thai literature at Silpakorn University. Her book on the traditional chanting of poetry, which is used as a text in universities, is accompanied by cassette tapes that are of great value since Thai poetry is chanted. The introduction to poetic chanting is invariably a stunning experience—especially for foreign students of Thai. Whatever ideas they may have had about Thai poetry based upon the laborious experience of reading it on the page are overwhelmed the moment the poet opens his or her mouth, and the mellifluous chanting begins.

Each year, the SEAWrite award is presented within a specific genre. In 1995, a year in which poetry was honored, the selection committee was somewhat surprised to receive a collection entitled *Lay suu thai* or *Laay sǔu thay* (Thai letters/words), by Anchan, who had won the award in 1990 for the collection *Jewels of Life*. Many people in the literary community had not known that Anchan wrote poetry, and they were amazed at the vitality, intensity, and innovation that characterized the nature-focused poems in this collection. Anchan did not win the award, however, which was given to Paivarin Khaongam, for the collection *Ma kan kluay*, or *Máa kâan klûay* (literally, "a hobby horse made of a banana stalk"). The chief reason given for choosing Paivarin's work over Anchan's was that he showed greater technical mastery of Thai poetic forms: this mastery must be considered the most important factor in choosing the winning collection, however exciting Anchan's less technically perfect poetry might be. No one questioned Paivarin's excellence as a poet. Anchan herself strongly supported the committee's decision, saying that she never expected to win with a first volume of poetry, and that in her opinion Paivarin deserved the award not only for the present collection but also for the body of work he has produced over the years. But some people who disagreed with the decision felt that in this case, the selection criteria had been misused in order to bypass an extraordinary work by a woman writer whose selection for the award in 1990 had engendered a storm of controversy. They pointed out that thirty years ago, the male poet Ankhan Kalyanapongse, now considered Thailand's leading poet, had been excoriated for his lack of attention to and occasional contempt for technical issues, among other things, but Ankhan had won literary awards anyway because his poetry was, if controversial, extraordinary. Why had that been more than enough, in his case? And what would the critics have made of some of Ankhan's poems, had a woman dared to write them?[43] Would she have been lionized, as the male writer Ankhan has been for three decades—or would she have been dismissed as mad, like Khun Suwan? Thus is the state of the debate, as of this writing.

WOMEN IN LIFE, LITERATURE, AND BUDDHIST PRACTICE

There are several reasons for completing this introduction with remarks on women and Thai Buddhism. The most important is that

43. For example, in a long poem denouncing the declining quality of life in Bangkok, *Baangkɔ̀k kɛ̂ɛw kam sǔan rɯ̌ɯ nírâat Nakhɔn Sǐi Thamarâat* (Bangkok: Sathian Koset Foundation, 1978), moral decay and the horrific traffic situation are combined:

> A new animal: A miracle!
> Half human, lovely
> yes but also
> half automobile
> and note the integrity of the whole
> See the *farang* give it "thumbs up!"
> Good for you, Thailand
> Countless autos radiating sex
> female, male,
> drunk, voracious,
> crawling, squirming
> in the streets,
> in transports of fornication,
> tasting the bliss, licking the rapture,
> the delicious garbage of Siam. (84–85)

many seemingly contradictory beliefs about Thai women and their natural roles and functions in the world are supported by assumptions that have their basis in Buddhism as it is understood and practiced by Thais.

In its 2,500 year history, Buddhism has developed a massive and massively complex body of teachings and commentaries. But popular Buddhism, the religion as it is practiced and understood by most believers, rests upon a relatively few straightforward ideas, or core beliefs. Taken together, these beliefs constitute a view of reality that virtually all Thai citizens share and understand, even the 10 percent of Thais who practice other religions. This view of reality is strongly reflected in Thai fiction. One reason for including the following introduction to some of the core beliefs, which is admittedly simplistic, is to make possible a deeper understanding of the fiction selections to follow for those readers who have little or no understanding of Buddhism.

There is one more important reason for concluding the introduction in this way. The place of women in Thai Buddhism is increasingly a subject of interest and discussion, and a feminist Buddhist movement is now under way, although it has few adherents and little if any influence, as will be seen. It is in fiction that some women are tentatively beginning to explore the effects of traditional Thai Buddhist practice on women's lives. The most conspicuous example to date is Sri Dao Ruang's short story "Matsii," which is included in this anthology.

THAI BUDDHISM

The form of Buddhism practiced in Thailand is called Theravada Buddhism. The following succinct definition from Charles Keyes, Laurel Kendall, and Helen Hardacres's *Asian Visions of Authority* will suffice for my purposes: "From the eleventh through the fifteenth centuries, Buddhist monks gained the patronage of most rulers of principalities and kingdoms in what are today Burma (Myanmar), Thailand, and Laos as well as Cambodia. These monks derived their understanding of Buddhism from interpretations of Pali texts that had become authoritative in the fourth century A.D. in Sri Lanka. These interpretations constituted what became known as Theravada Buddhism, or the "way of the elders." The *sangha,* or Buddhist order of monks, is seen as the exemplar, teacher, and embodiment of the *dhamma* [dharma], the message of the Buddha."[44]

In contrast, most Buddhists in the world—including those in China, Japan, and Tibet—practice Mahayana Buddhism, which incorporates many teachings and ideas developed subsequent to the teachings referred to above as the "way of the elders." Theravadans tend to feel that their understanding of Buddhism represents an older, purer version of the religion. The great majority of Buddhist women who have been ordained belong to the Mahayana tradition; the import of this, for Thai women, is discussed below.

CORE BELIEFS

All Thais recognize the Four Noble Truths of Buddhism.[45] The first truth is that all human beings are subject to *dhukkha*, a word that is usually translated as "suffering" but that in fact includes every kind of pain, sorrow, and misery, and also such abstractions as imperfection, emptiness, and dissatisfaction; even the frustration of not getting one's own way is dhukkha. All attachments are dhukkha, including those that are seen in the Judeo-Christian tradition as good and desirable, such as the love of one's parents and children. How can this be? Eventually, even the most loving and selfless relationship must end on a note of suffering, since one will either die first, or suffer the death of the loved one and then die. Dhukkha is inescapable, so long as one is attached to anything or anyone.

The second truth, which is suggested by the first, is that the origin of suffering and all kinds of dhukkha is craving or desire. Cravings and desires, no matter how honorable, give rise to all forms of suffering and the continuity of beings. For example, love between a man and woman leads to procreation, which leads to the suffering attendant upon birth, worries about the child, the frightful possibility of the child's death, and so on and on. The common term that encom-

44. Charles F. Keyes, Laurel Kendall, and Helen Hardacre, *Asian Visions of Authority: Religion and the Modern States of East and Southeast Asia* (Honolulu: University of Hawaii Press, 1994), 44.
45. Religious minorities in Thailand, including a sizable Muslim population in the south and members of various Christian denominations throughout the kingdom, have complete freedom of religious belief and practice. However, the influence of Buddhism is so pervasive that no Thai can grow up unaffected by it or unaware of basic tenets of Buddhism such as the Four Noble Truths.

passes all craving, desire, and attachments is *kilèet.* It implies "not only desire for, and attachment to, sense-pleasures, wealth and power, but also desire for, and attachment to, ideas and ideals, views, opinions, theories, conceptions and beliefs."[46]

The third truth is that the elimination of craving, desire, and attachments is *nibbāna,* usually represented in English as "nirvana." Countless words have been written in the effort to define *nibbāna.* It represents an end to *samsara,* the Wheel of Life, that turns relentlessly, carrying all sentient beings on an endless round of birth, desire, suffering, death, and rebirth. Commonly used definitions of *nibbāna* include "realization of absolute truth" and "the perception of ultimate reality." In any case, *nibbāna* is in no way synonymous with *heaven.*

The fourth noble truth is that the path to nibbāna is to be found in the teachings of the Buddha.

Other important Buddhist beliefs that influence the ways in which Thai Buddhists, including authors, interpret the meaning of life and of daily events are discussed below.

The Illusion of the Self

Walpole Rahula writes, "According to the teaching of the Buddha, the idea of self is an imaginary, false belief which has no corresponding reality, and it produces harmful thoughts of 'me' and 'mine,' selfish desire, craving, attachment, hatred, ill-will, conceit, pride, egoism, and other defilements, impurities and problems. It is the source of all the troubles in the world from personal conflicts to wars between nations. In short, to this false view can be traced all the evil in the world."[47] Obviously, this denial of a "self" and of "me" and "mine" is very far from ideas such as "know thyself," or the importance of either "finding oneself" or "being oneself," all of which play so significant a role in contemporary Western literature. From the traditional Thai Buddhist point of view, *there is no situation in which concentration on the self may be interpreted as positive.* Buddhist meditation, which appears to many non-Buddhists quite *self*ish, in fact involves a great deal of work on the dismantling of the notion of self.

---

46. Walpole Rahula, *What the Buddha Taught,* 2d enlarged ed. (New York: Grove Press, 1974; reprint, New York: Grove Weidenfeld, n.d.), 30.
47. Ibid., 51.

The Impermanence of All Things

All things are impermanent and in a constant state of flux; this applies to everything: people, societies, governments, philosophies, worlds—*everything*. Buddhism teaches that we human beings delude ourselves to think otherwise, and that in fact we spend a good deal of our lives deluding ourselves about nearly everything, including our inevitable decline and death. It is not unusual for a devout Thai Buddhist to possess images (usually photographs) of the decaying corpses of people who were very attractive while alive, as a reminder of the reality of life; and this is by no means a symptom of mental aberration. Indeed, many Thais consider the phobic attitude toward death evinced by many Westerners to be unrealistic, even childish.[48] Death rites and cremations are of great importance in Thai society; it is a much worse offense to miss a funeral than to miss a wedding.

Rebirth: A Continuity of Lives

Every birth is a rebirth into a state of being that is the inescapable legacy of both positive and negative actions of past lives. It is one's purpose in this life to accumulate merit by choosing right actions, so that one's subsequent rebirth will be an improvement over one's situation in the present life. Although the eventual goal is nibbāna, it is understood that one is probably many (perhaps countless) lives away from that achievement. Just as the notion of selflessness is very far from notions of knowing oneself or being oneself, the acceptance of many, many lives instead of one—with all the attendant pressures to accomplish, achieve, and succeed because "you only live once"— has significant consequences for Thai attitudes toward the human condition, and these are reflected everywhere in Thai fiction.

Responsibility for One's Own Karma

"Karma" is so common a word in English that I do not italicize it, yet it is used inaccurately by almost everyone except English-speaking

---

48. A Western-educated Thai professor told me that following the cremation of a writer who had been a close friend, she requested fragments of the woman's finger bones because the sight of the fingers with which her friend had written her works would be a comfort.

Buddhists. Karma may be literally translated as a "volitional act." That one is responsible for oneself, for one's own acts, is reflected in this teaching of the Buddha: "By oneself is evil done, by oneself one is defiled, / Purity and impurity belong to oneself, no one can purify another."[49] Thus, karma is not fate, nor has it anything to do with chance or luck. One's status in this life reflects the current balance of good and evil deeds performed in former lives and to date in this life, a fact upon which characters in Thai fiction are wont to reflect, perhaps in sorrow but inevitably with resignation. Another fact that is understood, in all traditional and many contemporary literary works, is that there can be no such thing as undeserved bad or good fortune. The first saying most students of Thai learn is "tham dii dây dii[,] tham chûa dây chûa" (Do good, receive good / do evil, receive evil). This Buddhist idea, in particular, is challenged by some contemporary writers who try to convince their readers that people need not bow meekly before "bad fortune" that is in reality the result of social inequities and injustices that could be changed by citizens who believe in their ability and their right to work for change. Woman writers are more likely to carry such ideas of personal responsibility and the right to challenge injustice into the domestic sphere rather than focus on society at large or on social and political institutions.

The Five Precepts

On the level of day-to-day life, Buddhists strive to adhere to the Five Precepts, which are similar to the Ten Commandments: one ought not to (1) take life, (2) steal, (3) be unchaste, (4) lie, or (5) take intoxicants. These are of less importance to matters of plot, plan, and characterization in Thai literature than are ideas such as the impermanence of all things, the role of karma, the origins of suffering, and so on.

The Thai Buddhist belief system allows individuals to rationalize and cope with the fact of unhappiness in human life, which is not to imply that Buddhists are less capable than other people of feeling sorrow or experiencing grief. But a lifelong exposure to reality as ex-

49. *The Dhammapada,* trans. Irving Babbitt (New York: New Directions, 1965), 27.

pressed in Buddhist terms does not encourage the individual to expect happiness as his or her rightful privilege in life; on the contrary, Buddhist teaching constantly emphasizes the *evidence* that everyone is subject to suffering and death. Even the richest and most beautiful people in the world will suffer and die like everyone else. The cry "Why me?" does not make any sense to the Thai Buddhist, for the answer must always be "Why not?" Since everyone's life and life span are the result of karma, painful and terrible events are understood, not as the result of fate or bad luck, but as the inescapable result of one's karmic balance sheet.

It is difficult to find a work of Thai literature from any period or any genre that is not permeated by at least some of the Buddhist beliefs described above. The virtuous character in fiction strives to live in recognition of these truths; villains and weak characters either reject them or fail to live by them. In any case, no one escapes them.

Dharma, the body of the Buddha's teachings (as recorded in written form much later by his followers), which includes the ideas introduced above, is accepted by all Buddhists, whether they follow the Theravada or Mahayana tradition.

THAI WOMEN AND BUDDHISM

By all accounts including their own, the great majority of Thai Buddhist women are satisfied with the status quo, in terms of Buddhist practice and their own opportunities, roles, and responsibilities. One woman, the administrative director of a large school, told me, "We are happy to support our male relatives, when they become monks. It is a hard life, and I for one am glad to leave it to them." Another woman, a Western-educated political scientist, said: "I never felt that women were inferior in Thai Buddhism. My grandmother was a Buddhist scholar and taught monks!" When I reported this to Chatsumarn Kabilsingh, professor of philosophy and religion at Thammasat University—and one-woman crusade for Buddhist women's rights, including ordination—she replied, "You may be sure that her grandmother didn't teach them Buddhism in a temple. I teach Mahayana Buddhism to monks every week, and not only do I have to teach them in a classroom outside the temple, but the official teacher of this course is a man. He doesn't teach at all, but it would be unseemly for the monks to be learning from a woman, so officially, they're taking the course from him."[50]

There have always been some Thai women who were disturbed by beliefs about woman's nature that have their foundation in popular Buddhist beliefs and traditional Buddhist practices. A few women now claim that these popular beliefs and traditional practices—such as the prohibition against the ordination of women—have nothing to do with the core beliefs of Buddhism or the Buddha's own teachings; they are social and political constructs that serve to justify discrimination against women.

The first cause for dissatisfaction on the part of women like Chatsumarn, and the one from which, in one way or another, all else follows, is that Thai Buddhist women cannot be ordained, although they may become Buddhist nuns, or *mae chii*—a vastly different and immeasurably inferior status when compared with the monkhood. Darunee Tantiwiramanondh and Shashi Pandey, in their essay "The Status and Role of Thai Women in the Pre-Modern Period: A Historical and Cultural Perspective," describe traditional (and, for the most part, contemporary) views of males and females who wish to live the religious life:

> According to religious interpretations, female gender was inferior to male and women were pollutants to the monastic order—a belief that Thai women have internalized. Instead of absolutely banning women from ordination, devout women were allowed to become *mae chii.* . . . Thai people usually see a *mae chii* as either a "destitute" or a "housekeeper" of monks at a temple. . . . A *mae chii*, unlike a monk, was neither a role model for female spirituality nor a venerable symbol of authority in other-worldly matters. The irony is that, what a man could do for "self-cultivation," such as leaving his familial responsibilities to become a monk, would be interpreted as "selfishness" if attempted by a young married woman.[51]

The reason why Thai women may not be ordained is described in a succinctly catch-22 fashion by Chatsumarn:

---

50. Chatsumarn Kabilsingh, interview with author, July 13, 1995.
51. *Sojourn* 2, no. 1 (February 1987): 140. In fact, a man is not supposed to be accepted for ordination if it is apparent that he is doing so to avoid family responsibilities.

[T]here can be no bhikkhuni ordination since this requires dual ordination from both the bhikkhu and bhikkhuni sanghas. Since there
has never been a Bhikkhuni Sangha in Thailand, such ordination is
not possible. However, Voramai [Chatsumarn's mother, who finally
founded her own Buddhist temple in Thailand] believed that as the
Bhikkhuni Sangha was established by the Buddha, any Buddhist
woman who wanted to become ordained should be regarded as a
bhikkhuni. . . . In 1971, she was ordained at Sung San Temple in
Taipei. . . . She is the first Thai woman to have received full ordination as a bhikkhuni in the Darmagupta sub-sect of the Theravada
tradition.

   To the general public in Thailand, Voramai is still only a mae ji [mae
chii] [italics added].[52]

In his book *Siamese Resurgence*, the independent scholar Sulak
Sivarak describes the same conditions and similar events quite dif-
ferently:

   To do the good work for society or to devote oneself for the Con-
   templative Life, an Upasiká or a devoted laywoman could do both
   quite effectively. . . . It is only due to *technicalities* [italics added] that
   they cannot receive the higher ordination of Bhikkhuni or even a
   lower ordination of Sámaneri; the Holy Order was simply discontinued and once discontinued, it cannot be revived.[53]

Earlier in the same essay, Sulak reports an earlier case involving a
woman seeking ordination: "In 1959, a Thai lady wished to revive the
Order of Almswomen in Siam. She was ordained in Taiwan and returned to Siam and established a nunnery with some public support.
Because Siam recognized only Theravada Buddhism as a state religion, what she did with her Mahayana belief and practice was her
own private affair."[54]

   This attitude was echoed by a woman language professor at a leading university who told me, "These women who want to shave their
heads and dress up in white robes, they can do it, but it doesn't mean

   52. Chatsumarn Kabilsingh, *Thai Women in Buddhism* (Berkeley: Parallax Press,
1991), 52. An ordained man becomes a *bhikkhu;* an ordained woman, a *bhikkhuni.* (It is
significant that the most important work on this subject written by a Thai woman was
not published in Thailand but in Berkeley, California.)
   53. Sulak Sivarak, "Buddhist Women, Past and Present," in *Siamese Resurgence*
(Bangkok: Asian Cultural Forum on Development, 1985), 60.
   54. Ibid., 59–60.

anything. They are not monks, and they are not even '*bhikkhuni*' because the Buddha didn't ordain any women after his mother and aunt died, and if the Buddha made that decision it should be good enough for us."

Sulak's essay begins with high praise for the Buddha's mother and aunt, and other early Buddhist women who are not to be confused, it would appear, with the contemporary Buddhist feminists, including such people as the Burmese scholar Khin Thitsa.[55] Sulak writes, "I have much sympathy with [her] position, although she has been too sweeping in her generalizations and unfairly blames Buddhism for all the social evils of contemporary Thai women." This is followed, in the same paragraph, by the opinion that "if feminists could be more careful in their analysis and study the subject more thoroughly, especially those dealing with spiritual tradition, their criticism would be much more convincing."[56]

In the current climate, a Thai woman who is a recognized Buddhist scholar or meditation teacher, or both (there are several such women in Thailand), would *lose* status by donning the white robe, shaving her head, and entering the official religious life that is allowed to women. In general, to be a nun is to become invisible; to become a nun who rejects invisibility is to be regarded as an eccentric. She is either a woman who doesn't understand Buddhism, or she is maladjusted or neurotic in some way, and therefore either does not want or cannot achieve a normal woman's life.

The key arguments posed by women who are challenging the status quo are firmly grounded in the teachings of the Buddha. In *Buddhism after Patriarchy*, Rita M. Gross writes, "Buddhism does, after all, teach that all-pervasive impermanence is the nature of things. To regard patriarchy as an impermanent set of social conditions, destined to give way to other conditions eventually, is both a welcome view to feminists and more in accord with fundamental Buddhist teachings than to regard male dominance and male privilege as unalterable and

---

55.   In Thailand, reactions to Khin Thitsa's monograph, *Providence and Prostitution: Image and Reality for Women in Buddhist Thailand* (London: CHANGE International Reports: Women and Society, 1980), predictably ranged from outrage to curt dismissal of her work on the grounds that she did not know what she was talking about.

56.   Sulak, "Buddhist Women," 63.

unchanging constants. If everything is subject to impermanence, there seems to be no reason to exempt male dominance and male privilege or to try to preserve them."[57]

Some male scholars writing in the 1980s offered the opinion that the subject of Buddhist feminism had been something of a flash in the pan during the 1970s and was already on the wane. For example, Reynolds opines that "the debate over whether or not Buddhism devalued women . . . came to an impasse . . . stalled, I think, because gender was not conceptualized as a discursive and changeable category that depends on context, institutional practice, and ritual." In a following note, however, Reynolds asserts, "I may be misreading what has happened."[58]

I suggest, to the contrary, that interest in the subject of women's role in Buddhism is on the rise, as evidenced by the great increase in the numbers of women who practice meditation, some of whom even choose to spend their vacations at rural temples that have become famous as retreats; by the work of people like Chatsumarn, for whom religion is the core of her career and her life; and by the new presence of this subject in contemporary fiction by women. I suspect that the flash observed during the 1970s may have been the faint precursor of a much stronger and better organized movement led by feminists who will, to borrow Sulak's words, be extremely careful in their analysis and study the subject quite thoroughly. And then, perhaps, their arguments will be much more convincing.

Thai and foreign scholars alike have tended to discount Buddhist feminism as "extreme"; or they politely suggest, as shown above, that the authors of essays and books critical of current Buddhist practice don't really understand that women are not discriminated against—it just looks that way. But it is not just a matter of ordainment. Despite the words of the Buddha quoted earlier—"By oneself is evil done, by oneself one is defiled, / Purity and impurity belong to oneself, no one can purify another"—the fact is that most Thai Buddhists believe that the merit a son gains through entering the monkhood can and should be accrued to his mother. As Khin Thitsa writes:

---

57.   Albany: State University of New York Press, 1993, 120–21. Gross is a professor of comparative studies in religion at the University of Wisconsin, Eau Claire, a practicing Buddhist, and a former president of the Society for Buddhist-Christian Studies.

58.   "Predicaments," 71.

She, deeply bound to her son, "gives" him to the Order. Being a female, she is believed to be more firmly rooted in her worldly attachments than a man and thus this act of renunciation is regarded as a prime source of merit for a woman. . . . A renowned monk . . . writes that "the mothers, who can never be admitted to the Order, really believe that if their sons become priests, their souls will be saved, and that they could cling to the fringes of the yellow robes of their sons, which would take them to heaven. Of course, this is not meant in a literal sense. . . ." (No part of a monk's person may come into contact with a woman).[59]

The belief described above or the belief that a man could be demoted in his next life by being reborn as a woman has significant potential effects on the attitude toward sons and toward daughters—and on both men's and women's feelings about the value of their own gender. That these ideas and beliefs reflect popular Buddhism, not necessarily the intellectual Buddhism of the "cognitive elite" in Thai society, does not ameliorate the effects of such ideas on the self-esteem of the vast majority of women or on the role they play in bolstering male perceptions of the superiority of men and of the supposed natural inferiority of women—or on the way many Buddhist nuns perceive themselves in relation to and in comparison with monks.[60]

Keyes begins his essay "Mother or Mistress but Never a Monk: Buddhist Notions of Female Gender in Rural Thailand" with this statement: "[C]ontrary to the argument of some scholars, that Thai Buddhist culture does not relegate women to a religiously inferior status relative to men . . . , both males and females who understand the world in Buddhist terms face the same problem of attachment to the world, although the characteristic tension between worldly attachment and orientation toward Buddhist salvation is expressed for females in gender images that are different than those for males."[61]

Keyes points out that women, as the mothers of monks (even, as the mother of the Buddha himself), are in effect the "mothers of Bud-

---

59. *Providence and Prostitution,* 18.
60. Contributing to the welfare of Buddhist monks, whether through food offerings, clothing, service, and so on, is one of the primary ways in which women can accrue merit. The importance of feeding and serving monks has been expressed to me by several Thai Buddhist nuns. In 1986, one chided me for doing research on a project to provide kindergartens for slum children by saying, "You should be doing things for monks [to gain merit], instead of wasting your time on those children."
61. *American Ethnologist* 11, no. 2 (1984): 223.

dhism," essential to all aspects of the faith. It is a very familiar argument to women of other faiths, in other nations: behind every monk or priest—or national leader or CEO—there was a mother; therefore, women should understand how valuable they are.

Gross expresses this rationale for an equitable future: "Buddhists have often relied on Hindu or Confucian norms for gender roles, but they . . . are not breaking with divine command or cosmic models when they break with older gender roles and patterns of gender interaction. They are only changing received social custom. Thus a lay Buddhist male who wants to retain gender privilege cannot call upon God or the cosmos to validate him. . . . This does not mean that change can come easily, for social customs are well entrenched . . . but at least [Buddhist] feminists do not first have to reconstruct interpretations of divine revelation or cosmic order to make their case."[62]

It will be interesting to watch the development of the Buddhist women's movement in Thailand over the next fifty years: for Thai Buddhists, the second half of the twenty-sixth century. And it will be particularly interesting to see who leads, who follows, and how Thai society at large will react to the ideas and the actions of people on all sides of this issue—all of whom have strong convictions on the subject.

Through their work, many successful contemporary Thai writers, men as well as women, have made quite clear their conviction that women need not be ashamed of themselves for looking beyond the familiar virtues of self-sacrifice, resignation, and denial of desire that are seen as Buddhist virtues for everyone, but especially for women if they are to fulfill successfully their supposedly natural role in the family and in society. Through the selections in this anthology, readers will see for themselves how both traditional beliefs and innovative, original ideas and perceptions concerning women's physical, emotional, and spiritual lives are presented in fiction, which is a most important site of contempory discourse on women's roles, rights, responsibilities, and opportunities in contemporary Thai society.

---

62. *Buddhism after Patriarchy*, 142.

1
MOTHERS

Grandmother the Progressive

Junlada Phakdiphumin

A humorous tale, set in the 1960s, about the beloved
dowager of an old Bangkok family, who guides her
granddaughters into adulthood with love and wisdom.

As Grandmother shook her head, her hair moved softly, that lovely
hair as white and soft as pampas grass.

"Well, I don't care for *her,*" she pronounced. "The girl is not—not
po-poo-lah, not a bit."

Popular, or "po-poo-lah," Grandmother's version, was one of her
few and favorite English words.

We cousins, the oldest then about forty, the youngest eighteen,
laughed heartily. We sat about our grandmother on the floor of her
sitting room, as we did nearly every day, while great-grandchildren
who were three and four years old played happily nearby.

The unfortunate young woman whom Grandmother had just dismissed was a grandson's fiancée. The young man had brought his intended bride on the obligatory visit to our family matriarch. The girl
had knelt before the formidable old lady, placing her palms together
before her forehead in a graceful, respectful, and very nervous *wai.*[1]
She attempted polite, awkward conversation for a few minutes; and
then, mercifully, she was carried off by her fiancé. As soon as the pair
had cleared the stairs, Grandmother started in.

"Sat there like a *took-a-ta,* like a doll," she sniffed. "Not a bit like
his brother Chatchai's wife. Now *she's* a good one."

This story was originally published under the title "Khun yâa phátánaa"; a photocopy
was sent to me by a colleague who did not know where the story first appeared, and
I have not been able to obtain this information.

1.   The wai is the Thai greeting: palms are together before the face, with a slight
bow of the head. Seniors and older people place the hands lower; younger people place
them higher.

Doy, who had just turned eighteen, wrinkled her nose. "Ee-ee, I don't like Chatchai's wife. She talks too much. And she puts on airs."

Grandmother rose immediately to the defense of Chatchai's wife. "She knows how to please people! A girl has to have a little charm, know how to talk to people, how to make them smile. I don't like a girl who sits there as dumb as a leaf on the floor. I like a *po-poo-lah* girl."

Oh, how we knew.

Grandmother held forth on the philosophy of Grandmother while carefully arranging betel leaf, areca nut, lime paste, and an exquisite gold mortar and pestle on the tray beside her. She pushed the tray across the floor to Doy, who obediently set to work, preparing the mixture for Grandmother to chew.

Most of her grandchildren lived with their parents, of course. But, from time to time and for one reason or another, several of us girls lived with Grandmother. In my day, Doy seemed to be the favorite. She was definitely the most outspoken and perhaps the smartest; and, of course, she was very "po-poo-lah."

Grandmother was in her late seventies, strong and spry, rigorous in her application of what she called "healthy principles." She got up in the morning, ate her meals, and went to bed at night—all on a firm schedule. She watered her own garden, a garden in which nearly all the flowers had been planted by her, not the gardener, and she was a great believer in exercise. She did her daily calisthenics, energetically bending up and down, and twisting from side to side.

When we giggled about "healthy principles," she would say, "Go on and laugh. You all are going to die young. Eating and sleeping whenever you like, going to the cinemas and plays whenever you please, sitting before the television until after midnight. You are going to be full of aches and pains before you are forty. I am nearly eighty years old, and I have never been ill, not once in my life." And she would go on bobbing and twisting.

We dared to tease her in the manner of the children of our rude generation. "You forget, you impertinent children," she would say reproachfully, "who is *finger,* and who is *thumb!*" Yet she knew that we not only adored but also respected her.

Grandmother had lived a full life, passing through times of happiness and of sorrow, seeing her material fortunes wax and mostly wane through the years. She was a perfect example to us of fortitude under difficult circumstances, including bereavement: not once had

Grandmother shed tears over her misfortunes. She relied upon her Buddhist faith.

"Impermanence," she told us, "and change—they are the only things, my dears, upon which you may depend in this life."

The only daughter of a wealthy man, Grandmother was born during the reign of King Rama V and married according to the customs of those days for young ladies of the aristocracy. She went to her husband with a dowry reflecting the status of her father, a dowry that would contribute substantially to the meticulous conduct of an aristocratic household.

In their later years, she and Grandfather had divided most of what was left of their assets between their ten children. Gradually, the family's land holdings in Bangkok and in Thonburi, across the river, dwindled away. When Grandfather died, she sold the palatial family home in Bangkok and built a simple, big wooden house in Thonburi. There she stayed and gradually drew to her the flock of rotating resident granddaughters. We came and we went; but our number seemed fairly constant through the years. Those who married came back to visit frequently, bringing their children, and so it remained a lively household.

We never ceased to be amazed by the eagerness with which our grandmother welcomed nearly every nuance of the modern world, considering that she had grown up, married, and borne children within a meticulous and rigid social structure that dictated every thought and word, every gesture and action, down to the last possession that was suitable for a lady to own, wear, or carry.

When she was what today we would call a "teenager" (there certainly were no teenagers at the turn of the century, she had informed us), she had learned a few words of English from her tutor. Although she never learned to speak the language, she had avidly accumulated the dozen or so words that would punctuate her conversation forever after. It was an early sign of her lifelong passion for everything that was "progressive."

"Po-poo-lah" was a favorite, a fascinating word signifying everything that the "progressive woman"—a woman such as herself—was all about. And there were certain Thai words that she ignored, preferring their English equivalents—or, at any rate, their equivalents as understood, pronounced, and used by Grandmother. "Ek-sa-hee-bichun" was her word for grand events such as world fairs; "bah-lee-ya-men"[2] was the lawmaking body of our nation; the "kawn-sti-tiu-chun" was the document according to which our "bah-lee-ya-men" carried out its duties.

"You girls must keep yourselves up-to-date if you want to be happy in this world," Grandmother warned. "Not simply hang on to the things you learned when you were young and refuse to learn anything new. Our Thailand remained a free country because our leaders understood that. Do you understand what I am saying?"

She paused, and when all eyes had obediently met hers, she continued. "Look at the countries that surround us. All colonized but Siam! If our leaders had conducted themselves the way theirs did, we would not be holding our face up in the world today, a free people." This, as far as Grandmother was concerned, was an entirely adequate explanation of our fate and theirs.

"It was necessary to be progressive in those days, and we need to be progressive in this day as well. The government is all for it—and certainly, *I* am progressive." So saying, she daintily expectorated a thin stream of betel juice into a silver spittoon.

"I remember when we bought our first radio, when your fathers and mothers were children. The speakers were great, monstrous things. And now, look, you walk around with whole radios no bigger than matchboxes."

Other old ladies might long for days gone by, but to our grandmother, all new things were wonderful.

Still, if we pestered her, she could be coaxed into reminiscing. We loved to hear about such things as, for example, the maids' belts.

"All right then, I will tell you again . . . the maids in my father's house were divided into three levels. The first level—that is, the ones who waited directly upon us—were given gold belts by my father. The second level wore belts of *naak*, the finest mixture of silver, gold, and copper. The rest of the girls wore silver belts. *Not*, of course, the nasty silver you see today but *pure* silver. When you rubbed pure silver, it shone like nothing you can imagine."

We could imagine it. We had definitely been born at the wrong time, but when we suggested as much to Grandmother, she had no sympathy for us.

2.   Parliament.

"There is an old saying: 'The rich will walk through the crooked, poor streets . . . the refuse of those streets will rise up and walk the avenues.' So why do you girls torment yourselves? It is only natural. This family has had its turn."

Doy gave a great sigh. "And today, your very own granddaughters have to go to the market and buy their belts. All the good jewelry in the family went to the maids!"

"For every day at home," Grandmother continued, ignoring Doy, "daughters of good families wore belts made of fine gold chains. They were quite different, I assure you, from maids' belts . . . and when they went out, they wore belts with gems set into the center. Rubies and sometimes diamonds . . ."

We sat and blinked our eyes, imagining having been born then and living thus.

Even now, all of Grandmother's personal possessions, such as her betel implements, were small, charming, and precious, the things of her youth. They were all made of gold or silver. The tiny mortar and pestle for preparing betel that she carried in her purse when she went visiting was made of naak and inlaid with a delicate design.

One afternoon, Noy came to call. She was then twenty-five years old and had been married to Manat for two years.

Kneeling before Grandmother with a sad, downcast face, she announced, "I am going to leave Manat. I simply cannot bear it any longer." Tears glistened on her cheeks.

Grandmother peered at Noy over the tops of her spectacles. "What do you mean, *leave Manat?* You haven't been married long enough to blacken the bottoms of your kitchen pots. Why, you haven't even had your first child."

This observation did not help at all. Noy's reddened eyes brimmed over. "Oh, Grandmother, haven't you heard that Manat is in love with another woman? I am so hurt. To think of Manat having a minor wife . . . *already.*" She dabbed at her eyes with an exquisite handkerchief. "I haven't made a fuss, of course. I wouldn't lower myself to compete with that—with *her.* Anyway," she added bitterly, "Manat isn't anything so special!"

"Compose yourself." Grandmother reached for her betel box. "I thought—and I continue to think—that you made a good marriage.

You are a lovely girl and a competent wife. Certainly, you can't be any worse at marriage than our Noot." Grandmother smiled grimly. "And Noot has two children already. How odd."

Noy shook her head dazedly. "I can't understand it, Grandmother. I don't know why this is happening to me! I keep a lovely home. You know I do! The house, the food, everything . . . I do everything I can to please that man. And Noot!" Noy's little jaw clenched, and she twisted the exquisite handkerchief in her lap at the thought of her cousin Noot.

"Have you ever seen Noot's house, Grandmother? It's dreadful. I can't imagine why Tote puts up with it. Messy, everything messy, no matter when you go there. I went to call on her a little before noon on a Saturday, and she was sleeping, I couldn't believe it, and the place was—*dreadful*." She shuddered.

"*M-m*, I know. Noot has been lazy from the day she was born. She was even a lazy baby. A perfectly content, jolly, lazy baby." She smiled slightly at the memory of the infant Noot, then sighed as she studied the face of the unhappy young woman who sat before her.

Noy was the granddaughter who had shown the characteristics and the behavior of a true lady from childhood. Even as a little girl, she had moved slowly and gracefully. As an adult, Noy's manner might be a bit distant, it was true, but always pleasant. And she was a beautiful girl. Certainly, a man could be proud of such a wife. You could depend upon her, and she was never, ever silly. While Noot could be, and frequently was, extremely silly.

Noot was clever enough, Grandmother had to admit. The girl talked, for one thing. On the other hand, there were the things Noot *said*, but no one had been more "po-poo-lah" as an eligible young woman, no one less likely than Noot to sit "like a leaf on the floor," as her grandson's poor stick of a fiancée had done. We all knew what you have no doubt guessed: of all the granddaughters, Grandmother loved Noot best. Which had not prevented her from predicting when Noot married Tote that the marriage would last three days.

How odd, our grandmother thought, that it was the incomparable, impeccable Noy who sat before her, sniffling delicately into a perfectly pressed square of linen and talking about divorce! Listening to Noy's version of the situation, Grandmother could not see where the child was in the wrong; but then, it was always so difficult to know.

Grandmother thought about the qualities of a lady as enumerated in the ancient writings of Sunthon Phu or Krisna, in those little books one read as a girl. Days long gone. Ideas that had been hundreds of years old when she herself was a bride. How her granddaughters screamed with laughter at the standards for ladylike behavior as enumerated by Krisna. By those standards, Noy would be the wife every man sought; and Noot's imperfections, endless.

She thought to herself, "I must try to do something for poor Noy." She would begin by paying a call on Noot.

The next afternoon, Grandmother sent a girl into the street to call a taxi. She dressed herself carefully and prepared the little bag of lady's paraphernalia without which she would not think of leaving home. Still, going out of the house in the old days, she had often told us, was far more of a nuisance.

Then, no lady of good family simply marched out the door. No, at the very least, one servant girl trailed after, carrying her things. And nearly always, she was surrounded by a chattering swarm of female relatives. Then, there was the matter of correct dress, about which infinite pains must be taken. And all these things were multiplied if the lady's destination was the temple. Then, balancing the required panel of silk neatly across one shoulder, she must walk slowly and with particular grace, and there must be no chattering. It was, of course, all quite different today.

"I am quite capable of going from place to place by myself in the jet age," Grandmother announced huffily, standing in the doorway, her handbag clutched to her bosom. We were insisting that one of us accompany her.

"Nonsense," she snapped. "If I get sick and die out there," she said, gesticulating with one arm toward greater Thonburi, "I have a card in my handbag with my name and address on it. The taxi driver will bring my body home to you people."

As Grandmother lifted her hand to push open the screen door, she heard Noot's voice.

"You come back here this *minute!*" Noot was shouting. The reply to this order was a gleeful screech and the swift patter of small, re-treating footsteps.

Grandmother stuck her head into the kitchen, a room used for a great many purposes in this modest home. There stood Noot, before the sink, doing the best she could to bathe her exuberantly splashing five-month-old son.

Her two-year-old daughter, she of the gleeful screeches, now came racing back into the kitchen, kicking her way through baby clothes, diapers, soap, and a great deal of water.

It was not a tidy scene.

The little girl was carrying a can of baby powder in one hand and banged it on the table top as she raced by, causing clouds of powder to fill the air and roars of laughter to emerge from the delighted, splashing baby.

At this point, a breathless young girl of about twelve burst into the kitchen from another room, pounced upon the two-year-old and at-tempted to drag her off, which she resisted with mighty kicks and howls.

It was at that moment that Noot turned swiftly and saw her grand-mother standing in the doorway.

"Oh, *no!*" she wailed, and then, stricken by her own words, she stood for a moment with her mouth open, then broke into her en-dearing, foolish grin, shrugged her shoulders, and said, "Well, Grand-mother, here you are . . . and here we are." She wiped one hand on her apron, attempted to perform a polite wai, and lost her grip on the slippery infant.

"Compose yourself, Noot. I came alone. There is no need to be up-set just because I stop by for a visit. Go on with—with whatever it is you're doing."

Grandmother sat down on a kitchen chair and reached toward the little girl, who had stopped screaming and was staring at her with in-terest. "Come, come." She smiled and raised her eyebrows. "Well, *come!*"

The child returned her smile and hopped over to her great-grand-mother, who pulled her onto her lap and began to stroke the little head tenderly. The girl who had pounced upon her fled happily, clearly de-lighted with the brief respite from her charge.

Grandmother studied the young woman at the sink, noting that she was soaked with soapy water from head to foot.

"Noot, where is your husband?"

"It's Saturday. This is Tote's day to 'buy grass and feed the horses' . . ."

"The *horses*? Do you mean he's at a *racetrack*? That's a fine thing to indulge him in. Where is that other girl, the one who's supposed to look after Goy? Why can't she give him his bath?"

"She's making dinner. So I have to bathe him myself. It's a wonder I haven't drowned him. He's been under three times. That naughty and that strong."

"Child, is there a single thing you can do properly?"

Noot chuckled. "Not really. That's the problem. I thought it would be easier to give Goy a bath than to make dinner . . . only, it wasn't. Still, I do this better than I cook. When I make dinner, Tote refuses to eat. He says if he ever had to eat my cooking ten days in a row, he'd be nothing but bones."

Grandmother watched with interest as Noot searched through the pile of baby clothes on the table, then the pile on the floor, tossing things aside until she found the garments she wanted for Goy.

"Noot, dear, you look like you got into the bath with him. You haven't changed a bit since you were a child, and here you are with two children of your own. When do you expect your husband to come home?"

"That all depends. If the horse kicks him—I mean, if he loses—he'll be home early. But if he wins, he'll come home later. If he wins a lot, well, then he'll come home a lot later."

"And that's all right with you?" Grandmother's voice reflected curiosity but not disapproval. She was here to learn. Everyone said that Tote was inordinately fond of his young wife. What was it that a woman did, as an up-to-date, progressive wife, to make her marriage work?

"Is what all right? You mean the horses? Oh, I never say anything about that. After all, if he makes extra money outside of his job, a thousand baht or even more, why complain? He likes to go out and have fun with his friends. They don't do anything bad. He meets them at the track, and they go out to play billiards, and then he comes home."

"I see."

"Grandmother, the fact is that I'd rather have Tote out playing billiards with his friends once in a while than sitting at home moping and picking fights with me." She grinned mischievously. "Besides, this way he's always a little in my debt. Do you know what I mean?"

Indeed, she did. Yes, the excellent Noy could learn a few things from her feckless cousin.

Noot turned at the sound of footsteps outside. "You're in luck. Here he comes." She glanced at a clock on the wall. "Only five o'clock? Oh, dear—this probably means we're fifteen hundred baht poorer than we were this morning."

At that moment, Tote walked into the room, a handsome young man whose eyes flashed from his wife to her grandmother to the state of the kitchen and back to his wife. He laughed nervously and said, "Why, Grandmother, what a surprise."

Noot giggled, bundled up the baby, and handed him to Tote, who gave his son a loud, smacking kiss, then bent over and hugged his daughter.

"So, the horse kicked you," Noot pronounced.

Tote blushed and made no reply to Noot's surmise, but when he looked at her granddaughter, Grandmother noted with some astonishment, his expression held the faint embarrassment, admiration, and fervent hope of a schoolboy with a crush on the prettiest girl in class.

"Tomorrow," said Grandmother to herself, musing at the spectacle of the young couple who grinned at each other amidst the chaos of their life, "I will go to see Noy. I think we need to have a talk . . . she knows how to be a good wife. But she knows nothing at all about how to be a *progressive* one."

O O   JUNLADA PHAKDIPHUMIN AND
        "GRANDMOTHER THE PROGRESSIVE"

Junlada Phakdiphumin is the pen name of Mom Luang Sri-faa Mahawaan; many of her very popular short stories and novels are written under the pen name "Sri-faa." Junlada was born in Bangkok in 1930 and began writing in secondary school. She is a most prolific and well-loved writer whose work, in general, reflects social and political aspects of Thai life. She also writes very popular lighter stories, of which "Grandmother the Progressive" is a typical example. Junlada has written dozens of short stories and nearly one hundred novels, many of which have received literary awards from the Ministry of Education and numerous literary groups.

This selection was chosen because it represents so well that genre of women's fiction in which poverty, injustice, and troubled hearts have no place. It meets the criteria set by the legendary United States television producer who is said to have ordered his writers to turn out "happy stories about people with happy problems." The popularity of stories of this kind in Thailand, both in fiction and in television sitcoms, indicates that in Thailand, as elsewhere, most of the fiction-buying public would rather escape into Grandmother's world than delve into the world of tragedy and inequity portrayed in much of the critically admired contemporary fiction.

Another reason for including this story is the interesting juxtaposition of values and lifestyles: the granddaughters feel the great contrast between the good old days of Grandmother's tales when even servants wore jeweled belts and the Bangkok of today when Noot's only servant is a little girl with no particular skills, much less a vocation in service. Nevertheless, the only glimpse the reader has of ordinary people is the sketchy portrait of this hapless baby-sitter— or, more accurately, "baby-watcher." Virtually everyone else in the story represents the old elite, even if, as Grandmother firmly declares, the family's reign is over: "The rich will walk through the crooked, poor streets . . . the refuse of those streets will rise up and walk the avenues."

Still, if most Thai readers feel that their own lineage may be closer to the latter status than the former, it is pleasant to read about elite, happy families with happy problems. I suspect that the proportion of women who read stories of this kind to those who read the literature of social conscience is not much different in Thailand from what it is in other nations with a similarly high rate of literacy (about 80 percent). One of the benefits of literacy, after all, is the right to chart one's own avenues of literary escape. Even in the translated English and American fiction that is widely available in Thailand, bodice rippers and light, humorous tales vastly outsell winners of the National Book Award or the Booker Prize.

Deep in the Heart of a Mother

Wat Wanlayankul

An amusing, bittersweet story about an aging mother
with disappointing children.

The old woman's eyebrows pull together in the middle, and her lips
open slightly, which makes her look sad, although she is not. Her gaze
meets that of the foreign lady on the playing card. The old woman is
frowning because the lady reminds her of someone, but she can't quite
get it. This happens to her all the time. Something will vaguely occur
to her, but then she can't quite get it.

She turns to look at Lover Boy, the old dog. Well, he's no help. If
Lover Boy were a person, he would probably show the same symptoms. Ten years old for a dog is—what? Sixty or seventy years for a
human being? She turns back to the picture of the foreign lady and
the other cards lined up on the table before her.

The result of concentrating on the foreign lady's face is a feeling of
loss. No, not loss . . . a perception of kindliness and of feelings hidden away. Is this our own face? So, this is what it is, being old.

A weak, unpleasant sensation slithers up from her chest into the
base of her throat, like a demon sucking, and gives her chilly shudders despite the intense heat of the afternoon. A dark shadow slides
into the house through the doorway and wraps itself in the dimness
of the room. What kind of a demon is that? Maybe it is just a shadow
and nothing more. Or maybe it is death.

Her children have studied and know more about life, in some respects. Their mother's doings, in the eyes of this group, are humorous or embarrassing, as her own parents' doings once were to her.
Therefore, they are not much interested in what she has to say. Or they

This story appears in a collection of Wat Wanlayankul's work entitled *Nakhɔn hɛɛ̀ng
duang daaw* (City of stars), published by Khon Wannakaam Press, Bangkok, in 1984.

laugh. Oh, my children. Old people are not up with the times, that is true. Everything they do is amusing.

When she meets this behavior in her children, she loses confidence in herself and doesn't feel like talking to anybody or thinking. She doesn't want to be interested in anything. Certainly, she is not up to fighting these weak, shuddery feelings, much less the demons that come with them. And, yet, she feels more—more *faith*, some kind of a faith that is like armor shielding her. She could not describe it, but she knows what it feels like. She notices it especially when she is with her son Berm, the oldest one.

She rose from the sofa and tottered across the room to switch on the fan. As the cool air began to blow over her, the constriction in her chest and throat slowly eased. She always thought the fan looked like a round, smart, happy face. Her son Bawm had saved up his money to buy her this fan. Such a small salary, yet he thinks of his mother.

A fan is the best thing for heart disease of the not-enough-oxygen kind. It helps keeps the person cool. On the other hand, after it blows for a while, it makes the lungs worse. You get something, you lose something.

That is how it goes your whole life, she mused, the gaining and the losing. You work, for which you get money, but in the end you lose your strength. Once she had wanted a daughter (because she already had two sons), but when she got the daughter, her husband, whom she loved, got killed in an accident. She didn't know whom to blame for that.

The old woman had discovered that the moon tree in front of their house grew visibly taller every day. She measured its progress against the glass slats of the louvered window, watching the leaves ascending slat by slat, day by day. Now, at noon, she could almost hear its tiny new leaves opening. That was peculiar, she thought. In the countryside, one heard such noises in the deepest part of the night. But here, the deepest silence lay across the middle of the day. Hard to believe, with all these houses stuck together in a row, what they called a townhouse. Some days, it was too quiet and frightened her.

In this whole street, there was no one at home during the day but old people, a few dull-witted girls sulking over washtubs, and men who had fallen into low jobs, working an hour here, an hour there. Once in a while, she heard the sound of a bicycle and would make her way to the doorway only to catch a fleeting glimpse of a blue and white uniform, as a student pedaled by. It always warmed her heart, that glimpse of youth.

Near the window was a small table, on which lay a gold-colored plaque that had been recently awarded to Berm. It was some kind of government award. She couldn't remember what it was, but his name was in the newspaper about it and his picture, too. What was it? Something about working with children. The boy in the house next door had been impressed.

"Berm is real smart," he said. Then he laughed. "It's funny that he got an award for working with children, because he looks so old and serious."

"He must have been drinking when they took the picture. He always looks like that when he's drinking. Old—old and flushed in the face."

At dusk, the neighborhood gradually came to life again. The cars returned; people got out and talked to each other. Stereo speakers spouted music up and down the block, and one by one the TV sets were turned on.

Most days, dusk brought relief from the heat but not today.

The old woman sat on, patiently dealing her cards, glancing at the doorway with each new sound of hurrying footsteps, each car slowing down and stopping. Every day was the same. Hour after hour, she contended with the quiet and the loneliness; and it was when her children's day came to an end that her real day began.

At last came the sound of footsteps that were, to her, long spaced, the steps of someone tall, the footsteps of her daughter, who suddenly walked through the door. Lover Boy opened his eyes, rearranged his chin on his paws, and promptly went back to sleep, not caring that her long calves in their white knee socks brushed his nose.

Clutching her schoolbooks closer in her arms, the girl put her palms together before her face in a wai, bobbed in her mother's direction, and rushed past her.

Her youngest child was now home, had burst through the door like a flower opening. The first flower to open in my garden today, her mother thought as she turned over another card.

The old woman listened to the thrumming traffic that now filled the street until she heard the distinctive, rumbling sound of Bawm's car coming closer, slowing, and stopping. She went to the door and watched him park the familiar, dented old green car beside the moon tree, as he did every day.

Ordinarily, Bawm kissed his mother lightly on the cheek as he came through the door, but tonight he paused for a moment, cocking his head and looking faintly dismayed, as if to ask, "What's wrong?" Then a glint of mischief began to transform his expression. Slowly, he raised his hands to the base of his mother's throat, where they paused for a moment above the slack folds of skin. Then his fingers dove lightly into his mother's flesh, and he began to tickle her, crying "*Jucker-jee! Jucker-jee!*" as one does with babies, tickling them at the top of their chest where they are especially ticklish, and where he knew his mother was, too.

She screeched with pleasure. "Oh, you fool! Stop, stop, I can't get my breath . . . oh, oh . . . ." She leaned against her son, gasping for breath and wiping the tears from her eyes.

As a boy, Bawm had been homely and dark skinned, and his manners were blunt. He wasn't clever at anything, unlike his brother. Bawm had graduated from school with ordinary grades and gone straight into an ordinary government job. He had been working for two years, and his salary paid the major share of the mortgage.

When the woman was forced to quit working because of her health, her retirement money provided just enough for the down payment on the house and for the old green car Bawm now drove. He had insisted they have a car of some kind because of her health. If Mama should become suddenly ill, they could take her to the doctor or the hospital at once. He had wanted his brother and sister to drive it, too. She had gone as far as getting her driver's licence but was not interested in driving. As for Berm, he ignored the car altogether and managed to give the impression that he couldn't see any reason for owning one.

She never knew when Berm would come home. Some days, he arrived early; other days, he didn't return until late at night. For a while, he would go off faithfully every morning; but after a few weeks of that, he might pass a whole week at home, doing nothing at all. And often, when he did come home, he was surrounded by a swarm of friends. They would talk, laugh, and drink; and eventually, they would fall asleep all over the house.

Tonight, the dinner hour had come and gone. Lover Boy was now fully awake and sat looking at the door with a lonely, hopeful expression. He waited eagerly for the one person in the house who played with him. Berm had brought Lover Boy home when he was a tiny puppy, and although he had become part of the family, the rest of them seldom paid any attention to him.

Outside the door, there were now many sounds besides the traffic. High-heeled shoes clattered by, bicycle chains grated, and a peddler shuffled past the door, crying out the names of the snacks piled high on baskets suspended from her shoulder pole. Neon lights from across the street glowed and were reflected on the leaves of the moon tree.

Images on the TV screen flickered continually as the heroine of a Chinese movie jumped around. The old woman didn't like it. It was like watching the Chinese opera. So much noise, all that fighting and jumping around, it could give a person a heart attack.

Lover Boy began to wag his tail. Then he jumped up and barked. Berm entered the room, his face solemn. He bent over to pet the joyful dog.

"Take a bath first," his mother said. "That's all you think about when you come home, kissing that dog."

Berm ignored her remark. "He needs exercise," he said. "Don't you, boy? Yah, yah—look at that gut." Lover Boy gazed into Berm's eyes, his tail wagging furiously. Berm turned around and went back through the door, the ecstatic Lover Boy at his heel.

They were gone a long time. Later that evening, after he had washed and done a few household chores, Berm sat down with a novel.

"The boy next door said you look *old* in that picture in the newspaper," his mother said without looking at him. She didn't mention that the boy had said Berm was smart. "It's the liquor," she said. "You wouldn't look so old if you didn't drink." She went on placing one card after another before her on the table, just as she had done in the afternoon when she was all alone.

Berm put down his book. As if he had not heard a word she said, he turned to Lover Boy and began to scratch his stomach.

She scooped up the cards and began to deal them anew. There it was again, the face of the foreign lady staring up at her.

"You still haven't learned how to drive the car. Good. Because if you did know how, I wouldn't let you."

Berm laughed to himself softly, then pressed his lips together swiftly in what might have been a smile. "If I was drunk, Mother, I'd either sleep it off where I was or come home in a taxi."

"And what would happen to the car?"

Berm shrugged. "Nothing."

"What would you do, just leave it?"

"Sure."

"And let somebody steal it."

Berm didn't reply.

"That's good. My son doesn't care if somebody steals from him, not even his car."

He had never been any different, not even as a boy. His friends could borrow money, never pay it back, take his things—he didn't care, never asked. Look at what happened when he won that award. Money came with it, so he took all the money and spent it drinking with his friends, buying drinks for everybody until it was gone.

"To tell you the truth, Mother, I don't want to drive. I don't even want to learn how. If I could drive, I'd probably end up wanting my own car, or I'd end up arguing over this one with Bawm. It's better this way."

"Having nothing. Doing nothing. Is this how you're going to be your whole life? Don't you worry about when you get old?"

Berm was silent for a moment. He turned to her and said, "Mama, don't you know that people like me never starve?"

Berm had started by working for the government, like Bawm. But he didn't like it. Too many rules.

Long ago, she had believed that he was indeed the kind of person who would never starve. Many of her relatives had said that Berm looked like her. She had always been a hard worker; Berm, too, would be able to take care of himself. He would have a good life. She had believed it would be so. Had she been so wrong about him? If only Berm didn't like to drink so much. What was he interested in? Things that were nothing, of no importance.

A week ago, during one of their arguments, he had said angrily, "Why don't you leave me alone? I'll probably be dead before long, anyway."

She was furious and scared. "What are you thinking of?" He was talking like an old man! "You are not old, but your mother is. Don't you think of that? There are ten years left on this mortgage. Your brother's salary is not so big. What about him? What about your little sister? Don't they matter to you? No. What happens to your family means nothing to you."

Now he was silent. His mother watched a bead of sweat form on his forehead and run down his face. Berm's brows protruded in a frown; his face was puffy and flushed, marked with faint lines. Angry as she was, the woman felt a stab of sorrow.

"Oh, my son, my handsome Berm," she thought. "You could be a good-looking man still, if only you would change."

Berm tossed his book aside. "I'll be back soon," he said and left the house.

The air had not cooled enough to make the room bearable. The damp, plastic skin of the sofa stuck to the skin of her arms. Outside, not a leaf of the tree moved, and the street seemed to be regaining the bleak quality it had had at midday.

A random collection of thoughts invaded her mind, succeeding and overlapping each other. Her memory was unreliable. It was so frustrating to forget the simplest things. Sometimes she couldn't even add or subtract a few numbers, and then things would occur to her, memories of things that had happened years before, and she could remember every detail about them. Who said what, and what happened. Not important things; in fact, they were generally useless or stupid things that she would never have made a point of remembering. But she found that it didn't work that way. She didn't remember things because they were important. There wasn't anything logical about memory.

She found herself thinking about a man and wife who used to live near her. The husband was keeping a minor wife, and when the legal wife found out about it, they had a big fight. In the end, they decided to sell the house cheap and split the profit. But on the day they were supposed to sell, the husband didn't show up. He said he would rather let the bank just take it all than give her half. What a shame. The downpayment, all those mortgage payments, for nothing. He didn't care. He would rather get nothing. Now *that*, the old woman reflected, was *anger*.

Why was she thinking about those people? Why should she think about them? People she had known once, not very well, and would never meet again. This was the kind of thing that came into her mind, some event that had nothing to do with her own life and was past, anyway. She couldn't figure out a bill, but she could sit there and think about those three, the man and his wife and his minor wife, and what did that whole mess have to do with her bad heart, anyway?

She switched the fan to high. How often had she got off the couch during this whole day? She could count the number of times. To go to the bathroom, to eat rice, to feed Lover Boy, that was all. The fan breathed, turning its face slowly from left to right; the fan was a living thing, and this was its job. It had its purpose, unlike a person who could only sit and breathe, all alone, to no purpose.

Her breathing was becoming more difficult, as if something were stuck. She coughed as hard as she could and groped for her medicine. Bawm came into the room and turned off the fan. There was nothing else to do but cough, nothing but make herself fight once more the terror against which all her courage, allied with her feeble breath, was less and less able to prevail.

Thoughts, so many thoughts, all fearful. Why had Berm gone out? He just got home. Maybe he didn't want to hear his mother going on and on again. For a month now, perhaps longer, she had been complaining about the drinking and other things.

"I'll be back soon," he had said, but an hour had passed since then. Lover Boy looked sad.

She reached out and smoothed the top of his head. "Poor Lover, poor Lover. Is Berm mad at his mama? Maybe he thinks I don't understand him. Old people are a bore, Lover Boy, yes, they are."

Why couldn't she understand her own son? He said he wanted to work for children and help society. Those were his own words. He was earnest about it, she could see, because somebody in the government had seen fit to give him an award and put his picture in the paper. People told her Berm was smart. Why couldn't she be proud of this son?

She felt ashamed, but this was succeeded by anger. Those people who thought so much of him that they gave him an award—had they thought about *his* problems? While he was helping children and society, what about his *family*'s problems?

Could it be getting hotter as the evening wore on? Bawm and his sister were asleep in their beds. She looked over at Berm's plaque. She worked hard her whole life, and nobody ever gave her any kind of award. This neither pleased nor dismayed her; it was just a fact. Her work had been her work; that was all.

She had been the housekeeper in a student boarding house, working hard until she couldn't anymore. All those years, she never missed a day, sick or not. She seldom slept through a night. There was always some student out after curfew, knocking softly at her door, asking to borrow her key. When the lady who was her boss found out, she said that was very unfair, that everyone had the right to be asleep by ten and stay asleep. No more getting up for those kids: they could pay a hundred baht fine to get in if it was so important to stay out late.

But she had felt sorry for them. Some didn't have the money, or they had a perfectly reasonable excuse for their lateness. Better for one person to be inconvenienced, she thought—herself—than for many people to be unhappy.

But she had been strict with her own children. Maybe that's what was wrong with them. But why were they still like children? Would they ever understand why she had tried to teach them to be reliable, to have discipline? So that they would not have to suffer when they were old. On the other hand, she had been reliable and disciplined, and she was old and suffering.

Suddenly, Lover Boy raised himself off his belly and stretched his neck toward the sound of men's voices at the door. Familiar voices. Berm and his friends, some carrying bottles and one holding a bag of snacks. This entrance was unlike Berm's first homecoming. Everyone was jolly.

The friends greeted her politely, bowing and wai-ing with respect as they settled themselves on the floor.

"You don't mind sitting on the floor?" Berm asked. Nobody minded. He unfolded a newspaper, and they set the bottles and snacks on it.

The woman sat quietly, observing this scene. Probably Berm's friends didn't think much of this place, without even a table and chairs to sit around. She stole a glance at a rotund young man who sat cross-legged, a position that made it difficult for him to reach the bottle.

Her heart fluttered under the damp skin of her breast. Great drops of sweat ran in rivulets down her throat as she sat and watched the young men drink and laugh together. She felt as though she were breathing in hot steam instead of plain air. Hot steam that invaded her throat and stopped there. This heat was like a stone rolled onto her chest. The stone grew heavier.

The tiny pill she put beneath her tongue did nothing for the tight feeling that climbed from her ears into her temples, then moved into her eyes and made her vision swim. She tried to focus on the shiny plaque, and as it became clear to her, a wave, not of pain, but of bitter disappointment flowed through her. She looked at her son Berm and his friends, their mouths opening in laughter, opening to gobble and swallow. The sounds they made were indistinct to her; their voices sounded like *er-r-r . . . an-n-n*. The heat within her increased until she felt that her blood was about to boil. She reached for the switch on the fan, but she could make only weak, grabbing motions toward it.

Berm turned and looked at her, so that the last thing she remembered, before the dark curtain dropped, was Berm's face, not looking away, not escaping, but staring straight into her eyes, her fear suffusing his face.

They took her home from the hospital a little early. She was exhausted; she couldn't sleep in that place because it was so crowded. Hour after hour, day after day, people who had been shot or in car accidents or were having babies. She amused them with a story about one of the gunshot victims.

"The bullet went in his lung and went out his arm. He kept shouting, 'Am I dying, Doctor? Am I dying?' I bet the whole neighborhood could hear him. What did he think? That if he were dying, he'd be able to yell like that?"

All three of her children laughed, and she laughed with them. How long had it been since she had sat in a car with all three of her children?

As they inched forward in heavy traffic, simultaneously the car bounced, and they heard a loud bang. Bawm jumped out to find the driver of the car behind them peering anxiously at their rear bumper.

"It's nothing," Bawm said. "A little dent I can hardly see."

The man smiled with relief, bowing and thanking Bawm as they both returned to their cars.

"He was in the wrong," the old woman said as they resumed their slow progress down the crowded street.

"So what? It's just a little nick."

She sighed. "You could have asked him for something."

"Mama, I don't know how I could ask him for something. For what? A little nick like that?"

"A little nick, a little dent. Soon, we have a pile of nicks and dents, metal scraps instead of a car."

"You are right."

She knew he didn't care. She sat quietly, stealing a glance at him without turning her head. Then she turned around and looked at Berm, whose face reminded her of the other night when she was playing cards and he was scratching the dog's stomach.

Getting out of the car at home, she said, "You're all alike. Not one of you ever understands what I mean when I talk to you."

The next afternoon, she carried out her plan, working very slowly and stopping every few minutes to rest. She was quite sure that she would find everything she needed behind the house, and she was right. First, she dragged a two-foot square sheet of plywood through the kitchen and set it on the living-room floor. Then, one at a time she brought in four blocks of wood, each a foot high.

She sat on the floor cutting pretty paper and gluing it to the blocks of wood, and when she was finished, she set the plywood on top of them and covered the plywood with a tablecloth. Sitting back on the couch with her hands in her lap, she admired her creation.

When Bawm and her daughter returned home that evening, they made a great fuss. She should have been resting, lying down. Why had she done such a thing?

"It was nothing," she said.

She waited for Berm.

He was the last to come home, as usual, and tonight two friends were with him. One of them carried a bottle. As Berm picked up a newspaper and began to spread it on the floor, the friend with the bottle set it down on the pretty, new table. His mother said nothing. She sat on her couch, dealing her cards.

Berm turned to her, still on his knees with the newspaper in his hands. "Mama, what is this?"

She met his eyes and said, "It's a drinking table."

"Where did you get it?"

"I made it myself." And then she shrugged, as if the making of drinking tables were no special feat.

Berm tossed the newspaper aside and moved toward her clumsily on his knees. She smelled the whiskey on his breath as he came near. His nose bumped into her cheek; then he pressed his lips to it and kissed her loudly.

The corners of her mouth began to twitch. As Berm leaned away from her, she turned over the next card. It was the foreign lady, and she was smiling.

O   O   WAT WANLAYANKUL AND
          "DEEP IN THE HEART OF A MOTHER"

This author's real name is Wirawat Wanlayankul. He uses the shorter name "Wat" in his writing: a partial pen name of this kind is not uncommon among Thai writers. Clearly, anonymity is not the goal; the pen name defines the writing self. Wirawat Wanlayankul is a businessman from Kanchanaburi; "Wat" Wanlayankul is an author.

Born in Lopburi Province in 1955, Wat began writing when he was fifteen years old. His work gained prominence in the mid-1970s, during the period of political and artistic openness that followed the political upheavals of 1973. He has focused on problems that individuals and Thai society at large have faced due to the nature and the pace of economic, political, and social change in recent decades. Two of Wat's stories have been awarded the Best Short Story of the Year prize by PEN-Thailand.

As of this writing, six collections of his short stories, seven of his novels, and three collections of his poetry have been published. Wat continues to write and to pursue a business career in Kanchanaburi.

I include this short story because of Wat's sensitive, dead-on portrayal of an average, lower-middle-class Bangkok family; its depiction of mother-son relationships; and its strong, subtle Buddhist content. In this story, as in many works of Thai literature, Buddhist beliefs are not alluded to in any direct fashion, yet they underlie and sustain the characters' perceptions of reality and their definition of self. Moreover, they have a great effect on the actions that the author arranges for the characters to choose. Karma, it must be remembered, is synonymous, not with *fate*, but with *action*. One's actions add to the all-important credit-debit balance with which one arrives in life; each action alters the balance with which one leaves this life and, it is hoped, enters the next.[1]

The kind of relationship that exists between the mother and Bawm, one of intimate, comfortable, lifelong interdependence, appears with some frequency in Thai literature.[2] This relationship is exquisitely drawn in the scene in which Bawm tickles his mother, "crying '*Jucker-jee! Jucker-jee!*' as one does with babies, tickling them at the top of their chest where they are especially ticklish, and where he knew his mother was, too.

"She screeched with pleasure. 'Oh, you fool! Stop, stop, I can't get my breath . . . oh, oh . . .' She leaned against her son, gasping for breath and wiping the tears from her eyes."

Bawm will never amount to much; Berm is worse, drunk most of the time and with shiftless friends. The point of the story, aside from the depiction of the profound love between mothers and sons, is the importance of accepting other human beings as they are and cannot help but be. The mother and both of the sons in this story are living a life that has, in many respects, been determined by their actions, or karma, good and bad, through countless lives. Why should she spoil her last, precious years in resenting what she cannot change? And so, she builds the very table at which her son Berm and his friends can go on drinking.

The relationship between the mother and her only daughter is something else again. The only role of the daughter, who is never given a name (even the dog is named), is to scurry through the house on her way home from school, "burst[ing] through the door like a flower opening. The first flower to open in my garden today, her mother thought as she turned over another card." The mother had wanted a daughter "because she already had two sons," a telling

---

1.   It is not at all certain, according to Buddhist belief, that one will die only to wake up as a human baby somewhere. There are many other possibilities.

2.   This relationship is particularly similar to that between Ploy and her youngest son in the famous novel *Four Reigns*, by M. R. Kukrit Pramoj. The son never marries, and despite a foreign university education, which he endured with great difficulty, he asks nothing of life but to stay at his mother's side.

remark that indicates the luxury of being able to wish for a daughter, once the birth of sons has been achieved. But it is the sons who have her heart. I do not wish to make too much of this; and I do not believe that the author meant to make a statement through the shadowy portrayal of this daughter.

From *People of Quality*
Dok Mai Sot

In this classic novel about an ideal Thai woman of
the upper class, written in 1934, the heroine helps
to save the family fortune while keeping her siblings
united and strong after their father's untimely death.
Two excerpts are included here. In the first, Khun Sae
writes a letter to Wimon. In the second, Khun Sae visits
the dying Khunying Saay-swaat.

*[As the novel opens, Wimon is preparing for the lavish party her father, Chao Khun
Amornrat,[1] will give on the following day in honor of her twenty-first birthday.*

*The letter from Khun Sae to her daughter Wimon, which follows, provides con-
siderable information about the characters in the story—and about women in Thai
upper-class life and in Thai fiction during the 1930s.*

*Khun Sae is the first (or "major") wife of Wimon's father. She chooses to live in
Chantaburi, which is approximately two hundred miles southeast of Bangkok, near
the Cambodian border. Wimon lives in Bangkok with her father.*

*In this letter, Khun Sae advises Wimon on how to be a good woman and a suc-
cessful* meh baan, *or* mɛ̂ɛ bâan *(literally, "mother [of the] house"), which cannot
be translated exactly. The meh baan, that is, the woman who is in charge of running
the household, is usually the major wife (or a minor wife if the major wife is not
resident), but there are exceptions. As I state in the introduction, the Thai woman
traditionally has managed family finances and borne a great deal of responsibility
for the family's welfare. In this case, Khun Sae clearly expects Wimon to become
the meh baan of her father's household, even though a minor wife of her father's and
some of that wife's children are living in the home. (They will leave, early in the
novel.)]*

The edition of the novel from which this translation was prepared was published by
Prae Pittaya, Bangkok, in 1970.
   1.   *Chao khun,* or *câw khun,* was one of the titles given to senior officials at court before the overthrow of the monarchy; such titles were held for life.

Sala Santi
Chantaburi

15 January B.E. 2477[2]

Little One, Beloved Child,
I await the twenty-first day of January with a most impatient heart, for I have found something for your birthday that pleases me greatly, and that I think you will like.

The workmanship of the goldsmiths here in Chantaburi is not particularly good. At first, I thought to send the stone just as it was and not have it set at all. But then, you would not have been able to wear it on your birthday. Begrudgingly, I let the jeweler set it. If you don't like it, do have it reset, and have the bill sent to me. I hope that it will arrive in time for my little one's birthday; I shall be so disappointed if it does not.

I have made up my mind to give you two gifts on this special birthday. The first is tangible and visible; you can hold it in your hand. The second is invisible and must be held in your heart. The first gift, of course, is the sapphire locket. The second consists of the remainder of this birthday letter.

Dear Wimon, beloved daughter, from this day forward everyone will consider you an adult.[3] When a young woman is twenty-one years of age, no one will say of a careless word or action, "Ah, but she is just a child . . ." Such excuses can no longer be made. Therefore, on this important birthday I wish to give you some words of loving advice on the principles by which a grown woman must live. Hold them in your heart, Wimon, and rely upon them to guide your behavior.

First, a simple rule for yourself: Guard against carelessness, whether in speech, in action, or in thought. Consider, before you speak, why you mean to speak. Is it love that prompts you to speak? Or feelings of anger, hatred, envy, or boastfulness? Before you take an action, ask yourself the same question. If you do this, my child,

2.   B.E. (Buddhist era) 2477 is equivalent to 1934.
3.   The term she uses is *phûu yàay*, literally, a "large person." In fact, the term has several meanings: a person over twenty-one years of age or an important person or both. In a household, to children of the family *phûu yàay* are the adults, such as grandparents, parents, older relatives; to servants, the family in general represents the *phûu yàay*; in society at large, the term refers to political leaders and wealthy, influential people in general.

you will behave sensibly, and others will have no cause to criticize you.

Second, a rule for the direction of your household. When you are an adult, you must conduct yourself according to your principles. People who do not do so are quite apt to say one thing and do another, and fail to think before they speak or to consider what is suitable to say, and what is not. They babble on, and their words are valued by no one.

You must be feared in your household. Not, of course, because you are unkind, but because you are just. It is your responsibility to set standards for the behavior of younger people in your house and of your servants.[4] They should know that you too are bound by standards. When anyone does wrong, you must recognize that person's error, and help him or her to understand and rectify it.

If you do these things, people will fear and love you. Like a good teacher, the meh baan who successfully manages her household understands that a good heart is not enough. The teacher who is most loved is strict but also kind. It is exactly the same for a meh baan. Though she may be good-hearted to a fault, a fault it will be if she does not also have the power to instill fear in her servants. They will smile to her face—and gossip behind her back.

Of course, the meh baan who instills only fear and inspires no love will have new servants every three days. You will win both fear and love when everyone in the household knows that misdeeds will be punished without prejudice or favor, and good deeds rewarded. Your everyday manner of speaking should be soft and kind. When a servant is unwell, you must provide good care, and no one who is ill should be sent away.

My little one must not suppose that these things are easy to accomplish. Nor would I have you fear that they are too difficult. But easy or difficult, you must do your very best. Do you remember how unsure you felt when your father announced his intention to send you to boarding school?

I remember when you graduated and came to visit me. I saw that your father's hopes for you had indeed been fulfilled, and I shall always be grateful to him for his decision. How proud he was when

4. The Thai word used here is *phûu nɔ́ɔy*, literally, "small people," referring to social inferiors. This term sounds less pejorative in Thai than the translation indicates.

you returned home even lovelier and more charming than you had been before. But now, my child, it is no longer enough to be Father's lovely, charming girl. You will be called *Khun* Wimon;[5] you must behave in such a way that your name will be a fragrance in the air and bring you honor and joy.

When you were a child, it was enough that you were a good girl in the eyes of your father and mother. But now, you must be a good woman in the eyes of the world. Moreover, you must know how to recognize good people and to emulate them.

The people who live in your house today, Little One, are not all servants. Your stepmother is there also and her two children. You must be a bit careful and realize that people may be devious, yet it is important that you are not overly suspicious of others, lest you cause estrangement. You should never be afraid of others when they have done wrong, yet you must avoid seeming to disparage them for their actions, lest they be embarrassed before others.

Listen to people when they want to confide in you, unless you perceive that they are attempting to turn you against others. Do not be irritated when people try to give you advice; consider what they have to say. People who fawn over you and flatter you can never be trusted. Do not trust people under your authority on the basis of what they tell you to your face; with your own eyes, observe what they do.

When someone comes to you with accusations against another, under no circumstances must you join in their folly and abandon your dignity. Nothing invites more scorn than a light ear that eagerly accepts all tales and a gossiping mouth that repeats them.

My final word of advice, Little One, is this: she who would govern others, must first be able to govern herself.

On this birthday, may you strive to be good, as I have taught you. May you continue to be blessed, to have no injury, to know no pain. May you live long and achieve honors; may your life be prosperous and your name as perfume. May all who see you, love you; may you

---

5.   *Khun* is a second-person pronoun used between peers and to superiors. (It also is used by Thais addressing foreigners as in "Khun Julia" but not "Khun Smith.") Today, it is the most common pronoun used between adults in ordinary social situations. Sixty years ago, *khun* bore a stronger connotation of class (the person being spoken to as "Khun" might well be far above the speaker in social class). Then and now, servants in a household would use "Khun" when speaking to superiors.

know happiness and health, and continue to be your father's joy all
the days of his life.[6]

o   o   o   o

[On the day following Wimon's twenty-first birthday, her father, Chao Khun Amorn-
rat, collapses and dies. To the consternation of all, it is discovered that he had been
in serious financial difficulty. Wimon, her older brother, who is studying abroad, and
her younger siblings—all face a troubling future.

Khun Sae had written a letter preparing her daughter for the life of a well-to-do
aristocrat's wife. Of what use are her cautions about the treatment of servants when
Wimon and her siblings move into the servants' quarters themselves and prepare to
rent the family home?

This was Wimon's idea. Having taken charge of the situation, she has decided to
rent the family home to Phraya Ponewat, a high official with the Ministry of Foreign
Affairs (who is referred to as Chao Khun throughout the novel); his wife, Khunying
Saay-swaat (who is dying of tuberculosis); and their young son, Sumon.

Characters in the following excerpt include Khun Sae and Khunying Saay-swaat,
who is arguably the most interesting character in the novel. Before her illness, this
lady, who is in her late twenties or early thirties, was a famous beauty, a woman of
wonderful energy and great enthusiasms. Now, tuberculosis has robbed her of all that.
Determined to die a graceful death, strong in her Buddhist faith, Khunying Saay-
swaat now faces the reality that even in this she will be thwarted. Her life has trailed
on, and fear and suffering have taken their toll. The once indomitable khunying *is*
becoming consumed with envy of those who will live on, with bitterness at her fate,
and with worry about her surviving son. And she loathes herself, despising the de-
pendent, complaining creature she has become.

This passage typifies the strong Buddhist message in Dok Mai Sot's novels. Once
the reader recognizes the fundamental themes of Buddhist philosophy, as represented
in the excerpt that follows, they become apparent in virtually all Thai fiction: One's
karma is the chief determinant of one's status and fortunes in this life. Karma is the
current balance of good and bad deeds performed in previous lives. It is incumbent
upon everyone to attempt to do good deeds in this life, so that the karmic balance will
be improved in one's next incarnation. One is unable to change the important facts
about one's life or the lives of other people, because of the workings of karma; all that
one can do is to accept reality, living and dying in true wisdom.

6.   This excerpt is translated from Dok Mai Sot, *Phûu dii*, 19–25.

Perhaps the oddest single feature in this excerpt, in comparison with a similar scene in a Western novel, is that Wimon is present but does not utter a word during the entire scene. The author means to show that Wimon is upset by other events in the story. But, even were that not so, the fact that she contributes nothing to the conversation does not strike Khunying Saay-swaat, or her mother, as particularly odd, since it is acceptable for a young, unmarried woman to sit in attendance upon her elders in respectful silence.]

Khun Sae prepared to pay a second visit to Khunying Ponewat.[7]

This time she came informally and alone. No one had come to introduce her, nor had she announced her intention to stop by.

Khun Sae walked up the front stairs and went straight to the khunying's bedroom, but as she began to enter the room, she stopped abruptly, seeing that her new friend was in bed, with the covers pulled up. Wimon sat quietly on the floor, in the center of the room. Khun Sae turned to leave, lest she waken the sleeping woman, but the khunying had seen her and called to her in a weak, hoarse voice.

"If you are going to come see me whenever you please, then you must expect to see me in this bed. Do come in."

As Khun Sae approached the bed, Khunying Saay-swaat sighed and said, "I shall be confined here for the rest of my time, I expect, until they lift me into my coffin."

A tear slid down her cheek as she spoke, and her visitor's face filled with pity.

"My dear, my dear," Khun Sae began, pulling a chair to the bedside. "Are you feeling so much worse?" Only the night before, she thought to herself, she had visited with the khunying's husband, and he had seemed quite cheerful.

"Very late last night, there was more blood. I shall not last to the end of this rainy season. Which is just as well. I am so ready for it to end; I hope I am nearing the place my karma and fate have been leading me to, because I am so thoroughly tired of being a dreadful burden to everyone."

"For shame, Khunying." Khun Sae recognized that the woman was quite willing to speak intimately with her, and so she would behave as if they were old friends. "If you want to speak of your own karma, that

---

7. *Khunying,* or *khunyĭng,* is a title given to the wife of a high-ranking official or the wife of a titled man. Her husband's name is Ponewat; her own given name is Saay-swaat. Usually, in the novel, she is referred to as Khunying Saay-swaat.

is your affair; but when you speak of being a burden to others, I must disagree. Persons such as yourself are not easily found, you know."

The other woman slowly shook her head but did not reply. She looked about the room, and her gaze fell on Wimon.

"Why are you sitting on the floor? Sit on the chair at my dressing table. Or perhaps it's too heavy—and I made Nang Piw [the servant] leave, oh dear . . . Wimon sits there as if she were waiting politely for my last breath. What do you think, Khun Sae?"

"Never mind about her," said Khun Sae. "You're sick, she's not. She can sit there. Have you told the doctor yet, about last night?"

"Oh, the doctor. He just left. Chao Khun[8] called him early this morning."

"Well then, what did he say?"

"What do you think he said? What is there to say? This illness is beyond the doctor's power. He can do nothing. Except to lie and tell me that nothing is really very wrong. How sick I am of it all."

Khun Sae, looking at the frail woman in the bed, believed that the khunying's own evaluation of her condition was correct. Today, she was much changed from the first time Khun Sae had visited her. It seemed that there was no blood left in her body: her face was white; her lips were greenish; her eyes, yellow. The thin hands that fluttered on the coverlet were as pale as her face. However, she was not coughing or panting for breath.

Khun Sae pronounced, "If you're going to give up that easily, then you are quite right, the doctor is useless; but nothing is as important to getting well, Khunying, as strength of heart. Doctors and medicines are—accessories; they cannot cure you."

They sat in silence for a few moments, and then Khun Sae began to speak again. "Old age, illness, and death: these things are coming to us all. We cannot escape them. The best we can do is to recognize the fact and die when our time comes to die. But until that time comes, we must be unafraid and struggle to live until it really is the end.

"My friend, you must keep your heart and mind clean, free of sin, free of anxiety. Not waste your energy trying to change or fix things over which you have no control. Conserve your strength of heart for your own struggle, Khunying."

8.   Referring to her husband.

While Khun Sae spoke, Khunying Saay-swaat's eyes never left her face. But when she had finished speaking, the other woman's gaze slowly shifted to Wimon and stayed upon her until the young woman shifted uneasily.

The khunying wiped a tear from her cheek and said, "I do not weep because I am afraid to die. I wish that I would die as soon as possible. But I cannot help but weep for those I love. Oh, I know that while I live, I am a burden to them. But when I die . . . when I am gone, I wonder how it will be for them."

"When you die," Khun Sae said gently, "they will be sorry and sad, and will think of you. As much as you loved them, that is how much they will miss you. But no matter how much we love other people, we will lose them, either through their death or ours. Worrying about them can only make us more miserable than we need to be. And you know the truth: Even if you were here for those you love all the days of your life, their karma would remain unchanged. They would be unhappy when bad things happen and happy when good things happen, with you or without you. Do not worry about them. It is a waste of time when you should be thinking of yourself. If there is anything that you can do to improve your health, you should be doing it—instead of lying here weeping about the things you cannot change."

"There isn't anything I can do to help myself," Khunying Saay-swaat said petulantly.

"Oo-ey! In these days, people get cured of tuberculosis, don't you know that? It takes a long time, but you mustn't be so eager to be conquered by it."

"Oh, Khun Sae, I have been sick more than a year already. I don't know how many doctors have attended me, and all that happens is that I get a bit better and then fail . . ." She looked earnestly at Khun Sae for a moment. "Do you really think that even I could get better?"

Khunying Saay-swaat's expression looked almost cheerful. It is only natural for a person to want to believe in the possibility that he or she most desires; and when that person is ill, both in body and in spirit, the ability to believe increases. Khun Sae, seeing that her words had worked a positive effect upon the patient, hurried to improve upon them.

"Why, don't you know that if a person is going to die of tuberculosis, it almost always happens in the first three months? Perhaps you will 'get a bit better and then fail,' just as you have said, for three or four more years. Isn't that worth something? I should think so. Or you could be ill for a few years, and then get much better and go on to be an old lady with a grown son. Now, do you think you ought to be in such a hurry to die?"

Khunying Saay-swaat sat up straighter in her bed.

"Let us talk of other things," Khun Sae said, hoping to steer the conversation away from illness. "The foreign food last night was quite delicious.[9] Did Chao Khun tell you how much I ate? I haven't had a dinner like that one in a long time. I do like foreign food, but I'm far too lazy to prepare it for myself. Imagine you, lying here in this bed and still thinking of us and providing all that lovely food."

"Oh, the *chao khun* thought of it, you know. I didn't do anything but lie here and make up the menu and order the food."

"Well, then. You share the *boon,* half and half.[10] Where is Sumon? He was with his father last night and sat so politely. No naughtiness in him at all."

"I sent him downstairs to play. I don't—I don't want him here when I'm so ill. I can't bear to look at him and think of him after I'm dead." Khunying Saay-swaat's face crumpled, and she began to sob quietly.

"If his mother dies, he still has a father," Khun Sae said firmly, dismayed by the sudden and unwelcome return of the conversation to the khunying's illness. "An only son! Why, the chao khun would cherish him all the more if you were not here."

"Oo-ey, who can know?" Khunying Saay-swaat's eyes flashed. "Men! They find some new wife and think of nothing but—but being with her. They forget all about their children."

"My dear, the chao khun is a very sensible man—"

"You don't know him. You have no idea. When he is interested in something, he becomes quite—beguiled."

"Everyone knows that he is beguiled by you. If it were otherwise, you wouldn't have had that absurd argument, trying to talk him into taking a minor wife."

---

9.   The previous evening, Khunying Saay-swaat had ordered her cook to prepare a foreign (European) dinner for Wimon and the visiting Khun Sae. Khunying Saay-swaat's husband, Chao Khun Ponewat, and their son had joined them.

10.   Acts of merit, boon, or *bun,* have a positive effect on one's karma. Common acts of merit include giving food to monks when they carry their bowls through the neighborhood early each morning or on special holiday; supporting temples or building new ones; and doing good works in general.

Khunying Saay-swaat smiled again and dabbed at her eyes. "We argued again last night!"

"Even though you see how good he is, still you—"

"No, no!" the khunying interrupted. "We didn't argue about *that!*" Her voice had taken on the impatient tone of a child. "It was quite a new argument. He has a friend, an important man from India, who has come to Bangkok. The chao khun received a card from him at his office in the ministry, and when he went to the man's hotel the next evening to leave his own card, they met by chance in the lobby and chatted for hours. When the chao khun came home, he told me that in a few days, he's going to take his old friend to dinner."

Having made this lengthy speech, Khunying Saay-swaat lay back against the pillow. Khun Sae saw with alarm that her friend was growing very tired but was determined to continue the story, and so, instead of imploring her to rest, Khun Sae sat back and listened.

"Before my illness, the chao khun would never have taken an important visitor from another country to dinner at a hotel. He always criticized men who did that. He loves to invite guests to his own home. And now, he was going to take this old friend—this man at whose house he had stayed—to a hotel! Because he didn't want me to be troubled." As she spoke, the khunying moved closer to the edge of the bed and Khun Sae. Now she lay on her side, solemnly looking into her friend's face. "I said, 'Oh, it is no trouble. I need not leave my bed at all. At least I can plan the menu, and you can see to the rest yourself.'

"But he said no, he couldn't, he wasn't able to do such things without me. How absurd! Before we married, I had studied *farang*[11] subjects and languages, too; but it was the chao khun who taught me most about their ways, you know. And now—now he says he can't do anything without me! Even when I suggested that you might help him— I knew you wouldn't mind at all—but no, that only made him all the more adamant. I am quite put out with him."

"My dear, he means so well; he is only thinking of you." The khunying opened her mouth to speak again, but this time Khun Sae raised her hand and said, "No more, you must rest. You've quite tired yourself out. Haven't you considered that this man, the chao khun's friend from India, would be naturally reluctant to visit his friend at home,

---

11.   The word *farang* means both "foreign" (Western) and "foreigner."

knowing that his wife is ill? Surely, he would refuse. However, if you really want him to come to dinner at your house, I shall speak to the chao khun myself. I was my own father's hostess when I was a girl. And Wimon here is quite clever at these things. But you, my dear khunying, must give your word: if he accepts our help, you must leave the matter to us entirely." She smiled and added, "I want to see you lying serene and prayerful upon your bed throughout; and if you will promise me that, perhaps you can have your wish, and the chao khun can bring his old friend home to dinner."

"Oh, thank you—I thank you with all my heart." Khunying Saay-swaat smiled, brought her palms together before her face, and bent her head in a graceful wai. "It is so dreadful, lying here and thinking of all the ways in which I hinder the chao khun's career now—in society and—and in his life."

"Enough, enough. I understand, and I believe that I know what is in your heart. But I also know that everything your good husband does for you, he does out of love. No one is forcing him. You might think of rewarding his devotion by caring for yourself the very best you can and by doing as your doctor tells you. And all those things you insist upon worrying about—let them go!"

Khunying Saay-swaat made another grateful wai and, in a low, trembling voice, said, "Besides my husband, you are the best person I know."

To this, Khun Sae made no reply but only smiled.

They sat in silence. Khun Sae looked about the room, from one object to another, to relieve the irritation and frustration she felt, scolding the khunying for her fretting. The sick woman stroked the edge of her pillow absently, seeming lost in thought until her eyes fell on Wimon, who had been turning a ring on her finger absently. Wimon looked up, aware of the khunying's eyes upon her.

"And you, Elder Sister,"[12] Khunying Saay-swaat said, "since you came into the room, you have not spoken a single word!"

Khun Sae looked at her daughter and, when Wimon continued to sit silently, spoke on her behalf. "We would like to see you have a real rest now. It is the most important thing, after all. It is rest that will heal you."

12. Khunying Saay-swaat has playfully taken to calling the younger Wimon "Elder Sister" (*phîi*) because Wimon has become like an elder sister to Sumon, the khunying's son.

Khunying Saay-swaat let out a great sigh of dismay. "Oh, *rest!* It is all I do. I would sleep, but sleep will not come. That is why I lie here and—and *think*. There is nothing amusing to look at. If I look up, there is the top of my mosquito net; if I look out, I see the walls. I am bored, bored, bored beyond endurance."

A person who is ill like this, Khun Sae thought to herself, needs someone to sit and to be a friend, to be there when she falls asleep and when she awakens. Someone to provide the small comforts, read from a favorite book, and nourish her spirit.

At that moment, the servant Nang Piw entered the bedroom to say that Chao Khun Ponewat had telephoned to ask how the khunying was feeling.

"And what did you tell him?" Khunying Saay-swaat asked, noticeably cheered by the news.

"I didn't tell Taan anything yet, Jao Kha.[13] Taan is still waiting on the telephone. I am supposed to ask you how you are feeling."

"Go and say that I am feeling quite well. Khun Taan[14] has come to visit me, and Wimon also." She laughed softly. "Tell the chao khun that we are sitting here gossiping about him."

Nang Piw left the room, returning a few moments later. "I told Taan what you said, Jao Kha. Taan said that he will be home at noon."

"Oh, dear, I say that I am feeling well, and then he says he's coming home at noon, as if he didn't hear a word. What else did you say?"

"I only said the things you said, Jao Kha. What I already told you. Taan said he is coming home at noon. But not to eat lunch."

"Well, then. He will do as he likes."

Khunying Saay-swaat pretended to be piqued as she watched the

13.   In this conversation between Khunying Saay-swaat and her servant Nang Piw, all the personal pronouns used are different from those used in the conversation between the Khunying and Khun Sae. These differences unfortunately cannot be represented without encumbering the dialogue so much that the reader loses track of the story in trying to follow the mechanics of the translation. *Taan,* or *thâan,* is a more polite second-person pronoun than *khun. Jao kha,* or *jâw khá,* is a phrase used at the end of a sentence by a lower-class person speaking to an upper-class person, especially one with a royal title. The initial words in the terms I have given as *chao khun, chao phraya,* and *jao kha* are spelled identically in Thai; the use of *ch* in the transliteration of the first two terms reflects common usage.

14.   *Khun taan* is an honorific pronoun phrase. Although it does not specifically identify Khun Sae, Khunying Saay-swaat knows that her husband will understand that she is referring to their guest of the past few days. An English equivalent would be referring to a member of royalty as "Her Highness" when the person to whom one is speaking understands which "Highness" is the subject of conversation.

servant leave the room, but Khun Sae noted the sparkle in her eye at the knowledge that her husband soon would be home.

"Khun Sae, do you have any errands to do today?"

"I am not sure. Perhaps, later this afternoon."

"It is nearly noon. Don't go out now when it is so hot. Why don't you wait and talk to the chao khun?"

Wimon's eyes flashed to the clock at the khunying's bedside. Khun Sae noticed and said, "I will stay for a while, but Wimon must go home. She left several tasks undone this morning."

Wimon made a parting wai and left the room. Khunying Saay-swaat's eyes followed the tall, slender form until the young woman had disappeared through the door.

"How I wish I could know," she said softly, "what the chao khun's new wife will look like. I would like to have known her before I die. I have asked him to let me find her, but he is implacable."[15]

Khun Sae did not reply. She had no wish to see the khunying further weaken herself by discussing this subject.

"Your daughter," the khunying said, "is both beautiful and charming. Why is she still alone? It is very strange."

"If the chao khun had not died,[16] I don't think we would see her alone," Khun Sae replied. In the next moment, she remembered that Wimon did indeed have a young man who was interested in her.[17] But she did not feel that this was a matter to discuss with Khunying Saay-swaat.[18]

The khunying moved as if to speak, then stopped, began again, and seemed to change her mind.

Khun Sae remained silent. She was content to sit at the bedside, provide insofar as she could the warmth of friendship and attempt to

---

15.   Traditionally, it has been quite usual for a major wife to bring other women to her husband's attention. If the major wife had a hand in choosing subsequent wives, she could ensure the continuance of her authority. A younger sister or cousin, for example, would almost certainly show her the kind of respect and attention that, in other cultures, might be compared to behavior toward one's mother-in-law.

16.   She is referring to Chao Khun Amornrat, Wimon's father.

17.   Wimon has a tacit understanding with a young man who is studying abroad.

18.   No well-brought-up young woman would discuss the possibility of an engagement or her interest in a young man, nor would her mother risk compromising her honor by speaking of it, lest the match fail to reach the point of marriage. To do so could seriously affect her chances of making another match.

avoid those subjects of conversation most likely to distress and exhaust Khunying Saay-swaat.[19]

[The dinner for the visiting Indian official is a great success. Wimon acts as hostess. Khunying Saay-swaat finds herself tortured between gratitude and overwhelming jealousy toward the young woman. The servant Nang Piw must run between the khunying's bedroom and the hallways outside the dining room, so that she can report to her mistress on Phraya Ponewat's every move and word, and on Wimon's also.

Soon after, Khunying Saay-swaat dies. Phraya Ponewat helps Wimon to recover part of her family fortune. As the novel ends, the reader is encouraged to hope that, after a decent interval, Wimon and Phraya Ponewat will wed.

Khun Sae returns to Chantaburi.]

o   o   DOK MAI SOT AND *PEOPLE OF QUALITY*

Dok Mai Sot is the pen name of the late M. L. Bubpha Kunchon Nimmanhaemin, the most admired and critically acclaimed female writer of the early modern period. She is one of the few writers of her era, male or female, whose novels are continually reprinted and discovered by new generations. The best of Dok Mai Sot's novels, while reflecting the society she knew, are timeless, reflecting personal values and aspirations that are considered as desirable and worth pursuing today as they were seventy years ago.

Born in 1905, Dok Mai Sot was the daughter of Chao Phraya Thewet, a close adviser to King Chulalongkorn. She has been compared with Jane Austen and other nineteenth-century woman writers, which may seem a fanciful comparison; nonetheless, it is an apt one. Dok Mai Sot married at forty-nine, until which time she lived in the family home, in the company of her many sisters (including the well-known author and educator M. L. Boonlua), under the care and direction of her elder brothers. In short, if Dok Mai Sot and M. L. Boonlua were not exactly Siamese versions of Jane Austen and her sister Cassandra, they shared an amazing number of similarities, among them, the influence of somewhat overbearing and sometimes resented elder brothers.

After publishing two or three early romances, Dok Mai Sot went

19. This excerpt is translated from Dok Mai Sot, *Phûu dii*, 544–58.

on to write a number of increasingly sophisticated novels—all set in the world of the Siamese elite. She brought a keen intellect to her work, as well as a highly developed moral sense firmly grounded in Buddhism. *People of Quality*[1] is one of Dok Mai Sot's finest and best-loved novels, and is included in this anthology for several reasons. First, the novel provides an excellent definition of the ideal woman of the post-1932 Thai world—restricted, by and large, to the Bangkok elite and a scattering of highly placed families elsewhere in the kingdom. I use the word *elite* advisedly, since some promoters of the 1932 coup d'état were antiroyalist and took pains to include in their government only as many tractable members of the nobility as necessary to avoid difficulties. This is very well exemplified in M. R. Kukrit Pramoj's novel *Four Reigns,* in which a mother of aristocratic birth is anguished to see her only daughter spurn the advances of a polite, intelligent, charming young nobleman, choosing instead an avaricious upstart with "no family." In the long term, the antiroyalist campaign never seriously eroded people's fascination with, and sincere respect for, people connected to the royal family.

In this novel, Dok Mai Sot makes certain references to the kinds of new ideas promoted by the government, especially at the beginning of the novel, then settles down to tell the story of a good-hearted young woman's struggles to keep the family mansion that her father nearly lost through his financial blunders; to get back the family fortune; and to keep all of her siblings firmly rooted in their privileged social niche.[2] It is clear, despite the references to the importance of a woman's education (as in the birthday letter from Khun Sae to Wimon)[3] and despite the much greater emphasis on character, that "what's bred in the

---

1. The Thai title *Phûu dii* carries connotations not only of virtuous behavior but also of upper-class origins. Dok Mai Sot clearly meant to imply that the true *phûu dii* is identified by character, not means.

2. Dok Mai Sot's political views are far more evident in some of her short stories, which are less well known than her novels. Several interesting examples appear in Manas Chitkasem, "The Development of Political and Social Consciousness in Thai Short Stories," in *The Short Story in South East Asia: Aspects of a Genre,* ed. Jeremy H. C. S. Davidson and Helen Cordell, Collected Papers in Oriental and African Studies, (London: School of Oriental and African Studies, University of London, 1982).

3. Dok Mai Sot was very well read, but her own education took place mainly at home and at St. Joseph's Convent School, where she was taught by European nuns. This signifies more education than it may seem; the atmosphere at Baan Maw Palace, where she lived for most of her life, was one of great intellectual and artistic fervor. Her father, Chao Phraya Thewet, was an expert on the Thai classical theater, and several of his wives were classical dance artists.

bone" still matters. The reader should remember that no one, in the Buddhist view, is born into wealth and a socially prominent position in life by accident.

Another important feature of *People of Quality* is the pervasive influence of the author's profound Buddhist faith. As I have said, virtually all Thai novels and short stories reveal the *influence* of Buddhist beliefs on characters, plot, and action, but in Dok Mai Sot's work, Buddhism sometimes plays an overt role. In *People of Quality,* the loss of faith on the part of the dying, despairing Khunying Saay-swaat is explored in ways that were truly groundbreaking for Thai fiction. It is, in my opinion, the most interesting of her novels. The matter of one's personal faith, much less the loss of it, is an unusual subject for Thai writers (certainly, it was for writers of the 1930s). Equally unusual is Dok Mai Sot's unsparing exploration of unwholesome and unacceptable feelings, such as jealousy and rage, in a female character (the dying Khunying Saay-swaat), who has been, all her life, a person of quality.

The reader may compare this portrayal of ideal femininity in the 1930s to the portrayal of a society woman of the 1960s in the excerpt from Krisna Asoksin's *This Human Vessel* in the next section, "Wives and Lovers." Not a few Thais would interpret the gulf between the former and the latter depictions of Thai society as the distance between the lost graces of the old Siam and the materialistic realities of the new Thailand.

— Death ~ loss of faith
— What is she hinting at
— Who is Phraya Ponewat (guest?)

From *A Child of the Northeast*

Kampoon Boontawee

This 1969 novel is based on the author's fond memories
of his boyhood in Thailand's rural northeast, Isan, during
the 1930s.

*[The simple plot of this novel (some critics have claimed that it has no plot) is the
story of a journey: after several years of drought, several families in a village decide
to take an ox-cart caravan to a neighboring province, Roi Et. There, the bounty of the
River Chi (pronounced "chee") will allow them to catch fish that they can preserve,
in various ways, for sale on the return trip and for their own use back in the hungry
village over the coming year.*

*Characters in the novel who appear in this chapter include Koon; his parents (re-
ferred to exclusively as Koon's papa and Koon's mama, which is true to life); his little sisters, Yee-soon and Bua-lai; Uncle Gah, leader of the party, and Uncle Gah's
wife; a man named Gad; a young man named Tid-joon and his bride, Kamgong (often called Pi, or "elder sister," by Koon); Koon's best friend, the irrepressibly naughty
and amusing Jundi; Jundi's parents, Uncle Kem and Auntie Bua-si; the* phuyaiban,
or "head man," of the village near which they are currently staying and his family.]

Chapter 21
Adventures of the First Night

That evening, a cool breeze from the River Chi blew continually over
the caravan. Sometimes Koon heard faint songs coming from the distance, mixed with the sound of flowing water.

The three dogs raced back and forth; first to the river, where they
would stop and howl energetically, then back into camp, where
they would run around and around the carts.

Uncle Gah sent Tid-joon and Gad to fetch water, and the women
to gather firewood. If anyone was hungry now, Uncle Gah said, he
should eat a little cold rice and *pla ra.*[1]

This excerpt is taken from my translation of the novel *Lûuk iisǎan,* which was published
by Duang Kamol, Bangkok, in 1987. The translation is based upon the 1985 Thai edition published in Bangkok by Baankit.
    1. Fermented fish, prepared with salt.

He was going to take Koon's papa with him to see the phuyaiban of the nearest village.

Uncle Gah stooped over the water basket, plunged the dipper into it, and tossed the water over his back. "Oh ho, that feels good," he said. "Maybe I'll find a nice widow in that village."

"You go right ahead," his wife said. "You go find some nice widow. After no bath for five days and five nights, the only female who wouldn't mind being close to you is Tid-joon's dog."   ˥ᵉ ˥ᵉ ˎˎ ᵎ

Koon's mother and Auntie Bua-si returned from the woods, dumped armloads of kindling on the ground, and went back for more. When Koon began to follow her, his father said, "Wait, you can go with us to see the phuyaiban. Go wash yourself first."

"Can Jundi go, too?"

His father sighed. "I suppose so."

Koon and Jundi happily followed Uncle Gah's example, pouring a full dipper of water over their backs, then hurried off after the men.

Uncle Gah walked ahead. It was growing dark, and he carried a torch to light the way. "The moon will soon be up," he remarked to Koon's father.

"Yes," Koon's father said, "this is the third night of the rising moon."

Jundi, looking worriedly to his left and right, asked Uncle Gah if it might not have been a good idea to bring his gun.

"No. Because the people here do not carry guns at night—or crossbows."

"What country is this, Uncle Gah?"

"It's not another *country;* it's another *province*—Roi Et."

"Where does the River Chi come from, and how far does it go before it ends?"

"It comes from big mountains, and it ends in another river far away. Enough questions."

Jundi didn't ask any more questions, but Uncle Gah offered the information that the village they were going to was called Nam Sai.[2]

They walked silently down the road, and presently they came to a house. A man sitting on the porch called down to them, "Where are you going, friends?" Uncle Gah said that they wanted to visit the phuyaiban.

---

2. *Nam sai* means "clear water."

"Go to the left until you get to the *wat*.[3] Then ask again."

Uncle Gah increased his pace. Now there were more houses, and torches were flickering in all of them. From some houses, they heard the familiar sounds of women making food, the *boke-boke-boke* of stone pestles and the *sup-sup-sup* of chopping blocks. And when a warm, sharp scent reached his nose, Koon realized how hungry he was.

"Somebody is making *lop*[4] from fresh fish," he said, swallowing the saliva that had filled his mouth.

Uncle Gah heard him and said, "Nobody goes without fresh fish in this place. Just wait, Buk-Koon.[5] Tomorrow you will eat fresh fish until your belly busts."

The house of the phuyaiban was not so different from that of the phuyaiban in Koon's own village. But he knew that this family owned more animals, because he heard a great jingling and clacking of bells and bamboo from beneath the house as they climbed the ladder.

The phuyaiban was sitting on his porch, wearing an old *pakomah*[6] and thoughtfully puffing on a cigarette. He was little and skinny like Uncle Gah, but he seemed very good-natured. Every time he spoke, he ended his statement with a sharp bark of laughter.

While Uncle Gah and Koon's father spoke with the phuyaiban, Koon and Jundi looked in the direction of the kitchen. They could not help themselves, for the delicious smell of roasting fish was coming from it.

After a few minutes, the phuyaiban's wife and daughter came out of the kitchen and joined them. Jundi stared at the girl. Koon thought that she looked about the same age as Wandam, the Vietnamese girl [in their own village], but this girl had a paler complexion. The cloth tightly wrapped about her bosom was made of silk, and she wore a pair of twinkling earrings that matched her necklace.

The phuyaiban told Uncle Gah that the place where they had camped was no good.

"Too many weeds in the river there," he said, "and a strong current in the water. If you go just a bit farther along the river, you will

---

3. A Buddhist temple.
4. A typical northeastern dish made of fish or meat or blood, briefly rinsed with boiling water, and then mixed with chili peppers; ground, toasted raw rice; herbs; and, if possible, lime juice.
5. *Buk* is a common northeastern prefix to a male name.
6. A length of plain or checkered cloth used as a garment, knotted about the waist; sometimes it is tied about the head or used to carry things.

have much better luck. Now, if you need anything, you tell me. And nobody needs to be afraid of thieves or ruffians around here, because there aren't any."

Uncle Gah thanked him and said that he had long known of the goodness of the people of this place.

The girl smiled at Jundi and asked, "Are you hungry, boy?"

"No," Jundi replied in a loud voice. "We just ate."

The phuyaiban's wife pointed to Jundi and said, "This boy, when -he gets a little older, will be a good one for the ladies. And with such a stubborn look in his eyes, he would make a good boxer or a policeman."

The phuyaiban laughed his strange, barking laugh and said that Jundi should come back when he grew to be a man and was looking for a wife. And when Jundi boldly replied, "Yes, sir—if all the girls here are as beautiful as her," and stared right at the girl, the phuyaiban laughed delightedly and said, "My wife is right—but what kind of son-in-law he would make, I am not so sure . . ."

Before they left, the girl went to the kitchen and returned with a banana-leaf packet. "It is a roasted fish," her mother said, "with a steamed turmeric blossom."

Uncle Gah nodded to Jundi to carry the packet, thanked the phuyaiban's family for their kindness and good advice, and also for the food, and they left.

The flower the phuyaiban's wife had packed with the fish was a kind Koon had eaten once at home. When the rain fell briefly the year before and the ground was wet, such flowers grew. His mother had picked two, a red one and a white one, each blossom almost [as wide as the span of his hand]. But he hadn't liked them very much; they were bitter, which surprised him, because they were so beautiful.

As they walked along the village path, Uncle Gah decided that they should ask for rice before returning to camp. He would take Jundi with him, and Koon could go with his father.

Asking for rice was something Koon had never done, and he didn't want to do it now. But he knew how it was done, because he had seen enough caravans come through his own village. At dusk, the people from the caravan would walk through the village, asking for cooked rice at each household; his mother always gave rice to these people.

"Papa, don't you mind asking strangers for rice?" he asked as they turned down a small lane.

"Not at all. It is nothing to be ashamed of, Koon. It is the custom of our people whenever we travel to another village. And in the morning, if we go to the temple, the monks and the people will feed everyone. I don't think we will do that—but we could, and no one would think badly of us. We do the same for strangers in our village."

"I know," Koon said. But it was different, he thought, being the ones who were asking.

His father stopped before the first house and called out, "Fathers and mothers! Brothers and sisters! We are travelers and ask you for rice for our supper." A moment later, a young woman appeared in the doorway carrying a ladle that held about two handfuls of cooked rice. She asked them where they had come from, and if they had anything to sell.

With both hands, Koon's father held up the hem of his pakomah, from the extra piece that was folded over in front. He told the woman that they had come from a village far away in Ubon Province, where the rain had not fallen for a long time, to catch fish in the River Chi. She put the rice into the pakomah, and he thanked her.

"We will be selling *pla som* and *pla daek*[7] and roasted fresh fish," he said.

"Good. You come back then. I will be glad to trade rice for fish. We don't go fishing so often now."

Koon understood. "Now" meant since the rain had fallen. Now they could work in the fields.

Koon and his father walked on, collecting rice at one house after another, and after they had collected rice at ten houses, they walked back to the main road in the village to join Uncle Gah and Jundi.

"That phuyaiban's daughter is all right," Jundi said, "but they have plenty of ugly girls here, too. A couple of them had real sour faces, and when they bent over to give us the rice, they had big, floppy breasts."

"You fool," Uncle Gah said. "Those weren't girls. They were young women with babies."

Back at camp, a fire was burning brightly, and Koon was grateful for its warmth. Tid-joon was sitting back, at ease, playing Koon's fa-

7.   Various preserved fish preparations.

ther's *kan.*[8] Uncle Gah asked if he had done all the work he was supposed to do. Tid-joon said that he had done everything. All the animals had been fed and watered, but there was nothing to cook and
not much to eat, as Uncle Gah well knew.

"We got a roasted fish and a steamed turmeric flower from the
phuyaiban's wife and rice from the villagers. Whatever we have, we
will eat now and then go to sleep. We won't have to scout fishing
grounds tonight, because we will move in the morning. The phuyaiban
says this place is no good. Too many weeds near the shore and a strong
current."

They formed their supper circle, and Koon's mother sat beside Uncle Gah.

"Yee-soon has a fever," she said. "Maybe you should look at her."

He rose at once. "Why didn't you tell me this before?"

"She didn't feel warm to me until after you had left for the village."

Uncle Gah left his food and went to Koon's family's cart. He shook
the sleeping girl gently.

Koon's father looked worried, and Koon took his hand.

"Papa, why did Mama ask Uncle Gah to look at her?"

"He knows more about healing than anyone else here."

Koon's mother held a torch above Yee-soon, so that Uncle Gah
could see. "She ate a little rice," she said, "and then she said her head
hurt, so I made her lie down. When I touched her, she was hot."

Uncle Gah sat down inside the cart and lifted Yee-soon onto his
lap.

Koon was surprised to see how gentle Uncle Gah was with his little sister. Usually, he was either mad at somebody or making jokes.

"Does it hurt very much?" he asked.

"Not very much," Yee-soon replied in a sleepy voice.

Then he began to mumble in a low voice. After he mumbled for a
while and rocked back and forth with her, he blew on the crown of
Yee-soon's head—once, twice, three times. Then he waited for a few
moments and asked, "How does your head feel now, little Yee-soon?"

"I think it's better," she said.

Uncle Gah told Koon's mother to let Yee-soon sleep until morning,
and then he returned to the supper circle and ate hungrily.

"I will go back in the middle of the night and blow the spell again,"

8.   A flutelike instrument made of bamboo.

he said. "In the morning, she will be running around between the carts, the same as ever."

Jundi looked up and asked, "What will you do if she isn't any better?"

Without looking up from his food, Uncle Gah said, "Probably give her three good kicks."

On some nights, Koon had slept beneath the cart with his father and the dogs. But that night, he slept inside the cart, because in his heart he was afraid that Yee-soon might be very sick, although of course he wouldn't say that to his mother. He lay quietly in the dark, staring at his sister's back, watching her shoulder rise and fall ever so slightly with her breathing.

When he awoke some time later, he heard the men talking outside. He crawled forward and stuck his head out of the cart and saw that the moon was floating high in the sky. The breeze off the River Chi was colder and gustier.

o   o   o   o

[Later that night, the men decide to go out fishing after all; Koon and Jundi are allowed to join them. The next morning, they joyfully return to camp, bearing baskets of shrimp and small fish.]

When they reached camp and showed off their catch, Auntie Bua-si and Uncle Gah's wife smiled and smiled. Kamgong and Koon's mother brought a large, flat basket, and the men dumped the fish and shrimp onto it.

"Make four crocks of pla som with that," Uncle Gah said, "one for each of the families." Then he went and sat under his cart and smoked a cigarette.

Koon helped the women pick out all the debris that had got into the baskets with the catch. When they were done, Kamgong poured a coconut shell full of salt over the fish, and the others mixed it in thoroughly with their hands. Soon, the little fish and shrimp stopped squirming around on the flat basket and lay still, coated with salt. Kamgong pounded dried garlic with a pestle, then began cutting a piece of lemon grass on the chopping block.

Jundi sat beside her, absently picking at the cold, charred part of a torch that had burned to almost nothing. "Pi, where did you get the lemon grass?"

"I brought it from home. What do you think?"

When Kamgong had finished mincing the lemon grass, Koon's mother scooped the pounded garlic out of the pestle and sprinkled that on the fish too and on top of that a good handful of ground, roasted raw rice.

"We need some cooked rice, too," Uncle Gah's wife said. "Kamgong, you go get a box."

Kamgong rushed off. Koon had noticed that the older women were always telling Pi Kamgong what to do, and she obeyed without complaining or even looking like she wanted to complain. Koon's mother said that Pi Kamgong was very sweet natured, and he supposed it was true.

When Kamgong returned with the rice, Uncle Gah's wife took a good-sized lump from the basket and broke it into fragments over the fish, salt, garlic, and lemon grass, then turned the mixture with her hands once again. Its fragrance was lovely.

When the pla som had been mixed enough, Uncle Gah's wife told Kamgong to divide it into four parts and to pack it into crocks. "Be sure you put those tops on tight," she said. "In three days, we can eat it." And she went to her cart to sleep.

"So that is how you make pla som," Jundi said.

"*Er.* Some people say 'pla som'; some people call it *som pla noi* or *som pla bom* or *pla jawm*. But it is all the same thing. Do you think you boys could make it yourself, now that you watched us?"

Jundi nodded and grinned. "Sure, why not?"

It didn't look too hard, Koon thought. There were only a few things in it besides the fish and little shrimp: garlic, lemon grass, ground roasted rice, and cooked rice. Four things. He could remember four things. He was curious about one of them, however.

"Mama, why do you have to put in cooked rice?"

"Cooked rice makes the nice, sour flavor. Otherwise, it would be a little flat."

"Three more days, and I'm going to eat som pla," Jundi said happily.

"Or pla som or som pla noi or som pla bom—" Koon added.

"Or pla jawm," Jundi said. "But whatever they call it, I like it."

Koon sat and listened to his parents and the other grown-ups talk until late; he was too excited to sleep. Even if the fish and shrimp were only little ones, he had never seen so many. Maybe tomorrow, he would be able to wade into that cool water with a dip net, too . . . wade back and forth with his father.

Just as Koon was nodding off, his head in his mother's lap, Uncle Gah leaned out of his cart and barked, "What is all this noise? Get in your carts. go to sleep. Anyone would think none of you had ever seen a fish before."

The people went off to their carts, carrying crocks of the precious fish, the first catch. Koon's mother let him carry theirs, and he held it with both arms, close to his chest.

Inside the cart, he set the crock on the floor and lay down beside it, with one hand touching the crock and the other touching Yee-soon's shoulder. Soon he was asleep.

O   O   KAMPOON BOONTAWEE
          AND *A CHILD OF THE NORTHEAST*

Kampoon likes to call himself the ambassador of Isan to the world, a title his devoted readers find entirely appropriate. Born in the early 1920s in the northeastern village that one day would become the model for Koon's village in *A Child of the Northeast*, Kampoon left home as a young man and traveled the length and breadth of Thailand for the next twenty years. He worked as a day laborer, horse trainer, pedicab driver, and Bangkok school teacher before settling into a long-term career as a prison warden. Kampoon was assigned to jails in various parts of Thailand, and it was in this position that he began to write short stories based on the lives and misadventures of the people he met on the job. He sent the short stories to Ajin Banjapan, the well-known editor of the popular magazine *Faa muang thai* (Thai sky), who was delighted to publish them.

Kampoon became an immediate and great success, and soon turned to full-time writing. Readers were enchanted by his stories, in which characters whom other writers might have presented as one-dimensional scoundrels—or as victims of society—were seen to be complex and also quite human in some unexpectedly endearing ways. The compassion and humor that permeate *A Child of the North-east* were present from the very first stories.

The most important reason for including this selection is its faithful portrayal of the lives of rural women. No single chapter in the novel focuses mainly on women, and women's experiences in *A Child of the Northeast*, faithfully reflecting life, are presented something in the manner of threads woven into a fabric of many colors.

Even at the close of the twentieth century, the lives of many Thai women are mirrored in Kampoon's descriptions of Koon's mother and other women in this small northeastern village. We also see the relatively egalitarian nature of life in a rice-farming village, where all people must work together, the tasks of men and women are complementary, and everyone's contribution is critical. It is Koon's mother who prepares virtually all of the family's food, and his father who hunts small animals and puts a new thatch roof on their house (with the help of every other man in the village) when the old one begins to leak. Yet men and women seem quite knowledgeable about their respective tasks; and readers will see far more congruence between female and male lives in this selection than in any other.

There is continual, easy banter and affectionate understanding between wives and husbands, and among neighboring families as all work to survive, play when they can, and help each other in raising the next generation. The perceptions of Thai women that are explored in the introduction are mirrored faintly, at best, in *A Child of the Northeast*. (Sometimes they are even spoofed, as in the hilarious depiction of a wedding in which the groom's family meets the traditional bride price with "three bahts and a chicken." One baht is worth about four and a half cents.)

The women in this novel speak up, and they talk back. When Uncle Gah muses about finding "some nice widow" in the nearby village, his wife's retort is "You go right ahead. . . . You go find some nice widow. After no bath for five days and five nights, the only female who wouldn't mind being close to you is Tid-joon's dog."

These women work in the fields, catch fish, weave cloth, and engage in all kinds of cottage industries—aside from their responsibilities for cooking, housework, and child rearing. Their relative independence owes a good deal to the fact that rural families depend, in no small part, upon wives' and mothers' economic activities.[1] At no

---

1.   Although one sometimes hears that poor rural women are the truly free women in Thai society, these claims are never made by women who are poor and rural.

other level in society are women's contributions more crucial to family survival. Moreover, issues of job discrimination and unequal educational opportunities that may be concerns for middle- and upper-class women are of far less importance to rural women who do not have enough time for the jobs already waiting to be done, much less the time (or the inclination) to vie for jobs traditionally done by men.

There is no denying that, although life in some northeastern farming villages goes on in much the same way as it always has, there is a considerable gap between the northeast as depicted in Kampoon's novel and the contemporary northeast depicted in three of the other selections: the novel *That Woman's Name Is Boonrawd,* by Botan; and the short stories "Greenie," by Manop Thanomsri, and "A Mote of Dust on the Face of the Earth," by Preechapoul Boonchuay. The two short stories, in particular, represent a relentlessly tragic view of northeastern life.

It is a sad commentary on changing times that when the movie version of *A Child of the Northeast* was filmed, a character was added: a girl who runs off to town, becomes a prostitute, and returns to show off her fancy clothes. As I viewed the film with Kampoon, he told me that he was not pleased about this addition, "but the people who made the movie wanted it to be more exciting, *and up-to-date."*

Yet contemporary northeasterners are not entirely different from Kampoon's villagers of the 1930s; like Koon's parents and neighbors, they are strong, enduring, and extremely proud of being "children of the northeast." And, like the villagers in the novel, they continue to rely upon humor to get themselves and each other through the worst of times; Isan humor is a staple of television sitcoms.

Kampoon showed the rest of Thailand that northeasterners are not just victims of poverty; they are as multidimensional and as complex as Thais living anywhere else, at any socioeconomic level of society. In 1969, the first annual SEAWrite award was presented to Kampoon Boontawee for *A Child of the Northeast.*

Matsii

Sri Dao Ruang

This 1985 short story is about a young woman who
leaves her children at a bus stop and refuses to take
them back. The excuses she gives for her behavior
made this a controversial story.

[Unlike most of the short stories in this anthology, "Matsii" requires some explana-
tion. Maha Wetsandon chadok, a beloved tale to which Sri Dao Ruang alludes in
this story, was composed in the reign of King Mongkut. It represents the work of sev-
eral authors, including King Mongkut himself, a high-ranking Buddhist monk of royal
birth who was also a great poet, and many other literary personalities, monks and
laymen.[1] According to the tale, Prince Wetsandon was the name of the Buddha in
his last incarnation before his last rebirth as Lord Gautama, who achieved enlight-
enment, or Buddhahood.

Unfairly banished from the kingdom of Sonchai by his father, the king, Prince
Wetsandon goes to live an ascetic life in the forest. His wife, Matsii, begs to join him;
when she does, she brings their two children with her. One day when Matsii is ab-
sent, a Brahman beggar named Chuchok asks for the two children, so that they may
serve his beautiful young wife, Amittada. Prince Wetsandon readily gives up his
beloved children. When Matsii returns to find her children gone, she does not re-
monstrate with her husband but continues to serve him as a loyal, loving, respect-
ful, and unquestioning wife. (At the end of the tale, Prince Wetsandon's children are
returned to their parents.)

In Women in Thai Literature *(see introduction, note 1), Matsii is described in*
admiring terms: "Matsii is a determined woman. She is adamant about sharing her
husband's fate. Her pleading with the King and the Queen on her husband's behalf
shows her to be a clever woman with an alert mind, and extraordinary power of rea-
soning."[2] Matsii's reaction to her husband's giving away their children is seen as re-
nunciation, displaying enormous strength of character.]

She sat before the police lieutenant with matted, dirty hair, her face
dotted with tiny white pimples. She forced a laugh, apparently un-

---

"Matsii" appears as the title story of a collection of Sri Dao Ruang's short stories: *Mat-*
sii (Bangkok: Love and Live Press, 1990).
   1. National Identity Board, *WTL*, 99–115.
   2. Ibid., 105.

concerned about the two missing buttons on her blouse or the sloppy knot that held the waistband of her skirt precariously in place.

"I already told everything about not wanting them—you gonna put me in jail? Good, put me in jail, but I'm not takin' care of 'em anymore."

The lieutenant shook his head. It required an effort of will to restrain himself before this unmannerly young woman. He pulled a cigarette from the pack, lit it, and inhaled. He let the smoke out slowly, looking carefully at the accused, who appeared to be imitating him, exaggeratedly inhaling and exhaling.

"If you didn't want them, why did you have them? Excuse my words, but even a dog loves its puppies." He did not bother to lower his voice; his expression made his feelings plain.

"What about their father?" she asked, her voice trembling with resentment. "Why don't you go arrest *him?*" "If I did wrong, then he did more wrong, because he's the one who—who *did* it. He left his children and left his wife to chase after some new c——.[3] I didn't leave them to get a new husband!" She lowered her voice, spoke more slowly. "Anyway, I have no feelings, Mr. Policeman.[4] Our body is born, but it isn't ours. Like the monks say in their sermons, we're born, and then we're dead . . . these children were born, but they're not mine. They—"

"What? All this nonsense is beside the point! What if someone were to take these children and raise them. What would you do?"

Bitterness shone in the large round eyes that swam with tears. She did not answer. At last he had to call for her attention. As she shook her head slightly, the tears brimmed, slipped down her cheeks. "I just want to be a nun. I've had enough of husbands and children. I mean it. You see—I can even cut myself off from my children . . ."[5]

The lieutenant leaned back, tipped his chair slightly, sighed with weariness and disgust. "How old are you?"

She looked up, met his eyes. "Nineteen."

"Nineteen, with three children. Who would believe it? So young,

---

3. In Thai, the words used are *h—— màay; h——*is a censored version of *hĭi*, the ordinary word for "vagina," equivalent here to "cunt"; *màay* means "new."

4. In Thai, the words are *khun tamrùat*, a polite way of addressing policemen frequently used by rural or urban poor people.

5. The Thai term used here is *tàt kilèet*, literally to "cut desires" or "cut attachments"; see the introduction for a brief description of *kilèet* and its consequences for human life according to Buddhism.

She wants to become a nun and in order to be one she can't have the kids so she abandons them.

and you have done this despicable thing. What happens when this husband of yours comes cajoling, eh? You'll be out there with another big belly." The lieutenant was becoming less polite.

"No, I learned my lesson. If I become a nun, I'll stay a nun. We've had our whole time together.[6] Nothing could start up again between us."

Difficult to believe, this. Her words and behavior had already convinced others that she was mad or perhaps mentally retarded. The lieutenant had sent the three children of this strangely behaved young woman to stay with the family of one of his underlings. The man's wife would care for them temporarily.

"So, you like going to the temple?"

"Yes. Before I had a husband, I went with my mother every holy day."[7] As she said these words, the woman's eyes began to shine happily. Suddenly, she resembled a child who has just received a present. "I listened to the sermons, and then I felt happy. I didn't worry about anything."

"Indeed. Well, I can see that you are a good-hearted young woman who loves to go to temple. What I don't see is why, when you are so good-hearted, you don't have a bit of pity for your own children. Or how you are able to leave them at a bus stop—where, fortunately, a squad car happened to be passing by. If it hadn't, then what? At a busy intersection, full of cars?"

The woman's expression grew sullen, and she stiffened her neck. "How many times do you want me to tell you that I don't want them— *I don't want them!*" Her voice rose as she shouted these words; one would not believe she would dare to speak in such a voice, in this place. "If you force them on me, Mr. Policeman, I will just leave them beside the road again. If they cry after me, they'll get hit for sure. It's not against the law for a mother to hit her children. I didn't kill them! When I was a kid, there wasn't a time my mother hit me that I didn't think, '*This* time I'm gonna die.'"

She drew her legs up, sat cross-legged on the chair. The edges of

---

6. In Thai, she says, "Khon raw tham bun rûam-kan maa khêc năay kɔ̃ khêc nán," a phrase that literally means that the couple's "mutual merit making" is now at an absolute end. The phrase signifies the marriage bond and is used here with irony.

7. The term in Thai is *wan phrá*, literally, "monk's day," referring to Buddhist holy days that occur on the eighth, fifteenth, twenty-third, and twenty-ninth or thirtieth day of the lunar month.

her thick lips grew dark as she anxiously pushed them in and out, in and out.

Not many hours before, she had lifted the middle child, dropped him roughly onto the passenger bench at the bus stop, yelled, "Whoever wants some children, here—take these!" The people waiting inside the bus shelter all scurried out, away from the woman and her children. She stood silent for a few moments, then turned to the oldest child, a small girl holding a baby, and said, "You all stay here. Don't you dare follow me. Ask the people who come in here if you can go with them. You understand? There's lots of people here, as many as worms. You'll find one with a good heart pretty soon."

She walked off. The three children, although they were too frightened of being hit to follow her, set up a howling. "Mama! Mama! Don't leave us!" the oldest girl cried. "Mama! I'm afraid!"

In fact, the young woman would have been successful in escaping the three little piles of suffering at the bus stop if a squad car had not happened to be passing by at that moment.[8] Now she sat before the lieutenant at the police station.

"Mr. Policeman, don't you believe in merit and in sin?"

What nerve she had! "I believe. I believe that a woman with sins as serious as yours will go straight to hell."

"You don't understand. If I'm such a big sinner, and I have to pay for my sins by going to hell, then why do you *arrest* me? Instead of bothering with me, why don't you just let hell take care of me?"

The lieutenant was becoming very angry. Most offenders, when you interrogated them, no matter how obstinate they might be, at least could come up with a more rational excuse for what they had done than this. The woman had nothing to say for herself besides these feeble-minded religious ramblings. He probably would have to send her off to the doctors at the mental hospital. That or just let her go. But the children would have to be sent to the welfare office—or he could give the story to *Thai Rath*. Just the kind of headline they were always looking for. At the least, some good-hearted people would read about

8.   "[T]he three little piles of suffering" is an exact translation of the author's words, "kɔɔng thúk tháng sǎam kɔɔng nán."

the children, maybe do something for them. Easy. On the other hand, he probably ought to talk to their father before doing anything.

"Their father?" the woman said suddenly, as if she were reading his thoughts. "The son of a bitch won't even admit they're his.[9] Can I have a cigarette?"

The lieutenant, further annoyed at her presumption, wondered suddenly if she might be a prostitute. But in the next moment he changed his mind, for a prostitute is likely to raise her own children. He looked at the lit cigarette in his hand, stubbed it out in the ashtray, then pushed his pack of 85s, with its one remaining cigarette, across the table toward her.

"I know you have troubles. Your husband won't support the children; he's infatuated with a minor wife—but the children, they don't know about any of this. If you toss them away like this, leave them at the side of the road, they'll become thieves, probably drug addicts. The girls will end up selling their bodies. Even if you give them to somebody else, it isn't the same as growing up with their own parents. They will feel inferior to other people when they grow up. You give birth to them, then you don't take care of them—think about it. If you want to find work, I can help you find work. Maybe in a restaurant, or cleaning house. I can help you find a cheap room to rent. The children can go to day care, but when you get off work, you have to pick them up, take them home with you to sleep. How about that? Here, eat your food," he added, gesturing toward the plate of food that had been put in front of her some time before. It had been a long speech, like a day's worth of the Annual Sermon.[10]

The woman inhaled deeply, seeming to think, as she slowly fastened the open buttons of her blouse. "Yeah, well that would be good. But I'd have to work really hard . . ."

"Everyone has to work. And there are plenty of people who want to work hard and can't find work. I am a police officer, that is my work, and you . . ." He struggled against his anger, to keep his voice low and his words slow, like a sermon.

9. The Thai phrase I have chosen to translate as "son of a bitch" is *ây hàa.*

10. Each year, an annual Sermon, which takes place over three days, is broadcast on radio. People believe that considerable merit attaches to listening to all three days of the sermon, which is given by a highly placed monk who is well regarded for his preaching abilities.

"Well . . . I never done that before. Worked."

"You never worked! But you got yourself a husband when you were hardly an adult—maybe he just got sick of being the only one working and supporting you and those three kids." This was sounding less like a sermon, more like the words of a man in a police uniform.

Tears began to drip down the woman's cheeks. She looked at him with something that might be fear, changed her tone of voice to a supplicating one as she said, "Please, please just let me go be a nun . . ."

This was it. The lieutenant rose, glaring at her and slapping the table loudly with the flat of his hands, barely able to suppress his rage as he said, "So you think you can just walk out of this! What kind of person are you—have you no sense of responsibility to society at all?"

The woman sprang from her chair, shuffled backward until she reached the wall. Sweat appeared on her face, trickled down from her eyes and her nose. The room had become absolutely quiet; flies buzzed over the cold rice and curry. Then she began to sob.

"Lots of *men* get to be *monks*, lots of them! Why doesn't anybody yell at them?" She didn't seem to have understood any of his sermon.

"But those men aren't escaping their responsibilities, holding up religion in front of their faces like you! Even if your poor children went willingly to be left at the roadside, how do you think that would show their mother to be a good Buddhist?"[11]

"Then why do *men* get to do it?"

"*Who* gets to do such a thing? Will you please tell me *what man does what you have done?*"

"*Phra Wetsandon did it!*"

Our big police officer is stunned. He is not sure what the woman is talking about. But slowly, he sits down in his chair and stares at her. He extends his arm, motions for her to sit down again. He picks up his pen, writes quietly, his shoulders hunched, head down. He calls one of his men into the room.

"Take this form and the accused, and send her to the doctors. And when they come up with some kind of result, I want a report."

11. In Thai, the actual phrase used by the police officer, which I have replaced here with "good Buddhist," is one the woman has used before, *tàt kilèet* (see this selection, note 5), meaning to "cut oneself off from desires" (which lead to dhukkha, or suffering).

O   O   SRI DAO RUANG AND "MATSII"

"Sri Dao Ruang" is the pen name of Wanna Sawadsee. She was born in 1943 in Phitsanulok, the third of eight children. Her father was a railroad worker; her mother sold sweets along the railroad line. Wanna tried to help her mother, running alongside passenger cars at the Phitsanulok train station. In a 1993 interview, she recalled "running along, yelling 'khanŏm jâa! khanŏm jâa!'[1]—but I was too shy to yell loud enough to sell any."[2] Both of her parents loved to read and valued old books, but there was little money for such luxuries. She went to school wearing a skirt given to her by a family friend.[3] When she was twelve, someone came to the village looking for children to go to work in Bangkok. Wanna's mother sent her away with this person, despite her pleas to be allowed to return to school. She felt betrayed then and betrayed again when her mother refused the offer of a local woman teacher to raise and educate her. These memories rankled for years.

Alone among the leading Thai writers, Sri Dao Ruang has only a fourth-grade education, the compulsory minimum when she was a child. As a young woman, she worked in factories and as a household servant. She is a self-taught writer, a fact that is of considerable significance, although she regrets her lack of education and frankly admits in interviews to vexing feelings of inadequacy when she compares herself to "the intellectuals." Yet it seems possible that her writing would not be nearly as innovative or as extraordinary had she gone through the educational experiences that have given some of her peers' work a certain sameness and predictability, however polished their efforts might be. For one thing, Sri Dao Ruang never protects herself in her fiction and sometimes allows herself to be perceived in unflattering ways through what she writes. (More sophisticated writers know how to avoid this.) Or, perhaps, she just doesn't care.

Since 1973, Sri Dao Ruang has been publishing short stories and novellas, many of which have won literary prizes. The most prestigious prizes (such as the annual SEAWrite award) have eluded her to date, perhaps because she continues to produce at least some stories with

---

1. "Sweets [for sale]!"
2. Sri Dao Ruang, "Nay wanníi khɔ̌ɔng Sǐi Daaw Ruang" (approximately, "Sri Dao Ruang's today"), interview by Wan Pen, *Prɛɛw* 14, no. 335 (August 1993): 265.
3. This was in fact a *phâa thǔng:* a wraparound length of cloth worn as a skirt.

unattractive characters—mad, crude, or socially marginal in some
other way—and plots or situations that are "excessive"[4] for many readers and not a few critics. Some of her technically most intriguing and
beautifully written stories are among her most controversial efforts;
for example, in "Has Anybody Seen My Dog?"[5] an abandoned, disturbed boy in a slum is discovered, at story's end, to have eaten his
own puppy; in "Snakes Court,"[6] a neurotic spinster watches a pair of
snakes copulating in a puddle all day and finally beats them to death.[7]
Sri Dao Ruang is, and no doubt will continue to be, a controversial
writer with staunch champions and righteous critics.

In his essay encouraging the expansion of gender studies by Thai
scholars in the social sciences, Reynolds writes: "Films and novels in
contemporary Thai popular culture are still overwhelmingly concerned with the theme of the family; threats to the family; conflicts in
the family; love in the family. The complicated tangles of relationships
in family life are what people want to watch and read about in popular culture."[8]

This is undeniable, yet the parameters within which authors are
expected to describe the "complicated tangles" are not so complicated:
people still want to watch films and read fiction that sanction certain
topics and prohibit others. In "Matsii," Sri Dao Ruang steps over the
line, managing to offend with her usual failings (nasty characters, vulgar language, depressing plot) and a new one: the use of a tale that is
revered by all Buddhists to try to make some sort of point about a
young mother who refuses to live a decent life or is just too crazy to
do so.

"Matsii" was chosen for inclusion in this anthology for two reasons: First, it is one of the few short stories by women that deals with
the very common situation of a mother having to accept the major or
total responsibility for her children when their father moves on. Cus-

4.   The Thai term I have heard more than once in regard to Sri Dao Ruang's work
is *mâak kɔɔn pay*—"too much."
5.   "Mǎa hǎay," in Sri Dao Ruang, *Matsii*.
6.   "Nguu gîaw," in ibid. Nguu means "snake"; gîaw means "to court" or "to make
sexual overtures."
7.   A translation of this story appears in a collection of Sri Dao Ruang's works: *A
Drop of Glass and Other Stories*, trans. Rachel Harrison (Bangkok: Duang Kamol, 1994).
8.   Reynolds, op. cit., 81. Reynolds is referring, in this passage, to a 1992 essay by
A. Hamilton, "Family Dramas: Film and Modernity in Thailand," *Screen*, vol. 33, no. 3
(n.d.): 259–73.

tody of children once was the prerogative and legal right of the father. But today in Thailand, as elsewhere, the sheer economics of child raising tends to make custody, for many men, more of a burden than a privilege. Thai men continue to practice the contemporary equivalent of polygamy, with minor wives and mistresses (women cannot sue for divorce on grounds of adultery), but few can afford it. The extended family that once could absorb a man's children without causing him any inconvenience is less able to do so nowadays; and the more affluent he is, the more likely he is to face the same problems divorced fathers face in other countries: lack of time to spend with his children, lack of help, and the inconvenience of fitting his children into his new life.

The second reason for including the story is its innovative use of a well-known and well-loved work of Buddhist literature to make a point about a serious contemporary social problem. *"Phra Wetsandon did it!"* the woman cries in despair. Prince Wetsandon could give up his children, become a monk, and be praised for his pursuit of a religious ideal, but no decent woman could. Women are considered to be more attached to the world of the flesh than are men in the Thai Buddhist view, partly because of the experiences of childbearing and motherhood. This naturally greater female attachment to the world is one of the reasons commonly given to defend the fact the men may be ordained as monks, but women may not. Yet men are also considered naturally less capable of controlling their sexual desires than women and far more likely to stray after marriage; and no one expects a young man to remain a virgin until marriage—although all women are expected to do so. These are some of the interesting contradictions that underlie "Matsii."

2

WIVES AND LOVERS

Snakes Weep, Flowers Smile

Suwanee Sukhontha

This 1974 story depicts the end of a love affair
between two eccentric writers.

That night, the air was hot and sultry. The leaves were peaceful; there
was no breeze. I sat on the porch that extended from the house out
over the pond. The soft, sweet scent of tamarinds filled the air in the
advancing darkness. Their leaves were wound into tight curls; the fat
buds of the *tamlung*[1] vine bobbed gracefully, and new tendrils lifted,
as if reaching for heaven.

I could hear the tender new fronds of palms splitting open and the
rustling of old, dry fronds scraping the murky surface of the pond. I
longed for rain, knowing that probably it would not come.

Mosquitoes stung me. I slapped at them carelessly, lacking any real
desire to kill one and let another life slip out of this world.

I thought about the poor farmers who get so desperate that they
shut a cat up in a cage and haul it around, tormenting it until the an-
gels, distressed by its pitiful yowling, relent and send rain.

I like the smell of rain and the fresh smell of wet leaves, grass, and
dirt afterward. But that night, none would fall. Dry, old palm fronds
went on scraping the pond's surface; fish sent shudders across its surface, which I first mistook for the gathering of a night breeze.

Near the house there was a rice field with no rice growing in it, only
bits of stiff grass trying to pierce the parched earth. For the sake of
the grass, too, I wished it would rain. Beyond the field is the *klong*.[2]

This story, "Nguu róong hây dɔ̀ɔk máy yím" (Snakes weep, flowers smile), appears in
the collection *Nǎaw khâw pay thǔng hǔa jay* (The cold that reaches the heart) (Bangkok:
Praphansan, 1974).
1. The *tamlung*, or *tamlʉng*, is a kind of gourd.
2. Canal.

From the porch of the house, you can see a thin white ribbon of water that winds through the fields, goes on and on, ending somewhere. I suppose I could find out where if I started walking one day and followed it.

He sat beside me, scribbling on the paper with those chicken scratches I thought were lovely. Smoking cigarette after cigarette, as if he could force the thoughts out of his mind in the streams of smoke.

The faintest breeze wafted over the porch, ruffling his page. I felt irritable, watching his hand move across the paper. What did he think while he wrote? I so much wanted to enter his thoughts, but that could never be. When he looked up for a moment, in my direction, his eyes were blank, as if I were nothing but air.

For a moment, thick streams of cigarette smoke concealed him; in another moment, the picture cleared. He had opened the top buttons of his shirt, and I could see his dark, bare skin.

Patches of yellow coreopsis gleamed in the darkness. Once I had stood in the midst of them, looking perky while he took my picture. "Don't waste the film," I had protested. "I'm not pretty." Don't think I said it so that he would contradict me; I meant it. He was stubborn, trusting his hand with the camera. I put on a yellow shirt and stood among the yellow flowers and let him take my picture. I had planted them with my own hands, and he had watered them every evening when he came home, rejoicing in them with his eyes, which was his way, not with words.

He used to complain to me that what he really wanted to do was paint. I always said that certainly he could paint if he had time to practice and develop his talent. He saw beauty in flowers, grass, everything. He had a quick and lively mind when it came to the beauty of women, of the petals of flowers . . . If only he weren't writing day and night, maybe he would paint, I thought. But, as I often told him, to appreciate beauty is something, too. Painting isn't the only thing.

Next to the coreopsis I had planted zinnias, showy flowers that swayed on tall, slender stems. There was a woman we knew whom he used to call Zinnia. He had many women. At dusk, he was mine. But I knew that later in the evening he would share his flesh with others.

I waited until he had written his last line and stacked the pages neatly. He was always orderly in his work, however disorderly the rest of his life might be.

"Want a drink?" I asked, splashing soda and whiskey into his glass without waiting for a reply. He handed me the manuscript and went to put another record on the phonograph. He liked jazz, I liked classical. It's not that I try to be an intellectual, but classical music arouses my emotions more than any other kind. To me, his music sounded like somebody shaking hot sand on a griddle. I couldn't hear anything beautiful in it. To please me, he had bought *Swan Lake* and the *Grand Canyon Suite*. We also had *Sleeping Beauty* and *South Pacific*. I still am very fond of "I'm in Love,"[3] which was popular then. I cannot hear it without thinking of the house between the edge of the rice fields and the bank of the klong, palm fronds, and the scent of tamarinds, the pure yellow of coreopsis blossoms, and the love we had for a little while, as brief as the shimmer of a reflection on the surface of a pond.

I like love. I think of love as a classical art although it is true that I love in a casual, careless way; and that he was just another reflection fluttering across the surface of my pond.

I like jealousy, too. It makes my heart dance, leap, and burn. I am not a stick or a stone, but a human being whose heart is full of cravings,[4] and therefore I have loved whatever provoked jealousy, love, lust . . .

Love, a reflection in a pond, and that is all.

Still, it hurt, that blank look in his eyes.

But I loved the pain, even when it was like a hot knife in my heart.

Hot, stifling . . . but a breeze was beginning to blow in earnest, helping the old palm fronds to lower themselves into the dark pond.

The young fronds rose up with dignity, gracefully flaunting their bright colors, their freshness, and their lovely shapes while the old ones withered, grieved, and sank.

I read his new story to the end; it made me feel nothing. Perhaps I had become used to his talent.

"So, how is it?"

I didn't answer. The jazz had shaken up my nerves; my brain felt

---

3.   In Thai, "Chăn mii khwaam rák" (literally, "I have love"). I am not sure of Suwanee's meaning; she may be referring to the *South Pacific* song "I'm in Love with a Wonderful Guy," the irony of which would no doubt have appealed to her—and may even have been intentional.

4.   The word I have translated as "craving" is *kilèet*, for which there is no exact English translation; it is usually translated as "craving" or "attachment"—to people, possessions, and so on. A lengthier definition can be found in the introduction in my discussion of the Four Noble Truths.

empty. All I could hear was that music, violence without depth. At least, that was my opinion.

I looked at him; my thoughts wandered. I do like to look at people. Faces are so interesting: eyes, two; nostrils, two; lips, two; all the same, it is true. What fascinates are the differences.

"I want to bathe . . ."

"Bathe, then," he said.

"You have to come too and be my friend."

He smiled. "Where, to the bathroom?"

"No, not to the bathroom. I'm going to bathe in the klong."

He cast a sharp glance at me. The two of us had seen each other do so many peculiar things; nothing was likely to surprise either of us, anymore. I wondered what he was thinking as he bent his head to light another cigarette, looking so smart doing it that I wished I were a man.

So hot, even with the breeze. We walked silently from the veranda to the bank of the klong. The vast fields that stretched in three directions beyond the small house now melted into the darkness, blended with the sky. Tiny screeching wings surrounded us, the sounds of insects urgently seeking mates. And then I heard it, the sound of a snake slipping through the grass very near us, a high, light whispering sound, like quiet weeping, and it struck me to the heart. I did not want to think about it, for I hate snakes more than I hate the person I hate most in the world.

He followed me, carrying his bottle. I seem fated to love people who love liquor more than they love me. The grass near the klong was tall and stiff and so rough that it cut painfully into my feet and calves. The water gleamed silver in the surrounding darkness, and the breeze was now quite fresh—cold, really—but I was determined to bathe.

We looked for a place where the grass was short, and sat down. He sat with his knees drawn up to his chest. We stared at each other in the darkness as he lit a cigarette and passed it to me. I took a few drags and passed it back. We often shared them, more out of laziness than any romantic intent. I listened to the water lap at the bank, watched the soft weeds shift to and fro, looked up to see that a hundred thousand stars had poked their winking faces out of the sky to chat with us. I took off everything but my thin underwear, tossing the other things in a heap and wrapping myself in a large, thick towel that belonged to him. He sipped his drink. A towel that other women had wrapped around their bodies, a towel that had fallen from their bodies. In a few moments, I dropped it and jumped into the water. With a shock of revulsion, I felt the bottom mud seize my feet like the coils of a huge, cold snake. I quickly lifted myself to the surface and floated on my back among the roiling weeds. He sat and smoked, perhaps watching me.

I splashed and kicked. If a policeman had been passing by, maybe he would have arrested me. All of Bangkok uses the water in this klong. People drink it. In my heart, I begged their forgiveness. I swam to and fro until I was tired, and when I grabbed at the bank, my hair streaming around my face, and he reached down and pulled me up, I realized that there would have been no easy way to climb out had he not been there. His hands were warm and dry. I realized that I must look dreadful. I quickly wrapped myself in the towel, then sat close beside him, dangling my feet in the water and looking up at my friends the stars.

"What about you? Aren't you going to bathe?"

He didn't answer. The insects kept up their screeching, and I was sure I heard another snake. I wanted to see his eyes. I wanted to know if that blank expression still hid his thoughts, now that he had no pencil in his hand, no story forming in his mind. But it was too dark. There was no moon.

Instead of turning to him, looking into his eyes, I bolted to my feet, threw aside the towel, and jumped into the klong again, but this time I sought the cold, thick mud eagerly. I dove down, held my breath, not wanting to return to the surface even if he would be there close beside me, even though my friends the stars would be flickering above us and a fresh breeze would be blowing from the fields.

At last I was forced to surge up into the night air. The first thing I noticed was that the screeching of the insects in search of mates seemed duller, farther away. Or perhaps my ears were ringing from staying underwater too long.

Just as before, he was there, the glass in his hand, the cigarette in his mouth. Just as before, he pulled me out, and we faced each other in the meager light from a hundred thousand stars.

O   O   SUWANEE SUKHONTHA
          AND "SNAKES WEEP, FLOWERS SMILE"

Suwanee was born Suwanee Sukhonthiang in Phitsanulok in 1932. She studied and taught fine arts at Silpakorn University in Bangkok during the 1950s, but with the success of her first short stories during the early 1960s, she turned to writing full-time. She also became the founding editor of *Lalana*, a magazine that published the work of many well-known female writers and helped to establish the careers of several younger women, including Sri Dao Ruang, two of whose short stories are included here. Suwanee had a wonderful ear for the style, slang, and cadences of everyday conversation, and was by turns hilarious, morose, wanton, and self-deprecating in her inimitably self-forgiving way.

"Snakes Weep, Flowers Smile" is included because it is a wonderful example of Suwanee's popular love-gone-wrong stories, full of the rich imagery her readers love: "I heard the sound of a snake slipping through the grass, a high, light whispering sound, like quiet weeping, and the sound struck me to the heart." There is the familiar unworthy lover who sullenly smokes a cigarette in the darkness and the woman who suffers—although the reader is led to believe that she rather revels in the titillating drama of it all: "I felt the bottom mud seize my feet like the coils of a huge, cold snake." A reader may wonder if the woman touching the cold bottom mud of the klong is thinking how she will describe the moment, when she returns to her typewriter the next morning.

Divorced early in life (she had married one of her professors at Silpakorn), Suwanee raised four children on her own. She wrote some wonderful short stories about family life, in which the narrator is clearly based on her own eldest daughter; invariably, these stories center around funny, touching reminiscences of "life with my mother"; no one ever accused Suwanee of a lack of self-esteem or confidence.

Perhaps her most popular works are the stories, like "Snakes Weep," that chronicle her long series of troubled romantic relationships—relationships she had no compunctions about revising as she saw fit. One story of a woman's terrifying revenge against a cheating lover bears a title that I labored to translate, finally coming up with "Alone in Her Room with Her Snake, Brooding on Thoughts of the Past."

No female author has had a more important effect on contemporary women's writing in Thailand than Suwanee. One of the most interesting aspects of her career is that unlike some other contemporary women writers who take risks, such as Sri Dao Ruang and Anchan, Suwanee never had to pay for the ones she took, with either critics or readers. Why not? Perhaps part of the answer lies in her being so understandable to most members of the literary establishment: she was the daughter of a physician, the wife and former wife of a professor, the possessor of a degree from an outstanding Thai university. She never was, in the things that mattered, an outsider despite her unconventional life; and she did not speak enough of any other language to form relationships with foreigners. Though she might sprinkle her work with such Western references as *Dr. Zhivago*, drinking scotch at bars, the *Grand Canyon Suite*, and Mia Farrow's current hairdo, she and her writing were quintessentially, understandably *Thai*, and although she was innovative, she did things in a recognizably and comfortably Thai way. For example, she was extraordinarily good at devising nature images to suggest sexual feelings and activities, a technique that has been used in Thai literature for centuries. However earthy her writing might be, there are no frank depictions of sexual relations in her work; the first recognized woman writer to dare such a thing was Anchan in "A Pot That Scouring Will Not Save," which appears in this section.

In one of Suwanee's most famous and admired stories, "Wan thi daed suay," or "Wan thîi, dὲεd sŭay" (On a day the sun was pretty),[1] the narrator, sitting in a stalled bus in the midst of a typical Bangkok traffic jam, sees an expensively dressed woman get out of a chauffeur-driven car to see why traffic has stopped moving. When the woman raises her arm to shield her eyes, her large diamond ring flashes in the sunlight. A thief dashes out from an alley, grabs her by the arm, and cuts off her finger to steal the ring.

In 1984, Suwanee was herself stabbed to death in the midst of a Bangkok traffic jam by two young men apparently attempting to hijack her car. Her friend Krisna Asoksin[2] composed the following words for the book distributed at Suwanee's funeral:

> You did not waste the opportunity of your birth, Khun Suwanee. Yours was the life of a woman who struggles with life, who fights with her arms, with her legs, with her whole body and being. In sorrow, you grieved the hardest; in happiness, no one was more

---

1. My translation of this story appears under the title "On a Cloudy Morning," *Tenggara*, vol. 29 (1990).

2. The pen name of Sukanya Cholasueks; an excerpt from one of her novels, *This Human Vessel*, is included.

joyful. Of good luck and bad, you had the most. In all of your life, nothing was moderate or average. *You should have been a man* [italics added], not a woman; but you were born a woman, and in your womanhood you were the equal of any man and sometimes stronger than a man. The opportunity of this birth was not in vain, [you were not like] so many women, who are born only to waste [their lives]. You tasted all of life, in all of its aspects.[3]

Suwanee continues to be deeply missed by all who knew her. Her death at fifty-four, at the height of her fame, was a tremendous loss— and as far as the literary community is concerned, no one can ever quite take her place.

3. From *Sùwanii Sùkhonthiang* (Bangkok: Burapha Khawmpiw, 1984), 65 (my translation). Since the late nineteenth century, it has been traditional to distribute some kind of book at a funeral if the family can afford to do so. This book is filled with the reminiscences and heartfelt eulogies of Suwanee's many writer friends. In one of the photographs in the book, Suwanee stands alone in a field of coreopsis, smiling at the photographer.

From *Behind the Painting*

Sri Burapha

This famous novel of the late 1930s is about a woman of
the aristocracy who marries late, at the age of thirty-four,
because her father has not been willing to sanction a less
than suitable match.

[*In the mid-1930s, Nopporn, a twenty-two-year-old Thai university student in Japan,
falls in love with Mom Rachawong Kirati,*[1] *the unhappy, recently married wife of an
elderly Thai aristocrat, Chao Khun Atikanbodi;*[2] *the couple is visiting Japan for two
months. Kirati befriends the young man and falls in love with him, but does not con-
fess her love and honorably rejects his advances. Six years later, in Bangkok, he is
called to her deathbed, where she confesses that she loved him, too, and that she will
die loving him.*

Although it was written in the late 1930s, Behind the Painting *has a distinctly
Victorian sensibility and mode of expression. The themes are dramatic, and the emotions are lavish—never more so than when suppressed. The novel is not only Victorian but also decidedly operatic. Its highly idealized characters are concerned with
tradition and honor, duty and loyalty, undying love and sacrifice.*

*Kirati has been raised in social isolation by her widowed father, confined to home
and the royal court, reserved for the perfect match he insisted her great beauty, wealth,
and social position deserved. The years pass, and when she is thirty-four years old,*

Many editions of this novel, which was written during the late 1930s, have been published. The one used for this translation was published by Baankit, Bangkok, and is
undated. A fine translation of the complete novel has appeared: Siburapha, *Behind the
Painting and Other Stories,* trans. David Smyth (Singapore: Oxford University Press,
1990). The translation that appears here is my own; readers interested in the subject of
translation may be interested in comparing the choices made by Smyth with my own.

1.   *Mom rachawong,* or *mɔ̀ɔm ráchawong,* is a title indicating descent from a Thai king.
Khunying is a name prefix (or title) that indicates Kirati's status as the wife of a titled
man. Both terms are used in the original Thai version of the novel, and both appear
here.

2.   The title *"chao khun"* was used in place of the individual's name when addressing
him. *Chao khun* was also used as a third-person pronoun when speaking of the individual. *Atikanbodi,* or *athíkanbɔ̀dì,* means "dean" or "rector." We never learn the given
name of this man.

her frightened and remorseful father urges her to marry his dear friend, an old man whom, as Kirati tells Nopporn, "cares nothing for moonlight . . . lives only in the past . . . and has no future."

The reader may be taken aback to discover that Chao Khun Atikanbodi is only fifty years old. When the novel was written, a Thai person of fifty years was considered old indeed—very likely a grandfather or grandmother, which is the definition of old age. The author himself was nearly as young as his protagonist, Nopporn, when he went to Japan in 1932 and decided to write this novel. Perhaps, from the perspective of youth, fifty seemed as reasonable an age as eighty to assign to the character of an elderly husband.

The greatly admired, elegant simplicity of the novel's original Thai cannot be adequately rendered even in the most careful translation. An absolutely faithful translation would render the language of the novel not elegantly simple but irritatingly simplistic; on the other hand, the creation of a kind of parallel expression in English, sacrificing the literal meaning and sense of the author's dialogue and descriptions, would be to take an even less justifiable liberty. I have tried to effect an adequate compromise; the style I have developed is somewhat stiff; however, the narrator is a rather stiff individual and appears so in the original Thai. The narration might have been made more attractive to the English reader at the expense of fidelity.

This translation is slightly abridged to avoid repetitive sentences; a few passing remarks that refer to incidents in the novel that are not relevant to these excerpts have been omitted.]

Preface

The picture had been hanging in my study for two days before Bree noticed it. "Where is that?" She put her face up to it. "Someone wrote 'Mitake' in one corner—the artist, I'm sure."

I started, but she did not seem to notice. "Yes . . . Mitake is a lovely place," I said. "People in Tokyo often go there for a Sunday outing."

"Did you buy it in Tokyo when you were studying there? I've never seen it before."

I looked down at the book I had been reading when she entered the room and said, "No, it was painted by a friend." I was not satisfied with my voice, which had the careful quality of an actor speaking from the stage.

"It is awfully—*ordinary,* don't you think? Or perhaps I'm not looking at it in the right way. I'm not a very good judge of art."

"You're much too close to it to see it properly. It is an oil, Bree; if you look at it from a distance, it will look quite different." But Bree had already lost interest. She did not bother to step back and look at it from a distance, nor did she ask any more questions, which was just as well.

The painting hangs above my desk. At first, I had thought to put it on the opposite wall until I realized how disturbing it would be, seeing it every time I looked up from my work. In truth, Bree was not wrong; it is quite ordinary. There is no comparison between it and the paintings that hang in our parlor or in the bedrooms.

In the center of the picture, a stream flows down a hillside; trees cover the slope to its left, and on the other bank a small path winds up, toward an overhanging ledge. There are a good many gnarled trees, wildflowers, and rocks of all sizes; on one great rock at the edge of the stream, you can just make out two people sitting together. They are small, at so great a distance from the artist that it is difficult to tell whether they are two men or a man and a woman; although, of course, I know. At the bottom of the picture are the words "At the Edge of the Stream" and in the lower right corner "Mitake," which Bree had noticed, and the date—six years ago.

The artist possessed a mediocre talent. You could call it a pretty picture, I suppose, and not be wrong; one who loves the outdoors might admire it and find it interesting on that account; but Bree has not such a nature, which is regrettable, for I have.

In any event, the fact that neither Bree nor anyone else sees much of interest in it is reasonable enough. To the objective eye, behind the picture there is only a sheet of stiff paper; and behind that, a wall. But for me, and only for me, the truth is quite different. I know very well what extraordinary life there is behind this picture, a life that is fixed forever in my heart.

When I am alone, looking at it closely, I see that the stream flows gently in some places, fiercely in others. I am aware of the soft light of autumn that surrounds the couple sitting side by side on the rock beside the stream. I can even see that one of them, the woman, has marvelously long eyelashes and a charming, curiously triangular little mouth, with fine, narrow lips meticulously rouged.

I know that the artist who painted this picture did not work carelessly. On the contrary, it was painted meticulously, this ordinary, peaceful scene; one scene from a tale that has recently ended, to my inexpressible sorrow.

Chapter 1

When Chao Khun Atikanbodi brought Mom Rachawong Kirati, his new wife, to honeymoon in Japan, I was studying at Rikkiu University. I was then twenty-two years old. I had known the chao khun in Thailand; he was an old friend of my father's and had always been kind to me. I had known his first wife and was saddened to learn, two years before, that she had died of influenza. I had heard nothing of Chao Khun Atikanbodi since then, until I received the letter in which he told me he would soon be coming to Japan with his new wife, Mom Rachawong Kirati. He would be most appreciative if I could locate a suitable house for them and make all the arrangements necessary for a stay of two months.

I must say that "honeymoon" was a word that came to my mind, not one that appears in his letter. He wished to make a trip of some duration, so that he could enjoy himself in a leisurely way. But the most important reason for the trip was to give his new wife a change of scene; he was anxious that she have a wonderful experience in Japan.

"I love her, and I must say that I feel sorry for her as well, for she has seen unusually little of the world for a lady of her age. I shall take pleasure in seeing Kirati move beyond the narrow sphere in which she has lived all of her life, and in seeing her learn something of the world. I wish to make it possible for her to travel, not only in Thailand but far beyond its borders. It is my hope that I shall be able to make her happy, not sorry she has married me. (I am somewhat older than she.) At the least, I pray that she will not feel that her life wants meaning. I am sure that you, too, will love her, dear Nopporn. She is a bit on the quiet side, particularly with people she does not know well. But she is very kind, and I have not the least doubt that she will take to you at once. I have told her so much about you . . ."

I was sure that I had never met Mom Rachawong Kirati, and as I reread Chao Khun Atikanbodi's letter, despite all he had said, I did not feel that I had learned very much about her. She would be about forty, I supposed, perhaps a few years older than that. His remark that she was "a bit on the quiet side" made me suspect that she was rather grand, as ladies of her class and age tend to be. She might well be thinking that it would be something of a trial to have a bumptious student about the house. In truth, I was no bumptious student; on the contrary, I was a rather solemn young man, already set in my careful ways. It would present no difficulty to be careful of my manners with Khunying Kirati.

In his letter, Chao Khun Atikanbodi had also written that he had no great liking for hotels, particularly grand ones, such as the Imperial Hotel in Tokyo. He did not like being constantly surrounded by people he did not know and having to dress up every time he left his room or wanted something to eat. He would greatly prefer to rent a house, where he would be free to do as he pleased. What it would cost to rent a house for two months was clearly of no importance to him. He was a man known for his immense wealth and also for his generous, good heart.

I found a house for them in a suburb of Tokyo, conveniently near a train station. It was not very large, but it was one of the most charming in the neighborhood. From the outside, it had a Western appearance, but its interior structure and design were thoroughly Japanese. The house stood upon a slight rise. The wall that encircled it was constructed of large rocks at the base; earth was packed above the rocks, and graceful plants had been placed at measured intervals. Within, there was a lovely, well-tended garden, the crowning glory of which was the pair of great trees that stood before the house. The leafy profusion of their spreading branches bespoke abundance, cheer, and welcome to the cozy house that nestled beneath them. As you may surmise, I was very fond of this house myself and felt that the two hundred yen per month the owner asked was not too much, especially considering that it was in perfect condition and fully furnished.

I hired a servant girl with a sweet, pretty face. Do not suspect that I engaged the girl with the idea that Chao Khun Atikanbodi might view her in a capacity beyond her official duties. In my opinion, if one must choose between a servant with a face like a *yakshni*[3] and one who is lovely, one ought to pick the latter, for when we are faced with beauty every day, whether it be in a person or in a work of art, our disposition cannot help but be improved. The salary this young woman required was considerably more than one would pay an average servant. It was not her pretty face that made her so valuable, but the fact that she spoke some English, an ability that I had no doubt

---

3. A yakshni is a female version of the demonic giants that appear in the *Ramakien* (the Thai version of *The Ramayana*).

would save both Chao Khun and his wife a good deal of inconvenience, and enhance the pleasure of living in the charming house.

The first time I met Khunying Kirati, at the Tokyo train station, was also the first time in my life that I found myself at a complete loss for words. Chao Khun Atikanbodi stepped down from the train first, then proceeded to help two women disembark. One was middle aged, with a somewhat forbidding expression slightly relieved by the uncertainty and agitation occasioned by her new surroundings. Indeed, she perfectly fulfilled my expectations of Khunying Kirati. The other woman was young, quite lovely, and fashionably dressed; her expression, far from being one of uncertainty or agitation, suggested boundless delight restrained by good manners. I knew that she could not be Chao Khun Atikanbodi's daughter, who had married some years before. Who could this young woman be?

I had not long to wonder, for no sooner had we exchanged a few words of greeting than he turned to her and said, "I should like you to meet my wife, Khunying Kirati." Her smile was warm and gracious, as she returned my prompt wai. I was nearly struck speechless and felt a fool, although no doubt only a fraction of a moment passed while I searched that charming face for any clue by which I might have identified her as the woman in Chao Khun's letter. As the other woman turned to speak with someone nearby, I realized that she must be the cook. In his letter, he had said that his cook would be accompanying them, a fact that I had completely forgotten until this awkward moment. Amazed at the assumptions I had made concerning her, I quickly accustomed myself to the fact that the lovely young lady was indeed Khunying Kirati.

On that day, I was wearing my university uniform, which was the first thing Khunying Kirati commented upon. She admired it, pronouncing it very smart and pointing out that my navy blue suit quite matched her own. Her dress was dark blue, with a design of white flowers. It was not the showy sort of flowered dress but a graceful garment; I am not good at describing such things, but I would say that, white flowers and all, she looked quite dignified.

As the car I had hired turned into the driveway, Chao Khun Atikanbodi patted my shoulder and said, "You have found a splendid house." Truly, none of the houses we had seen along the way had looked as appealing. The pretty servant stood on the front stairs dressed in an immaculate kimono, bowing repeatedly, as is the Japanese custom. When Chao Khun Atikanbodi spoke a few words to her in English, and she answered nicely, he looked enormously pleased. He walked through the house, inspecting all the rooms and appointments, continually expressing his delight and his gratitude for my trouble. Everything had been prepared for their comfort, including a hot bath. Clearly, nothing in their new surroundings disappointed or failed to live up to their expectations. Later, I would be embarrassed, but as happy as anyone else would be, when people told me that Chao Khun Atikanbodi had shared with them his opinion that I was a young man of uncommon good sense and ability.

That evening, I took them to a Chinese restaurant, the famous Ka Jo Eng, where they admired the splendid dining room and enjoyed the excellent food. Chao Khun Atikanbodi repeatedly declared that it was quite the equal of Hoi Thien Lao in Bangkok.[4] When we returned to the house, they exclaimed over the exquisite care with which the servant had prepared their futons for sleep. At last, I returned to my home, my heart brimming with happiness and satisfaction. The arrival of Chao Khun Atikanbodi and Khunying Kirati, and all that had occurred during the day and the evening, had been all that I might have wished and so much more.

o   o   o   o

Chapter 9

[Nopporn has become the constant companion of Khunying Kirati during the first three weeks of her stay in Japan.]

After we had eaten lunch and rested a bit, the khunying and I went off for a walk on the main road in the direction of the foothills. There were no houses along this road, but in the distance one could make out four or five huts scattered over the gentle swell of a rise, each surrounded by a neat garden; I knew at once that this rise comprised the entire world for the people in those huts. We never saw another tourist on the road until we reached the rise and paused to rest beneath a large sapodilla tree whose graceful foliage we had admired as we approached.

---

4. The multistoried Hoi Thien Lao Restaurant still operates, virtually unchanged.

I shall describe only the part of our conversation in which I learned the tragic history of Khunying Kirati.

"I should like to know, if I may be so bold, how you arrived at the decision to marry Chao Khun Atikanbodi."

"You seem quite interested in the subject of matrimony. Perhaps you are preparing yourself for the state?"

"Not at all," I replied quickly. "It isn't matrimony in general that interests me, but your case."

"Really, and why such an interest in my private affairs?" she asked, her tone of voice less stern than the words themselves.

"Because you have never spoken of it to me, even though you have assured me that you have no closer friend."[5]

"Nevertheless, I do not see why you wish to know these things," she replied wearily. "My life is the life of an unlucky woman—especially unlucky in the matter of love. The details would only make you feel sad, Nopporn. I think it will be best if you satisfy yourself with the present and do not inquire into the past. Why spoil your happy mood on such a lovely day?"

"I am not a coward. In trying to persuade me that I should not ask after the reasons for your unluckiness, you have only succeeded in convincing me that I must know."

"Nopporn, you are so earnest, and your smile is so dear; it is quite impossible to resist you."

"You have two younger sisters, I know. Are they also married?"

"Yes, one married eight years ago; the other, a year later. They live happily with their husbands, neither of whom is old; and they are more than happy—they are in love."

"What a pity."

"That they are happy and in love with their husbands?" she asked, her eyes twinkling.

"Not at all. I am happy for them and sorry for you."

"Do you wish to tell me your opinion or to listen to my story?"

"I am prepared to listen."

"You already know that I married Chao Khun without love," Khunying Kirati began. "And what you wish to know is *why*. But in order to understand what I shall tell you, you must first understand

---

5.   The expression used here is *phûan taay; phûan* means "friend," and *taay* means "to die"; thus, a *phûan taay* is a "friend to the death."

how I came to be unmarried at thirty-four, an age at which few women marry for the first time. You know that most women marry at twenty or twenty-five—thirty, at the very most. And please—I beg you not to tell me how young I look for a woman of my age. If you wish to understand my situation, there are two circumstances that I must make clear to you, as clear as a cloudless sky." She smiled and added, "Because I know that otherwise you shall never cease to pester me."

We had brought a large cloth with us. We might both have reclined at our ease upon it, but we did not. Mom Rachawong Kirati sat with her back against the sapodilla tree, and I sat patiently at her feet, waiting for her to begin her story. Until this moment, she had been looking straight into my eyes, but now her gaze shifted into the distance.

"I am sorry." I said, "but I truly wish to know why you waited so long to marry; perhaps I have been a fool not to ask before."

"You have been a fool only for insisting on praising my 'youthful' good looks," she said in a half-joking manner—but only half. "It is not quite correct to say that I have *waited* so long to marry, Nopporn. And I may as well save you the trouble of imagining that my youth was dramatic and eventful—full of love and sorrow, dreadful disappointments and copious tears—for it was not. My chief disappointment was that my young life was so very ordinary, and that, by degrees, ordinariness seemed to transform itself into bad luck."

"I do not mean to contradict you, but it is very difficult for me to believe that there was not some strange event, some occurrence in your life that you are keeping to yourself. Please forgive my suspicions."

"My dear Nopporn, you must quit your studies and become a fortune teller—you are so certain that you know my life better than I know it myself! The world of my childhood was small and offered no opportunities for frolic or play. Before the change of government,[6] the aristocracy lived in a world of its own. When I finished school, my father drew me into that world with him and forbade me to associate with people beyond it. Of course, he meant to protect me. From then on, I continued my studies with an elderly foreign governess. Inside the house—or rather, the residence, as it was called in those days— between my old governess and the Thai house servants, you may

6.   Mom Rachawong Kirati is referring to the overthrow of the absolute monarchy in 1932, which is identified here, as always in Thai, as the "change in the form of governing" ("kaan plian pleeng kaan bòk krɔɔng").

imagine the sort of conversation to which I was exposed. The virtues of a lady . . . the proper conduct of a household. I had *Vogue* and *Mc-Call's* magazines to read, from which I learned to care for my beauty and to preserve it as well . . . something like caring for a hydrangea in a vase, which will stay fresh for an amazing number of days if you care for it properly.

"I lived at home and studied with my governess. Occasionally, Father would send me to the palace for a while to stay with ladies of our family. And for many years, that was my life, moving between home and the palace. During those years, I had no idea of the value of youth, particularly for a woman. It never occurred to me that I should be using my precious youth on my own behalf. Nor did I ask myself why I troubled to make myself beautiful, to enhance the freshness of youth—only to hide my efforts from the eyes of the world outside. I was not a very clever girl, you see; but then, we were not brought up to be clever—to *think*. The path had been laid out for us. We were set upon that path and followed it, narrow as it was, according to traditions we would not have dreamed of questioning."

She was silent for a moment, and I took advantage of the opportunity to say, "But the khunying whom I have come to know is nothing like the girl you describe; she is a lady of considerable intellect and judgment, and a good deal more clever than ordinary people such as myself."

"Please, do not say that I am more clever than you or anyone else. Over the years, the circumstances of my life have given me a great deal of time, and so I have learned to think. And I owe much to my governess, who purchased excellent English books and urged me to read them. Of course, being a biddable young woman, I did as I was told; but soon, I came to love books. And art, I loved art and beauty of all kinds. Gradually, a lonely girl became a thoughtful woman; I think now that it was in my nature to be so, however I might have been raised. As for my appearance, caring for myself became a matter of—well, a matter of art, if you will; I cheered myself by creating beauty in my own person. But, as I have already told you, I never thought of my beauty or my youth as an *asset*."

"I think I am beginning to understand."

"Painting was a great comfort to me. It saved me from my loneliness, and it absorbed time wonderfully. Painting became one of my two preoccupations; the other, as I have already told you, was myself, my beauty. I moved from the canvas to the mirror and back again. Eventually, my personal preparations for the day required several hours."

"Several *hours?* That is unbelievable," I said. "What could you do, for several hours, every day? What could you possibly require? A dash of powder, a bit of lipstick . . ."

She laughed, and her eyes lost their sadness for a moment. "Dear, dear Nopporn, you know nothing at all about women. Before you think too harshly of me, wasting the hours of my life in such a fashion, I beg you to try to understand what it is to live as women do. We are born to decorate the world and to pander to it. And to do our job properly, we must keep ourselves as decorative as possible. I do not say that this is our only responsibility, but you cannot deny its importance."

"I shall not contradict you. It is true that a man seeks a woman who is good—but also beautiful."

"Yes . . . and sometimes the matter of goodness is entirely overlooked. I had not thought much about love until my youngest sister fell in love and was married; and then, two years later my second sister was married, also a love match. After that wedding, I began to think of myself as an unlucky woman. I was twenty-six years old, Nopporn. Both of my sisters had married at nineteen. When I observed their happiness, a pain began to grow within me. I was not jealous of my sisters—I adore them. I was simply dismayed at my own situation. It was a bad time . . . please understand, I am not telling you these very private matters to boast of the difficulties of my life."

"You have called me your dear friend; and if you believe that it is so—and I know that it is so—you must realize that I cannot fail to understand you."

"Do you believe that I am a good person, Nopporn?"

"I have not the slightest doubt."

"Are you sure?"

"Absolutely. Unshakably."

She smiled and said, "Very well, then. Since you have vowed to believe in my essential virtue, I shall reveal all of my feelings and the truth of my life without fear of your disapproval. Her eyes sparkled as the result of our banter, but the sadness remained. "When I was twenty-nine years old, it is the simple truth that I was still more beautiful than my younger sisters. I told myself that it was one stroke of good luck to have been born beautiful—and one stroke of bad luck, never to have been in love. And then I slowly came to realize that luck was not altogether to blame. You see, my well-meaning father had purposely kept me confined between our home and the palace *because* I was the most beautiful of his daughters. My younger sisters were given far more freedom; perhaps Father thought they needed to be out and about in the world to attract suitors. But I, the great beauty of the family, needed to be protected from them—from the world, in fact. Had I been born plain, even ugly, I should have been free. I wondered why I had been given great beauty, only to be destined to loneliness because of it.

"After my sisters had both married and had homes of their own, our house was unbearably empty. Each time I passed a mirror, I paused to comfort myself with the fact that I was still pretty, and that, at twenty-nine, I should surely find someone to love. Nopporn, please do not think me shameful for confessing how greatly I desired to love someone and to be loved. It was my greatest wish. Like everyone else, I dreamed of love and of marriage. I wanted to be able to speak of such things, know them for myself, to live in that world where my sisters already dwelled. But I was given no such opportunity. I wanted my own home, into which I could bring the outside world, and from which I could go out into it.[7] I wanted children upon whom I could lavish my love, a family to serve—oh, and there were other things I wanted to do and to achieve. But all of them depended upon my finding . . . love.

"I thought that having lived to the age of twenty-nine without love was bad enough. I did not dare to think that the years would all but dissolve, and that I should find myself thirty-four years old and still alone in my father's house. It was then that Chao Khun Atikanbodi came into my life. Not for the first time, of course; he had always been my father's great friend. He asked for my hand, the hand of the eldest daughter—the one who had been left, the one who still lived at home at the age of thirty-four. My father considered the matter briefly, and then of course he gave his consent, provided that I agreed to the match. He was quite understandably afraid that if he did not enthu-

7. As an unmarried woman, Kirati would never have any of the social freedom of her younger, married sisters. She would have to remain in her father's home or, eventually, in the home of one of the sisters.

siastically accept his friend's proposal, I might never have the opportunity to enter the world of marriage. And he was equally afraid that I would refuse, condemning myself to spinsterhood forever. Had I done so, he would have grieved dreadfully over my fate. I knew that he loved me very much, and I believe that he felt remorse about my life, my unlucky life . . . as I have said, he always worried more about me than about my younger sisters. He wanted me to be happy and said that he could not bear the idea that I might, with all my beauty, go through life without a husband. And so, although he left the final decision to me, he implored me to accept Chao Khun's proposal."

She looked into my eyes then and smiled; and my heart trembled as I met her eyes, those beautiful eyes so full of pain.

"When I first learned of Chao Khun's intentions, I was stunned; and when Father told me that he hoped I would accept the proposal, I burst into tears. Do not imagine, Nopporn, that he was surprised by my reaction. He understood very well—I think he was appalled by the pass to which we all had come, in the matter of my future. He tried to comfort me; I remember every word.

"'My dear Kirati,' he said, 'I understand how you must feel. You are the best of my daughters and the loveliest. I am more proud of you than I can ever say. I realize that a man of Chao Khun's age is not the most desirable match for you; if it were up to me, I should see you married to a man who is your own age and whom you love—and, of course, whose family background is appropriate. I deeply regret that your goodness and beauty have not been better rewarded. But the fact remains that you will be thirty-five years old on your next birthday, and I must urge you to accept our friend's honorable proposal. Chao Khun may be an older suitor than you or I would prefer, but I assure you, and I believe you already know, that he is a very good man.'

"In the days that followed, we scarcely spoke. All I can remember is my weeping, hour after hour. My father, trying to comfort me, could only kiss me on the forehead, with the saddest look in his eyes. One evening, I dressed myself with particular care and stood before the mirror in my bedroom for a long time. I studied the person in the mirror: Why should a woman who appeared so fresh and lovely be considering marriage with a man of fifty? Could it be possible? How could such beauty have failed to find love? But then I remembered that I was thirty-four years old, and my heart sank. In that moment, standing before the mirror in my room, I knew that Chao Khun's proposal signified the end of hope. Whatever the mirror might reflect, my youth and the likelihood that I would ever marry for love were gone.

"Father waited patiently for my decision. I had asked for a certain number of days to clear and calm my mind, insofar as that was possible, and to give the chao khun's proposal the thoughtful attention that it deserved. In the end, as you know, I accepted him."

"Why didn't you say no? You were—you are—still so lovely! You would surely have met someone who loved you—you should have refused and waited!"

She smiled faintly and said, "Nopporn, you speak as if the decision had not yet been made."

"The world is too cruel."

"No. Human beings may be cruel, but the world itself is beautiful. Now, if you wish to hear the rest—"

"I am sorry, but I cannot accept the reasoning behind your decision —I cannot!"

"My dear Nopporn, you must not be angry. There is nothing over which we might quarrel, for all that I speak of today is in the past. You must accept the fact that all of my decisions have been made."

o   o   o   o

Chapter 13

Mom Rachawong Kirati continued her story.

"My father's pleading was one reason I accepted Chao Khun's proposal. I knew that he would be heartbroken if I refused. But that was not the most important reason. I had reasons of my own, Nopporn. For thirty-four years, I had lived in a very small world. I was lonely, and I was bored. When a young bird grows into its wings, it forsakes its nest and flies off into the great world. But a human being who is a female must remain in her cage. I had remained in mine and longed for that great world, craving change and another life than the one I had been living all those years. Only one thing would enable me to realize these dreams: *marriage.* So, I had been unlucky in love; what of it? Would I be the wiser to stay in my little cage because of it? How clever whould I have been, Nopporn, to forsake the world, close my eyes, and close my feelings against all the pleasant experiences that could be mine—if only I had married a good man whom I did not love?

"What had I to lose by marrying him? Yes, he was too old for me; but, Nopporn, what was I waiting for? Where would I meet my true love? Perhaps my true love had already died or was not yet born. I had come to desire reality, for I had tired of dreams. I accepted Chao Khun because he was real, and what he offered was real. The life I could have with him would be real. Despite my sorrow, I was thrilled to know that I was about to meet the great world at last, to see strange and wonderful sights; and I was content, Nopporn—even without love."

Mom Rachawong sat up a bit straighter, sighed deeply, and dabbed at her eyes with a handkerchief. "Nopporn, I feel as though I have told all of this to you in a dream—in a state of delirium, more nearly. I beg you, please—do not ask me more."

"Is it possible that you may come to love him?"

"No, it is not possible. There is no way that I could come to love him. He eats; he goes to sleep; he has his amusements. He is not interested in moonlight, much less in words of love. He has no future; he has only the past and the present. He is old. Love could no more bloom with such a man than a rose could grow through the stones of a paved lane."

"You have said that you are content—but is contentment enough?"

"Nopporn, do not bind me about with your words, or I shall be unable to breathe. Give me freedom, please!" She opened her compact, looked at herself, repaired her makeup, and patted her hair into place.

She was so beautiful that I could feel my heart beating. "Khunying, are you happy today?" I asked, aware of a trembling in my voice.

Instead of answering in words, she slowly nodded and, still looking into the compact, glanced at me in the tiny mirror from the corner of her eye, which caused my heart to beat all the more quickly.

"It is getting late, Nopporn. We must start back." She drew her feet beneath her and prepared to rise, then quickly sat down again. "Oh dear, I am afraid that my foot is quite asleep from sitting on it for so long."

"Have no fear, I shall carry you!" I said.

She laughed, but after she had allowed me to help her to her feet, she pulled away quickly. "I am quite all right, thank you. In a moment, I shall be quite able to walk." I paid no attention to her insistence on standing alone but continued to hold her arm and pressed close to her side.

"Khunying, are you happy?" I asked, so breathless that I could barely force the words from my throat.

"Look, Nopporn—how small the stream below us seems from here. Have we really come all that way? I shall have to find the strength to go back down."

I pressed closer. My chest nearly touched her bosom, and she leaned away from me, steadying herself against the tree. I could hear my breathing—and hers.

"I made two sketches of the river, you know . . ."

"I am so very happy when I am with you, Khunying."

"Do let go of my arm, Nopporn. We must gather our things and return."

"I do not want to let go of you, to be away from you, not ever," I said.

"Nopporn, you must not look at me that way." Her voice was shaking as she said, "Please, I must insist—let *go* of me. I am quite able to walk on my own."

But I had lost the power to restrain myself, and instead of releasing her, I buried my face in the rosy softness of her cheek. I kissed her, adoring her, nearly unconscious with longing.

Mom Rachawong Kirati wrenched free of my arm and leaned back against the tree, gasping for breath, her face flushed. "Nopporn, have you any idea what you have *done?*"

I did not move. Suddenly, I felt as meek as a lamb. "Khunying, I know only that I love you."

"And this is the way you show your love for me?"

"I do not know. I only know that I was overpowered by my love, that I was out of my mind!"

"Out of your mind . . . have you never observed that men explain their most regrettable acts with the excuse that they were 'out of their minds'?"

"But I love you—honestly, terribly . . ."

"What meaning has love when you express it while out of your mind?"

"I love you with my heart, my life . . . it is written on my heart for-ever—that I touched you, that I held you in my arms."

"Can you think that it will profit you to have this written on your heart?"

"Even in love, must we consider profit?"

"Have you given any thought to—who I am, and who you are?"

"A great deal, Khunying."

"And, still, you have behaved in this manner toward me."

I lowered my head and crossed my arms, hugging them to my chest. "I do not know what to say, except that I was overcome by my natural feelings. I tried not to succumb, but when I was tempted by love, I failed. If you speak of reason, of morality and tradition, I can make no response. But I believe that we all are capable of being felled by nature, however we may struggle against it."

"Nopporn, we cannot live our lives on this hilltop. All that you say may be true—and yet, eventually, we must descend to the world be-low and live in the society of our fellow human beings. In a few weeks, your head will be filled with your studies at the university and your plans for the future. As for me, I must be loyal to Chao Khun and fol-low him wherever he goes. I must care for him and perform the du-ties of a good wife as long as he wants me and as long as he cares for me. You and I will part before long and spend our lives among peo-ple who care much for matters of decorum and tradition. Could you have expected that I would say anything else to you? Do you think that society would be impressed with 'nature,' as an excuse for your actions? Nopporn, I beg you to believe that you must confront reality and only reality; let it be your judge and your guide in life. Idealism is far more attractive—but believe me, it is of little worth in practice."

I realized then that I was looking into the eyes of a woman who was so intelligent and so wise that I could not begin to follow her. Such a woman should have been a great figure in history, not merely Khun-ying Kirati. I said, "I am very sorry if I have made you unhappy with me." I could think of nothing else to say.

"It is not unhappiness that I feel, Nopporn, but—frustration."

"Tell me this, at least—do you believe that I love you?"

"My good Nopporn, I believe you."

"Khunying, shall you always think harshly of me?"

"Someday you will know the answer to that question."

"Have you already begun to hate me?"

"Not at all. If you never behave in such a way again, I shall consider you my old Nopporn, a friend for life."

"But I shall go on loving you, all of my life."

"That is your choice, of course; but in time, you will renounce that right, and you will do it of your own accord."

"I know otherwise."

"The very young have such faith in themselves; I congratulate you on that enviable faith, Nopporn."

"Then, you forgive me?"

Mom Rachawong Kirati stepped forward slowly, rested her hands lightly on my shoulders, and said, "I have forgiven you already. We will forget what happened this afternoon, and you will be my old Nopporn . . . now help me gather our things. Chao Khun will begin to worry if we are late."

Suddenly, she reminded me of a queen giving orders; I continued to stand with my arms crossed, watching her as she knelt over the hamper, until she repeated her orders, and I did as she had asked.

On the way back, we chatted and laughed as we had always done, as if nothing unusual had happened—much less, the marvelous event that had impressed itself on our minds and hearts on the hillside that afternoon, and that would never be forgotten.

o   o   o   o

Chapter 19

[In this, the last chapter of the novel, six years have passed since the day on the hillside at Mitake. The recently married Nopporn is visited by Mom Rachawong Kirati's aunt, who tells him that Kirati is dying of tuberculosis. He goes to her and is with her when she dies.]

Bree and I were married on the day we had chosen. I shall not relate the particulars of a splendid and joyful wedding, or the happiness Bree and I felt. My own happiness was spoiled only by my keen disappointment when Mom Rachawong Kirati did not appear. Instead, she sent a note in the afternoon, saying that she was ill. She sent her blessings and the assurance that she would come to visit us as soon as she was feeling better.

I had arranged to take my new wife to the seaside for two weeks. Three days before we left for Hua Hin, Mom Rachawong Kirati still had not come to visit, and I decided to take Bree to meet her at her home. She welcomed us, assured me that she was feeling a good deal better, and insisted that she had every intention of visiting us soon. I thought she looked pale, but when I inquired about her illness, she said that it was nothing much; she had felt rather weak on the day of our wedding, then discovered that she had a fever, and so thought she ought not to go.

She seemed a bit drowsy and said little, but insisted that we tell her all about the wedding. She listened intently, occasionally interrupting us to inquire after one detail or another. She seemed particularly interested in Bree, in how Bree had felt on the day of her wedding. We stayed for only an hour, fearing to tire her.

When we were outside, Bree offered the opinion that Mom Rachawong Kirati was "sweet and still beautiful—and very mysterious."

Two months later, on an evening in December, the shattering events of which I shall soon speak began to unfold. On that evening, I had just returned home. Before I had time to change my clothes, a servant came to say that a lady was waiting to see me and seemed in a great hurry. In the sitting room, I found Mom Rachawong Kirati's aunt.

"The khunying is very ill," she said.

"I had thought she was improving," I replied, trying to quell the sense of foreboding in my breast. "Madame, what exactly is the khunying's illness?"

"Tuberculosis." She explained that her niece had become ill two years before, but it had appeared a mild case; the family had been assured that with proper care and rest, there was no reason to fear that her life might be threatened. And yet, two months before, her condition had begun to decline alarmingly; and in the past three days, her symptoms had become truly frightening. The situation was grave: the fever was strong, and she had begun to experience hallucinations. At those times, her aunt said, Mom Rachawong Kirati would ramble on deliriously about Japan and speak my name repeatedly.

"Whenever she knows that a visitor has arrived, she asks, 'Is it Nopporn?' When we tell her who it is, she only sighs and says nothing. When I ask her, 'Would you like to see Nopporn?' she becomes extremely agitated. She has forbidden me to come to you. 'Do not bother

Nopporn,' she says. 'I will not have you intrude upon his happiness.' And then the next time she hears a visitor, she asks again, 'Is it Nopporn?' I cannot bear to see her so unhappy and so ill. I know that she dearly wishes to see you, so I slipped away, telling her that the doctor had asked me to fetch some medicine. He knows that I am here."

I could scarcely believe what the woman was telling me. How could Mom Rachawong Kirati's condition have become so grave in so short a time? And why, in her delirium, did she call out my name? Yet the sad face of the woman who sat before me pushed these doubts and questions aside, and in a moment, we were on our way to Mom Rachawong Kirati's house. I gave my word that I would not reveal the circumstance that had brought me.

She left me in the sitting room, and in a few moments, the doctor entered. He told me there was no hope that Mom Rachawong Kirati would recover. The only question was whether she would linger for many days or few. Because her aunt had told him that his patient and I had a very special friendship, he had agreed to allow us this opportunity to speak with each other before her death. Outwardly composed, I sat and listened to the man, while anguish and unspeakable sorrow consumed me.

Mom Rachawong Kirati's aunt reappeared, saying that her niece was conscious and lucid.

"Then I may see her?" I asked, swiftly rising to my feet.

The lady smiled. "You may as soon as she has dressed."

"*Dressed?* In her condition?"

"This is the first time I have seen her smile in many weeks. Khunying is very ill, yes, but when I objected to the idea of her dressing, she said, 'Dear Aunt, when I see my dear old friend Nopporn, I want to be pretty. Suthan will help me.' Then she turned to her sister and said, 'Suthan, you know how I like to look. Do my hair and put my lipstick on the way I do it . . . you know. Please, make your big sister beautiful once more before she dies.' The way she smiled when she said that, Suthan and I could barely control ourselves."

As she spoke, despite her attempts to maintain her composure the tears flowed down the woman's cheeks, and finally she broke into sobs. The doctor said nothing but sat respectfully, his head bowed in an attitude of calm and resignation.

"She became suspicious at one point and asked me if I had told you that she was near death. I had to tell a lie, for fear of upsetting her. 'Good,' she said to me. 'You can tell him that I'm not very well today, but you mustn't upset him.'"

You may imagine the silence that descended upon the doctor and myself when the lady left us. After ten minutes, she reappeared to say that Mom Rachawong Kirati was now ready to see me.

When I entered the sickroom, I was momentarily confused. I had expected darkness, medicine bottles, two or three weeping relatives beside the bed of the dying person. But my imagination had painted a scene that did not exist. The room was bright and airy; the soft light of early evening poured in through open windows. Mom Rachawong Kirati sat atop the bedcovers, resting comfortably against fresh, smooth pillows. A beautiful Chinese coverlet, white with green embroidery, had been tossed artfully over her legs. Under a black velvet jacket, her blouse was the same color as the embroidery of the coverlet. These garments concealed all but her face from my eyes, and at once I understood that the body cloaked by these gorgeous folds of silk and velvet must already have begun its journey to the land of death. Yet her hair and face had been prepared with meticulous care; the familiar, uniquely shaped little mouth looked just the same, a triangle of bright color; and I thought that, even now, if one glanced only briefly at Mom Rachawong Kirati, one could believe that she had not changed at all from the woman who climbed Mitake with me.

On a small table beside her bed, a cut-glass vase was filled with red flowers, a cheerful Christmas bouquet.[8] Little birds hopped and twittered merrily in two ornate cages that hung in the open window. Everything in this room was beautiful and carefully planned to be so; nothing reflected the fact that the person who lay on the bed was near death. You will not wonder, then, that my first reaction, once I stood inside the room, was that I must have been somehow deceived.

Mom Rachawong Kirati put down the book she had been holding, as if I had interrupted her reading. "Nopporn, do come sit beside me. So sorry to have to see you here, but I'm not feeling very well."

---

8. This reference to Christmas indicates the worldliness and foreign experience of the characters. The Buddhist influences in this work are embedded in the plot and in the traces of karmic factors that are never spoken of. The surface of this novel is a veneer of Western ideas about individualism, the right to self-determination, and the evil effects of the class system in Thai society.

At once, my heart sank, for the voice that came out of the lovely mouth was so dry and faint that I could barely understand her.

"I have been thinking of you, Khunying."

She smiled and said, "Thank you so much. I knew that you would not forget me." Turning her gaze to an anxious-looking woman who stood nearby, she said, "Nopporn, this is Suthan, my sister. The one who found love and happiness in marriage. I told you all about her."

I bowed to Suthan.

"Why don't you all leave us for a bit?" Mom Rachawong Kirati said. "Even you, Suthan. Nopporn and I would like to chat for a while . . ." The others exchanged meaningful looks, and I sat motionless. "Well, *go on* with you," she said. "I shall be quite all right with Nopporn here." Suthan and the aunt left the room, and the doctor followed, saying in a low tone as he passed me, "Not long."

When we were alone, she looked into my eyes for a long time with what seemed to me an expression of contentment. I pulled my chair closer to the bed.

"I did not think that I would see you today, Nopporn. Or ever again in my life." Her eyes did not leave mine for a moment.

"Well, here I am before your very eyes. And I shall be here, Khunying, as long as you wish me to be here."

"That cannot be, Nopporn, because you are not mine."

"I—I do not understand."

"That is correct. You do not understand. You never have understood. Not from the first day we met." There was a faint, mocking glint in her eyes.

"Tell me what I do not understand."

"Everything. Anything. You understand—nothing, least of all yourself." I could only sit dumbly, at a complete loss for words, feeling as I had felt on the day we met. She reached beneath the coverlet and withdrew a piece of stiff paper. "This is a painting I did after I returned from Japan. Let it be my wedding present."

In the center of the picture, a stream flowed down a hillside; the slope was covered with trees. On the other side of the stream, a small path wound through rocks, some large, some small. Well, you know the picture. It is painted from a substantial distance, but one can make out two people sitting on a rock at the river's edge. In one corner of the painting is the word "Mitake."

"It is not very good work, Nopporn, but my life and heart are in it, and so I thought it was appropriate for your wedding day." When I looked up from the painting, she asked, "Do you remember what happened there?"

I remembered very clearly; and I began to understand. "My love was born there," I said.

"Our love, Nopporn," she said and shut her eyes. I had to lean very close to hear her next words. "Your love was born there, and it died there, but love thrives in another body—one that is ruined and soon will be no more." Tears began to seep from her closed eyes. Mom Rachawong Kirati lay motionless against her pillows, with the serenity of utter exhaustion. And I could only sit and stare at that still form, consumed by my love and grief, and feeling as if my heart must break.

Seven days later, Mom Rachawong Kirati died. I sat beside her, among her relatives in that dark hour. Before she died, she motioned with her hands that she wished to write, and someone rushed for a pen and paper. She tried to speak to me but could not, and instead scrawled these words on the paper: "Though I die with no one to love me, still my heart is full . . . for I die loving someone."

[handwritten: → duty vs. love .]

O   O   SRI BURAPHA AND *BEHIND THE PAINTING*

[handwritten: → strong metaphor of their love .]

Born in Bangkok in 1905 as Kulab Saipradit,[1] this writer had the most adventurous and perhaps the most difficult life of any represented in this work. His father, a clerk in the Railways Department, died as the result of inadequate medical care when Kulab was six years old. According to David Smyth, in his introduction to *Behind the Painting and Other Stories*, "Years later, the inadequacy of medical provisions for the poor was to become a recurrent theme in Kulap's novels and short stories."[2]

Despite his humble origins, Kulab studied law at Thammasat University, yet he was most interested in literature and journalism. Over the next two decades, he was involved in founding or editing socially progressive journals, the most famous of which was *Supaap burut* (The

1. The author's given name has been spelled, in English, in many ways, among them, "Kularb," "Kulab," and "Kulaap."

2. David Smyth, introduction to *Behind the Painting*, by Siburapha, 1. This introduction contains the most complete biography of Kulab available in English.

gentleman). Since he was a courageous critic of injustice in society, particularly on the basis of class, his fortunes waxed and waned with the tolerance level of whatever administration happened to be in power. One thing that was never denied, even by his enemies, was the excellence of his writing. Many of his eighteen novels and some forty short stories are considered literary masterpieces. He also produced a great many political essays, and these led to his downfall.

In 1932, Kulab went to Japan to observe the practice of journalism, a trip that inspired him to write *Behind the Painting* soon after his return. In the late 1940s, he studied political science in Australia. By 1952, his writings were considered "dangerous" by Field Marshal Sarit Thanarat, who had seized control of the government in a coup d'état and instituted a strong anticommunist policy.[3] Kulab was arrested for attempting to overthrow Sarit's government and was jailed for five years. When he was released, he accepted an invitation from the Chinese government to visit Beijing. He began his journey by going to the USSR to attend the fortieth anniversary of the revolution, where he learned that Sarit had imprisoned hundreds of journalists and writers. He had no choice but to go on to China, where he lived until his death in 1974; his ashes were returned to Thailand in 1994.[4] For the twenty years he lived in China, this formerly prolific author did not write. Some who knew him believe that it was because he missed the stimulation of his Thai literary colleagues; others maintain that his heart was simply broken by his exile from his beloved native land.

The writer Witthayakorn Chiengkun has said that Kulab was "a democrat" who never had any connections to the Thai Communist Party. Witthayakorn recalled being told by the late journalist Supa Sirimanon that "Kularb was a Buddhist more than a Marxist and he was more of a social leader than a revolutionary."[5] This description applies to many Thai writers and journalists on the left, over the past six decades.

The journalist Sathian Juntimathorn explains the popularity of Kulab's work with contemporary readers: "First, Khun Kularb created a new trend of thought in Thai literature and journalism. Second, most of his novels and articles were written about people struggling for jus-

---

3. Some information on this period appears in the introduction.
4. Some of this information is taken from Nithinand Yorsaengrat, "Sriburapha: A Time for Revision," *Focus* (Bangkok), June 15, 1994.
5. Ibid.

tice and a better life. Third, he dedicated his whole life to fighting for the nation's absolute independence and democracy."[6]

The reader who does not know of Kulab's reputation as a fiery socialist critic of society and of the privileges of the Thai elite would be unlikely to come to such a conclusion from reading this relatively early novel. Not only is Mom Rachawong Kirati a beautiful, if unhappy, bird in a gilded cage, but the novel also depicts a whole world of gilded cages; there is not a glimpse of life beneath the upper tier of Thai society. Even the Japanese servant Nopporn hires for the wealthy Thai newlyweds speaks fluent English—a find, indeed, in 1932 Japan.

This selection was chosen for several reasons. First, it is a novel entirely focused on the life of one woman, and it has been praised and popular ever since its initial publication. In Mattani Rutnin's words, it "still moves many young women readers to tears and leaves them dreaming about melancholic, platonic love obstructed by conventions."[7] Another reason for its inclusion is that the selected chapters amount to a version of the ideal woman that thrives in popular literature: beautiful, dutiful, and wealthy, qualities that, in this case, have the disastrous effect of destroying her life. "I told myself that it was one stroke of good luck to have been born beautiful—and one stroke of bad luck, never to have been in love. And then, I slowly came to realize that luck was not altogether to blame. You see, my well-meaning father had purposely kept me confined between our home and the palace *because* I was the most beautiful of his daughters. . . . Had I been born plain, even ugly, I should have been free. I wondered why I had been given great beauty, only to be destined to loneliness because of it."

But Mom Rachawong Kirati is not only beautiful, she is also, in Nopporn's view, intellectually awe inspiring: "'Nopporn, I beg you to believe that you must confront reality and only reality; let it be your judge and your guide in life. Idealism is far more attractive—but believe me, it is of little worth in practice.'

"I realized then that I was looking into the eyes of a woman who was so intelligent and so wise that I could not begin to follow her. Such a woman should have been a great figure in history, not merely Khunying Kirati."

6. Ibid.
7. Mattani, op. cit., 31.

Another interesting aspect of the novel is the agency the author assigns to Khunying Kirati in her relationships with her husband and with Nopporn. She describes herself as powerless in many ways—a woman who has made an intelligent bargain with life in order not to waste it entirely. Yet Khunying Kirati is very much aware that she did, and does, make her her own decisions. She alone has the power to make her husband's last years pleasant and even happy. She could, of course, make him miserable by throwing fits and sulking because of his boring senescence (which she describes with considerable bitterness, hinting strongly at sexual impotence); or worse, she could subject him to the humiliation of being cuckolded or left, but such alternatives are detestable to her. (And, she would lose, if not her title, her place in society.) She also has great power over Nopporn; at least, over the youthful Nopporn whose infatuation, she suspects—with good reason—will soon wane.

Each reader will bring something different to the interpretation of Khunying Kirati. Certainly, Thai readers have widely different reactions to her and to the novel. Some find her the ultimate expression of ideal womanhood and the novel itself beautiful; others see a spoiled aristocrat, whining about a fate that she did nothing to shape[8]—and an enviable fate at that, if considered alongside the life of the average Thai woman who has, unlike Khunying Kirati, managed to marry young and probably for love.

Finally, as I have suggested, there is something distinctly operatic about this novel. It is larger than life; Khunying Kirati is an exaggeration of the Thai female aristocrat; Nopporn is the epitome of the idealistic, handsome young student. Professor Chetana Nagavajara of Silpakorn University has frequently spoken and written on the subject of poetry, not prose, as the true literary medium of the Thai.[9] Until only a century ago, both the classical dramas performed at court and the tales told far from court were often related in song and in chanted poetry.

The filmed version of *Behind the Painting* was a great success;

---

8. For all that is traditional in this tale, Kirati conspicuously avoids the stoic references to karma that so often appear in tales of disappointing lives.

9. The subject of the oral tradition in Thai literature is discussed in considerable depth in Chetana Nagavajara, "Literature in Thai Life: Reflections of a Native" (paper presented at the Fifth International Conference on Thai Studies, School of Oriental and African Studies, University of London, July 1993).

Khunying Kirati's deathbed scene, in particular, had a huge impact on audiences. In Chetana's opinion, this scene, while it was performed very well, sacrificed much to the limitations of prose dialogue.

Khunying Kirati's final words have been translated many ways; none of them is satisfactory. In fact, no one (including this translator) has been able to do much with that problematical, supremely frustrating last line: "chǎn taay dooy praasajàak khon thîi rák chǎn[.] tɛ̀ɛ kɔ̂im jaay wâa chǎn mii khon thîi chǎn rák." Smyth, in his translation of the novel, renders it as "I die with no one to love me, yet content that I have someone to love."[10] Two other versions I have seen are: "Nobody loves me as I die; but I'm happy that I love somebody," and "I die without having anybody who loves me; but my heart is full because I am in love with someone."

[margin handwritten note: I die / ? un love / but / content / b/c I / love .]

If none of these does justice to the original sentiments, what, outside of an operatic aria—or chanted poetry, in the Thai case—could? Chetana, in his 1993 essay "Literature in Thai Life, Reflections of a Native," asserts that any appraisal of Thai literature that fails to assess the primary role of the oral tradition must produce a distorted image of the Thai literary heritage. After the sack of Ayuthya by the Burmese in 1767, nearly all of the written literature was burned. During the next two decades, learned men of the early Bangkok era were able to recreate the literature from memory because their primary associations with it were *aural*, not the result of reading. Chetana recalls his grandmother's storytelling ability:

> She was endowed with extraordinary memory (which was common to her contemporaries) and possessed a very large repertoire of literary works that she could recite. It was perfectly natural for her to recite, say, *Phra Aphai Mani* for a . . . few hours. . . . To be able to recite effectively, one has to be a "performer" of some kind, and I still recall how my grandmother chanted and sang her favourite literary pieces and how she would manipulate her voice to suit the emotional contents of the respective texts.[11]

Despite the excellence of Sri Burapha's prose writing, and the acclaimed performance of the actress who portrayed Khunying Kirati in the film, the entire story, and especially its deathbed finale, were in Chetana's opinion "meant for poetry, for song."

10. Siburapha, op. cit., 152.
11. Chetana, "Literature in Thai Life."

In the first line of his essay "The Development of Political and Social Consciousness in Thai Short Stories," Manat Chitkasem echoes Chetana when he states: "Traditionally, the medium for imaginative writing in Thailand was poetry, and it is only in the last hundred years that prose has become a medium for fiction."[12] Perhaps more than any other work of modern Thai fiction, *Behind the Painting* reminds us of that fact.

12. Manas, op. cit., 63.

Thai culture does not mix duty & other obligations — duty as very important.

. Kirati stuck in a r/s that she has a duty on. — noble-r/s w/ husband - not romantic.

. Ploy - romantic r/s w/ husband.

From *That Woman's Name Is Boonrawd*

Botan

This novel is set in the late 1960s, when thousands of
American troops were stationed in Thailand. Boonrawd
wages a struggle against poverty and discrimination, finally
succeeding in establishing a successful business career. She
is courted by an American engineer, whom she marries.

*[In chapters 12 and 13, Boonrawd and her teenage brothers, Tham and Sin,[1] move
from their home (and bakery) into Robert's house. There is no marriage ceremony;
an official marriage apparently takes place at some unspecified, later time. (In the
book's preface, Boonrawd, Robert, and their two daughters are shown at Don Muang
Airport, ten years after the events in the novel; we are told that they live in Texas.)]*

Chapter 12

When her brothers arrived home, Boonrawd told them that they
would spend the evening packing; the move would take place late
the next morning.

"What are you thinking of?" Sin asked, frowning. "You go out with
Ay Bob once,[2] and now you're going to move in with him—and not
just you, but me and Tham are supposed to go, too?"[3]

"That's right."

Sin blinked. He could not believe his ears. "This is crazy. Why should

This novel was published during the early 1980s (the book is undated) by Chomromdek,
Bangkok, the publishing company Botan and her husband founded. They publish children's books and for the past several years have also published all of her novels and
two collections of short stories.

1. Boonrawd and all of her siblings' names begin with *boon,* or *bun,* "merit" in the
Buddhist sense: Boontham, Boonsin, Boonlam, and so on; to avoid confusion, these have
been shortened to their second syllable. It is significant that the second syllable of her
own name, *-rawd,* or *rɔ̂ɔt,* means "to escape, to be free, to stand on one's own."

2. Sin refers to Bob as "Ay Bob," which is very rude (and which he would find offensive). Bob has given jobs at the base to both brothers; they respect him but are embarrassed by the new situation.

3. Sin is about twenty and works at the air base where Robert helped him get a
job. Tham is several years younger and goes to secondary school.

we go live with some farang[4] when we have our own house, we have jobs, and you make a lot more money than you did when you worked for Khun Pawm at the restaurant? If you need any more help with your bread, you could hire somebody. Or Ting[5] could come and live here with us. But, no, you want us to drag our stuff over there, go live with some guy you went out with once. I suppose money is part of this deal . . ."

"I'm not selling myself to Robert," Boonrawd snapped.

"Yeah, well who do you think is going to believe that? Who do you think will believe that you moved in with Ay Bob just because you two like each other? *Nobody*. They can think only *one thing*."

"The hell with them, and what they think. I haven't asked Robert for anything. Now shut up and start packing."

"You gonna keep the bakery?" Tham asked. "Will I still be delivering?"

"Everything will be the same."

Sin's expression changed from anger to bewilderment. "Why? If you go live with him, why shouldn't he support you? You mean, you're still gonna work all day and night? If you're going to be like regular married people, and you're no rented wife, why shouldn't he support you?"

"Don't worry, he's going to support me in the usual ways; I'll be living in his house, won't I? And you two will have nothing to worry about. He knows I want to keep working. It's all right with him. Anyway, what happens between Robert and me is none of your business."

"Yeah, well, I just might not be making this little move," Sin muttered.

"Oh, so you're going to support yourself on what you make, eh? If you live with us, you won't have any rent to pay; you won't have to spend your own money on anything except lunch. If it's the gossip you can't stand, you're going to have to move pretty damned far away—the rest of this family is no secret, you know. A few miles away, Ma has Lam's boys—one, a little Negro, the other one, a redhead. So now you've got me to live down—and so what? Don't be stupid, Sin. A *man* ignores gossip."

4. Caucasian foreigner.
5. Another brother.

Sin, unable to come up with a response to this, continued frowning and turned away.

"Aw, Sin," she continued, "don't get crazy. You know I always think before I do anything. Not just for me but for all of us. If I can keep saving money, if you can work hard and save, too, it won't be long before we can lease a building in town. You'll have that machine shop, I swear. But I'm not using Robert to get it; I'm not moving over there because I can't get what I want on my own. I like him, and he likes me. And what people say—you can't stop them, and you can't let yourself care. That's what I think, and you've got to think like that, too."

"But he'll go home to America someday. They all do. And here you'll be, with your little redheads, just like Lam."[6]

Boonrawd shook her head. "I don't have them now. You've got to plan, but at some point, you've got to let the future take care of itself. Women get left by men every day, all kinds of women by all kinds of men—Thai, Chinese, farang. As long as I have a business of my own, I'll be all right. Can you imagine me depending on some man—and then he leaves, and I'm destitute? *Me?* I'll never understand Lam. She goes off with some guy, she has a lot of money for a little while, spends every bit of it, and then there she is again—dragging a baby home to Ma, and broke."

"If Ma knew what you've done, she'd curse you good. And this guy—your precious *Ay Bob*—let me tell you, he's fussier than a woman. At the base, everybody has to work like hell, everything has to be perfect, and it has to be done just his way, you know? I wouldn't be surprised if he thinks he's getting a free maid, a free washerwoman, a free cook—" Sin lowered his voice, backed off a good arm's length, and added, "And a free what else, Sis?"

Boonrawd only bit her lip and made no reply. Sin, who had fully expected to be slapped across the face, at the very least, was astonished.

"Why is it only when the man is a farang that people criticize the woman?" Boonrawd asked. "What about all the girls who went with Sia Song, back home? Are you going to tell me they didn't sell themselves? And who looked down on them? Nobody."

---

6. "Red-haired children," *dèk phŏm dɛɛng,* is a common, vulgar reference to children of mixed (Caucasian and Thai) parentage, especially the offspring of GI-prostitute or "rented-wife" relationships. It is never used to refer to the children of legal mixed-race marriages, who are called *lûuk khrûng,* literally, "half children."

Sia Song was the owner of the biggest rice mill in their district. He was always willing to loan money to a family with a pretty young daughter—especially if she had a pale complexion and a full bosom. She would become his minor wife, and he would forgive her family's debt; and as long as she lasted, she would have money to spend. If she was clever, she might walk away with a few thousand baht, but she had to be quick, because Sia Song was easily bored. No girl stayed longer than a year, before being sent back to her parents to make room for her successor. Boonrawd's sister-in-law, the wife of her eldest brother, had been one of Sia Song's girls, and their mother had never thought the less of her for it.

Tham and Sin fell to work and conversation stopped. It was very late before they slept, because Boonrawd had to finish the bread. It never occurred to her to skip the next morning's bakery run just because they were moving. Tham would deliver the bread, the same as on any other day; and then he would take the day off from school to help with the move into Bob's house. Sin would go to work at the air base as soon as the move was completed.

"I can't spend the whole day unpacking," he had said. "Are you kidding, with my boss? And it isn't only my main boss, either—who would curse me good—but there are two other guys who get to tell me what to do, and they're just as bad. The only good thing about all this is, they won't dare curse me as much, after today."

"Listen," Boonrawd said, turning swiftly, "you owe Robert for getting you that job. Don't you dare make him look like a fool— you should work all the harder to show you're not trying to take advantage."

She was sure that Robert had hired people to help with the move, just as he had hired a truck and driver on the day the new refrigerator was delivered, and she was not wrong. Late the next morning, as they were finishing the packing, a truck turned the corner, rumbled down the street, and stopped before the house. In what seemed no more than a few minutes, the driver and his three burly helpers had carried out everything she owned and neatly loaded it onto the truck.

"Are you supposed to unload everything, too?" she asked the driver.

"Oh, yes," he said, quite respectfully. "Wherever you and the boss tell us it goes, that's where it goes. He stayed home to wait for the new furniture," he added with a friendly grin. He eyed Boonrawd with polite curiosity. This one was different from the others, he thought. Who had ever heard of a rented wife with her own business? But there it was, on a sign above the door, Bakery—Home Delivery. And she was clearly the boss! All the things she owned were high quality: the refrigerator, the big stove, the sewing machine. Very peculiar, he thought. This farang has never had a rented wife before, and now he gets a woman who obviously has never been one. Beyond that, he not only takes her—but he also takes her two kid brothers and sets them up in a fancy bedroom. As for the boss's own bedroom, it had been done over completely. There was even a lady's dressing table in there, now—*very* peculiar . . .

Or was it possible that the tall, blond farang was really *marrying* this tall, dark, sharp-eyed woman?—she was sharp tongued, too. He wondered what their kids would look like. Would they have brown skin and yellow hair? Or white skin and black hair? He grinned to himself. They'd be peculiar, too. Anyway, that was none of his business. All he and his men had to do was deliver the woman, her brothers, and their possessions to the boss's house, put everything where they were told to put it, and get back to the base.

When they arrived, Robert beamed happily at Boonrawd, then hurried the boys off to see their room, leaving them to consider the conditions of their new life.

Tham was struck speechless. Everything in the whole room was new! Two beds, two small chests, and a big desk with two chairs facing each other. All the windows were screened, and although the room was not large, it was big enough for the two of them. "*Look* at this place, Sin!" Tham exclaimed, like a child surveying a room full of toys. "Our sister, she really—well, she's a smart one, that's all I can say."

Sin was silent, too, but for a different reason. Tham, he thought, was too young to know the difference between a man getting himself a rented wife—and getting married. But Sin knew very well, and looking around, he realized how very wrongly he had judged the situation. Their sister had gotten herself—*married.*

•   •   •

After Boonrawd had got the kitchen the way she wanted it, she went upstairs. Robert followed her, lugging the last of her suitcases. He set it down, proudly pointing out the new additions: the dressing table, the chest of drawers, the great armoire. They were plain pieces from the market, but they were durable and well made. An air conditioner hummed noisily in the window. Boonrawd shivered slightly. She had never slept in a room with an air conditioner.

"Oh, you're cold." Robert quickly crossed the room and gave the control a turn to the left. The hum abated to a low drone. "I want it to be comfortable for you," he said. "You have to tell me where I should set it."

"Aren't you going to work?" she asked, snapping open one of the suitcases. She lifted out a dress and hung it in an armoire so new that it reeked of shellac.

"Not today. This is the day I get myself a wife, remember?" Boonrawd felt her face grow hot. "I told them at the base, if there's anything really important, call me on the phone. Otherwise, leave me alone . . ."

"Who cleans this place—you? It looks pretty good."

"A woman comes in every afternoon to clean and do the laundry. I'll have to pay her more, of course, now that you and the boys are here."

"What do you give her now?"

"Twelve hundred baht a month. What do you think—four hundred baht more for the extra work?"

Boonrawd nearly dropped the dress she was holding. "You pay her *twelve hundred baht a month?* A Thai family wouldn't pay more than three or four hundred baht, plus room and board. And for that, the woman would work day and night."

"But she doesn't stay here, she lives out. And I can trust her. Nothing has ever disappeared. I wanted somebody with experience, not a kid. This woman is married, with two children. Her husband is a welder at the base."

He began to help her unpack. Boonrawd had a lot of clothes, all of them the bright, flamboyant colors she loved, and that he had come to love because she wore them. As they worked together, walking back and forth across the room, she affected not to notice when he stroked her arm or when his shoulder lightly grazed her own as they paced back and forth between the suitcases and the armoire. When there was nothing more to unpack and the suitcases had been snapped shut, he put his arms about her and hugged her tightly.

"No, no," she mumbled. "I stink, Robert—I'm all sweaty. I've been hauling boxes all morning and sitting in a hot truck and—"

"And I like it," he interrupted her. "I think you smell good, sweat and all. Anyway, we're not in the middle of the street now, are we?"

She couldn't help but smile. What a dear he was, this tall, blond young farang, to remember a phrase she had taught him—so that now, he could use it on her![7] His hands grew bolder, but it was a loving urgency; he made her feel swept along. She had wondered if she would be able to make herself forget, when this time came, the terrible things that had happened to her when she was a girl. That proved impossible; she could not put away the memory of the cruel, repulsive old man, her terror and pain, the humiliation of being treated worse than a prostitute—a prostitute was at least willing. And yet this man, her new husband, made what was happening something . . . else. Both his words and his body were gentle and loving. He talked to her constantly; he did nothing without asking her first, which amazed her, so that finally, despite the bitter memories, Boonrawd responded to him, and the most amazing thing of all was that she felt pleasure when she had expected to feel only fear. Could he tell that he was not the first? People said that farangs didn't care so much about that, but she wasn't sure.

"Boonrawd," he whispered when it was over, "did I make you as happy as you made me?"

"When you went to bed with Sunee, did you ask her that?"[8]

Robert blinked and stared at her for a minute, as if trying to decide how to answer her. "No, Boonrawd. When I was married before, I asked my wife. And I ask you. But for Sunee, it's a job. It's not the same. As a matter of fact, if you want to know, I just laid back and left everything up to her."

Boonrawd, who had been so bold with her question, felt suddenly shy.

"I didn't insult her, Boonrawd, or look down on her. I paid her, and that was that. But you—you are my wife."

---

7.   The phrase she had taught him, once when he had tried to hold her hand in public, was *klaang hŏn*, literally, the "center [of the] path," equivalent to "in the middle of the street," i.e., "in public."

8.   Sunee is a prostitute whom Robert had visited before he met Boonrawd.

Boonrawd smiled and sat up. "I'm going to take a shower. Where's the bathroom, downstairs?"

"No, it's right there, behind that screen." He pointed to a wooden screen that stood a few feet from the opposite wall. Boonrawd hadn't even noticed it while she was unpacking.

"When you've finished your shower, Boonrawd, we need to have a talk."

Standing in the shower, Boonrawd wondered what Robert wanted to talk about. Probably, she thought to herself with a smirk, the same kind of "talk" they'd just had. But when she reentered the bedroom, he was lying on his side with the newspaper in front of his face and didn't say anything. She had put on clean clothes before she left the bathroom. Now she sat before her new dressing table for the first time. She could never bear to look at her bare face and was never without makeup until she scrubbed her face to go to bed at night. Yet she didn't waste much time on the process either; in less than five minutes, she turned to Robert, her face as made-up as it was going to get.

"So, what do you want to talk about, boss?"[9] She snapped the lid of her compact shut and put it away in one of the small drawers of the dressing table.

Robert folded the newspaper and set it down. "Well, don't you think you need to know a few things about this place?"

"You want me to take care of things? Pay the bills?"

"Well, I should hope so. If the lady of the house doesn't, who should? Hey, I have a wife now." He grinned. "I figure that should leave me with more time for fun."

Robert explained how much money he made each month, and what his expenses were. "I used to have to pay alimony to my first wife. But she got married again, so that's over. After taxes, I make the equivalent of about forty thousand baht a month.[10] So, here's where my money's been going: the maid, the club,[11] expenses when I go to Bangkok once in a while, utilities—but not rent, that's taken care of; and the money I spend at the Rot Thip Restaurant. That's about it. At the end of the month, that leaves about twenty thousand."

9. In Thai, *naay châang yày*; Boonrawd is teasing Robert by addressing him as the workers, including her brothers, do.

10.   About US$2,000.

11.   This club is never explained and never appears again; presumably, the author is referring to the Officers Club at the air base, to which a professional civilian employee like Robert could belong.

She looked at him gravely. "So, what you're saying is, you're rich."

Robert laughed. "I'd be a long way from rich if I were back in the States. Anyway, with you and the boys here, the food budget has to go up. How much do you want me to give you every month?"

"Whatever you were saving before, you should still save, even with us here. I can feed the four of us for a lot less than you've been paying to eat at Rot Thip, that's for sure." She frowned, thinking of the huge markup there. She didn't want to say anything that might make Robert think she was either stingy or greedy. But she couldn't pretend not to be stunned—stupefied was more like it—at finding out that Robert ended up, every month, after the bills were paid, with *twenty thousand baht.* She thought about the farang men she had observed. Most of them spent a fortune on their rented wives and on going out to restaurants and bars. She doubted that they ended up with twenty thousand left over at the end of the month; but then, she was also sure that few of them started the month with forty thousand.

"Besides food," she said, "your own expenses should be the same—cigarettes, beer, your club, some meals out, whatever you spend when you go to Bangkok—"

"I won't be going to Bangkok anymore. I only went down there to look for women. Not anymore. And why can't I eat at home? I can come home for lunch every day and eat your food, which I'd rather do anyway. So now, how much do you need every month?"

Working for Khun Pawn at the Rot Thip Restaurant, Boonrawd had learned to add, subtract, multiply, and divide almost as fast as the abacus; she quickly arrived at her answer. "If you want me to manage this place and handle your salary, give me half, and I'll take care of everything. If you eat out, you take that out of your pocket. You'll still end up saving half at the end of the month, just like you've been doing."

"What about money for yourself?"

"I included myself. And another thing—remember, I don't want to give up my work unless I find some other work I'd rather do." She thought about the machine shop she had promised her brothers but didn't mention it.

"All right, then," said Robert, "it's a deal." He reached for her hand and pulled her from the dressing table chair. She laughed and tumbled onto the bed beside him. Just as he wrapped his arms about her, they heard a knock at the door.

o   o   o   o

Chapter 13

Boonrawd opened the bedroom door to face a neatly dressed, middle-aged woman who looked past her with a ferocious scowl. Tham stood behind the woman, looking distressed. "I told her not to bother Nai Farang,[12] because my sister just got here today, and he said he didn't want anybody bothering him, but she wouldn't listen. She said—I'm sorry, Sister, but—she said, 'He wouldn't *have* one of those creatures in his house,' and that I was a liar."

"What do you expect me to do?" the woman asked, her eyes blazing. "Not come up here and find out for myself? I came to clean, like always, and do the wash." She took one swift glance at Boonrawd, from head to toe, her expression filled with contempt.

Boonrawd's hand seemed to move of its own accord, covering her chest. "Why don't you start downstairs," she said evenly. "Nai Farang's clothes are in the wicker hamper, out behind the kitchen. By the time you've finished, I'll be downstairs, and then you can clean up here."

"Nai," the woman said, as if Boonrawd had not spoken a word, did not exist, "what do you want me to do?"

"You'll have to work that out with my wife, Somchai."

"Your *wife*? Oh, ho, you're putting her way up there, aren't you?" The woman's thin lips moved in and out, in and out between her spiteful comments. "How many months is she gonna be here?"

Boonrawd decided to ignore this. "I understand that until now, you've earned twelve hundred baht a month, isn't that right? But now you'll have three extra people's laundry. Mine and my brothers'. And there will be more dishes to do, too. What do you think would be fair? Another three hundred baht? That would make it fifteen hundred in all."

"Another three hundred baht?" She looked down at the floor and said, "I worked here because I didn't have to wash the clothes of her kind. If I had to wash her underpants, I wouldn't be able to eat my

12.   Literally, "Mr. Caucasian Foreigner."

supper. If you gave me another *thousand* baht, I wouldn't stay in this house."

"Then leave," Boonrawd said.

"Boonrawd," Robert said, "Somchai has been with me since I came here. I can trust her, and if we have to get someone else, maybe that person won't be so reliable." He turned to the glowering Somchai and said, "Why don't you just tell me how much more you think is fair instead of saying these ugly things?"

Boonrawd said, "Oh, Robert, don't you understand? It isn't the money, it's the damned underpants. Some women think it's unlucky—I don't know how to explain it, exactly. They're afraid of—there isn't any English. We say, *haay phra* . . ."

Robert's brow creased with concentration. "*Haay* . . . that's 'lost'—and a *phra* is a monk. She's afraid of losing a *monk?*"[13]

Tham snickered, and Boonrawd grinned in spite of herself. "You're right. It's more like something sacred inside her is violated. Well, she's going to leave no matter what you do, Robert—and good riddance. Don't worry, I can take care of this place, and the boys will help."

Somchai sneered at this. "You think she's going to keep this place clean? Hah! Some of them can't even boil rice. She and her brothers will turn your place into a pigsty. Every cup and dish in the kitchen will have stinking fish paste stuck to it.[14] A clean man like you, Nai, you won't be able to stand it, and that's the truth."

The woman had spared nothing in her diatribe. Boonrawd saw that Tham's fists were clenched at his side and sent him a look that said, "*Don't!*"

"Pay me for the twenty days I worked already this month, and I'll go."

Robert now looked as angry as Tham. He crossed quickly to the dresser and counted out a number of bills. "Here, this is for the whole month. Take it."

13.   All of this conversation between Boonrawd and Robert is, of course, in Thai. Robert says, "Phrá aray nii?" (What monk?), and Boonrawd answers, "Phrá nay tua" (literally, "the monk within"), an idiom that refers to one's own moral purity. To *hǎay phrá* is to jeopardize or lose one's purity.

14.   Fermented fish is the protein staple of the very poor, especially in the northeast. This is the very kind of food Koon and his family were thrilled to be able to make on their fishing expedition to the River Chi in *A Child of the Northeast*. To Somchai, Robert's maid, it is the food that prostitutes, who grew up poor, would eat.

Somchai took the bills, shot one venomous glance at Boonrawd, turned and stalked from the room. Tham followed her. Boonrawd shut the door, being careful not to slam it.

"Boonrawd, can you really do everything yourself?" Robert asked. "My clothes aren't easy to wash. Sometimes I come home with motor oil all over my shirt, my pants . . ."

She laughed. "Robert, you have no idea. This place?" She gestured with one hand, dismissing it. "I've worked much harder than this. And the boys are good at housework, you'll see. Anyway, I don't want them to be lazy. It's better this way. We'll have the house to ourselves, and we'll be able to do things our own way."

"I'm afraid you'll be exhausted."

"I won't. Look, don't you understand that I want to keep your house clean and cook your food and wash your clothes? Don't you like the idea?"

"Sure, who wouldn't? But," he added, switching into English, "I'd like it even better if you left time for—other things."

"Not now," she said, pulling away from him. "I have to start tomorrow's bread. And then there's the laundry, the ironing, and cleaning . . ." She smiled and added, "Tonight is another matter."

Robert picked up a towel from the end of the bed and swung it over his shoulder. "Then I might as well go back to work. Otherwise, I'll just be hanging around here, trying to drag you out of your kitchen and up the stairs." He smiled sweetly. Boonrawd responded with a happy grin, keeping her distance, then resolutely descended the stairs to start bread for the first time in her new home.

Tham was less than happy to be put to work on the laundry.

"You could have somebody else do this, but no," he grumbled from the corner of the kitchen where his sister had installed him with a pile of clothing and a huge wash pan. "We wouldn't even have to pay our own money for it, but no . . . 'oh, Robert,' she says, 'don't think of it— my *brothers* will be glad to do your laundry.' That's my sister."

"Don't be a fool, Tham. We're saving fifteen hundred baht a month—that's a fortune! I have an allowance to use for the house, and it stays the same, no matter what I spend. Don't you get it? Wouldn't you rather have the fifteen hundred baht a month going toward our future than to some maid? It's enough to send our little nephews to a good school."

Tham sat back and wiped his forehead. "A good school? Just what good school do you think is going to take those two little bastards? No place, except for the public school."

"All they need is fathers, and I have some ideas about that. They don't need real fathers, you know; they just need farang names to put on their school applications. When they get a little older, we can enroll them in a boarding school that has farang children in it, and then no one will tease them."

Tham laughed, shook his head, and went to work on the laundry.

He was a good boy, she thought. She never had to worry about the bread delivery, because she could count on him.

"Sis, you're always thinking about doing something for somebody else. Starting the machine shop for Sin, getting the little boys into a good school. When do you think about yourself?"

"What should I think about?"

"Well, what you should do when people act like that bitch today, treating you like a rented wife and being mean. You just stood there."

"Don't worry about me, Tham. I can take care of myself just fine." Boonrawd bit her lower lip thoughtfully. "If people want to hate you, there's nothing you can do about it. You just have to live for yourself. The neighbors at home gossip behind our backs—about how Lam sold herself, about the little boys. But does that stop the same people from running to Ma to borrow a little rice when they're low?"

"Yeah, and they borrow money, too—and you know those clothes you send for the boys? When they outgrow them, there's always somebody waiting to take them."

"There you are! And it should be that way between neighbors. Really, a small town is just a big family. When a child outgrows his clothing, why hang on to it if another child in the neighborhood can make use of it? The clothes I buy for the boys are all good, not little five-baht things from the market, but shirts and pants with strong seams; they should survive three little boys."

They heard footsteps on the stairs above, and then Robert appeared, dressed for work. Boonrawd raised her floury white hands and held them in front of her smiling face, in striking contrast with her healthy, bronzed complexion. Tham did not look up from the laundry, so Boonrawd allowed Robert a brief hug while whispering, "You shouldn't touch me in front of him. Thais don't like it."

"I understand," he whispered back. "Not in the middle of the street, either. Because Boonrawd isn't that kind of girl."

"You've got it."

He planted a swift, furtive kiss on the back of her neck and went striding off.

Boonrawd spent the rest of the day happily cleaning the house. When she had finished, she ironed the clothes—only moments before they would be fully dry, so that they would be very smooth—put them away, and started preparations for dinner. By the time she had showered and changed, the last batch of bread was ready to knead. The alarm clock in the kitchen ensured that every step in the bread-making process was timed just so, and that the bread never, ever burned. It was not in her nature to waste a minute. When she had lived with her teacher, Kruu Orapin, the woman had fondly teased her, calling her Miss Fidgety or Mrs. Hurry-Scurry. She also teased Boonrawd about the fact that Mrs. Hurry-Scurry might be able to put supper on the table the moment the rice was done, but she was hopeless at needlework. Boonrawd had tried her best, but she had no patience for it and certainly no gift.

"See, Tham? We got everything done by ourselves. Who needs that nasty woman, anyway? We're better off doing everything ourselves and saving the money."

Tham had now been set to frying fish for supper. He was standing at the stove, staring into the pan.

"Why don't you do something else while it's frying?"

"How can I? What if it burns?"

"You can keep an eye on it while you clean vegetables or chop onions. You don't have to just stand there, staring at it."

Tham muttered to himself.

"Tomorrow morning, you'd better be up on time to make the bread delivery. It would be easy to sleep in, on that nice new bed."

"Yeah, it's really soft," he said, his face brightening. "And the desk is huge, did you notice? It has a little partition down the middle; one half for me, and one for Sin. Only Sin doesn't go to school, so he doesn't have any homework. Do you think I could use the whole desk?"

"Maybe—ask Sin. But he might need it. I'm thinking of sending him to learn more English. Then he'll be able to read those manuals at work for himself. He can ask his boss the words he doesn't understand."

Sometimes Tham was jealous of his younger brother, Ting, who lived at home with their mother, where he did exactly as he pleased every day of his life and never got yelled at. "Ting has the easy life," he said. "Ma doesn't boss him around, like you boss me and Sin. The only one she hits is Lam's little blackie."

Three days later, Boonrawd opened the front door to find her mother glaring at her.

"So here's the smart one, the one who knows everything—living with a farang and not even getting paid for it!" These were her words of greeting. "The whole *tambon*[15] is talking about it. I don't know where to hide my face."

She followed Boonrawd into the kitchen and sat in a chair. Boonrawd said nothing but resumed kneading her bread.

"So you're still baking bread? Your farang won't support you?"

"I didn't sell myself, like Lam," Boonrawd said, trying to control her temper as she kneaded the bread harder. "Would you like a cold drink? Tell me about the little boys."

Her mother ignored the questions. "You can't even get somebody to do that, knead that bread? Look at her, she works all day. Not just in the bedroom—in the kitchen, too."

"Leave me alone, Ma."

"Leave her alone, she says. So she can bring me another redhead to raise."

Boonrawd's hands stopped kneading. "I have my work. Whatever happens, I'll be able to take care of myself, don't worry. If we ever do break up, I can do this or open a restaurant. Anyway, what do you care?" She set the bread into a large bowl and washed her hands at the sink.

"How much does he give you a month?"

"Enough. You don't have to worry." She took a bottle of soda from the refrigerator, poured some into a glass for her mother, and sat down at the table across from her. "Who's been telling stories about me?"

"Everybody. The whole district is talking about how Boonrawd, who thought she was better than everybody else, ends up just like her sister." She finished her drink and said, "Bring me some rain water. This sweet stuff, the more you drink, the dryer your throat gets."

15. A district or group of villages.

"I don't have any rain water. Just plain boiled water in the refrigerator."

"Better than this." She heaved a weary sigh and repeated, "How much does he give you?"

"Why do you need to know? You'll get your money every month, the same as ever."

"Ting is growing up," she said, her voice taking on the whining note Boonrawd knew so well, "and the little boys, you don't know how much they eat. It isn't enough, what you send. Not nearly enough."

And so, Boonrawd thought, we're down to the reason for the visit. "You want more money. Aren't you growing anything anymore?"

"How can I? Ting is in school, and I have to look after Lam's boys. I thought I'd get Wing to help me, but all he thinks about these days is chasing girls."

Wing was Boonrawd's cousin. He wasn't capable of farming his own family's small field and worked for others, when he worked at all. For years, he had helped Boonrawd's family—for wages that she paid him.

"Ma, if you don't work the field we leased, the owner is going to take it back, don't you know that?"

"I don't know where we'll live, then. He hasn't done it so far, because it's all dried out; but if he does, we're ruined."

"Do you want to buy a field, so that Ting can farm it?" It was a possibility she had toyed with; she wouldn't mind having one of her brothers on the land.

"He doesn't want it! He says he hates farming; he doesn't want to stink from water buffaloes. What he wants is to go to Bangkok."

Boonrawd sighed. How many boys wanted to go to Bangkok . . . in a few years, who would feed Thailand? "What does he think he could do there?"

"He wants to be a singer—and he's real good, too,"[16] she added, beaming with pride in her youngest son. "He wins first place at the wat fair every year."

"What about school?"

---

16. In Thai, *nák rɔ́ɔng lûuk thûng,* a country ballad singer.

"Not so good," she shrugged, undismayed. "He can't read a single sign when we go to town," she announced, as if this were an achievement.

Boonrawd had to bite her tongue not to say, "Send him here." Maybe when Sin was off on his own but not now. She couldn't fill Robert's house with her relatives.

"Who's watching the little boys?"

"Wing's mother."[17]

"Well, stay until Tham and Sin get home, and then you'd better get going. You don't want to get home after dark. About the money—I'm willing to give you another hundred baht a month."

Her mother exploded. "One hundred baht? Are you crazy? You're living with a farang, and you're going to give your own mother *one hundred baht a month?* I would be ashamed for anyone to find out!"

"It's a lot. The boys aren't going to eat up another hundred baht. And when it's time for them to go to school, I'll pay for it. Ma, you shouldn't spoil Ting the way you do. It isn't doing him any good. He should be in school, learning to read. What kind of a singer will he be if he can't even read the words to a new song?"

Her mother was unmoved. "Why should he waste his time sitting in a school?"

"Why do you *do* this, Ma? You've raised your sons to be gods and your daughters to be slaves! Don't you see that you're ruining Ting?"

"Huh! All I see is Kruu Orapin falling down in a faint if she knew what you've done. She sends you to school, and you go chasing after a farang—and so crazy about him you do his business for nothing."

"Is that so? If my teacher knew what I've done—the truth, from me, the way it really is—she would congratulate me," Boonrawd said with a smile, which so incensed her mother that a stream of obscenities poured from her mouth, describing Boonrawd's relationship with her husband in the most obscene terms she knew.

"Shut up, Ma! I'm not here because of what happens in bed. Anyway, I was no virgin when I came into this house."

17. Although the woman is a relative and her best friend, Boonrawd's mother refers to her, not by her own name, but as "Wing's mother"; this is a common way of referring to a person who has a child. In *A Child of the Northeast*, Koon's parents are never identified by name.

Her mother's eyes widened. Now, this was news.

"You gave me to that disgusting old man—what did you get for your daughter, eh? A few hundred baht, so he could treat me like a whore? You pushed me into the tiger's mouth."

"You never said," her mother whined.

"No, I never told you. But would you have cared? Why do you think I ran to Kruu Orapin? Just because the old man didn't pay me my salary? Face the facts, Ma. What are my prospects? No Thai man wants a woman who's been used; I've got a sister who's a rented wife; and then there are my nephews—a redhead and the other one with kinky black hair. Do you think any decent man is going to come begging for my hand? Any Thai man who would marry me would know he could walk out any time, and nobody would think worse of him, because I was spoiled when he got me, and my family is nothing. So I've got a farang husband, and everybody says, 'Yah, Boonrawd—she sold herself.' Is it so impossible for you to imagine that we love each other? That this man really cares about me?"

"As dark as you are, I'm surprised a farang would go for you."

"You think it would be just wonderful if I took this man for everything I could, don't you? If I just laid around the house eating and sleeping, waiting for him to come home. Never! I will go on working just like I always have. Why should I care what other people think? Robert likes me just the way I am. Why don't you ask him for yourself? He'll be home any minute."

"How? I won't understand a word he says."

"He speaks Thai—pretty good, too."

A car pulled up to the house and stopped. Robert called out to a neighbor in English. A moment later, two young men—one tall and dark, the other tall and fair—entered the kitchen. Sin looked from his mother to his sister with apprehension.

"My mother is visiting," Boonrawd said, rising to greet her husband. "I put some snacks out on the dining room table for you to eat before dinner."

Boonrawd's mother was covered with confusion when Robert turned eagerly toward her, put his palms together before his nose, and bowed his head in a respectful wai.

Her own hands moved clumsily to reciprocate.

O O   BOTAN AND
          THAT WOMAN'S NAME IS BOONRAWD

"Botan" is the pen name of Supa Luesiri Sirising, who was born in Thonburi, across the Chao Phraya River from Bangkok, in 1947. This unique author, who wrote the highly acclaimed autobiographical novel *Letters from Thailand*[1] when she was a twenty-one-year-old graduate student at Chulalongkorn University, is the epitome of the self-made woman. Botan's father and uncle were Chinese immigrants; the main character in *Letters from Thailand*, Tan Suang U, is a composite of the two men. Her father saw no need for a girl to be educated; and had she not won the first of many scholarships at the age of nine, schooling would have ended for her with the compulsory four years (now extended to six).

The women in Botan's novels reflect her own struggle. They are ambitious, driven, and single-minded. They are deeply concerned with independence—and with *money,* for which she makes no apologies.

The phenomenally successful *Letters from Thailand* was awarded the regional SEATO Award for the best work of Thai literature for the year 1969, raising Botan to a prominent position in the Thai literary world at a young age. It was a controversial novel because Botan had made no attempt to soften or leave out aspects of Chinese-Thai culture, opinions, or family matters that another author might well have decided were better left unexamined or unexposed. Many Chinese Thais were offended. The depiction of ethnic Thais was no more flattering and equally disturbing to some ethnic Thai readers. Nevertheless, it is to the credit of the SEATO Awards Committee that its members stood firm; this is a wonderful novel, they insisted; there could be no question that its world was the world as this writer had experienced it, not one created to appeal to a segment of the reading market. Eventually, the novel became required reading for high school students, in the interest of promoting understanding between the two major ethnic groups in Thai society.

---

1.   In Thai: Botan, *Jot mǎay jàak mɯang thay* (Bangkok: Duang Kamol, 1969); in English: Botan, *Letters from Thailand*, trans. Susan Fulop Kepner (Bangkok: Duang Kamol, 1977).

Two chapters of *That Woman's Name Is Boonrawd* were chosen for inclusion because the novel's heroine is the most fully realized of Botan's independent women. Boonrawd is born into a large, poor family in the northeast. In the family, she is the only child who loves school, and who dreams of a better life. (One weak point of the novel is that Boonrawd is so superior to everyone else in her family that the reader may wonder how she ever got the way she is.) Her mother, a vulgar, sly, lazy woman who coddles her sons and ignores her daughters, sends Boonrawd to work for a pittance in the home of a man notorious for preying upon his young female employees. After months of sexual abuse, Boonrawd runs away, seeking refuge with a former teacher. Living with the teacher's family in a more or less au pair status, Boonrawd furthers her education and plans a future in which she will not only triumph over her sad beginnings but also pull her family along with her into a world of order, achievement, and respectability.

When Boonrawd meets Robert, she is running a bakery from her home near Takhli Air Base. He is an American engineer, a civilian employee at the base. This is a real marriage, and both parties consider it permanent. Unlike her sister, Lam, Boonrawd is not a "rented wife," hired for the duration of a man's tour, a common feature of the air base scene during what Benedict Anderson and Ruchira Mendiones, in their anthology *In the Mirror,* call the "American era."[2]

Safety and security are paramount concerns in this novel. Although Botan makes it clear that they love each other, even the scene in which Boonrawd and her husband, Robert, make love for the first time is dominated by money. The marriage is efficiently consummated, whereupon the new couple settles down to a cozy but meticulous discussion of their financial assets and attitudes, and of how his income will be used in the marriage. The non-Thai reader may well find Robert an unconvincing character. Surely, he is Botan's creation; his words and actions—particularly, his reactions to some of his new wife's questions and pronouncements—do not always ring true.

The three primary messages in this novel appear, to one degree or another, in all of Botan's work. Once the reader understands the importance of these issues to Botan, everything that Boonrawd does and every element in her story seem reasonable. First, a woman who is

2. Anderson and Mendiones, op. cit.

without money of her own (whether she is married or not) is dan-
gerously vulnerable; second, the choice of a marriage partner is too
important to be dictated by affection alone—marriage is a serious *business* for a woman; third, daughters are valued much less than sons by
Thai or Chinese-Thai parents, and this is a situation that must be
changed.

Is Botan a feminist writer? If so, such an identification will be made
by others. She is really not interested in labels but in writing books
that show life the way it is. She is considered didactic and rigid, and
some readers are offended by the continuing emphasis on money.

The unreality of the Robert character is more interesting than may
first appear. Men do not often fare well in Botan's work; and Robert
is an ideal necessarily brought in from a foreign society. The society
with which she is familiar (in some sense, two societies: Chinese-Thai
and Thai) has not provided models of male behavior that have greatly
appealed to her. In *Letters from Thailand*, a young Thai man who marries one of the daughters of the family (the one modeled on Botan herself) seems such a model; but his character has the same unreal cast
as Robert. Rarely are Chinese-Thai men presented as worthy mates
for her strong, morally exceptional women.

Women, however, do not always fare well either in Botan's work.
Lazy, shiftless, self-obsessed women are as numerous as admirable
ones. Boonrawd's mother is a fine example of Botan's useless women,
as is the mother in the novel *Letters from Thailand*. The latter is not a
sluttish Thai, like Boonrawd's mother, but the spoiled, willful daughter of a Chinese-Thai merchant who is afraid of her temper. She marries Tan Suang U, the protagonist, and in a few years has become an
indolent, embittered woman and indifferent mother.

In Botan's novels, the reader is told that people ought to help themselves, work hard, and treat each other with respect; that daughters
ought to be raised with every bit of the love and encouragement with
which sons are raised; and that women ought to have every opportunity men have—*and* their own, private financial resources.

⚹ Deaf Sim

Prabhassorn Sevikul

In this 1984 story, an old deaf, homeless woman who
sews for passersby on a busy Bangkok street remembers
the important events in her life.

An old Chinese woman crouched on a low bench at the edge of a busy
sidewalk before a row of shops. She bent closely over a pair of worn
trousers, darning the knees. Every day, her eyesight grew worse, so
that the spectacles that slipped to the end of her nose were of little
use. Worse, they were sometimes a nuisance; they got in her way and
made her feel irritable. Only her two hands worked as reliably as ever.
Even so, the task of getting the new threads to blend in with the old
was becoming more difficult, and she couldn't do it as neatly as she
once had. Many times, she had made up her mind not to do any more
of this kind of work, but women paid more for this than for embroidery or patching or hemming.

Occasionally, she would raise her head and look off down the busy
road. Cars sped by continually; crowds of people filled the sidewalks
from early morning until late at night. It was a busy, noisy world, but
there was no noise in it for her.

Because she was deaf, it was as though she observed the life of the
street from a secret place. She removed her spectacles and laid them
on the lid of the bamboo sewing basket, which was her means of liveli-
hood and also her best friend. The old woman raised her hands to her
eyes and rubbed them hard; they hurt from hours of work.

Since her sight had begun to worsen, the pain also had worsened.
But if she ever gave in, closed her eyes, and let her head droop forward, in a moment she would be jolted from her repose with a start
to begin work again. Fear kept her eyes open. Fear that the customers

This is the title short story in the author's collection *Sim bây* (Deaf Sim), published by
Wannakaam Thai, Bangkok, in 1984.

would walk by, afraid to disturb her. Fear that she would not be able to call out to them in time, that another woman would get the work—for she was not alone on her small square bench at the curbside, beside her bamboo basket full of needles and thread, darning eggs, and scraps of fabric. There were other women on other small square benches, any of whom would eagerly snatch away her regular customers if an opportunity appeared. No, she had no choice. Nor did they.

Would anyone come to this place to offer a compassionate hand when such women were hungry or too ill to work? While they had skill in their hands and eyes to see, they must earn as much as possible to stave off for as long as possible the poverty, misery, and hopelessness they knew old age would bring.

Today was a sunny, clean-looking day, for three days of rain had washed the streets. But those three days! Rainy days were evil days for her. Not only did water spill from clogged drains, flooding first the sidewalks and then the whole road, ankle or knee deep, but cars and trucks splashed the dirty water onto the sidewalk as they churned past.

Then, the old woman hid herself in a narrow alley beside the row of shops, craning her neck to spot anyone who, despite the weather, might be carrying clothes to be mended.

Early in the morning, awakening to the sound of rain on the roof of the shack where she lived, she sometimes considered crawling back under her blanket to close her eyes and return to sleep, and not going into the street at all. But she always did. She could not resist taking up the bamboo basket and the paper umbrella under which she usually sat, and going to the street, even though she would end up in the alleyway, with the little umbrella folded tight, peering out sadly at people hurrying by with their heads tucked down, heedless of an old woman nearly hidden in a narrow crack between two blocks of shops.

This had been her life for so many years. She could not remember the first day she had sat on her bench among the clothing menders and set her hands to the work she had done every day since. Perhaps fifteen years or twenty. Or it might have been twenty-five years. But she did know that on the first day, her sight had been clear and sharp, her fingers nimble and exacting.

Today, her jade bracelet gleamed in the afternoon sun. Rich and warm-looking, yet cool and smooth to the touch, the bracelet pleased her every time she looked at it. Her husband had given it to her. She stroked it tenderly. She knew very well that it signified nothing of love and never had. It was a symbol of possession. Women were born to be possessed: by parents, then by husbands and children, and, at last, by grandchildren. She had been possessed but had been judged a worthless piece of property. There were no grandchildren. Still, she had the jade bracelet.

Her childhood had been predictable, in view of the undesirability of girl children and the far greater undesirability of one who had been born deaf. What a piece of ill fortune for a family was a defective girl! Although they did not abandon her, she was nonetheless forsaken.

She had not received even as much attention as the other girls in the household, which was not very much; and she was not capable of comparing herself to the boys, who had been wanted and were loved. Yet she was not entirely ignored; there was plenty for her to do.

Whenever she was alone, the little girl wept and wondered whether it could be her fault that she was deaf, or whether somebody had done this to her. But who? And why? She wondered why everyone in the house treated her with such contempt and anger, why they blamed her for things she had not done. At last she stopped wondering and began simply to hate herself for having been born as she was, whatever the cause might have been.

Other children despised and taunted her, and there was no one to stop them. If she came too near, they struck her. As an old woman, she could still remember running in terror from other children. She had never expected comfort, and she had never been given any. She learned the life of a solitary person very early while surrounded by a mother and father, brothers and sisters. She was deaf to them, and they were blind to her. Later, it was difficult for her to learn how one lives with others, even near others. She had been nothing but an oddity all her life and a terrified, trembling one at that.

In spite of everything, she did have her happy memories from those years of childhood. She remembered cool breezes in the night during the rainy season. And a big tree with branches that swayed in the breeze and leaves that floated to the ground. She remembered a tiny bird, flitting from one flower to another. She had felt that the bird was very happy. She was ignorant of birdsong, of the chirping and twittering of little birds, but the beauty of this creature, its quickness and grace, were marvelous to her.

She married at a very late age, the last of the children to leave home. By then, she had ceased to dream about marriage, having realized that it was a hopeless matter for a girl like her. Before she had fully understood this fact, however, she had daydreamed . . .

In her dreams, she walked gracefully and modestly in the red silk bridal dress, her face covered by a veil set with pearls. She raised one cup of wine after another in toasts to the assembled relatives. Later in this dream, she shyly turned her face to one side as her husband lowered the bamboo blind and lifted the pearl-studded veil . . .

That lovely dream had slowly faded. She had felt excited and curiously pleased when her eldest sister was married and also when the marriage of the second eldest took place. In her way, she shared the happiness of these great events in the family. But when, at last, her younger sister—younger by eight years—had worn the red gown and the pearl-studded veil, she had felt only envy and bitterness. It was then that she noticed her parents looking at her in a new way. Not only did they despise her, but they resented her the more, because they now saw her as a burden that would not be lifted from them until the day of their death.

And then, long after hope had died, she became a bride after all. Her husband was a man of the Kwo clan, from Sikkiang. He was old. She could not understand why this old, ugly man was to become her husband. She had known him all her life, for he did business with her father. But never, never would she have dreamed that she would become his wife. When the go-between first came to the house to ask for her hand, she did not feel happiness at the prospect of the marriage, but she did feel relief and a kind of gratitude, for she knew that this would be her only chance to leave her miserable home.

After the marriage, she learned why the old man had married her. Her father and mother had urged him to take her, saying that the sum of money ordinarily given to the bride's family upon the occasion of an engagement need not be thought of, under the circumstances. And there was something else: the old man believed that deaf women had stronger and more unusual sexual desires than normal women. When she discovered how she was valued in the eyes of her husband, she wept as she had not done since her childhood.

The old woman was startled from her reverie by a cluster of small girls on their way to school, whispering and giggling together. Their eyes were bright; their fresh young cheeks, smooth. The moment one of them met her gaze, she looked away.

She had writhed on the hospital bed in silence for many hours, staring up at the dark, rain-streaked window. Rain fell relentlessly throughout that night, and with each gust of wind the branch of a tree blew against the window. It was a night of fear and pain, and was succeeded by another agony. The serious faces of the doctor and nurse told her what she had feared to learn: they believed that the baby girl to whom she had just given birth would be deaf. Her husband's expression was a mixture of embarrassment, anger, and disappointment.

When the baby was a few months old, the man disappeared. He could not bear the shame of it, although he had sought this woman as his wife, had fathered this child. The neighbors regarded the mother and child as curiosities. Deaf mother, deaf child!

She remembered holding the baby through the nights, looking at the door, waiting for it to open, waiting for him to return to them. She thought about the future of her baby, of how her daughter's life would be, growing up as a stranger in the world. She imagined the child, weeping, enduring the taunts and cruel insults of other children. Imagined her marrying, after many years, only to learn the sole reason why a man would seek out a woman like her. Imagined her bearing a child, only to learn that it was as cursed, as useless as she herself was, as certain to know despair and loneliness all the days of its life.

That day was very hot. The baby cried ceaselessly, and although she could not hear her, she saw the little face, distorted by crying, frantic and miserable. A very hot day and the poorest day of the woman's life. It was the day on which she had nothing left at all, nothing but the jade bracelet. There was no food of any kind in the house, no vegetables, not even rice. She was hungry, and she knew that the baby was hungry. Again and again, she removed the jade bracelet, placed it on her open palm and looked at it. If she sold it, they would have food for a few days.

The bracelet was the only thing he had given her. It must do, in place of all the things she would never have in her life. Such a thing could never mean to another woman what it meant to her, she who had never been wanted by anyone, never been given anything. She could not bring herself to sacrifice it.

The baby cried on. Its face looked twisted and ugly, inhuman. She began to feel dizzy. Her own pain became one with the dread she felt for her child. She pulled the baby to her, looked for a long time into the tiny, tormented face, studied the open mouth that moved spasmodically with its constant howling. She was consumed by sorrow and despair and rage. She held the baby close, then closer, closer, until at last her child lay still across her lap, at peace.

The afternoon sun began to fade; the shadows of the row of shops reached across the road. The old woman looked up, grasped the spectacles that lay on top of her sewing basket, and set them back on her nose. With a slightly trembling hand, she rethreaded her needle and began again to mend the trouser knees. Cars and trucks crowded the road and moved slowly into the rush hour; crowds of people hurried and jostled each other, eager to be going home.

The old woman worked on, in perfect silence.

○   ○   PRABHASSORN SEVIKUL AND "DEAF SIM"

Prabhassorn, who was born in Bangkok in 1948, writes under his own name. He is an official in the Ministry of Foreign Affairs and is often posted abroad, yet since the early 1970s, he has also managed to find time to write his impeccably crafted, unusual short stories. Most of his work focuses on social and political problems in contemporary Thai society.

Prabhassorn has received numerous literary awards for his work, including the short story collection *The Broken Web*[1] and the novel *Power*.[2] It seems unlikely that Prabhassorn will ever repeat the com-

---

1. In Thai, *Khrîip hàk.*
2. In Thai, *Amnâat.*

mercial success of his 1978 novel *Wela nai kuat gaew,* or *Weelaa nay khùat kɛ̂ɛw* (Time in a bottle). Told in the form of a memoir, it follows a group of teenage best friends during the turbulent year of 1973. The friends must cope not only with family problems but also with the dangerous political events of that year. The Jim Croce song "Time in a Bottle" is printed, translated into Thai, as the frontispiece and is referred to throughout the novel, which is arguably the *Catcher in the Rye* of Thai fiction. It has been reprinted many, many times and was made into a popular film. Eight collections of his short stories and eleven novels have been published; unfortunately, to my knowledge none of his fiction has been translated into English except "Deaf Sim" in this work.

One reason "Deaf Sim" was chosen for inclusion is because it provides such a powerful depiction of urban poverty from the vantage point of an old woman, alone in the world. Such old women surely do exist in urban Thailand, on the fringes of crowded markets and busy streets. (The fact that this woman is Chinese Thai is noteworthy, I believe, only in terms of the details of her story.)

A more important reason for including this selection is the matter of its style. The sense of place in the story is perfect; one can easily picture the busy sidewalk in front of the row of shops; the muddy alleyway during the monsoon rains; the skinny old woman huddled on a small bench, with her sewing basket beside her. (Nowhere does Prabhassorn tell us that she is skinny, but could a reader imagine her otherwise?) The majority of Thai writers, especially before the past two decades, would have padded these scenes with dramatic details, as if the reader must be convinced of how bad things really are for Sim, how bad they have always been.

The story of deaf Sim is horrifying, but unlike many Thai short stories about poor people in desperate situations, including some in this anthology ("Greenie," "A Mote of Dust on the Face of the Earth"), it contains not a scintilla of sentimentality or melodrama. The spare, unsentimental, highly intelligent method that underlies it represents something of a trend in contemporary Thai writing; surely, it has characterized Prabhassorn's writing over the last twenty years. In this anthology, the same spare, restrained quality is evident in Sri Dao Ruang's "Matsii," included in the first section, and also in the story that follows this one, "A Pot That Scouring Will Not Save," by Anchan. Although the latter story ends in violence, the events leading up to it are related in scrupulous fashion; from the first page, fear is methodically constructed by a highly disciplined and restrained author.

Prabhassorn's contributions to the growing sophistication of the Thai short story have been substantial. It is his genius to let the horrors of a story such as "Deaf Sim" take us unawares. We may need to reread some passages to be sure that we have not missed something—some foreshadowing, some signal that would have warned us that the suitor will have monstrous ulterior motives for giving Sim the opportunity to wear the coveted red wedding dress and the pearl-studded veil; that would have put us on our guard for worse things to come after the marriage; that would have cautioned us that an unspeakable crime is about to take place. But he never does. At the end, cars and trucks fill the road, moving slowly into the rush hour; crowds of people hurry and jostle each other, eager to go home; the old woman works on, in perfect silence.

A Pot That Scouring Will Not Save

Anchan

This 1987 story depicts the life
of a woman married to an abusive man.

I

The rice porridge rose in the pot, bubbled, foamed over the top, streamed thickly over the sides and down into the fire with furious hisses, *cheee . . . chaaa . . .* When no more could escape, the remainder contented itself with boiling furiously on the bottom, *boot-boot, boot-boot . . .*

A child's voice cried out, "Mama! Oo-ey—smoke everywhere! The rice porridge is burning! Hurry, Mama!"

Nien set down her iron beside a pan heaped with damp twists of clothing, ran from the little yard behind the house into the kitchen to encounter a sight familiar to any housewife, a forgotten pot boiling over. But this housewife was overwhelmed by the sight, felt her knees turn to water. By now, the flames of the gas burner lapped ravenously at the blackened porridge that encrusted the pot, unmindful of the woman who scuttled about helplessly, grabbing first this, now that; whose attempts to control the situation were useless, pointless.

"Mama, *do* something!" shouted the boy, whose name was On. His sister, Am, looked wildly about the kitchen, then lunged for the fan that dangled from a rail beside a few knives, some smaller pots, an old frying pan. They coughed and choked, trying to suppress the sounds as Am fanned the smoke toward the open window. Nien at last managed to turn off the flame and faced her children with more pleading than anger in her voice.

"Didn't you smell it burning before now?" The children nodded. "Then why didn't you run to turn off the stove?"

"But, Mama, you know Papa won't let us touch the stove." Am's

"A Pot That Scouring Will Not Save" ("Mɔ̌ɔ thîi khùt mây ɔ̀ɔk") appeared in Anchan's 1990 SEAWrite award–winning short story collection, *Anmanii hὲɛng chiiwít* (Jewels of life), published by Khom Bang Press, Bangkok, in 1990.

dark eyes widened with disbelief that her mother would suggest such a thing.

"It's the new pot, the one Papa just bought!" On said, adding, in a sighing undertone, *"dai la-wa-a-ah,"* an exclamation replete with dread of the likely consequences, implying an educated idea of the possibilities. His glance slid toward his mother and at once away. He did not want to observe what he knew would be as easy to see as a banana was to peel: a deepening of the fear that had filled her eyes when she first comprehended the disaster of the ruined pot.

But On needn't have worried, for his mother scarcely heard him, so great was her consternation at this unexpected misfortune.

She had got up very early to begin making their Sunday breakfast. She loved the ritual of it, the comforting aroma of spicy *kun-chieng* sausages; the deep pink color and appetizing, oily sheen of the salt-preserved eggs. She sniffed the sausages as they sizzled and browned, chopped the pink eggs into a bowl. At the last moment, when the family was seated around the table, she would beat a spoonful of fish sauce into a bowl of raw eggs until they were frothy, slip them into a hot greased pan, watch them puff and turn golden. By then, the rice porridge would be ready, fragrant and smooth.

Rice porridge must simmer long and slowly, so that it will slide smoothly down the throat. Nien had set the new, shining white enamel pot onto the gas burner, turned up the flame, and gone outside to begin ironing the great pile of clothing she had sprinkled the night before, thinking that she would iron for just a minute or two, then return to the kitchen to turn down the flame. But she soon became absorbed in her task and forgot all about the porridge.

Now, with a small, worried face on either side of her, she inspected the pot, carefully scraping the inside with a large spoon. The rice came off in blackened chunks. The outside was worse. She knew that the enamel, so white and shining only an hour before, would come off in flakes the moment she touched the scorched and blackened crust. Scouring would not save it, nothing would. It would remain ugly, ruined. She had ruined it.

The fate of the previous pot had been similar, the result of her handiwork. Thrown away because of her carelessness, her forgetful and heedless ways. Unsightly because of her, a thing from which a person would avert his eyes. And so her husband had taken the matter in hand, and on the previous day, Saturday, a day on which he could have done many things, he had gone to the market and bought the new white-enamel pot, had stalked into the house, his footsteps heavy with resentment, the new pot under his arm, his anger filling the small kitchen.

"Mama, it's almost eight o'clock," said Am. "Papa will wake up soon."

Am's words turned a switch in her mind. When she opened her mouth to speak, it seemed to her that the quiet, insistent voice came from someone else, that all three of them were listening. "Later, when—if Papa asks what happened to the new pot, tell him—tell him Yai Man next door, she borrowed it. Yes, and if he doesn't ask, don't say anything." She swallowed, reached into her pocket, and in a voice scarcely above a whisper added, "Yes, and I will give you each ten baht for—to buy candy, then."

The children grabbed the money eagerly.

Upstairs, she crept into the bedroom. He lay fast and peacefully asleep although the morning sun poured through the window. The warmth of the sun reminded her of a second pan filled with clothing, things she had washed the night before. Later in the afternoon, when they had baked dry in the warm sweetness of the sun, she would iron them meticulously. The thought of the finished laundry—dry, pressed, and fragrant, no mistakes—for a moment caused the reality of the charred pot to recede. Perhaps everything would turn out all right after all, and he would never know.

Her reflections were interrupted by the *jawk-jack* of sparrows in the mango tree outside. A flock of them descended into the tree every morning, causing the branches to brush against the eaves of the house and the window of their bedroom. He hated those sparrows.

She tiptoed across the room, took a broom from the corner, slowly opened the window screen, and, holding the broom in both hands, leaned out the window and began to brandish it vigorously, thrusting it back and forth among the branches until the birds fled.

On some mornings, when school was not in session and her husband still lay asleep, she bade Am take over the daily task of banishing the sparrows. The girl would sulk, but she would do it because she was afraid to disobey her mother, a fact that had nothing to do with her mother and everything to do with her father. But not today.

It was not worth taking the chance that Am might make a noise as she opened the screen, or might accidentally knock the broom handle against the windowsill and waken her father before Nien was able to get the burned pot safely out of sight.

Even more than sparrows, he hated *jing-jooks*, the tiny gray-green house lizards that made the sound *juk-jak-juk-jak* as they chased each other up and down walls and across ceilings. Any day that Nien found jing-jooks in the bedroom, she would brush along behind them with the fly swatter, gently urging them out the window. It was worth these small tasks to avoid his reproaches: "This place is a *nest*, not a home. One of these days there won't be room for people at all, it will be a filthy *nest* and nothing more." This morning, as she was about to withdraw the broom from the tree and fasten the window screen before a jing-jook could slip by, a voice interrupted her thoughts.

"Lady, what are you doing up there? Every morning I see you up there with that broom."

Nien leaned out the window cautiously. Beneath her in the lane, the old woman who sold *bah tong go tawt*[1] leaned against her pushcart. At this hour, it was full of the steamed buns and Chinese rice pancakes that she would hawk up and down this lane, on her way to the busy street beyond the corner. She peered quizzically up at Nien, who, having no idea how to respond, smiled down at her timidly. But even if she had been able to think of something to say, there was nothing she could do. She felt sorry that she could not explain herself to the pushcart woman, but of course that was impossible, because he would awaken. The bah tong go tawt woman waited for a few moments, then laughed, braced herself against the handles of the cart, and slowly pushed off toward the mouth of the lane.

Nien quickly closed the screen, set the broom to rest, and tiptoed from the bedroom.

She returned to the disorder of the kitchen, where she, On, and Am worked with hands as quick as spools, seizing this, grasping that, completing each other's tasks without a word. When, from the corner of his eye, On glimpsed two cockroaches skittering across the floor, he leaped for the broom, whacked them, and leaned to one side just as Am slid the dustpan beneath their stiff, dark bodies.

---

1. A Chinese doughnut made of two small fingers of dough that produce an X-shaped product about three inches square.

In the very instant they finished tidying the kitchen, a groan sounded above them, freezing them all where they stood. The rhythm of Nien's heart speeded up in the instant she heard the groan, as if it had been waiting for this signal. She took a deep breath, exhaling slowly as she set a freshly cooked pot of rice porridge in the center of the table. "There," she said, "everything is just in time."

"Who turned on the *television?*" came the querulous voice from upstairs. "Does the whole damned house have to fall around your ears before you can turn it *down?*"

No one had turned on the television.

"Don't you hear me? Turn it *off! Now!*"

The children's faces radiated fear, engendering a flicker of courage in Nien's breast. She pulled her hair back and fastened it with a rubber band at the nape of her neck as she climbed the stairs, composing her face into a good-morning smile.

He was sitting up in bed, his face creased with sleep and vexation. He did not look up or respond to her presence.

She smiled and said, "Good morning, Khun," began to talk to him as if he had smiled back or looked at her or acknowledged her in some way. "No one turned on the television. You know the children would never think to do such a thing while their papa is sleeping, not that I would permit it, no. I am afraid it is the television next door, at Yai Man's. It is such a shame, really. Here you are, with a morning when you could sleep in, but then, of course, Yai Man's children are home because there isn't any school, and when they're home, it is on all day, just deafening, really."

She tried to look concerned without losing her smile, cheerful yet sympathetic, inclining her ear toward the sound that was more like the buzzing of mosquitoes than deafening. But, of course, it was not actually quiet; a person could hear it if he was trying to sleep.

"Stop yapping and get over there and tell them to shut the thing up." He scratched his head irritably.

She would have to do it or one of the children.

Theirs was one unit in a row house, with just enough room for the four of them: Nien; the children, On and Am; and her husband, Tahni, though she had never called him that or even *phii,* "elder brother," as women often did, but only *khun,* which was awfully polite but then she had not known when or how to change this after they were married, and now it would be too odd to call him anything else, and so to her, he would always be Khun.

There were two bedrooms and a bath upstairs, a kitchen and sitting room downstairs. The backdoor faced a paved slab where a large earthenware water jug collected rainwater, and where she did the laundry and ironing, and washed dishes. The front door faced a tiny square of grass and also the mango tree that lent its cool and leafy shade to their home.

There were seven or eight buildings like theirs in the neighborhood. In the last few years, the residents had achieved a gratifying upgrading of status by the simple expedient of appropriating a foreign word: *town house*. Whatever the word, foreign or Thai, the walls between families were too thin for privacy. Sounds that were not meant to be shared thus passed with some frequency from one *town house* to the next, occasionally bringing a quiet smile to Nien's lips.

She was a woman who felt the importance of friendship and of small kindnesses. She would have enjoyed her neighbors, but her husband could see no point in reaching beyond the walls of their own four rooms. What, he demanded to know, was there to be gained from the prattle of neighbors? And, besides, he was fed up with the way she let people walk all over her. Which neighbors were bound to do, and she would be fool enough to let them, for in any dispute, large or small, nothing would induce her to do or say anything that might offend or upset another person, however right her cause or wrong theirs.

"On!" she called down the stairs. "Run next door to Yai Man's and ask them to please turn down the television. Tell them your father is trying to sleep."

"You'll have to do it yourself," came On's loud reply. "I'm going out to buy Papa's newspaper."

The boy's voice, suddenly insolent, chilled her. So conscious was he that Papa was listening, so full of the power of his refusal on the grounds of Papa's newspaper. Suddenly, the charred pot appeared before her eyes. She blinked it away, called down the stairs again. "But you can stop at Yai Man's on your way. You can—" The door slammed.

"You're a pair, you are," Tahni said, pushing himself from the bed onto his feet. "Bickering like two kids. You don't even know how to be a mother. Even that. Another minute, and I'll go over there myself, and then we'll see if they shut the thing up. And you won't have to worry about looking them in the eye, because they'll be afraid to look *you* in the eye."

"Oh, no—don't, please, Khun. I will go myself."

His readiness for a fight made her stomach hurt, made her feel strangely afraid for the neighbors. Who knew better than herself what there was to fear? As for her own embarrassment over facing Yai Man and her family about the television, the discomfort of facing Yai Man herself was nothing, minuscule, a speck of dirt under a fingernail, in comparison with the picture in her mind of her husband storming into the neighbor's house, shouting and swearing.

To her relief, he wrapped a clean pakomah about his waist, picked up the fresh towel she had set out for him, and headed toward the bathroom, banging his heels on the floor and yawning. In another moment, she heard the shower running.

A good sign. He would be in there a long time, for he was a man who loved to be clean and prided himself on impeccable grooming. By the time he left the bathroom, he would be wide awake and almost certainly in a better mood. He might even have forgotten about Yai Man's television or ceased to care.

Whatever Nien did today, she must get rid of the burned pot. That he might never inquire after it was beyond possibility, for he was a man who noticed everything, including and particularly anything that was his and missing. He was meticulous in his attentions to the household; his eye, fine as a sieve, missed nothing. Oh yes, he would ask.

She would go to Yai Man and ask for help. If Yai Man would tell him herself that she had borrowed it . . . and then she could say that she had lent it to another neighbor, who . . . but then what? Before long, the entire neighborhood would be embroiled in the story of the burned pot, and how would it end? Never mind, she would think of something. Nothing else mattered but keeping him from learning the truth today.

It was said of Nien that she possessed every quality of a true Thai lady. Her docile manner, her soft words, even her narrow waist and delicate figure seemed to belong to another time. The hopeless thing, the unsolvable problem, was that it seemed precisely these qualities that ignited the terrifying temper of the strapping man who had become her husband.

II

And yet, in the beginning, this strapping man had attracted her in no small measure. He was handsome and strong, with powerful shoulders and forceful ways; but that was not all. He was witty, he made her laugh, and he was quite the cleverest person Nien had ever met.

Indeed, not only Nien but also her family had considered it a most fortunate match for her, as did her envious friends. Aside from his other qualities, Tahni possessed enormous charm. He charmed her and her family and everyone else he met. She was proud of him, proud to be seen with him. She herself never could think of the right thing to say; invariably, Tahni could. Nien had never imagined that anyone could have such perfect self-confidence. And the most amazing thing of all was that he, who could have charmed and chosen anyone to be his wife, had chosen—*Nien!*

Tahni was the deputy director of a branch of a successful private bank. He had achieved this position at an impressively young age and entirely through his own ability and ambition. Indeed, he could have attained the position in no other way, due to his single flaw, if it could be called such: his family.

Tahni had risen, or rather clawed his way upward, from origins that only charity could describe as humble. Not only had they been desperately poor but (however Nien tried not to judge or disparage them) they were not—well, not the sort of people one thought of as the "humble poor." They were more—the frightening poor; the poor who survived any way they could, to whom certain ways of behaving, which people like Nien would consider simple human decency, were regarded, if they were regarded at all, as affectations.

Upon his family's very principles, Tahni had clambered over their backs and onto the next level of society and then the next. Who could help but admire such unfailing determination and courage?

Nien had grown up in what may be described as an old-fashioned family, which is to say that they were amiable, politely affectionate with each other, and, if not wealthy, comfortable enough on money that had accumulated over several generations. Another old-fashioned quality was their generosity, extended to all who were in need, whether the need be for a full belly or a kind word.

Nien was the youngest daughter. Her father had died when she was a baby, and she was the joy of her mother's heart. Her upbringing was the kind of which Thai people say, "No ant dared to bite her, no cloud dared to rain upon her head." She had never encountered a situation that required her to resist, oppose, or even disagree with anyone, for her mother, at the first sign that something might displease or offend Nien, always managed to adjust the situation before her daughter could fully realize the sensation of displeasure or offense.

Still, the girl was sensible of pain and grief in the world, for she observed these things as she went about the streets of Bangkok. Scenes of want or obvious unhappiness troubled and saddened her, for she had a tender heart; while she may have been raised indulgently, she had never been encouraged to accept her own good fortune as her due and other people's bad fortune as the just expression of an unfortunately less deserving karmic inheritance.

Who would not, like Nien, troubled and saddened after an excursion into the mean streets, return gratefully to the warm bosom of such a family? She believed that everyone who was near to her was possessed of only the best intentions, a belief in which she was entirely justified. She never thought of looking for faults in those she loved or ascribing unbecoming motives to their words or actions. Nien knew that evil existed, just as she knew that grief and unhappiness existed. But evil, like grief and unhappiness, was a thing that lurked somewhere on the other side of a river so wide that her eyes could barely make out the features of the opposite shore.

This was the sum of Nien's preparation for her journey into life. As her family had adored her, she would adore her husband and children, without qualification. Taken all in all, she was not unlike a person who has been raised in a germ-free environment, but who must, at last, go into a world teeming with disease. Against the specific diseases of cruelty, meanness of spirit, and greed, she had neither immunities nor defenses.

During the first year of their marriage, Nien and her husband could not afford a home of their own, so they lived with her mother, who considered this a most desirable situation. As she was not only an indulgent mother but also a wise one, she carefully divided her house to give the young couple complete privacy and the sense, if not quite the fact, of independence.

Nien soon learned that her husband had yet another phenomenal ability beyond those she had already admired.

"Nien, you look at art through the eyes of a child," he remarked in a tone of voice that combined amusement and exasperation. "As if a five hundred baht painting might well be the equal of one listed at five thousand. What a little fantasist you are."

She shrugged and smiled helplessly. It was true. What did she know about art? Really, she had no right to question (however privately) his definition of taste, which appeared to be the ability to guess the price of any object after a cursory glance. Should one of his friends seek his opinion of a painting or sculpture that hung or stood in some studio about town, which frequently they did, he would invariably delay giving an answer if he had not yet discovered the answer to the only question that truly mattered: *how much?*

She was infatuated with him. He *knew* so many things! True, his concern with the price of everything and some of his odd habits of thrift were a bit vexing, or would have been vexing had she not reminded herself that his thrifty ways were quite what she needed. She was far too careless with money. Even Mother teased her, calling her Miss Basket with a Hole in the Bottom.

In a serious attempt to reform herself, Nien planted a garden with herbs and peppers, gourds and vines and flowers, a project that was born one Saturday morning as he pulled vegetables from her market basket, pretending (she was sure) to be quite put out with her for not driving a harder bargain with the women in the market.

"You want to be like Makato, little Nien. Do you know the tale?"

"No." She felt embarrassed, for she knew almost none of the stories that he delighted in telling her, and that she loved to hear. Wherever had he learned them all?

"Well, then. Makato was a boy who cut grass for elephants. That was his job. One day, he found a tiny coin in the grass, only a *bia*,[2] but he thought that he would take it to market and buy himself a nice lettuce with it. Of course, the market woman laughed in his face.

"'One bia?' She laughed with her mouth wide open, Nien—like this—*Haw haw haw!* 'You expect to buy a lettuce with only one bia?' She took the coin and contemptuously tossed it onto the ground.

---

2.   A bia was an ancient coin equivalent to $\frac{1}{64}$ of a baht, which is worth slightly less than five cents.

Makato was not daunted in the least. He picked up the coin, held it out again, and said, 'Well, then, Mother, I see that you have a bag of seeds beside you. Wouldn't you please sell me just one lettuce seed for this bia, so that I may grow a lettuce in my own garden?'

"The old woman chuckled to herself, and thinking to have a little fun with this fool, she said to him, 'All right, then. Stick your finger into the bag of seeds, and perhaps a magic seed will stick to it. Any magic seed you find is yours.'

"And so, little Nien, what do you think the clever Makato did? He stuck his finger into his mouth and then into the bag—and, naturally, when he drew his wet finger from the bag, it was covered with 'magic' seeds. The old woman could only shake her head. 'You're a clever boy, you are,' she said—for she now realized that Makato was not at all the fool he looked. 'With such a brain, you could grow up to be a politician.'

"But Makato did not become a politician. He became a *king!* The king of the Mon people, who called him Phra Jao Fah Rua. He ruled during the same era as our own king, Phra Ruang Jao. My mother loved to tell this story, no doubt because our family has Mon blood.

"Did you ever hear the saying that in every Mon stomach, there are seven needles and seven scythes? No? Then let me tell you a secret, little Nien. It is not quite true. You see, the scythes are not in here," and he touched a finger to his belly, "they are *here.*" He raised his hand to his head, tapped a finger to his temple, then extended his arm toward her slowly, so slowly that she felt quite mesmerized, and drew his index finger across her throat, straight across, from beneath one ear lobe all the way to the other, with a touch so light that a shiver ran from her throat to the tips of her toes.

He dropped his arm and turned away from her. "If only you could have known my mother." He stared out the kitchen window with a forlorn look on his face, but when at last he looked back at Nien, a twinkle came into his eye. "Shall I tell you an absolutely astonishing story about my mother?"

Nien settled herself happily for another tale and put the seven scythes firmly out of her mind.

"Mother was pregnant with our youngest brother. The baby was due any day, but do you think that would stop my mother from selling tripe in the marketplace? Not my mother—and if you have ever wondered, by the way, if I was ever ashamed that my mother sold tripe in the marketplace, you would have been quite wrong."

Nien shook her head quickly and laughed to show the absurdity of the idea.

"Only minutes after our brother was born, Mother dragged herself from the bed, carrying the afterbirth in the bowl in which my grandmother had placed it, and what do you think she did with it? She dropped it into the stock pot! Grandmother had already whacked off the cord, and without a blink, she tossed it onto the block, chopped it up, and threw that into the pot along with the rest. Our family didn't have to waste so much as a satang at the butcher's that day, and no one was the wiser. Everything—afterbirth, cord, and all—*boop-boop, into the soup!*"

He studied her face for several moments, then slowly broke into a wide grin.

Oh, he was *teasing* her! It was a joke! She began to giggle hysterically.

"Aow!" he cried. "Are you laughing at my mother?" His smile faded. "Don't do that, little Nien, not ever . . ."

Tahni was a man of eloquent speech and dazzling words, full of hilarious tales that occasionally caused his listeners to wonder, hours or days later, what the tale had really meant. There was, however, another side to Tahni's golden tongue. When he became angry, which happened with a frequency that began to alarm Nien, his tongue could be as sharp as a razor, could slash and cut without warning or restraint. After several months of marriage, Nien realized that she was becoming the chief target upon which he practiced his art. It hurt and saddened her, but never once was she able to think of a retort to one of his wounding remarks.

Nien's mother loved to surprise them with food. She would appear at the kitchen door, her merry face above a steaming bowl of her famous *gaeng liang*, redolent with the fragrance of *krachai* herbs and shrimp paste, peppers and onions and fish.[3] For this dish, she used the leaves at the tenderest tips of the tamlung vines, the prettiest of the gourds that Nien had planted in the garden behind the house, and that

---

3. Gaeng liang (kɛɛng liang) is a kind of curry. Krachai is called lemon grass in English.

now grew in splendid profusion. From time to time, she would save herself a trip to the market by pinching off a few mouse-turd peppers or a handful of pungent, minty *horapa* leaves from the inexhaustible abundance of the garden.

One morning, Nien's mother called through the kitchen door, "What is wrong with your Tahni today? He passed me on his way to work with scarcely a word, and with such a face! If it wasn't a frown, *well*—it wasn't a smile, either."

"I don't know," Nien replied, flustered and embarrassed. It was the truth; she didn't know what had sent him out of the house in such a bad humor that morning, but she did know that suddenly she felt the dull pain in her chest, a pain that was becoming dismayingly familiar.

As the next day was the first of the month, when he rose from the breakfast table Tahni withdrew a small roll of folded bills from the inside pocket of his suit jacket and laid it on the table. Nien had, with great diffidence and a good deal of indirection, prevailed upon him to contribute to the upkeep of the house they shared.

"But, Khun," she began in a small, breathy voice, seeing that the amount of money was smaller than it ought to be, "I'm afraid this isn't enough."

"You may tell your mother," he replied as he strode from the room, "that the rest paid for watering the vegetables she swiped from our garden."

When he had gone, Nien continued to stand before the table, staring at his breakfast dishes, not wanting to believe that she had heard him speak such words. Not for anything would she tell her mother what he had said, so clearly did it reveal a quality in her husband that was mortifying to her.

From that time forward, such behavior on Tahni's part became quite ordinary, particularly when he suspected that someone was trying to take advantage of him or, worse, when he feared that he was losing an opportunity to take advantage of someone else. He would have found many more such opportunities in his mother-in-law's house, had not Nien's older brother at last perceived the kind of man his sister had married and taken steps to prevent another such event as the levying of the garden water fee.

"Your Tahni is a man of stone," her brother remarked drily. "As hard as stone and stingy as well, but—Nien, my dear, the truth is that you encourage him."

When Nien responded only with a look of bewilderment, he said, "Because you give in to his every act of meanness. But—you really don't understand, do you?"

She knew that she was not doing quite the right things, but what the right things might be, she could not imagine. Of course, she was not nearly as clever as her husband; but, she reasoned, she did have a good education. And so she decided that she might solve several problems at once by going to work.

Unfortunately, the state of the economy in that year did not support her ambitions. In the end, it was Tahni who found her the job, who negotiated the terms of her employment as a salesperson in an air-conditioner store downtown.

The first week, she wondered if she would ever make her sales quota. She knew perfectly well the reason for her poor start: it was obvious, simple, and fatal. Each time she looked into a potential buyer's face, she began to shake with fear, and before she could gain control of herself, the uncomfortable customer had moved on. Day by day, her faith in her ability to succeed in the job waned.

"Nien, you need to get a little—you know—'hardened up,'" one of the other saleswomen advised her sympathetically. "The customers are just people, you know; it's not so bad."

But behind her back, the others shook their heads with a mixture of amusement, pity, and irritation. The way Nien scuttled away from people, as if they were pursuing her, when she should be pursuing them and making a sale—it was very peculiar. Soon, she had earned a nickname, Literature Lady, after one of the men had remarked, "She is exactly like one of those well-born heroines in the deadly old novels they made us read in high school."

As they were having tea one afternoon, Nong-noot, the youngest saleswoman, remarked, "Nien, it's not enough anymore to have a quick ear, a quick eye, and keep your hands and feet in motion. The truth is, you've got to shake your ass, too!"

The others broke into laughter, not only at the truth of Nong-noot's observation but also at Nien's reaction to the word "ass." For her part, Nien understood that the laughter was not unkindly, and that they regarded her with a certain affection. And so she laughed along with them, gripping the edges of her desk to stop the detested shaking, which had overtaken her once again, telling herself all the while that it was only normal, normal to be surrounded by people, talked to, and teased.

Not long after, she was fired. The explanation the manager gave her was straightforward. She had no personality. And none of the qualities of a good salesperson, least of all the ability to talk anyone into buying anything.

One of her colleagues rushed to comfort her. "Oo-ey, the hell with him!" she whispered to Nien about their boss. "Anyway, you don't need a *sungkabooey* little job like this, an educated woman like you. You know what? I'll quit, too, and then he'll be sorry."

But she didn't quit.

At the end of the day, Nong-noot, who always topped her weekly quota, took a gold-plated pen from her pocket and held it toward Nien with a smile. Nien's heart swelled, lightening miraculously with this simple gesture. Her eyes burned, and her throat hurt so that she didn't dare to speak.

"It's yours, Nien. You left it on my desk yesterday."

The girl might as well have stuck a pin into Nien's swelling heart. Nong-noot was not giving her a gift. No one would. How stupid she had been! As Nien reached for the pen, Nong-noot quickly drew her hand back, looked away, and in a rush of words said, "You know, I'd really like to keep it, because then every time I use it, I'll think of you, Nien. I mean, I really liked you." Interpreting Nien's silence as acquiescence, she put the pen into her pocket and walked away.

Thus did Nien lose both her job and her pen in one day. And came to understand very well how inadequate she was to deal in the world outside, as other people seemed to do so easily.

Much chastened, she fled to her home, where before long she had a small child to care for and then another. Home, Nien had learned, was the only place a woman like her belonged. Unfortunately, from the day she returned from the air-conditioner store in disgrace, her husband treated her with even less respect than before. But how could she blame him? After all, he had earned a good job and was successful at it. It was not his fault if she could not make a success of even a simple sales job in an air-conditioner store.

The unfailing and unconditional love of her mother sustained her while she cared for her babies and tried to please her husband. And then the catastrophe occurred: her mother fell ill and died.

Nien inherited enough money to buy the town house, with the addition of a small amount from Tahni's private account. It was after they moved that his rages over their household expenses became constant and frightening. The only money Nien saw was her allowance, doled out according to his calculations of household needs, not a satang more than was accounted for on the list he prepared meticulously each week. It was nearly impossible to feed them all on what he gave her, but she dared not complain, since she never had been good about money, as no one knew better than he. In fact, the allowance was probably good for her; and anyway, she reasoned, it was he who had earned the money, not she. Why shouldn't he have the right to say how it should be spent?

The condition of the bar of soap in the bathroom was a weekly crisis. "From now on," he yelled down the stairs at her one morning, "you can start carrying a handful of Fab up the stairs for your shower. Look at this! This bar has been in here less than a month, and it's nothing but a crumb!" There was no solution to the bath soap problem, as he used most of it himself.

Gradually, happiness for Nien became entirely defined by her husband's state of mind. A day when he awoke and seemed in an inexplicably good mood was a gift, a happy day. If, as was far more often the case, he was full of anger, cursing her and terrifying the children, she and they endured. Such was the climate of this household. It was good or it was bad, but in any case neither she nor the children had any power to alter or affect it.

The world outside, full of people and events, now seemed barely connected to the mouse-hole world of her home. But it did not occur to Nien that she might move from the mouse hole. She had gone into the world outside once since her marriage and had failed there. The only answer to her predicament was to learn how to survive and to enable her children to survive in the mouse hole.

One evening, Tahni arrived home from the bank in a state of high excitement. "Wait until you see what I have to show you!" he announced, smiling so broadly that Nien felt a thrill of delight and hope. He rushed upstairs to bathe, and when he returned, he opened his briefcase, removed a torn sheet of newspaper, and flattened it on the kitchen table.

"Look at this, Nien—it's perfect. 'No experience needed—' See? They've described you already. 'Now hiring salespeople to represent finest brand-name china. Pays top commissions.' I called, and I got all the details. Even you could do this, believe me. At first they said they require a refundable security deposit on the china, twenty thousand baht, but it can be negotiated. So, what do you say? Your customers would be just housewives, Nien. Even you could sell to other housewives."

Terror filled her. "Oh, Khun, I—I don't think so. You have to haul a huge, heavy case of dishes all around town. I know, because a long time ago, I had a friend who sold china like that. It was—I mean, I'm sure I could never . . . you have to go to people's houses who didn't invite you, and—well, my friend only did it for a little while, but she said it was like—like being a coolie, dragging that case, and then . . . nobody wanted the china." She stared fixedly at the ad as she spoke, her hands twisting damply in her lap. "Khun, it was . . . very difficult, she had to go to all these little lanes she'd never seen before in her life, up to her knees in mud in the rainy season and then in the hot season, dragging that case. And she was afraid in some of those places, too, afraid of those men who watch for women alone, you know, Khun, to rob them, and they have guns, and they—they watch for you . . ."

Despite her fear, she was unable to stop talking, stop defending herself against the terrible prospect of dragging a heavy case of china into thousands of little streets she had never seen before, knocking on the doors of strange houses. But stop talking she did, for he jumped to his feet, grabbed the sheet of newspaper, crumpled it into a ball, and flung it at her, grazing the side of her head.

Nien braced herself, but instead of lunging at her he turned and stalked into the other room. The children disappeared upstairs at once, and a few moments later, she heard them straightening and cleaning their room. She wished with all her might that she had the power to shrink herself, to become the size of an ant, so that she would not affront his eyes. She knew exactly how he looked without so much as a glance in his direction: his face dark with anger, his eyes bulging.

As she could neither shrink herself nor dare to think of leaving the house, she tried instead to pacify him with the sight of her devotion to their home. With her broom, with her dust rag, with her industrious light steps up and down, back and forth. Even if she didn't have a real job, she would show him that she did not expect to live off him like a parasite, eating his toil.

This tactic had to be abandoned when he bellowed from the next room, "I've had quite enough of your doleful little drama. The news is coming on in a minute—so *shut up.*" Nien at once set aside her whisk broom and carefully pushed the small pile of dirt onto the dustpan with the side of her hand. The news was coming on, and she hadn't noticed.

He liked her to sit next to him during the news, and she looked forward to it. It made her feel close to him, especially when he shared his views on national political events. She had quickly learned that he did not intend for it to become a discussion. All she needed to do was nod often to show that she was paying attention.

Despite the pounding of her heart, she slipped in beside him on the couch. It was worth a try, because sometimes after he had yelled at her, if she simply acted as if nothing had happened, he would begin to behave as if it were true. Since the commercial was still on and the news had not yet begun, she picked up a magazine and flipped through it, looking for something that might interest him.

"Here's an article about the police breaking up another one of those prostitution rings in the Klong Toey slum. The things people do—I mean, wouldn't you think those women would be ashamed, getting arrested like that? There's a picture, too."

In truth, Nien had no opinion about the police or the prostitutes or the Klong Toey slum, but it seemed like a subject on which he would have a definite opinion, and when he expressed it, she would have an opportunity to agree with him, which might begin to reverse the direction of the evening.

But that was not to be. When he turned to her and looked at her for the first time since his outburst in the kitchen, she was stunned by the contempt in his eyes. "In any case, little Nien, they seem to have figured out how to make a living, haven't they?" He was quiet for a moment. "I said, *haven't they?*" She nodded. "I should think that a woman who can do nothing competently might well feel ashamed by comparison with a whore, who is competent at least in bed."

Strangely, she felt as though she had been expecting these words, or something like them, for a long time. An unerring slash from the razor tongue, a perfectly aimed thrust that would answer, for all time, any questions that might have lingered in her mind.

She rose and went out the backdoor, began to wash dishes, wept into the tepid water, scrubbing and weeping until her entire body thrummed with grief. She lifted a glass to rinse under the running water, felt it slip between her soapy fingers, tried to catch it, cracked it against the faucet. Some of the fragments went into the pan, some fell to the cement floor at her feet. A stab of pain focused her attention on a finger from which great drops of blood fell steadily. She separated the skin, saw the smooth white of the shaven knuckle, pressed the wound firmly against the palm of her other hand.

Something plucked her attention from the throbbing finger and the shards of glass that lay about her bare feet on the cement floor: the sight of a jing-jook that had been unlucky enough to choose that moment to tumble from the wall, and sever its tail on a large fragment of glass. Tail-less, it could not move and squirmed helplessly in the fine, bright rubble, unable to escape.

In that moment, her husband burst through the door in response to the sound of the breaking glass. She held up the injured hand and blurted out, "I'm sorry, Khun, I'm so sorry—my hand was soapy, I was washing a glass, and it—it just slipped."

Now she did not wish to be as small as an ant. A molecule, she thought, an element, a particle too small to be seen with a husband's naked eye.

"Well, it looks like you fixed one of your little friends," he said, bending over to look at the mutilated jing-jook. "Hand me the sponge."

He took it from her, laid it atop the jing-jook, and stepped on it, grinding it into the cement as if it were an enemy of whose annihilation he had long dreamed.

"Clean it up, little Nien," he said softly and returned to the living room to watch the rest of the news.

She took a spatula from the dishwater, squatted beside the broken glass, lifted the sponge, and scraped the bit of green pulp from the floor.

III

As her husband entered the bedroom after his shower, Nien pulled her consciousness back to this day. He had spent an hour in the bathroom, a precious hour during which she had been able to find a place to hide the burned pot until tomorrow, when he would be at work and she could take it far away. She was relieved to see that, as she had so fervently hoped, the sourness of early morning had given way to a look of mild pride that bespoke the effects of fragrant lather and gentle spray.

He strode to the dressing table and began to comb his hair before the mirror. The sleek wetness of his hair emphasized his shapely head, the straight, narrow line of his nose, the curve of his lips, his strong chin. The tight, gleaming muscles of his shoulder and back flexed with the motion of his arm as he drew the comb back and forth. He was still a wonderfully handsome man.

In the mirror, behind this robust man with his ruddy complexion and fit body, Nien contemplated with dismay her own small face, pale and narrow, the hair that was pulled back hastily, emphasizing the faint lines around her eyes and mouth. A frowsy woman, not yet thirty years old, a woman whose image barely suggested the radiant young girl who had once been pleased to regard herself in a dressing table mirror. How could she expect him to love her?

She crossed the room, stopping just before her hip touched his, and glanced down at the damp, loose knot of the pakomah tied beneath his flat belly. She was intensely aware of the soft fragrance of soap that lingered in the creases of his body; and as he moved, despite herself Nien could not keep her eyes from the bewitching shifting of wet fabric that clearly revealed him. Astonished and disturbed by her feelings, she looked away quickly. But it was too late; he had caught her eye, and the corners of his mouth twitched into a grin.

"Lock the door."

He picked up the pair of freshly pressed slacks she had laid over the back of a chair and began waving them in front of her. "And then you can help me put these on." He continued to wave the pants slowly in front of her face, grinning at her embarrassment, then tossed them aside, untied the knot of his pakomah, and let it drop to the floor.

"Come closer." He seized her hand and began to caress himself with it, firmly guiding her fingers.

He pushed her backward onto the bed, fell over her, penetrated her at once. She wrapped her arms about him tightly, strained against him, greedy to absorb the delicious pleasure with her whole body. Breathless with excitement and the joy of his desire for her, she was barely aware of the whispering in her ear.

"Little Nien had better be sure there's nothing on the stove, or she'll have to get down there and turn it off, little bare-tits Nien, bare-ass naked just like she is now—and who knows who might get a good look at her through the window, little Nien hustling her skinny bare ass around the kitchen . . ."

Whispering, whispering as he always did, words to arouse not her passion but her humiliation, which, reflected in her face, heightened his lust and his pleasure, as she well knew. But today, when he lifted his head to look down into her face, what he saw was not embarrassment but desire. Heedless of his words, she moved against him in a frenzy, clutched him fiercely, then stiffened, held him fast, shuddered.

His face was suffused with confusion and disbelief, and then with outrage, because he had gone too far and now could not hold back. And also because she had cheated him, had grabbed her pleasure from him, and now he could not withhold himself, get out of her, take it away. He was powerless; he could do nothing except to move faster and faster, get it over with as soon as possible. With the last pulse of his own climax, he rolled off her and away. A moment later, he leaned against the headboard, lit a cigarette, and stared fixedly out the window into the branches of the mango tree.

Nien crawled across the bed to him, stroked him tenderly, scarcely daring to breathe lest the sweet moment be threatened in any way.

"Get off me," he said. "Your hands are sticky."

The sun was high now and baked the room. Her thoughts drifted lazily to the clothing she would hang out after breakfast. She blushed to regard the bedspread, wrinkled and soiled. I will have to wash it too, she thought, pleased at the evidence of their passion, two people in love, *no matter what,* heedless of a clean bedspread in the urgency of their need for each other. She rolled over onto her side and propped herself on her elbow. If only she could lie here all day, reliving at her leisure the delicious things he had done to her.

Her hand flew to her throat at the sudden clamor that emanated from the next room. The children were shouting at each other; something metal clattered loudly across the bare floor.

All feeling drained from her body, leaving her hands and feet too numb to move. Tahni leaped to his feet, grabbed the pakomah and knotted it about his waist, pounded on the wall.

"On! Am! Have you gone crazy?"

Incredibly, despite his pounding and shouting, the noise did not diminish.

He fumbled with the lock, flung open the door, and bolted down the hall with his banging-heels walk, threatening to settle their dispute in a way they would not soon forget.

Nien dressed herself with shaking hands, each button a challenge, but she wanted to be slow, wanted to stand forever beside the bed, as rigid as stone, hands and feet so icy that it seemed her blood had ceased to flow and now lay cool and dead in her veins. She could think of only one thing: *the pot, the dreadful ruined pot.*

Nien gazes at the window with longing. Should she run to it, leap from it? Or will it only mock her, withhold death's emancipation, punish her instead with long years of agony in a maimed body? But, no, neither death nor life will be of her choosing. The footsteps of the executioner draw ever nearer.

Oh, help! What escape, what refuge is there for Nien? She cries out, but no sound escapes. Is there no compassionate angel who will save her? She claps her hands to her face, covers her eyes with her fingers, a small scream at last escaping into her sweaty palms as the vision she has already seen in her darkest imaginings fills the doorway: her husband, transformed into a demon, clutching the charred pot she hid beneath her daughter's bed. In a hundred days, a thousand years, he would not enter his children's bedroom, but on this of all days he has, and now, there he stands—holding the pot in one hand, twisting his daughter's ear with the other. The girl dances and writhes in pain beside him, whimpering, biting her lip to keep from crying out. Behind his father and sister, On trembles like a baby bird in a chill wind.

Her husband holds the pot high, swings it back and forth before her, showing off its condition to fullest advantage.

"What is *this*? Can you speak and explain *this* to me?" He strides toward her, still clutching the ear of the agonized girl, and thrusts the pot directly against Nien's face. She turns away. Until this moment, she still has not met his eye, but now she must, for he releases his daughter with a vicious shove to free his hand so that he may clutch his wife's face, jerk it toward him so that she cannot look away.

He pushes her chin up, up so that she must stand on her toes. Her voice is hoarse, bleating; she fears that she will faint. "Khun—oh, Khun! I started the rice porridge, and then I went outside to iron, and I—I forgot about the porridge, I don't know why, and it burned, and I tried and tried to clean it, but I could see that it was too—that scouring would not—clean it . . ."

"Scouring would not *clean* it?" He rubs the pot against her nose.

"Indeed it wouldn't! So what do you do? You decide to trick me, conceal your dirty little secret under a bed like the slovenly, lying slut you are. Yes, that is exactly what you would do, isn't it? Ruin the pot, and then deceive me as if I were as big a fool as you."

"Khun! Please! I promise I'll never, ever do anything like this again. I swear it." She is shaking from head to foot now, moaning her litany of repentance over and over. "If I ever do anything like this again, do anything to me, but this time please believe—" Her voice rises in terror as she cries out, "Oh, Khun, I am so afraid, so afraid!"

It was this despairing cry, this splash of fuel that set all ablaze. He raised the pot above his head and with all his strength hurled it to the floor with a crash that sent On and Am leaping straight into the air. As it went clanging across the floor, he seized Nien's shoulders, lifted her from her feet, and dashed her to the floor. He bent over her and began to pummel her with his fists; but the awkwardness of the position soon frustrated him, and so he began to drag her across the room, his powerful hands clutching her thin arms. He ripped the screen from the window, lifted and tossed her until she felt her lower ribs and the bones of her pelvis crack against the sill. Although she was in terror for her life, she had no strength to resist, could only hang there as about her head the startled sparrows screeched and flapped, frantic at the invasion of their tree. People beneath her walked on, not bothering to turn their faces up to see what had caused the commotion among the birds.

Although no sound had escaped her lips, he clapped his hand over her mouth and hissed into her ear, "Once more, *once more,* and you'll be lying down there with a busted neck, you miserable creature. You cannot *do* anything. You are *not* anything! Will I never be rid of you? Why can't you die before you drive me insane? *Because of you I am going insane!*"

Beneath her terror, beaten and paralyzed with fear, hanging from her bedroom window, held back only by his tormenting hands, she accepted with a certainty that was absolute, even calm, two facts: he was mad, and she would die. Her feet flopped against the wall with the force of the pull that jerked her back through the window. She landed on the floor, heard the crack of her forehead against the boards before she felt the pain. A high *whiw-whiw-whiw* sound filled her head, and the room whirled about her. He had not eased his grip on her arms. She raised her face to him, barely seeing him through the blood that gushed down her forehead and into her eyes, begged him for mercy, but his hatred, which year after year he had allowed to escape in measured doses, would not be contained.

The chaos in her mind gradually was distilled into a single, pure emotion: the will to survive. Tahni, not expecting any resistance now, was taken off guard as suddenly she tore her arm from his grasp and crawled clumsily backward into a corner, beyond thought, beyond pride, beyond shame.

He turned to the children, who stood transfixed near the door. All that had transpired had taken—how long? A minute? Less?

"Don't think of running," he shouted as he lunged toward them, "don't think of it!" They raised their arms to shield their faces, dodged his blows as best they could, stifling their screams so that no one would hear. Although they had never been told that the privacy of their affliction must be protected at all cost, they understood that it was so.

"Oh, Khun—not the children!" Nien cried out, "Please, Khun, no!"

He clutched Am's arm, held her fast. "You are like your mother," he jeered, "you pitiful thing, I should beat you to death, all three of you."

"Papa, I didn't do it!" Am shrilled. "Mama put the pot under my bed, so I took it and put it under On's bed because it wasn't my fault, and anyway—it was his idea! Not me, Papa—I didn't do anything!"

"She *lies,* Papa!" On's back was against the wall, and his arms flapped frantically, the baby bird now in full view of the cat. "I saw her trying to hide it under my bed, but I wouldn't let her, Papa. She's the one who took the ten baht Mama gave us not to tell you about the pot, and she went down the street and spent it on candy right away, but my ten baht is right here, Papa. I knew it was wrong." On reached into his pants pocket, pulled out the wrinkled note, held it out with a quivering hand. "Here, Papa, you can have mine."

Nien stared at her children: Am, crumpled and sobbing beside the door; On, holding out the ten baht note in a fervent, hopeless gesture of appeasement. Her son and daughter, who had shared her breath and blood as they grew beneath her heart. Why, they were— orphans! What did they know of the safety of home, the love of mother and father, loyalty to those they loved? Nothing, nothing at all! What hope had been nurtured in their young hearts? Survival and nothing more.

If they were unnatural children, she was an unnatural woman. What kind of mother was she, what kind of wife? Crouched in the corner, her body bruised and bloodied, as was her spirit, she wept now with knowledge of the entire truth, that she was—and had—nothing, possessed nothing, had nothing to give, not even to them, these children she adored, who now kicked and punched each other as they tried to get through the doorway at the same time. Their small, wildly scampering feet were her last image of them, as they made their escape without a glance in her direction.

Her husband stood for a moment, his chest heaving, then turned and stalked into the bathroom, slamming the door. As she crouched unmoving in the corner, an image formed in her mind, the face of her own mother as she had looked up into Nien's eyes in the last moment of her life.

Above all, her mother had valued compassion for others. This she had not needed to teach to Nien, for it was evident in every action of her own life: compassion was the crowning glory of the daughter of woman, an ideal she had fulfilled to the last breath she drew. This was her dowry to her daughter. She had nurtured, in this beloved daughter, a beautiful tree that would offer cool shade to all who were weary and sun parched, sweet fruit to all who might feel the pangs of hunger. Never did she suspect that the beautiful tree would one day be cut to the ground by one who had rested beneath its verdant shelter and dined upon its fruit only to rise, cool and sated, to heft an axe and strike it down.

Nien could hear her mother's voice: "The woman must be like the hind legs of the elephant, Nien, the husband like the front legs, which, though they must always lead, cannot move the elephant by themselves." And: "A woman must be like a reed, my daughter. In the dark of night, it may be whipped by the fiercest storm, yet we always find it the next morning, swaying in the breeze, glistening with dew drops, its gentle strength a miracle."

The face of her mother faded from Nien's thoughts and was replaced by vague images of the world outside, a world for which she had been too timid, a world full of people who had been too sharp, too quick for her. She never knew what they might do or say; it was like being surrounded by wild animals who were temporarily at rest, their bellies full—for a while. And so she had retreated to the lair of just one wild animal, clinging to the belief that there must be a way to placate him, keep his belly full, his wrath at bay; and thus she and her children might, after all, survive.

Even now, Nien clung to one, saving reality: though she might live under the tyranny of a beast, she herself was not a beast. She was not a dog or a pig that can be driven into a pen and locked up. She had walked into this place of her own free will, eaten and slept and lived with this man, borne his children. She was not a dog or a pig. She had a mind and a spirit, hands and feet. She could unlock the gate of the pen and walk out.

In the early darkness, the pale silver of dawn began to lighten the sky in the window above her. Cautiously, she reached out with aching arms to touch the children who slept on either side of her. Even the slight shift of position sent a searing pain through her ribs. The night before, she had waited for On and Am to fall asleep, then pushed their beds together and crawled between them. She stroked her daughter's warm, smooth back, cherishing the even rise and fall of her breath. At least, he had restrained himself this far; his hand had not fallen as heavily on the children.

He had left the house, not returning until long after midnight. She had lain rigid between the children, knowing from the stumbling of his footsteps that he was, as she had been sure he would be, very drunk. She had forced her breaths to be shallow, even though her heart was pounding in her chest, until she heard him snoring through the wall.

Now, she dressed as quickly as her pain would allow. In the kitchen, she prepared soft-boiled eggs and Ovaltine for On and Am. The charred pot lay in the basin where it had soaked overnight. After he had left the house, she spent an hour on it, though it had done no good at all.

Almost six o'clock. She set the mugs of Ovaltine and the eggs on the table and went upstairs to wake the children, get them into the bathroom to wash and brush their teeth, and help them dress for school. Before long, the *tuk-tuk*[4] driver who picked them up each school day

---

4. "Tuk-tuk" is the onomatopoeic name for a three-wheeled vehicle with a bench behind the driver; an awning covers the vehicle.

would stop before their door, revving the engine, peering impatiently from under the awning of his vehicle. The children would rush out the door, jump onto the plastic-covered bench behind him, and disappear into the traffic for another day in their other world. She envied them.

As On and Am sleepily tied their shoes, she tiptoed down the short hallway, her heart in her throat. The door was ajar, and she was able to slip into the room without touching it. He lay sound asleep beneath the folds of the silky coverlet. She sank to her knees at the foot of the bed, sat back on her heels and studied the graceful planes of his face, his lashes dark against his cheeks. A man sleeping peacefully, she thought, not a demon, just a man. She sat dazed, her hands folded on her thighs, her slender arms bare, mottled with dark bruises above the elbows.

Her eyes moved from his face to the picture that hung above the bed: Tahni and Nien, On and Am, smiling into the camera. The family portrait seemed to float toward her. Something was moving—not the picture, something scarcely glimpsed from the corner of her eye. Was it only her imagination?

No, it was a pair of jing-jooks. They had dashed past the picture, just above it. One chased the other, overtook it, climbed onto its back. Nien rose up on her knees, watching, fascinated. After a moment, the one on top clambered away. Immediately, the one on the bottom scurried after it. Halfway across the wall, with a lightning quick contortion of its lithe body, the first jing-jook turned and bit the other's tail. *Jik-jik-jik!* the injured jing-jook trilled as it dashed into the corner.

Tears stung Nien's eyes. "Don't follow him, you stupid thing! Don't screech and run away into your corner. Have you no shame, no shame?" She could neither bear the sight of the tiny lizard nor take her eyes from it. She swayed back and forth on her knees like a madwoman, her mouth wide open, salty tears falling into it, howling soundlessly. *"Don't follow him! Get out! Get out, you stupid animal!"*

A gentle rustling sound began as the sparrows started their soft descent into the branches of the mango tree. Her husband stirred. Nien rose to her feet, tiptoed to the corner, picked up the broom. Slowly, she opened the screen, leaned out, and began poking the broom among the branches.

"Don't be mad at me, lady, but I really want to know—what is it you do up there?"

It was the bah tong go tawt lady, shielding her eyes with a hand, grinning up at Nien.

Nien smiled back at her, as before, but made no reply. At last the old woman gave up and began to push her cart down the lane. Nien leaned forward, gripping her broom more tightly, and resumed her silent battle with the sparrows.

○ ○   ANCHAN AND "A POT
         THAT SCOURING WILL NOT SAVE"

Anchan (Anchalee Vivathanachai) was born in Bangkok in 1953. She graduated from Chulalongkorn University and received her master of arts degree in English literature from the City University of New York. She currently lives and writes in New York State, where her husband has started a business.

Both her nonfiction writing, including *New York, New York,* a brilliant and hilarious memoir of her first years in New York, and her short stories have been popular and highly praised. Some of her work has also been controversial, especially "A Pot That Scouring Will Not Save."

This selection is included for several reasons: it is a highly realistic exploration of an area of male-female relations that has never been dealt with in such frank terms in modern Thai literature; it displays female attitudes and behaviors that may not be immediately evident (or may not occur at all) to the non-Thai reader; and it represents a benchmark in women's writing in Thailand. Beyond all of this, however, is the relevance of this story to the growing dialogue between Western feminists and women in what is called, for lack of a better term, the third world.

A significant segment of Thai society, representing not only men but also women, dislikes and disapproves of certain subjects (not necessarily sexual but "private") in literature. This is due less to prudery than to the conviction that information that reflects badly on the family—including the family of the nation—ought not to be a subject of *public* discourse.[1] In the case of literature, there is always the possibility that someone is going to write an article or translate and publish a story (or, worse, include it in an anthology), providing a potential source of disapproval or contempt on the part of non-Thais.[2]

---

1. This is discussed in the introduction.
2. However, it is a fact that the emphasis on the public-private dichotomy is also strong *within* Thai society.

It is also particularly offensive to many people when it is a woman who writes fiction or nonfiction containing questionable content: in this case, wife abuse and class hatred that finds expression in the connubial bed. (Some members of the literary community have expressed the opinion that it is *class*, not *sex*, that is the primary subject of this story.)

Why should it be worse for a woman writer to commit these transgressions? Because she has traditionally been considered to have a special responsibility to write stories that are uplifting and improving, and that provide good role models for young Thai women who may read her work. This is changing—largely because of events such as the publication of this very story and the fact that it was recognized via literary prizes, no trifling matter[3]—but the issue is far from resolved.

Anchan insisted upon writing a sexually explicit, harrowing, realistic story, knowing perfectly well that it would be savaged by some critics and disapproved of by some readers. That she wrote it anyway, and that by and large the results were positive, despite some vicious critical attacks,[4] cannot help but encourage other women writers to write short stories and novels they might not otherwise have written, with characters they might not have included, and themes they might not have had the courage to explore.

The non-Thai reader will have several questions about this story. An obvious one, having nothing to do with Thai literature, is: how prevalent is family violence of this degree in Thailand? First, there are both religious and social sanctions against violence. Obviously, despite these sanctions, in Thailand as everywhere else, some men beat their wives. However, there is nothing in Thailand that nearly approaches the publicity that attends the subject in the United States. Two major factors mitigate against this: men have no intention of allowing such a thing to happen, and they continue to have the power

---

3. It is quite possible that the story would not have won any prizes, nor the collection in which it appeared the annual SEAWrite award, were there no women on the selection committees.

4. An entire volume of essays criticizing the individual short stories in *Anmanii hɛ̀ɛng chiiwít*—particularly, this one—appeared immediately following the announcement that this collection had been awarded the SEAWrite award. (Naren Jantaraprasut, *Wípâak rûang sân raangwan siiraay pii 2533* ..."*Anmanii hɛ̀ɛng chiiwít*" / *katáw plùak tua aksɔ̌n khɔ̌ɔng* ... *Anchan* [approximately, "criticizing the short stories that won the SEAWrite award in 2533 / (1990) ... *Jewels of Life* / peeling the words of Anchan"] (Bangkok: Klum Saayleen Wannakaam Suksaa, 1990).

to see that it does not; and women are blamed and blame themselves when they are abused. In the case of a divorce, even when people know that the husband is at fault, it is still common to blame the wife for not knowing how to keep her husband happy.

Writers have a privilege no one else has: they can say exactly what they have observed, and what they feel; they can speak their truths through narrative and dialogue, and then defend themselves against critics with the trump card of fiction. This passage from a short story by Boonlua, translated as "The Enchanting Cooking Spoon" in Herbert P. Phillips's *Modern Thai Literature: An Ethnographic Interpretation*, reflects the traditional view of a wife's role. I include this passage because of its relevance to the psychological profile of Nien in "A Pot That Scouring Will Not Save," and because it illustrates so well the importance of ideal behavior to the woman who has been able to achieve it. She clings to the role partly because she has internalized it and partly because she is good at it, even when she is painfully aware that it is not working for her:

> Phachongchid had carefully prepared all the with-rice dishes and the dessert, had arranged the dining table, the living room, the recreation room, and the patio, had trimmed all the flowers in the garden, and had done everything to make the house a place that was pleasant to the eye and to the heart. And then she dressed herself carefully, not to be too beautiful but to be beautiful in a way that was flawless. Everything that Phachongchid did was done with grace and proportion. To glance at it was to see its beauty. To scrutinize it was to see its suitability. . . . [S]he had been taught never to bore a man with arguments. A man does not want to argue with a woman he loves. If he wants to argue, to sharpen his wits or for some other reason, he will go do this with his male friends. . . . When he comes to see a woman, he comes to obtain happiness.[5]

In this story, written more than thirty years ago, and also in Anchan's story, the ideal behavior so painstakingly learned and practiced unfortunately has ceased to work for the woman; in Boonlua's story, it is because the husband has been educated abroad and wants to establish his new marital relationship on a "modern" footing. He wants stimulating conversation and honesty. Phachongchid, who has no idea what this might mean in practice—or even in theory—is bewildered

5. In Phillips, op. cit., 163.

and frightened. In Anchan's story, the only value of ideal feminine behavior, in Tahni's eyes, is the pleasure he gets from cutting down his limpid, pathetic little wife—an available stand-in for all the people who ever looked down on him,[6] his family, and especially his mother, the kind of woman who might be called an authentic non-ideal Thai woman.[7]

All people, including women, cling to the attitudes and behaviors that they have been taught will assure them first survival and then success in fulfilling the expectations of family and society. If a woman has been able not only to internalize certain socially approved feminine attitudes and behaviors but also perceives a benefit from them, the likelihood of her continuing to hold and to use them is very great indeed. One of the problems Western feminists continue to face in attempting to understand, much less evaluate, the situation of women in the third world, and one for which they have been rightfully criticized by some of the women in whose lives they claim to be interested, is the unwillingness—or the inability despite willingness—to accept the fact that a woman in another culture may never appreciate the logic that seems so obviously sensible and useful to the Western feminist.[8]

Some Western readers of this translation have also suggested that it is about class, not sex. Because this is a reasonable supposition, I asked Anchan to comment on the subject, and I found so many ele-

---

6. Some Thais have told me that they think Tahni is meant to be Chinese; if so, the significance of such an intention is beyond the scope of this brief analysis. However, an interesting, related fact is that during the 1980s a group of Chulalongkorn University students produced their own version of Tennessee Williams's *Streetcar Named Desire*, in which Stanley is a lower-class Chinese, Stella and Blanche are impoverished Thai gentry, *phûu dii kàw* (i.e., old *phûu dii*, from families with well-known names), and the action takes place in a tenement on Yaowarat Road, a commercial section of Bangkok largely populated by ethnic Chinese. The play was a great success.

7. By the term *authentic, non-ideal*, I mean a woman who is undeniably Thai in every respect—a market woman such as Tahni's mother, for example, who may have been a villager, that quintessential example of "a real Thai," yet no one's vision of the ideal Thai woman with fine manners and lovely ways. Thai literature is filled with women, at all social levels, who represent one or another point on the spectrum of non-ideal identity or behavior (viz., servants, spinster aunts, homely best friends), but until the last two decades, such a woman was rarely featured as the main character of a short story or novel.

8. Few of the Thai women with whom I have discussed this subject seem aware of the fact that only a minority of American women would describe themselves as feminists; the word *feminist* is frequently understood to be virtually synonymous with "Western woman" and fully relevant only to her.

ments of her answer fascinating that I decided to include her remarks almost verbatim:

> The story is about sex, not class! The woman in the story was brought up to be a good woman. And everybody ignored her true self. She thought that she herself was a good person, because she never knew her true identity. She had natural sexual desires, and for certain reasons in Thai society, the only way for a woman to have access to sex is to have a husband. Men can do whatever they want, but affairs are beyond [Thai women's] thoughts. She has to cling to him. Her nature is, she is weak and dependent, indecisive because she is the only daughter of the family, pampered all her life; and beyond that, she desires sex, but she can have just this husband. She's afraid, that's her character; otherwise, she might find some other way to satisfy her sexual desires; she might have second thoughts.
>
> The husband is not evil; he's just a selfish, insensitive, very callous person. When he married her, he was a confident male, and he instinctively wanted someone to support that, by contrast. He wanted a feminine, quiet woman who was his opposite; we say, white makes the black look blacker. But when they live together, it's another story. He realizes that he doesn't want that feeling anymore, that contrast; he's finished with that already. He wants a smarter woman who will be a partner, help support the family. He has to see her weakness day in and day out—she's so indecisive, she has to obey him like a dog—and it makes him feel disturbed. He's just a simple self-centered man and terribly disappointed in her. So he becomes abusive to get revenge, even looking at her makes him mad, her pathetic weakness. What he wants now is a selfish, pushy woman like himself, not the quiet feminine woman he wanted when he was younger, when he married her.
>
> I wanted to show that [Thai] society is not fair in terms of sexual desire. This woman has strong sexual desires, and she cannot escape them or the man. If society were fair, women would have equal sexual possibilities. There is no hope for these two.
>
> The pot is a common Thai symbol for the female sex; a [crude Thai] expression for having sex is "to beat the pot."[9] The burning pot in this story is her burning sexuality, which is hopeless. Nothing can mend this woman or save her.[10]

9. *Tii* (to beat) *mɔ̌ɔ* (pot).

10. Anchan, telephone conversation with author, October 1, 1995. I do not suggest that there are no other possible readings besides the one Anchan has given. However, it is unlikely that the non-Thai reader would perceive these elements of the story without having read her explanation.

The process of trying to understand another woman's culture and the realities of her life through her eyes is extremely difficult and one in which the reader must accept success as something measured in inches, on a journey of countless miles. Anchan, with "A Pot That Scouring Will Not Save," has introduced the reader to Nien, a woman who is doing what she knows a woman is supposed to do and suffering for it. "A Pot That Scouring Will Not Save" was written to tell one woman's story, not to provide solutions to the problem it so brilliantly portrays. But, if the first step in solving a problem is to describe it exactly, Anchan has taken the first such step by describing family abuse in Thailand. And in so doing, she has accomplished more than opening doors for other woman writers; she has cut doors into walls where they did not exist before.

When She Was a Major Wife

Subha Devakul

This humorous short story of the 1970s follows a
jealous wife as she follows her husband around Bangkok.

Quite unexpectedly one day, news came to Plaeng-pin that Bop, her
husband, had altered her status from wife to major wife.

It is a fact that most women, once they get their hands on a duly
signed marriage license, have every intention of living not merely as
a wife but as *the* wife, and this is a state that they expect to remain
permanent. Plaeng-pin was no exception. Some of these women,
Plaeng-pin included, believe that it is unnecessary to make this expectation known to the husband, especially when there has been no
sign, thus far, of a threat to the status of solitary wifehood. And, thus
far in Bop and Plaeng-pin's marriage, there had been not a glimmer
of such a sign.

"Ooy, Plaeng-*pin,* you are so *dumb!*" said her friend at the office. It
was she who had brought the evil news of seeing Bop with another
woman, and who had driven it home with words that stabbed like
little knives. "No matter what that man says, you believe him. And
what do you get for your see no evil, hear no evil? Your darling Bop
cheats on you while you keep your nose in your work and bring home
your paycheck."

Another woman assumed the role of cheerleader.

"I saw it coming from the beginning, Plaeng-pin, when you got the
second car. That's the way it begins. You go your way, he goes his.
How do you know where he goes with his car? Before you know it,
he's at a hotel with curtains around the parking spaces."[1]

The story appears in *Baang sùan khɔ̌ɔng hǔa jay* (Some parts of the heart), published by
Praphansan, Bangkok, in 1978. The original title, which has almost exactly the same
meaning in Thai, is "Mûa təə pen mia lǔang."
    1. A "privacy hotel," which exists for the purpose of assignations.

Plaeng-pin was unwilling to believe in the possibility of Bop's infidelity. So she took the matter to a better friend, looking for words of wisdom and comfort.

"Ooy, Plaeng-pin! I say it is two hundred percent possible. That woman at your office is right. One marriage, two cars, you work in opposite corners of Bangkok . . . and look at his job—advertising and public relations! The perfect job for cheating on a wife."

"Why?"

"He has an excuse to come home from work any time, at any hour of the night. He goes to see someone here, he goes to 'entertain' someone there . . . who knows what he's really up to?"

Plaeng-pin went to work and, try as she might, all day she could not stop hearing her friend's words. What *was* he up to? At first she felt as if her heart were being poked, then as if it were pulled with little jerks, and, finally, as if it were beating—*pahng-pahng-pahng*—like a war drum.

After all, it was true that Bop's job in advertising and public relations allowed him to justify every occasion upon which he had to return home late. Or not at all.

And then there was the onerous matter of the curfew.[2]

What better excuse could a man hope for than a curfew? Many were the times when the phone had rung—*griiiing! griiing!*—just as she was preparing his dinner, and it was Bop. Calling from a hotel— *a hotel!*

"Plaeng-pin, I'm still with this client, and now it's too late to get home before the damned curfew. I'll just have to stay at the hotel and come home first thing in the morning to change. Don't misunderstand, darling."

And she hadn't misunderstood. Or so she had thought. All those times, Plaeng-pin had believed him. But now—she wondered whether, by agreeing not to misunderstand what he said, instead of understanding what it was that he was probably doing but didn't want her to understand, she had not, after all, misunderstood.

Plaeng-pin and Bop had been married for nearly three years. They conducted their life together in the "new age" style, which is to say

---

2. Due to political demonstrations against military rule.

that they lived on their own instead of with her parents or his. They bought a house; both worked to pay off the mortgage, and they had agreed that for the first five years of their marriage, they would have no children.

"We should have a home of our own before we start thinking about children," Bop had said, and Plaeng-pin, after some private feelings of ambivalence on the subject, agreed. Besides, every day in the office she had to listen to the unceasing complaints of the women who did have children.

"In the old days they used to say that the mother and father were poor seven years for each child. Seven years! Nowadays it's more like twenty!" And so on and on.

The subject of instant and permanent poverty caused by children was *hit*[3] subject number two in the office. But hit subject number one was, and always would be, minor wives.

Plaeng-pin had listened to the tales of children and poverty and of minor wives every single day since she had started her job. At first, she had been amused, but at last she became bored and finally irked by both subjects. She had congratulated herself on her good luck in having no opportunity to amuse, bore, and irk other people with tales of her own. And now, like a bolt of lightning from the sky, came the scurrilous suggestion that her Bop had a minor wife.

Could it be true?

"With my own eyes, I saw your Bop walking arm in arm with the same girl on two different occasions."

So what? Bop had told her himself that sometimes he went to meetings with women from his office.

Yet she could not stifle a small sensation of alarm when another woman added, "Oh, I've seen them too. Laughing, whispering . . . well, you can be sure he never noticed me. I thought of telling you, Plaeng-pin, but you know me, I'm not one to start something between a husband and wife, so I just kept it to myself. If she hadn't told you first, I would never have breathed a word. Never a word."

Several other women who never would have breathed a word now

---

3. The word *hit*, borrowed from English (as in "*hit* song" or "the idea was a big hit!"), is commonly used; there is no Thai term that is exactly equivalent.

rose from their desks like a crack platoon advancing. This one had seen them eating lunch, that one had seen them sitting in a car, talking. Another had seen them ambling through a market together, with their heads close, laughing.

And then one of the women moved majestically from the rear of the ranks to drop the clincher: she had seen them going into a hotel.

Plaeng-pin struggled with her emotions. She told herself that Bop would never, never do such a thing. *Pahng-pahng-pahng!* It was no good. Her heart would not cooperate. In addition to the *pahng-pahng-pahng,* she felt as though someone had lit a tiny fire beneath her breastbone.

That evening, in a manner that she tried to make sound offhand, she asked Bop about the girl.

He frowned. "A girl? What? A girl who's seen with me all over town?" Bop looked very confused and totally, thoroughly innocent. Then his expression brightened. "Oh—a *girl* . . . I'm sure it was my friend's little sister. She does ad listings for one of the radio stations and brings them to our office. Hah! That's what you were worried about? Forget it."

After a moment, he frowned again, ever so slightly, and said, "Plaeng-pin, suspicion isn't becoming, you know."

There was something in Bop's tone of voice that made Plaeng-pin feel very uneasy. Something that sounded almost like—well, like anger.

Since she had fallen in love with Bop, they had never had a single argument or been angry with each other. Now, when she saw that she had made him angry, she felt remorse and made up her mind that she would never, ever be suspicious of him again, no matter what those women in the office said. He was right; it was definitely unbecoming.

"Ooy, Plaeng-pin!" her friend said, shaking her head sadly. "And just like that, you believed him, you poor little thing. Men are so clever. Like a parade of turtles burying their eggs in the sand and then digging them up again when the coast is clear. Do you think any man would be so crazy as to tell his own wife about his other women?"

"And when you believe their lies," another added, "they laugh behind your back."

"And then they go on their way!" said a third, sidling over to

Plaeng-pin's desk. "Just like my sister's husband. Everybody told her he had a minor wife, but she wouldn't believe them, oh no. Then he dropped dead, and when the will was read, there stood his other children with their hands out. Heart disease and bad nerves have been eating her up since that day."

Plaeng-pin's resolve crumbled, and at last she began to consider taking certain steps that, only a few weeks earlier, she would not have believed herself capable of. Suspicion, she was learning, is a good teacher.

Ordinarily, Plaeng-pin rose before Bop, made his breakfast, and then drove to work. Her office kept government hours, but Bop could go to the office at any time, since his company assessed its employees' worth solely in terms of the amount of business they brought in and didn't care about hours.

Now, Plaeng-pin began a new routine. Each morning, while he was still in bed and before she left for work, Plaeng-pin gave Bop's car a thorough going-over. First, she checked the glove compartment for little feminine artifacts. Then his Kleenex box. Bop and Plaeng-pin both kept a box of Kleenex on the front seat of their cars. She scrutinized his daily to see whether an unusual number of tissues had been used since the day before.

One morning, as she squatted beside Bop's car, feeling around under the floor mat on the passenger side, she was startled by a noise. It was Bop, standing at the kitchen door.

"What are you doing out there?" he called sharply.

Stupefied, frozen in a squatting position with one hand holding up the floor mat and the other hand underneath it, Plaeng-pin felt the surge of panic that is experienced only by those who have never done anything wrong, and who have been caught in the midst of a first offense. But when she peeked over the car door and saw Bop's face contorted with anger, saw his bulging eyes and his furiously knit brow, anger drove out panic, and she remembered the words of the women in the office.

"I know that you men have many ways of making women shut up and not ask about other women!" she said, her voice shaking but surprisingly strong. "You put on an honest face. You deny everything and pour smoke all over the place, even swearing that you have no other women—'I have no one! I have no one!'—Hah! And when we don't believe you, you change your strategy. You pretend to be angry, you frown and yell so that we will be—*intimidated*. Well, not me. I am *not intimidated!*"

Plaeng-pin paused for breath. "I have a right to look," she continued, "to see whether some girl has accidentally left something in my husband's car."

Bop's eyebrows lifted almost to his hairline. "Plaeng-pin, you are mad."

In the past, she and Bop had often used this word playfully. They had giggled and teased each other: "Ooh, you are *mad*—" Certainly, they had never said it through clenched teeth, their faces red with anger.

"Plaeng-pin, listen to me. You had better watch out and stop listening to those interfering, big-mouthed gossips in your office. If you keep this up, this marriage could very well—collapse!"

"Collapse!" she repeated after him as he stalked back into the house and slammed the door. "Yes, let it collapse! If it's that or having everyone laugh behind my back because I was a fool and my husband had a minor wife and I was too stupid to do anything about it, then that's just fine. Let it collapse!"

So saying, Plaeng-pin picked herself up off the ground, marched to her own car, and drove to work.

She would not give up as easily as that. Let him get angry and try to intimidate her. It wouldn't work anymore. At night, she checked his pockets and sniffed his shirts. When he went to the bathroom, she quickly searched his briefcase and wallet.

Inevitably, one evening while he was looking for something in his briefcase, Bop realized the truth. And this time, his rage exceeded anything that had gone before. But Plaeng-pin was fearless, having learned from her friends at the office more of the kinds of tricks he might employ.

"You have no cause to be angry," she said smoothly, "because, if you are innocent, you have nothing to hide from me."

To this, Bop made no reply. He simply stared at her for a moment, gave her the bulgy-eyed look to which she was now immune, and stormed out of the house.

That evening, Bop did not return home, and there was no telephone call to tell her where the curfew had stranded him. He repeated this behavior several times within the next few weeks.

"Of course!" said one of the women at the office. "He pretends to be so angry that he doesn't even want to come home, and then he spends the night with his little friend."

The experts agreed.

"Still, I don't know," said Plaeng-pin. "It isn't as if I had *caught* him with someone. I still don't *know* that he has a minor wife."

"It isn't so hard to get proof," said one, "and until you catch them red-handed, arguing with him is just banging your head on the wall. When you catch them—you know, *in the act*—well, that will be another matter. A man becomes as tame as a kitten, then!"

It sounded good to Plaeng-pin. Bop as tame as a kitten was infinitely preferable to her giving up and his laughing behind her back to his heart's content.

She became a spy in earnest. After work, she followed him in her car. Before leaving the office, she called him. Sometimes she would identify herself to the receptionist; sometimes she would get a friend to call and ask to speak to him on business. If Bop was not in, the friend would ask where he had gone. If they told her, Plaeng-pin would know where to look.

But most of the time, when she got to the place, she would find Bop alone in his car. Or with a male friend. Sometimes he was with a woman but never the same woman twice.

"He knows better," her friends said. "He knows you're watching him now. He's not stupid, your Bop."

Plaeng-pin agreed. Of course, Bop wasn't stupid. If he were, how could he have got a job in advertising and public relations?

Plaeng-pin spied on.

And then, early one evening, as Plaeng-pin was following her husband's car at a careful distance, he pulled up to the curb and opened the door on the passenger side. A young woman who had been standing on the sidewalk hopped into the car. Plaeng-pin couldn't see the girl's face clearly. She didn't dare get nearer or Bop would see her. She had to catch him red-handed. This girl exactly matched a description one of the women in the office had given her. Plaeng-pin's heart raced. "Tall and slim, with long hair, and very young, like a schoolgirl . . ."

Pahng-pahng-pahng! Although Plaeng-pin felt the blood rush from her head, leaving her almost too dizzy to steer, she forced herself to follow them through traffic.

Bop's car turned into the parking lot of a hotel.

But this was a first-class hotel, not the kind that has curtains around the parking spaces. Anyway, what reason could he invent for taking this girl to a first-class hotel at dusk?

"Oh—now I see it!" she said to herself. "First, he takes her to the first-class hotel." She gripped the steering wheel and jabbed the accelerator with her foot. "Makes the big impression. Orders the expensive food. Then what? Then they go from the restaurant into the hotel bar. And then? They order drinks. They listen to the singer. They dance together, they get all worked up—and then? *Then,* they leave and go to the hotel with the curtains around the parking spaces!"

Plaeng-pin's vision began to blur, and suddenly she understood the meaning of blind jealousy. The next thing she knew, she had jammed on her brakes, leaped from her car, and was clutching Bop's left arm in a fierce grip. The young woman who was tall and slim and had long hair and looked like a schoolgirl stared at her in horror, her eyes wide. Plaeng-pin heard herself making high, screechy noises that were barely recognizable as words. She saw Bop's expression change from astonishment to rage. She saw people turning to see what was going on, until a crowd had gathered and was watching them as with one eye.

The result of this occasion was that, on the following morning, Bop and Plaeng-pin drove, in separate cars, to the district office, where they filed divorce papers.

Plaeng-pin had given him the ultimatum. "Choose. It's her or me. If you love her so much, then fine, it's over. We'll get a divorce."

But Bop would not talk at all—not about whether he loved the young woman with the long hair who looked like a schoolgirl or how much or whom he would choose.

Bop had responded with a single word: "Agreed."

They split the proceeds of their home and divided everything they owned. Plaeng-pin took her things to her parents' house and moved back with them. Bop packed a suitcase and moved in with a friend.

And now the women at the office became very quiet. Strangely enough, not one of them seemed to have an opinion about the divorce.

Two months later, as Plaeng-pin was walking down the street, she was astonished to see, walking toward her, the young woman who was tall and thin and had long hair and looked like a schoolgirl. Plaeng-pin tried to escape, but it was too late.

"Oh, so it is you!" the girl said. "I was so sad to hear about—well, about your divorce."

Had she no shame?

"I have to tell you," the girl continued, "you made a big mistake. What happened was—well, let me explain the whole thing. You see, I work in Bop's office, and he's a friend of my older brother's. Last year, before I came back from the States, I married an American. I came back to Bangkok before he did, and that night—the night when, you know—when you saw us, I was going to meet him at that hotel. I didn't want to walk around in the lobby all by myself,[4] and so Bop was sweet enough to offer to go with me. You know, to meet my husband . . ."

Plaeng-pin stood speechless.

"I mean, you misunderstood everything . . ."

Plaeng-pin continued to stand like a stone.

"You didn't have any reason to be mad at him. Well—anyway, there's no way you'll get him back now, because—you know that friend he went to stay with, when you separated? Well, Bop has become very fond of a friend's little sister after all. But it isn't me. Still, I'm sorry about everything . . ."

As the girl turned away, Plaeng-pin could barely see her, because her eyes were blurred, just as they had been on that night. But this time, blind jealousy had nothing to do with it.

o   o   SUBHA DEVAKUL AND
        "WHEN SHE WAS A MAJOR WIFE"

[handwritten: able to express her own emotions, jealousy anger -]

Subha Devakul was born in 1928 in Bangkok and has been writing for nearly fifty years. Her short stories and novels, which she writes under her own name, are notable for their range of settings, subjects, and characters. Subha has been particularly successful as a writer of screenplays and television scripts. The author of nearly a hundred short stories and dozens of novels and screenplays, she is one of the few writers in Thailand who is able to make a living through full-time writing.

4.   She does not want to be mistaken for a prostitute.

"When She Was a Major Wife" is a story plainly devised to entertain. It is a humorous spoof of the lives of a couple of Bangkok yup-
pies, Plaeng-pin and her husband, Bop, whom she suspects of having
taken a mistress, or minor wife. A century ago, even fifty years ago,
the extended family in which a major wife (almost always the first and
eldest wife) and several minor wives lived more or less amicably
within one large compound was the norm. While this situation still
occurs, it is far less common today, and the term *minor wife* is far more
likely to connote a mistress or lover.[1]

Bop works in advertising; Plaeng-pin goes to a government office
every morning in her own car. They make a good deal of money and
are putting off having children until they have even more. Egged on
by her coworkers, against her better judgment Plaeng-pin succumbs
to their suspicions that Bop is not the mild-mannered husband he
seems but a conniving liar and cheat. It is all very silly and reminiscent of the television sitcoms the author is so successful at writing.
Indeed, American or European readers will have no difficulty imagining some version of this story on television in their own country.

However, Western readers will not necessarily comprehend this
story as Thai readers do, or laugh at the same things, or have the same
reactions to it—or even, perhaps, agree on what it is about. Thai readers I spoke with said that the moral of this story is that Plaeng-pin
was a fool to risk her marriage just because her husband might have
had a minor wife. So what if he *did?* She would still have been his major wife. When asked the same question, non-Thais who read the translation thought that Plaeng-pin was very silly; however, some women
offered the additional opinion that if a man is indeed guilty of adultery, the ends justify the means. While they focused on the probabil-
ity of Bop's guilt, no Thai reader seemed interested in the subject of
Bop's guilt; they tended to think that the author was making fun of
women who risk their marriage just because their husband might have
a lover, and who abandon their feminine dignity.

My initial reason for including this selection was to provide balance to such unremittingly tragic stories as "A Pot That Scouring Will
Not Save," "Greenie," or "Deaf Sim." Additionally, Subha's farcical

---

1.   A Thai woman may not sue for a divorce on grounds of adultery. Society does
not denounce a man for having minor wives, but he will be more respected if he provides for his children by these women than if he evades his responsibilities.

tale of ill-advised suspicion is a good example of the somewhat neglected subject of women's humorous writing in Thailand. In fact,
humor is a great staple of Thai fiction writing in general, although this
is not reflected in the majority of short stories and novels that have
been translated into other languages. Most Thai literature available
in translation reflects the attitudes and objectives of politically active
leftist writers with ties to Western intellectuals. There is nothing
wrong with this, but it does have the effect of canonizing certain kinds
of writing while ignoring others. Humorous writing by Thai women
is one such underrepresented segment of modern fiction.

Several Thai women writers are willing, even eager, to use humor
in order to comment on life as they see it and to expose previously
suppressed grievances, not only to other females but also to males, at
least some of whom may be expected to read their work. Not surprisingly, it is the women who choose to employ humor who also seem
the most eager to reject or at least to question the authenticity of the
culturally defined ideal woman—a woman who would, whatever her
suspicions of her husband, demurely look the other way and hope
that his gratitude for her fine behavior would ensure her continuing
security.

While the weighty subjects of women's rights, opportunities, and
disadvantages are the subtext of such stories, they are woven from
the small, not ostensibly political details of ordinary lives. They ex-
aggerate to the point of farce women's disappointed hopes and discouraging failures, their unmanageable desires and bad decisions.

Besides Subha Devakul, women writers whose work frequently includes humor are the late Suwanee Sukhontha, Krisna Asoksin, and
Sri Dao Ruang, among others. Each uses humor in her own way. In
Suwanee's work, it is never the point of a story; laughter just seems
her natural response to stress. No sooner has she apprehended some
injustice or catastrophe in a story than she sees something that strikes
her as funny; it is the giggle one struggles to suppress at the funeral.
After describing her outrage at seeing a crowd of children ignore the
fact that a dead man is blocking their path to a roast chicken[2] stand,
so that they almost have to crawl over him to get to their destination,
she suddenly goes off on a tangent about the chickens: "Everyone says
the 'kay yaang' at those stands is delicious, but I can't help thinking

2. *Kàay yâang.*

of the chickens as they were, full of life, skinny of shin, cheerfully stalking about, pecking and gabbling their way through a life that is short at best. Some of them may never have realized that they were alive at all—some of them may even have been virgins!"[3] Not only is this a classic expression of the earthy variety of Thai humor, but it is also classic Suwanee.

Krisna Asoksin's humor, which is very well exemplified in the excerpts from one of her novels that are included in this section, is based upon the folly of striving for things one would be much better off not having—a place in the firmament of high society, for example, or luxuries one has done nothing to earn or deserve.

The mocking tone of "When She Was a Major Wife" exemplifies the Thai love of sarcasm and cutting people down to size: "And . . . you believed him, you poor little thing," the gossip at the office says to Plaeng-pin. "Men are so clever. Like a parade of turtles burying their eggs in the sand and then digging them up again when the coast is clear."

A good deal of physical imagery is also carefully used for humorous effect, for example, when Plaeng-pin is caught, "[s]tupefied, frozen in a squatting position with one hand holding up the floor mat and the other hand underneath it." She does not mean to abandon all dignity; on the contrary, she longs to see Bop "tame as a kitten," but the reader knows that Plaeng-pin, having abandoned the behavior that any good wife would have, will come to no good end.

The theme of the jealous wife is handled in a very similar, also humorous fashion by Sri Dao Ruang, in her short story "Sita Puts out the Fire."

> Sita was sure that this woman he had found must be beautiful—in the way women who worked out in the world were beautiful. In fact, she was probably—*oh, no!* She was probably—*an intellectual!* And what was she, Sita, by comparison? *A plain old up-country factory worker,* that's what! The kind of woman who washes her face and combs her hair once a day, maybe twice, a woman whose clothes have never known the heat of an iron, a woman who never, during the course of a whole day, gives one thought to *"two-way powder, 280 baht a box!"*

---

3. From my translation of "Wan thîi dèɛd sǔay" ("On a Cloudy Morning"). The original Thai version was first published in the magazine *Lalana* in 1979, and appears in a collection of the author's work entitled *Baang-thii phrûng-níi ja plian jay* (Perhaps tomorrow I'll change my mind), published by Duang Taa, Bangkok, 1983.

... She sobbed miserably, silently into her pillow. The flames of her hurt and anger billowed and subsided, fanned by awful thoughts that she could not suppress. ... She was forced to admit that she would have been spared these dreadful thoughts and suspicions, had she not discovered his secret by sneaking into his diary—*a thing a truly good wife would never have done.*[4]

While it may be true that Thai women do not expect much in the way of fidelity from men—for women have been told all their lives that men's nature mitigates against it—Subha can write, "It is a fact that most women, once they get their hands on a duly signed marriage license, have every intention of living not merely as *a* wife but as *the* wife, and this is a state that they expect to remain permanent." From a perspective of despair, the same plot could easily have been written as a tragedy; but Subha chose to laugh.

---

4. From my translation of Sri Dao Ruang's short story "Sǐidaa dàp fay" (Sita puts out the fire), in a work in progress, "Married to the Demon King." The story originally appeared in 1985, in Thai, in *Lalana.*

Sai-roong's Dream of Love

Sri Dao Ruang

In this humorous 1984 short story, Sri Dao Ruang
lays bare the extraordinary dreams of an ordinary woman.

Sai-roong was an ordinary woman, except for her dreams. She was a
superb dreamer, an artist. They were dreams of extraordinary vividness and filled with meaning for her. Each night, as her household
slept soundly, Sai-roong proceeded to the elaborate, secret productions
in which she played two roles: the star and also the audience.

Her dreams were, she knew, the source of her strength. They permeated and energized her. Life rioted in her dreams, myriad scenes
and countless stories in which Sai-roong often changed form entirely,
becoming pure spirit in pursuit of the subjects of her own imagination. There had been times of late when she would wake in the morning so exhilarated that she could scarcely crawl out of bed.

Once upon a dream, Sai-roong fell in love.

It was true love, and Sai-roong's love was unique. The love she felt
toward the man of her dreams was profound. And not only profound
but a secret, mysterious love, and so it remains to this day. Even her
husband is jealous.

When a young man and a young woman meet, when each understands the desire of the other—when, like drops of mist, they melt together and are one . . . well, that was the sort of thing it was. Sai-roong's
heart was filled with gladness in those days or rather those nights; she
felt inundated, flooded with love as she kissed and caressed the face
of the young man with the line of stubble that was so sharp and pleas-

This story, "Făn rák khɔ̌ɔng Săay Rúng" (the meaning of the title is identical to the English title given here), appears in the collection of Sri Dao Ruang's stories entitled *Bàt
prachaachon* (Personal identity card), published by Met Sai, Bangkok, in 1984. The translation is slightly abridged. Another translation of this story, more abridged and also
expurgated, appeared in the September 1992 issue of *Sawatdee*, the magazine of Thai
International Airways.

ing above his upper lip. Had she ever really looked at eyes before? Not like these eyes, so charged with desire and meaning that she felt an overwhelming desire to be . . . vanquished; to be . . . senseless, warm, willing, and eager to feel her lips, her own delectable and smoldering lips, crushed with abandon.

The morning after, Sai-roong fought valiantly to remain in this electrifying dream of love, struggled with all her being to return to her garden of love, her lair of lust. *Please* . . . just another minute, one second, that is all she asks. To murmur a word of parting, to look once more upon the beloved face. But it is no use. However deep her love, however incorrigible her infatuation, she must accept the truth: this man cannot be dragged from the dreaming world into the waking world. (And if he could, she reflects, it would be inconvenient, and that was a fact.)

Sai-roong gathered her strength and rose from her bed. In the mirror, she blushed to see it in her face: yes, the sweet agony of desire. A suspicion entered her mind: in the waking world, could there be others like her? As she stepped from her bedroom, her eyes drifted toward the window, the path, the gate beyond. And what she saw made her uncombed hair stand on end, her skin tighten and shiver. Swiftly, she drew back, hiding her unwashed face behind the door.

What could have shocked her so? Only the sight of the new neighbor, the very young gentleman next door, striding past her gate. She was sure! How could she not be? Why, this was the very man from whose ardent embrace she had been dragged at dawn!

How could she not have realized it? There he lived, so near and yet so . . . unconcerned. Had he given her so much as a sidewise glance since moving in?

No.

Sai-roong breathed out a patient sigh. After all, what had she to blame him for? How could he possibly know that he had walked into her dreams? (Much less, what he had done when he got there.) It wasn't his fault. She turned back into her bedroom, pleased that her husband had gone into the bathroom. She picked up her pillow, gently hugged it, then threw herself down on the bed and tossed back and forth a few times. When she got back up, she felt much better. She thrust her arms and legs out vigorously. Everything seemed fresh and beautiful. She would be troubled by nothing today, by no one. A chord of natural music welled up within her, the internal music that might cause a woman to break out in tears while her household apprehends her joyous sobs in consternation. But not Sai-roong, who would rather keep it to herself.

Looking about her, she became aware of the embarrassing yet genuine fact that every item in and around her house, from the toilet to the front gate, had assumed a new importance. She would go now to wash her face, as soon as her husband got out of there, until it gleamed. And the house—everything must be cleaned meticulously. After all, he was a neighbor. One never knew when he might . . . enter.

She turned and inspected herself in the mirror, from head to toe. She was careful not to flatter herself. The face, she decided, was rather pretty. Other parts might not be as good. As for the house, however, it was too plain, a downright *homely* home. It no longer satisfied her.

The young man had not lived next door very long. Sai-roong had barely met him—and then, *that dream!* Quite astonishing, really. They had never spoken; their eyes had never met. Therefore, his image was in some ways cloudy in her mind and had been so in her dream, as well. This, she decided, was satisfactory. He was not a young man with strong features that would announce themselves to a young woman, causing her to turn around and have another look. No, it was definitely his role, in the theater of her dreams, that made him interesting. His performance.

It was at this time that Sai-roong began to change. Her family and neighbors could hardly fail to notice that whereas Khun Sai-roong had been a woman who heretofore had gone out to work every day wearing a nicely cut dress, invariably the proper color of the day,[1] these days she went out the door and down the street wearing big-flowered prints, short skirts with fringed hems—and once she had even been seen wearing a polo shirt and pants that were tight all the way up and down her legs. Most of her hair, which she had always worn long, suddenly disappeared, replaced by a short style that anyone would recognize who has seen the Princess of Wales. She worked on her eyebrows until she thought they looked very like Jane Fonda's and darkened her eyelashes, then pushed them up until they curled, disdaining the little rod in the mascara tube in favor of a little brush,

---

1. Traditionally, each day has its own color. Although wearing the "color of the day" is not nearly as important as it once was, most women still know which colors are related to which days of the week.

so that they would look natural. Sai-roong decided against eye shadow and regarded her nose approvingly. In truth, her nose was her best facial feature, straight and narrow, and she was a bit vain about it. Just—a touch of lip gloss—*yes*. Finally, the earrings, the little hoops. In the mirror, she practiced making the wide-eyed, sparkly look of the models in the women's magazines. Ooy! She grinned at herself.

He would be impressed. No one could think of the new, improved Sai-roong as—as what? Oh, dear . . . the expression that inexplicably floated into her mind caused the wide-eyed sparkly look to be eclipsed by a frown. It was *yai gae raeng tung*—a raggedy old lady ready for the vultures.

The kinds of fastidious attentions to body and face that Sai-roong had found irksome and boring before, now became the hit activities of her evening. She would do everything for him; she would never be tired or discouraged; she would always be willing, always eager. Everything from the heart and with love.

A day became a week; a week, a month; a whole year passed. In Sai-roong's dreams, the intimacy between them not only failed to wane, but it raged.

In the waking world, they met only at a distance, and never a word passed between them. On an ordinary day, both of them went to work. If he left his house first, Sai-roong watched him, stroked his back with her eyes, caressed his shoulders with her smiles, gloated happily behind her window. But there were times when Sai-roong stepped out of her front door just as he opened his, and then she could not avoid walking right past him. Those were dreadful times; they played havoc with her emotions. Her heart would race, skip beats; her blood would rush hotly to her face while her hands and feet became cold and sweaty.

She had practiced the way in which she would sail gracefully by him, head held high, aloof; the way she would walk with the slightest sway in her hips, as if she were crossing a stream on a narrow plank, carefully placing one dainty foot before the other, her neck slightly extended, her eyes radiant, her expression mild and sweet, yet holding a definite suggestion of straightforwardness, of sincerity and strength.

But all was to no avail. When she came face-to-face with him, she would shrink away, evade his glance, stare into her paper bag of groceries or at her handbag until she tripped over a stone and staggered forward, overcome with shyness, grinning foolishly. She became so excited each time she knew she would be near him that sometimes, seeing him from a distance, through her window, she decided that it was easier simply to stay indoors until he was gone. This happened with depressing frequency.

Nonetheless, Sai-roong clung joyously to her new feelings. Their love was a profound mystery, a precious secret. And it was all hers. No one knew. No one meddled in it.

One night, she met him in a new story (the plots tended not to vary a great deal). In the new dream, he was the same, of course, yet she could sense a new flowering, along with the addition of some other, rather amazing events. If their previous assignations had been paradisal, suffice to say that on this night paradise itself shuddered.

After this, certain images of him were ever in her mind, even on days when she was so busy and harried that you would have thought nothing could distract her from her tasks. Sitting on the bus on her way to work, if Sai-roong saw an accident along the road, she would imagine that he was the injured person . . .

She screams for the bus to stop, rushes out into the road. Sinking into the gutter, she cradles him with exquisite tenderness until at last he begins to regain consciousness. He clutches her hand feebly, gratefully, peers deeply and groggily into her dark and troubled eyes, and mouths the words "Thank . . . you."

Or the bus might pass a line of people outside the unemployment office.

He is out of work, wretched, desperate. She, powerful and well connected, pulls every string she can to get him a job. And what does she expect in return? Nothing, nothing at all, not even thanks. It doesn't matter.

That one wasn't much. She changed the scene. The one about the train wreck . . . yes! The train wreck was excellent.

Sitting across from each other on the train, suddenly they are thrown from their seats by a tremendous crash. It is a train wreck to be sure, but no one is hurt, except for a few bumped heads and ordinary bruises. Night has fallen, and all the lights in the train have gone out with the crash. Before the crash, each has been intensely aware of the other's knees. It has been impossible to avoid brushing knees as they shifted position. Now, he reaches for her, seizes

*her shoulders to prevent her from being harmed. But that is not all—he pulls
her fiercely to him. Without a word, they hurry from the train into the dark
night, clinging to each other. The train has been on its way to—where?—all
right, up-country somewhere, and now they huddle together in sweet warmth,
defying the blear cold of the dark, lonely night. Bangkok is far behind them.
Bravely, they set off for—wherever—to face whatever hardships . . .*

The train wreck was one of her favorites.

One day, after work, as Sai-roong trudged up the bumpy path to her
house, rain suddenly began to pour from the sky. She hurried on as
best she could, alone in the deluge and without an umbrella. The rain-
drops were fat and clear, she noted, as she pushed the tendrils of sod-
den hair back from her face. She looked down and saw that in only a
moment the rain had soaked her from the damp curves of her breasts
down to her feet. Unfortunately, the mud beneath her feet splashed
up with each step, making ugly dark splatters on the backs of her
calves and her skirt. She slowed her steps, placing her feet carefully,
wiping her eyes with both hands so that she could see where she was
going. And then, as suddenly as it had begun, the torrent ceased.

But her imagination remained in the storm . . .

*They meet just as the rain begins to fall in earnest. She raises her umbrella.
What to do? With a demure smile, she invites him to share her umbrella. They
walk on, side by side, but this umbrella is not large enough, not wide enough
to cover two bodies. They are forced to press closer together. It is so cold now;
the wind blows, chill and clammy, but under the umbrella they breathe in the
mingled, fragrant vapors of two warm, damp bodies. She wonders if he will
encircle her waist with his strong arm and pull her close, and if he does—yes,
he has done it now—and she fits against him snugly, deliciously aware of the
broad chest that, under his raincoat and shirt, is covered with fine, soft hair,
and then, without a word, they pass the gate that leads to her house and turn
toward the gate to his own . . .*

In a small society—a neighborhood, for example—long before the
event the preparations for an auspicious occasion, or any sort of celebration on the part of one household, tend to become the chief subject of conversation in all households. The news of his impending marriage set this process into fervent action.

Yes, he was going to be married.

Every mouth spoke as one, extolling the felicity of the match, the perfect rightness of the bride and groom for each other, whatever may have been said before the date was set. For the excitement of a wedding has the effect of dissipating previous cavils concerning any incompatibilities of social position, disposition, and the like. It was now perfectly clear that the couple was a perfect match—a jade leaf for a golden branch—and so on and on. Soon, the neighborhood was aflutter with those cards of invitation that show respect for the invited, proclaim the intentions of the betrothed, and tacitly announce that gifts will be graciously accepted.

Naturally, Sai-roong and her family received such an invitation.

"Please accept our best and most sincere wishes . . ." *No.* "We wish every happiness . . . to the bride and groom . . . forever . . ." *No.* How dreadful it was. Sai-roong sighed, tore up her tenth attempt, and began again. Having at last recovered sufficiently from the shock of the announcement, she faced the wearying task of composing the requisite note to the bride and groom.

At first, her heart had withered like a flower ripped cruelly from its earthy bed. What pond was there from which to draw the water that could restore her faded petals? None, none. In the first, terrible weeks her dreams were visited only by disappointment and fear. Sometimes she dreamed that she was trying to board a train that had already left; running with all her might, she knew that she could never catch up. Once she sprang up to fly into the sky, as she had done a thousand times in other dreams, but her arms had not the strength to lift her up. And then there was the horrible snake dream. A huge cobra reared up, flared its hood, began undulating toward her. It was indescribably disgusting as it writhed about, coming ever nearer. She was petrified for a moment, then looked about wildly, her glance at last falling upon the garden spade, which she grabbed and raised above her head. She brought it down with all her might and smashed the hideous snake to a pitiful little pile of pulp. She awoke with a pounding heart.

Sometimes the bride herself would appear in a dream, standing in Sai-roong's way with a sulky face. Whatever the story, nearly every dream these days was another slash at her heart.

. . .

On the day itself, according to custom, the young man followed his father into all the neighboring houses, formally inviting everyone to his nuptials. When the two men came through the gate of her home, it was all Sai-roong could do to flee to the back of the house, leaving her husband to welcome them. Not so much as her shadow would fall upon the happy occasion itself. She knew that she had not the courage to pour the water of blessing over the happy couple's hands; she could not trust herself to look down upon the bowed heads joined by the white thread—no, she simply could not do it.[2]

For many nights, she lay brooding into her pillow, interrogating herself. How had he disappointed her? What sin had he committed against her? What had she lost to him? And, finally, what had his bride stolen from her? Nothing. Neither bride nor groom had done her injury.

As time passed, and she observed him, as far as she could observe him from the corner of her eye, she saw that he behaved with as much respect toward her as he ever had: a proper nod, a slight bow as he hurried off to work or returned home. But he was gone from her dreams.

And then, one night just as she was drifting off to sleep, there he was, waiting. He had returned to her. That night, he made her very happy.

She wondered if he would have as much time for her in the future.

As she thought through her situation, over the weeks that followed, she came to realize the truth. She had it all: not only perfect love but also absolute freedom. Miraculously (for miracles do happen in life), everything had worked out perfectly. He was married, happily it seemed; and then, the children came. He was busy, but he came to

---

2. In a Thai wedding, the bride and groom, who are joined by a white thread that encircles the head of each, kneel side by side. Before each of them is a small table upon which they rest their elbows; their hands are placed in the wai position, palms together, over a basin. Each wedding guest pours a small amount of holy water over their hands as a blessing.

Sai-roong regularly, if not quite as frequently as before. She was satisfied. After all, she had never meant to be greedy.

No one lost anything. His wife and his sweet children were obviously content. Sai-roong saw them nearly every day. The children were darkly handsome, like their father, which was not surprising. The surprising thing—in fact, the truly *amazing* thing about them, Sai-roong gradually discovered—was their unmistakable resemblance to herself.

She continued to observe him from a distance, but she became quite friendly with the children. She never failed to stop and admire their bright eyes and fresh faces, their adorable smiling mouths, the white teeth that showed when they cried out to her—"Auntie! Auntie!"[3] She would hold out her arms to them, and they would run to her—yes, they loved her! They let her hold them fast—his children—let her press her face to theirs. At those times, the fragrant baby powder that clung to their tender cheeks would cause a sharp pang in her breast, recalling the clean scent of their father's face on some recent night.

His wife was always friendly and pleasant.

Really, there was no reason at all for the dreams to change, much less cease. Should he and his family ever fall upon hard times, she would consider it her moral duty to do everything in her power to aid and assist them.

It was quite the usual thing, in her dreams, for Sai-roong to sprout wings; she had always been able to do it. But now she realized that the force that propelled her flights through the sky came from within, from her love for him. Truly, this love had enabled her to overcome many difficulties in her life and to achieve her most important ambitions.

Years passed. Sai-roong remained a person who was respected throughout the neighborhood. "Khun Sai-roong? A quiet lady," people would say, "but a good-hearted one. It is wonderful how efficiently she does everything, even now that she is getting on. A good worker, Khun Sai-roong. And the husband, too."

---

3. This line, which represents very clever, dry humor in Thai, will be lost on most non-Thai readers without a few words of explanation. The pronoun I have translated as "Auntie" is *pâa*, which indicates the older sister of one's parent; but Thai people also use this pronoun when speaking to a woman who is, or who appears to be, older than their parents. Thus, the author indicates, with a single word, the fact that these small children think of her as an older woman.

To this day, Sai-roong has never looked directly into the eyes of the man next door. She prefers not to, lest his image become too clear. She likes him just the way he is: a little blurred, a little distant, a mystery, a dream of love.

And, after all, any time she wants him to come a little closer . . . *there he is.*

○ ○   SRI DAO RUANG AND
         "SAI-ROONG'S DREAM OF LOVE"

"Sai-roong's Dream of Love" is perhaps the best example of Thai women's humorous writing that has appeared during the past two decades. While Subha Devakul's story "When She Was a Major Wife" and the following excerpts from a novel by Krisna Asoksin are also good examples of this subgenre, "Sai-roong" is in a class by itself— or, rather, herself. Of all the translations in this anthology, this story and "Deep in the Heart of a Mother" invariably inspire comments from readers such as "I don't know what I expected, but I didn't expect a Thai story to be like this; this woman seems so . . . familiar."

I have written (following the story "Matsii" by the same author) that Sri Dao Ruang has only a fourth grade (Prathom IV) education, and that I suspect one result of her lack of the kind of education all the other writers have is her willingness to tackle subjects that other writers (especially women writers) have learned, somewhere along the way, to leave alone. "Sai-roong's Dream of Love" is a case in point. The mere fact of a woman writing such a story (in Thailand or any-where) is more than an assertion that women have sexual fantasies: it is an admission that *this* woman, the author, apparently does. It isn't that there is anything so wrong with that—but *writing* about it moves a private matter into a public space, an act that often draws criticism.

It seems unlikely that any other Thai woman writer would describe, in the way Sri Dao Ruang cheerfully does, Sai-roong's private prepa-rations for running into the neighbor: the eye shadow, the lip gloss, the Jane Fonda eyebrows, the Princess of Wales hair, practicing the wide-eyed sparkly look of the magazine models. Or the terrible real-ity of her shyness when she actually runs into her dream lover. In-stead of walking the way she has practiced, "head held high, aloof . . . with the slightest sway in her hips, as if she were crossing a stream on a narrow plank, carefully placing one dainty foot before the other,"

she panics, "[staring] into her paper bag of groceries or at her handbag until she trip[s] over a stone and stagger[s] forward, overcome
with shyness, grinning foolishly."

When she runs home through the rain one day, with each step she
takes, mud splashes on her, "making ugly dark splatters on the backs
of her calves and her skirt." Indeed, Sai-roong is a good candidate for
the ultimate authentic non-ideal female character in contemporary
Thai fiction. Surely, it would be difficult to imagine a character who
more deserves to be described as a Thai everywoman—at least, in her
urban manifestation.

Sai-roong is a good wife who is respected by her neighbors. But in
the privacy of her dreams: "*under the umbrella they breathe in the mingled, fragrant vapors of two warm, damp bodies. . . . she fits against him
snugly, deliciously aware of the broad chest that, under his raincoat and shirt,
is covered with fine, soft hair, and then, without a word, they pass the gate
that leads to her house and turn toward the gate to his own . . .*"

Sai-roong's adventures are not at all like those women have in short
stories by Suwanee—real, waking adventures, with disaster lurking
around the corner. On the contrary, they are the kind of adventures
in which Sai-roong muses but does not lose anything: neither husband
nor home, nor the regard of society. It might seem that this kind of
safe fantasizing would be endemic in a society in which women are
expected to come as close as possible to an ideal of grace, beauty, and
virtue that is all but unachievable—and perhaps it is—but this is the
first work of popular literature, to my knowledge, that suggests and
explores the therapeutic (or simply pleasurable) role of fantasy in
women's lives.

Another interesting feature of this story is its rather unusual gentle self-mockery. The objective is not, as so often in women's fiction,
the presentation of a woman striving to achieve her (or someone's)
ideals but the revelation of a few private truths about an ordinary
woman's life that are harmless, fun, and rather touching. More significant, when compared with a humorous story such as Subha
Devakul's "When She Was a Major Wife," this story is not laughing
at women, for their follies—in a cautionary, not especially kind way—
but laughing *with* women, congratulating them on the inventiveness
of their imaginations: "[Sai-roong] was a superb dreamer, an artist.
They were dreams of extraordinary vividness and filled with meaning for her. . . ."

"Her dreams were, she knew, the source of her strength."

Some readers may feel that there is a sad side to this story. After all, Sai-roong only feels completely alive when she is asleep. But such a conclusion would miss the point of the story by a wide mark. As Sai-roong says, "However deep her love, however incorrigible her infatuation, she must accept the truth: this man cannot be dragged from the dreaming world into the waking world. (And if he could, she reflects, it would be inconvenient, and that was a fact.)" She is not an unhappy woman, nor is she dissatisfied with her life, her society, or even, presumably, her husband. She is in charge of her life, and she certainly is in charge of her dreams. Sri Dao Ruang has often written about the importance of "the dreaming state" to the writer. One of her short stories, the frankly autobiographical "The Letter You Never Received," takes the form of a letter to Suwanee Sukhontha, in the week following her death: "Didn't you once say in an interview (somewhere, I don't remember exactly where), that one reason writing is hard is that one is mired in lavish private dreams, dreaming within oneself all of these stories and *words, words, words* . . . ? It is just as you said: dreaming all the time, and no end of it until there is an end of us."[1]

Although much of Sri Dao Ruang's writing is concerned with dreams and with the importance of the dreaming state in her life as a writer, it is equally concerned with the unending quest for the friend, the reader, the empathetic other who will validate her own fears, disappointments, joys—and, sometimes, her private laughter.

---

1. Sri Dao Ruang, "The Letter You Never Received," trans. Susan Fulop Kepner, *Two Lines: The Stanford Journal of Translation* (fall 1995): 135–42.

From *This Human Vessel*

Krisna Asoksin

This 1968 novel covers a year of crisis in
the life of a middle-class Bangkok family.

*[Maturot Kalyanope is unhappy. She longs to break into a higher echelon of Thai so-
ciety and is frustrated by life with her husband, Plao, an unambitious, honest civil
servant. Plao and Maturot have three children; the eldest daughter, Pimrot (usually
called Pim), is sixteen and, as the novel opens, pregnant by Chaiporn (also called
Khun Chai), son of a wealthy businessman, Khun Dej. This situation provides one
of two chief elements of the plot; the other is Plao's affair with their fourteen-year-
old house servant, Giaw, which begins in the following excerpt.]*

Chapter 21

*[Giaw's family lives in one of a cluster of shacks at the end of the Kalyanopes' lane.
She has been encouraged by her mother, Saay, to take advantage of the vexing problems currently threatening the stability of the comparatively splendid Kalyanope
home. (Pim, the pregnant daughter, has recently gone to live with her boyfriend, invited by his father into their family home, as the least unattractive solution to the
problem.) Saay tells Giaw that by making herself attractive and by showing that she
is more than willing to console her master, Plao, who feels depressed and overwhelmed,
Giaw might reap the benefits of the crisis by winning his affections and even becoming his minor wife. Giaw enthusiastically falls in with the plan.]*

Plao drove home at noon to fetch the documents he had forgotten.
The child Giaw came out to open the gate. When he had driven
through and parked the car, she lingered until he had opened the door
and go out.

"Are you sick?"

Plao turned and glanced at her without interest. But then he felt
compelled to look again, for something about the face of this girl—
young woman, almost—seemed different.

The edition of the novel from which this translation was prepared is *Rɨa manút*, published by Chokechai Thewet, Bangkok, in 1970. See the biographical note following the
excerpt for the explanation of this title.

"Ah, Giaw, practicing with the lipstick, eh? And the eyebrow pencil?"

Giaw grinned shyly. "Only lightly. Auntie Bao's daughter gives me her extra ones. You don't think it looks good?"

He shook his head as he turned the key in the lock. Because Maturot had no great trust in Giaw, she locked the house whenever she went out; only Plao and their son, Pochana, had keys to the front door.

Giaw followed Plao into the house and began to open the shutters.

"Don't, Giaw. I'll be going right away. I only came home to pick up some documents I forgot this morning." He began to climb the stairs.

"Sir, where did Khun Pim go?[1] I really miss her."

Plao's foot stopped on the first step. He turned, and in the darkness of the shuttered room, he saw only a pale face suffused with the creamy glow of youth and dark, restless eyes that reflected the narrow streams of faint light that trickled through the shutters. She was a tall child and plump. Her unpermed hair was cut just below her earlobes and left plain, parted in the middle, and pushed back on both sides, the simplest of styles. It was simplicity that most enhanced the bloom of youth, the natural glow of young, healthy flesh. No decoration was necessary. And yet, oddly enough, the colored lips and brows seemed right; they invited another, longer look.

"I didn't pay attention," he said, intending to cut short the conversation, "and anyway, that is no concern of yours."

Giaw followed him and stood holding the stair rail. "I just miss her, that's all . . ."

"Then miss her, but you don't have to know where she is."

"My mother asked me."

"Then tell her you don't know. Is that all you market people up there think about, other people's business? No wonder every time I turn into the lane they look at me like—like they never saw me before."

But he didn't look angry with her, Giaw thought. "Is he rich?" she persisted.

"Why would you want to know that?"

"If he's rich, then Khun Pim will be all right, won't she?"

---

1. Giaw is well aware of all the details of Pimrot's pregnancy and the potential family disgrace.

The insolence of the girl. "I don't know," he said irritably, but another feeling had begun to displace his annoyance. "Giaw, do you know how to give a massage?"

"Yes, massage and stepping on the person, too. I can do both."

"Are you clean?" he asked suspiciously. "Your hands and feet, I suppose they smell like the kitchen?"

"I just washed myself this morning," she replied and stretched her arms toward him. "Here, smell for yourself! And my *panung*[2] is clean, too."

Plao smiled, turned away. "How often do you wash your panung?"

"Every day—it's the truth!"

"You scrub it? And hang it out to dry in the sunshine?"

"If you don't believe me, I'll go out back right now and wash it again, and my hands and feet, too."

"Good, make them really clean. Use some nice-smelling soap. And then come upstairs. I—I could use a massage."

The daring girl hurried away to do his bidding.

She knew that she would find him in his library. When she entered the room, he was reclining on the chaise.

"Where do you hurt, sir?" she asked brightly, dropping gracefully to her knees.

"Everywhere," he responded shortly, his eyes moving quickly from her hair down to her feet. "How old are you, Giaw?"

"Almost fifteen. I'm almost a woman," she added proudly. "Pretty soon my mother will be able to get me a job. I'm going to make lots of money."

"Where?"

"I'm not sure. I think in a place where you give baths to people, and they pay you a lot. It has to be better than this—being a servant, I mean."

"You know how to give somebody a bath?"

"No. But they pay you a lot of money to do it, right?"

"Oh, yes. But you're taking some chances."

"What kind of chances?" Giaw moved her face closer to his.

"You haven't thought about someone reaching out to tickle you

---

2. A simple length of cloth worn as a skirt.

while you're giving him that bath? You could, you know—spoil your-self, Giaw."

"Are the men naked?"

Plao nodded.

"Have you ever done that? Gone to a place where a girl gives you a bath?"

"Never."

"Then how do you know?"

Plao grinned. "I've heard," he said, lifting one leg. "Aow! Let's get on with this massage."

Giaw laid her hands on his leg and began to knead his flesh.

"Why don't you sit up here with me," he said, "instead of down there on the floor. You can do a better job."

She complied and lifted his foot into her lap.

"You got your hands and feet nice and clean, did you? How many times did you wash them?"

"Three times. Here—smell." She held up her hands, leaned forward.

"Ah. Go on, go on with the massage."

"Don't you worry," Giaw boasted, "my mother makes me practice on her all the time, and I'm real good. Sir, can I ask you a question? I'm thinking about changing my name. What do you think?"

"Changing it to what?"

"Kliang Tong."[3]

Plao laughed. "*Woy!* Such a name—*Kliang Tong!*" He felt his spir-its rise for the first time in many days.

Giaw pouted prettily. "What's wrong with 'Kliang Tong'?"

"I think perhaps it's a bit . . . *much*, Giaw."

"What do you mean, *much?* You don't think it suits me?"

"Not quite."

"Then what name would be good?"

"What's wrong with 'Giaw'?"

"Oh, sir. What girl nowadays has such a plain name, with only one syllable? Everybody has a long name with at least two syllables, a name that's hard to remember."

"If you had one of those long names with lots of syllables, how would I remember what to call you?"

3. Approximately, a "strand of gold."

"Pretty soon, you won't have to call me anything."

"What do you mean?"

"As soon as my mistress can find somebody else, she's going to get rid of me. She can't wait."

"Don't worry about that."

"Why not?" Giaw asked, leaning toward him.

"Why don't you move up here?" He patted the cushion, beside his waist.

Giaw promptly walked up the chaise beside him on her knees.

"You aren't afraid of me?" he asked, somewhat abashed by her eagerness.

"No. You have a good heart. But I am afraid of *her*. She's so mean."

Plao lightly stroked her arm. "So nice and cool, your skin."

"Because I just washed it. With nice-smelling soap, too." Then she shivered, tucked in her chin and said, "Ooh—it makes my skin all shivery when you touch it lightly like that."

Plao laughed aloud. "Giaw, you are a funny child. You are becoming quite lovely, you know. I never noticed until today."

"I know. Boys think so, too. Plenty of them come around to see me, don't you know."

"I suppose they do. You've begun to dress yourself nicely."

"Yes. But I don't want any of those boys. I'm not going to end up in some dump, with only a handful of rice to eat from one day to the next. That's what it would be with them. I know."

"You're wise, Giaw. You should find someone who can take care of you."

"Where will I find somebody like that?"

"Will you believe me if I tell you something?"

"I will believe you."

"I can help you and take care of you." Plao took one of her small hands in his.

"You know all about palm reading," Giaw said.[4] "What do you see in mine?"

"It doesn't appear that you will have any troubles," he said, stroking the lines of her palm. "Providing that you don't go around

---

4. Plao stops at a nearby temple on his way home, most evenings, to talk about astrology, fortune-telling, palmistry, and so on with the monks.

giving a massage to just anybody. In fact, if you only give massages to me, you might find it rewarding."

"I'd give you a massage for nothing, anytime."

"You are a good girl." He lifted his head and said, "Like this, with you—Giaw, it is—I like it very much . . . do you understand?"

"My mistress would rip my skin off."

"Not only won't your mistress rip your skin off—I doubt if she would even be interested."

Giaw nodded thoughtfully. "I guess that's true. She doesn't care about you."

"Even you know it."

"Why wouldn't I know it? In the morning, you go away, she goes away, you both come home late. You hardly talk to each other. Do you love her a lot?"

"Do you think I love her?"

"Well, you still live with her. Otherwise, why would you?"

"It doesn't necessarily follow, Giaw. Many people live together like this."

Giaw tucked this puzzling information away, to think about later.

She had grown up in the warren of tumbledown shacks at the head of the lane, where it met the broad, busy road beyond. Hers was a small, teeming neighborhood within a neighborhood, swarming with people and gossip. Some of the people who lived there drove pedi-cabs; others drove taxis; some hawked ears of roasted corn or cheap sweets. Saay, Giaw's mother, sold toasted banana leaves filled with sticky rice;[5] her father was a construction laborer. Since the birth of her children, Saay had never left home, and this was true of most of the women who lived around them. Whenever anyone entered or left the lane, they knew about it. It was their chief entertainment. They knew everyone in the lane, both rich and poor, by name and their history, too. Every precious shred of information they could garner traveled swiftly from door to door and over the rooftops. When they had sold their sweets or corn or sticky rice, Saay and her neighbors drifted from one shack to another, savoring the delicious and abiding satisfactions provided by scrutinizing the lives of Master This and Mistress

---

5.   Glutinous ("sticky") rice is the staple food of the poor northeast; this single bit of information says volumes about the family's social status.

That,[6] who were neighbors of a different sort, in their big houses deep in the lane.

Giaw would see her mother bustling about, readying herself to go out, panting with eagerness. "Giaw, you watch the babies. I'm going."

"Where?"

"To find out whether Tuan and Chit have really broken up. Yesterday, they had a big fight, hitting each other, everything—you watch those babies, you hear?" And she would go scurrying off across the lane.

Sometimes she would even contribute a few baht to someone who was willing to go out and do some real spy work. "That Pao—she left her husband and her mother, both; we know she rented a house someplace, and we'll find out where . . ."

Giaw had learned curiosity from her mother and the neighbors. She too treasured the bits and pieces of titillating information that she was able to garner and proudly dispensed them up and down the lane. As for her maidenhood, she neither treasured nor was proud of it. It meant nothing to Giaw, but to call this a flaw in the child would not be fair; for all that she had seen, in her short life, was the casual couplings of the men and women around her. There were no weddings here. People ran off together, and girls with big stomachs weren't always sure who to blame. Giaw's own parents had never considered teaching their children how to live moral lives. What was important to them? Filling their children's bellies, trying to figure out how to get lucky in the lottery, arguing with each other: such was life. Their children had not been raised in this place so much as they had wallowed in it. They ran wild from one hovel to another. Who knew where they were, and who cared? When a girl's belly began to swell, she realized that eventually there would be a baby. Giaw and her friends had grown up brash, bold, and fearless. *Pua* was a word they understood: a pua was a man with whom one did things; a word signifying less, perhaps, than *husband* meant to people further down the lane. To have a pua was a very clear idea to Giaw.

"You mean it?" she asked Plao. "A husband and wife can live together—just *live* together, and that's all?"

---

6. The terms I have represented as "Master This and Mistress That" are "khun khon nán thâan khon nóon." The respectful pronouns *khun* and *thâan* emphasize the social gulf between Plao's family and Giaw's.

"Oh, yes. People grow older together, they have children, the children grow up. And then they just . . . live together, you see—in the same house—but not . . . *together.*"

"You like living like that?"

"I'm thinking about it," he said, impressed with the girl. Not bad, this one. "Perhaps you could help me."

"How do you want me to help you?"

"Like this," he said, putting his arm around her waist and pulling her close. She was a common little thing, Giaw was, and yet so like a bud just opening into bloom. Her young flesh was warm and exciting, and Plao felt himself awakening from the long stupor of his own senses, coming alive again. For so long, so long he had been buried under the weight of his job, the responsibility of earning a living to support this family, not even hoping for more. He felt like a tree that has long stood in parched earth, barely alive.

"Sir!" Giaw cried, gently pulling his hand away—just for a moment —before she relaxed into his embrace.

"You have nothing to be afraid of. I can give you more money than any of those boys. And you won't have to give anybody a bath. If you want to bathe somebody, you can bathe me, Giaw!"

"If my mistress finds out, she'll have a terrible fit—if that happens, you have to promise to help me."

"I promise. I won't desert you," he said in a shaking voice, stroking the girl's young body.

"He's old," she thought, "but so what. He has money. And who knows, I might end up in that car, driving right by everybody." Giaw closed her eyes, happily lost in the wonder of her new life, the status that would be hers. Everyone she knew—all of them—would be out there in the lane, their eyes bulging with excitement, standing aside as she and Plao drove past.

"Sir . . . I love you," she murmured sweetly into the curve of Plao's arm. "Will you come home at noon tomorrow, too?"

"Yes, Giaw. If you really were gold, you would be one hundred percent."

o   o   o   o

Chapter 103

[Giaw and her mother's, Saay's, plan to entrap Plao succeeds all too well. Giaw be-
comes Plao's minor wife, moves away with him to another house, and gives birth to
a son. Born prematurely and suffering from hydrocephaly and other birth defects, the
infant is placed in an institution soon after birth. The relationship sours, and Plao
moves back into his family home. As the following scene opens, the embittered Giaw,
bent on revenge, has decided to humiliate Plao and the proud Maturot by pursuing
their daughter Pimrot's young husband, Chaiporn. This marriage has not brought
happiness to either of the teenagers, who are now parents. The other characters who
appear in this excerpt are: Pochana, Plao and Maturot's son, a boy of fourteen; Nitima,
Plao's virtuous and reliable niece, in her midtwenties, who lives with Plao and
Maturot; Dom, Khun Dej's other son, an upstanding and outstanding young man
who is Nitima's fiancé; and Chuda, Dej's young, neglected second wife.

Plao and Maturot are standing just outside their front door, being harangued by
Saay. Their son, Pochana, looks on in great distress. Giaw has run off, and no one
knows where she has gone.]

Maturot felt the hair on the back of her neck lift as she listened to the
accusations of the sticky-rice woman. She clenched her fists at her
sides, forcing herself to contain her rage.

"You must talk to your daughter about all of this, Saay, not to me,"
Plao said gently. "If she is not blind, she should be able to wait."[7]

"I haven't even thought of helping her," Saay retorted. "It's useless to talk about it. Listen, my daughter *has* a man,[8] the man whose
baby she gave birth to not even half a year ago. What do you expect
me to do, poke my nose into her business and try to find her a new
husband, so that my neighbors will say that Saay goes around selling
her daughter like a vegetable, like a fish? The girl's father curses me
every day . . ."

Saay ranted on. Every word pierced Plao like a knife. That a man
such as himself should have to endure the curses of a woman like
Saay. That he should have to stand here in silence on his own property, accepting her insults. But could he make so much as one retort

---

7. The implication is that if Giaw keeps her eyes open, she will find someone new.
8. Saay uses the word *pua,* or *pŭa,* where I have used "man." Although the word
pŭa is commonly used to mean "husband," the implication here is of someone Giaw
would live with, another benefactor, but not a legal husband.

to her sarcastic harangue? No! Not when every word she said was the truth.

As for Maturot, she was so furious that she could feel her whole body trembling.

Pochana, who stood just inside the door, sharing his parents' agony, could bear it no longer and shouted, "Arrogant bitch! I'll knock you down this minute!"

"Saay, what do you want me to do?" Plao asked, feeling defenseless.

"I don't know! Wait for her to come back . . . oh, my Giaw, my poor baby chick," she began to wail, "just hatched, and already she has fallen into the mouth of the crocodile!"

Plao gasped. "What good can it do, coming here to revile me like this? It's all history!"

"You have never been a mother! Here I am, a poor woman who sells sticky rice in this lane—all I've known in my life is trouble and sorrow. And don't anybody dare to blame my poor baby—what did she know of the world, a young girl like that? You, you're old, you're a big man—you should know better. You asked for her, and did I stand in your way? No! All I asked was that you take good care of my child, and what did you do? All you could think of was to get rid of her. Maybe I should be thankful my little girl isn't already on the streets, because of you . . ."

Pochana bounded from the doorway. "Papa, how can you let her talk to you like that? Throw her off our property!"

Saay turned on the boy, hands on hips, and snarled, "Nobody has to throw me out. I'll walk out myself, and the sooner the better—unless somebody here would like to try and *make* me leave."

"You get out of here, you crazy woman, before I smash you—"

"Stop! Stop this at once!" Plao moved quickly to separate them. "Pochana, you are a boy. You don't belong here. This is grown-ups' business."

"But she cursed you, Papa!"

"Never mind. She is angry and hurt. She loves her child and worries about her, just as I love you and worry about you." Plao took his son by the arm, urging him into the house.

Saay turned to go, muttering, "Yah, yah, these big people, think they're so good, and look at them. They always take advantage of poor folks."

Plao called out, "Wait a moment, Saay. If Giaw returns, she is welcome to come back here and work, just as she did before."

"*Khun!*"[9] Maturot cried out. "What are you saying?"

"Maturot, I must accept responsibility for what I have done."

"Khun . . . oh, Khun!" His wife all but staggered toward the railing of the veranda, clung to it with both hands. Her heart, which had been pounding against her ribs, felt now as if it were withering inside her.

"Khun 'Rot . . . you must accept reality," Plao said softly. "How do you think I shall bear it if a person like this goes about our neighborhood telling people that I have no more heart than a beast? I tell you, I cannot bear it."

"But we have already made arrangements to support them,"[10] Maturot said, her voice shaking. "Isn't it enough?"

"When they say it is not enough, we must give until they say that it is. There is nothing that I fear in this world more than the accusation of injustice."

"But where is that girl's[11] sense of justice? Or loyalty? Has she any? Even when you were with her, she was unfaithful to you."

"But she[12] can say that it is because of us that she is like she is."

Maturot turned swiftly from him and called out, "Saay! How much do you want? How much is enough for you and your daughter never to set foot here again?"

Saay raised her eyebrows. "Ooh, madame—the value of my child is great."

Maturot wanted to scream, to reach out and strike the woman, but she restrained herself. "I asked you, *how much?*"

"Well . . . I can't say right this minute . . . I'll have to think it over." Saay felt triumphant. Her playing hard to get made Maturot even more furious. "Khun Nai,[13] what is your husband worth to you? That's what my daughter is worth to me."

---

9. This neutral second-person pronoun is often used by a woman speaking to her husband in the presence of others, especially in the middle and upper classes.

10. Plao has accepted full financial responsibility for the permanent institutionalization of his child by Giaw.

11. The pronoun Maturot uses in this instance is *man*, which is used only in reference to inanimate objects, animals, and persons of the lowest status; at one time, it was used to refer to foreigners, as well.

12. Plao uses the pronoun *khǎw* where I have translated "she"; this is a neutral pronoun, unlike Maturot's *man*.

13. A second-person pronoun used by a servant addressing his or her employer, *khun nai* could be translated as "boss."

Maturot felt the hairs on the back of her neck rise. Her face flushed darkly. "The *insolence*—," she hissed through her teeth.

Saay let that pass. She strode to the gate and disappeared, leaving Maturot with her disappointment.

Maturot had decided to offer the woman ten thousand baht[14]—Plao for Giaw—certain that Saay, faced with the possibility of such a wind-fall, would all but tremble in anticipation of holding the bills in her greedy hands. But Saay had turned her back and simply walked away. She was more clever and more patient than Maturot had imagined.

Saay was halfway down the lane when she recognized the famil-iar figure of her daughter, laughing and chatting with some familiar-looking young man, as bold as you please.

"Where have you been?" she shouted at the top of her lungs, stand-ing with her hands on her hips.

"Ma! Ma!" Giaw ran to her mother and grabbed her hands. "You don't have to throw a tantrum in the street like this."

"Where did you go? Where have you been?" Over Giaw's shoul-der, Saay looked at the young man who stood with his arms crossed over his chest.

"I went with Khun Chai."

"What 'Khun Chai'?"

"Oh, Ma. What other 'Khun Chai' could it be? Khun Chaiporn, you know, the one who married Pimrot—my daughter-in-law . . ." She giggled.

"You crazy bitch . . . *why?*"

"Aow, Ma . . . what a strange question. If I didn't love him, why would I have gone with him?"

Saay was dumbfounded. "You love him. How many days have you known him?"

Giaw held up one hand and counted on the fingers. "One . . . two . . . three . . ." Her eyes sparkled merrily. "Let me think—we've been together for two days, and then there were six days before that . . . so that makes eight days. More than a week. But, really, you shouldn't ask."

"You'd better get out of here, you'd better run, because you're just begging for a beating!"

14. A little less than US$200, a sum that, especially at the time Krisna was writing this novel (late 1960s), would have seemed a fortune to Saay.

"Why don't you *think*, Ma, for once? You should be congratulating me, not threatening me."

Saay was silent.

"I'm not angry anymore, Ma, and you shouldn't be either. It's all over now. I'm no longer bitter. Khun Chai has rented the house, the same house where I lived with Khun Plao. How do you like that?" Giaw snapped her fingers. "He got eight hundred baht from his wife. He pawned his watch, his Buddha necklace,[15] and his ring for another four thousand. After paying three months' rent in advance—*fifteen hundred baht, Ma*—we had enough left over for blankets and stuff. You don't even need a net in that house; there're screens on all the windows; you can sleep anyplace you want. The rest of the money I kept for food. So what do you think now, Ma? Didn't I handle it well?"

Saay was awestruck. "Ah, Giaw—you're beyond your old Ma, and that's the truth."

"We're going to pay a visit down the lane, me and Chai, just for a laugh. I can't wait to see their faces."

Giaw turned, went to Chaiporn, and linked her arm in his. "We're off to give Khun Plao the good news that he's free. I won't be bothering him for nothing now."

Chaiporn blanched, wrenching his arm away from her. "What, are you crazy? You want me to go to my in-laws' house? No way!"

"Aw, so you're afraid of them?"

"No. I just don't want to get into trouble, that's all."

"I'm going. I want to end the whole thing my way."

"So, go. Do whatever you want. I'll wait here."

"Come on, Ma, come with me." Giaw took her mother's arm instead, and they set off in high spirits.

Pochana opened the outer door and asked glumly through the screen door, "What do you want now?"

Giaw smiled brightly at him. "Nothing. I came to say good-bye to Khun Plao, that's all."[16]

---

15. A necklace consisting of a gold chain with a small Buddha-image pendant, worn by most Thai Buddhists under their clothing.

16. Readers who are familiar with Thai may be interested to know that the Thai line reads, "Maa laa khun phûu chaay." In using the term *khun phûu chaay* instead of addressing him as "Khun Plao," Giaw is saying, in effect, "I have come to say farewell

At these words, Pochana opened the door wide. "You're really going away?"

"If I'm lying, I'm not a human child," Giaw said, her expression triumphant.

Plao and Maturot, having heard Giaw's voice below, hurried down the stairs.

"Where have you been?" Plao asked Giaw. "Your mother has been looking everywhere for you."

"Well, she won't have to look for me anymore, will you, Ma? I came to say good-bye."

"Where are you going?" Plao asked.

"I'm going away with—" Giaw turned to her mother, her eyes gleaming with their secret. "Should I tell him, Ma?"

"Tell him."

"I'm going away with my new boyfriend. Yes, I have a new boyfriend," she said, responding to the surprise on their faces. She looked straight into Plao's eyes and said, "That should make you happy."

"So that's where you've been," Maturot said, her heart beginning to lift.

"We needed to rent a place."

"I see."

"Yes, and we found a good one. Five hundred baht a month."

"Well," said Plao, "it seems that your boyfriend has a good income."

"Not exactly. He's only about four years older than me. But his father's a millionaire."

Maturot frowned. "Who is he?"

"He's waiting for me down the lane. I wanted him to come with me, but he didn't want to. He was afraid."

A feeling of uneasiness was creeping into Maturot's breast, drowning the faint hope that had begun to grow there. The sly expressions of the two women were so . . . so what? She could not avoid the word that came to mind: so *triumphant.*

It was then that Nitima and Dom entered the room. Dom spoke. "Did you know that Khun Chai is at the end of the lane? He's just standing there."

---

to the master of the house," a choice of language that implies that she is abandoning her role of minor wife.

Maturot's hands flew to her chest. "Chai—Chaiporn? My daughter's Chaiporn?" Uttering a small shriek, she turned and ran to the telephone. Her hands shook as she dialed. "Let me speak with Pim. Please hurry. Pim, dear! It's Mother! Come to the house at once—this minute, do you hear me? You can stop looking for Chaiporn—he's here. *Hurry!*"

"Right. He's out there waiting for me," Giaw said.

Nitima repeated her words in a daze. "Waiting for you? Does this mean that?—"

"Yes. He was with me last night."

Nitima felt faint. Dom muttered, "Nit, you stay here. I'll drag that stupid kid every inch of the lane." He bolted through the door and was off.

The rest of them stood in silence until Dom reappeared, dragging Chaiporn by the hand. "You stand there, and you face them," Dom said, forcing the boy to stand directly before Plao and Maturot.

"How could you even think of doing such a thing?" Dom demanded in a voice that betrayed as much sorrow as anger.

But Chaiporn only hung his head and said nothing.

"Go on and tell them, Khun Chai," Giaw urged, her eyes sparkling. "Tell them it's true, that we're living together. Tell them we rented the house where I used to live with my old husband."[17]

The silence in the room was so profound that they could hear each other's anxious breathing. Maturot felt as though a sudden fever had struck her down. In the blink of an eye, the small hope she had allowed herself to feel at the thought of Giaw's having found a new boyfriend was smothered to death. And in that moment, Maturot the mother no longer cared that her husband had had a minor wife. She would gladly beg Giaw to return to him, she would plead with Plao to take the girl back.

"Oh, Giaw, have you any idea of what you have done?" Maturot said, all anger drained from her voice. "This must not—must not be, Giaw. You have borne Khun Plao's child, and you should—you must stay with him. Please, stay with him, here."

"It's too late, way too late." Giaw lifted her chin and said, "I don't want him anymore, see? If I'm going to be somebody's minor wife, why should I settle for an old man? It's more fun with a nice, young

17. In Thai, *pŭa kàw.*

one." She sidled up to Chaiporn, slipped her arm through his, grinned up at him, and said, "Isn't that right, Khun Chai?"

Chaiporn's face became even paler than before. At that moment, they all turned at the sound of a car approaching. In the driveway, the large, expensive automobile of Khun Dej, Chaiporn's father, came to a screeching stop. The door burst open, and he all but bounded out, followed by Chuda[18] and Pimrot.

When Pimrot saw Giaw glued to Chaiporn's side, she looked first paralyzed, then horrified. The only word that came to her lips was "Chaiporn!"

But Chaiporn never heard her, because his father was furiously pounding him with both fists. "You despicable little scoundrel," he panted hoarsely, between slaps and punches. "Is nothing too vile? What is left? What misery will you bring me next?"

"Ow! Ow!" the boy yelled, trying to protect himself with his hands. "I'm scared—I'm scared already—stop! Don't hit me anymore, Father!"

Plao seized Dej's arm. "Khun Dom, come help me—I can't pull him off the boy alone."

The two men were barely able to hold the tall, powerful man, who gasped for breath and shouted, "Don't hold me back—I want to beat him to death!"

"For what, Khun Dej?" Plao asked. "What would be the point of it? Don't you see that all of us have fallen and become the slaves of our own passions?" Speaking slowly, as if considering each word, Plao continued, "If our anger is so great that we will even murder each other, my friend, what hope is there for us to rise above our sorry state? We are all, each one of us, in the wrong. We have created our own troubles. But we refuse to accept the responsibility. We insist on putting the blame on someone or something else—anywhere but the place it belongs, which is on ourselves."

Nitima put her arm around Pimrot's shoulder to comfort her. The girl's flesh felt like ice. Maturot then pulled her gently from Nitima's arm and embraced her. "My poor child," she thought to herself, "if your selfish mother had faced reality for even a moment, you might have been spared this misery."

Chuda spoke to Giaw and Saay. "Go home," she said. "I will come to see you tomorrow, I promise."

18. Chuda met Dej when he was a widower; she is younger than his oldest children.

Mother and daughter looked at each other, considering what to do. "Yeah, all right," Giaw said at last. "But don't forget, you owe me. All of you."

"No one is denying that," Chuda said.

"Listen, I get to stay in that house for three months. I'm not going back to that rat's nest of my mother's."

Saay bristled. "Go anywhere you want," she said, the brief camaraderie with her offspring apparently at an end, "and don't think I'm not fed up with you." She opened the door and stamped out of the house.

Giaw paused and considered her two former husbands: first Plao and then Chaiporn, who, released from his father's fury, had fled outside to lean against the hood of the car and sob his heart out. "I'll take either one of them," she announced. "Or both of them together—what do I care? Just so long as I get to keep that house."

Giaw then followed her mother out of the home of the Kalyanope family—all of whom stood in perfect silence, like so many leaves on a breathless night.

O O   KRISNA ASOKSIN AND *THIS HUMAN VESSEL*

Krisna Asoksin, the pen name of Sukanya Cholasueks, was born in 1931 and became a leading figure in the generation of Thai writers who came of age in the late 1950s, and who achieved success during the politically, socially, and artistically tumultuous 1960s and early 1970s. Krisna, who graduated from Thammasat University, began writing fiction at the age of fifteen, publishing her first short story at twenty and her first novel at twenty-seven.[1]

In 1968, Krisna received the first annual SEATO Literature Award for the novel *This Human Vessel*. Of all the selections in this anthology, the original title of this one, *Rua manut* (or *Rʉa manút*), has most successfully defied an appropriate translation. The word *rʉa* means "boat"; the word *manút* means "human being" or "human creature." I had first translated the title as *The Ship of Humanity*; but this was not at all what Krisna had meant, as I learned from the letter that accompanied her corrections of the translated excerpts. For those readers

---

1. This information appears in Sukanya Cholasueks's [Krisna Asoksin] essay, "On Being a Novelist in Thailand," *Tenggara*, vol. 19 (1986).

who have an interest in the process of literary translation, I am including most of the text of her letter.

Krisna writes:

> It just occurred to me that you might not have heard of a nursery rhyme on which the title *Rua Manut*[2] is based. [This was correct.] The rhyme goes like this:
>
> > The boat, the human boat,
> > Your ultimate length is only a *wah*[3]
> > Lustful desire has brought you here.
> > Do you know where you're going?[4]
>
> It is obvious that the human boat here refers to the human body (an infant's in fact; as a mother is rocking her child to sleep, she is looking at the child). The idea here is very Buddhistic—the reference to the principle of the renunciation of desires. So, the title . . . may be more appropriately translated as *The Human Boat* rather than *The Ship of Humanity*. The title also gives you the key to the crux of the story.[5]

Much as I wished to comply with Krisna's desire in this matter, I did not agree that the title *The Human Boat* would give English readers the key to the crux of the story. A compromise was suggested in a note from the Thai professor of literature Nitaya Masavisut, helpfully penned at the bottom of Krisna's letter: "I myself would prefer *The Human Vessel*."

These excerpts are included in the anthology for several reasons. First, *This Human Vessel* is the best example of a popular subgenre of contemporary Thai fiction that may be described as "dysfunctional families comprised of selfish, materialistic adults raising resentful, unhappy children in the morally bankrupt atmosphere of mid-twentieth-century, urban, 'developed' Thailand." If this novel does

---

2. When writing about the novel in English, Krisna Asoksin spells this title *Rua Manut*.

3. About two arms' length or eighty inches.

4.   Rɯa ǒəy rɯa manút
        yày yaaw sùt phiang khɛ̂ɛ waa
        tanhǎa phaa jâw maa
        rúu rɯ̌ɯ jâw ja pay nǎy.

5. Sukanya Cholasueks [Krisna Asoksin], letter to author, September 7, 1995.

not depict the land of smiles, still it has provoked smiles from readers. They rejoice in the sardonic humor with which Krisna keeps this saga of a hysterical pregnant teenager, her social-climbing shrew of a mother, and her neglected, depressed father, who divides his free time between visiting astrologers and locking himself in his study to brood—until he sets up house with a fourteen-year-old lover—from teetering into outright bathos. It is very difficult to reproduce this prodigious balancing act in English, and I am well aware of the deficiencies of the translation.

And, yet, the anthology would be incomplete without it. *This Human Vessel* has great significance, not only because of the depiction of middle-class urban women in contemporary Thai society but also because of its display of feminine ideals—and their opposites. The story of the proud Maturot's downfall and re-creation as a submissive wife strongly suggests the taming of a modern Thai shrew. In the end, she might well qualify for membership in an extraordinary society women's organization of that era called the Safety Pin Club. No less than M. R. Kukrit Pramoj—Oxford graduate, author, prime minister, and denizen of the classical theater—gave his public approval to the Ten Oaths of the Safety Pin Club, which comprise an embodiment of the perfect woman that almost puts to shame the Sukhothai-period depiction of the perfect woman quoted at the beginning of the introduction:

1. We (women) will always accept that men are superior to us.
2. We will try as much as possible to be gentle, sweet and beautiful.
3. We will give our love freely to our husbands, because we realize that men cannot be complete without women to love.
4. We will try our best to bring good health, happiness and satisfaction to our husbands.
5. We will educate ourselves in order to be our husbands' best friends, because we know that a body needs a heart to govern it.
6. We will try in every way in our power to protect our husbands from all suffering with the knowledge that suffering and happiness are common phenomena, but that nature creates women to have greater endurability.
7. We will try in every way to bring peace into the world, our homes, and the lives of our husbands.

8. We will always be grateful to our husbands for everything they give us, whether children, home or the simple satisfaction of seeing them.
9. We will try our best to perform all activities which will make our husbands proud to say "This woman is my wife. She is really good."
10. We will pin a safety-pin on our chests as the symbol of our club with great pride and a consciousness that we are women, and with a realisation that without women, no man could have survived until now.[6]

The Safety Pin Club was symptomatic of the alarm felt in some quarters, during the 1960s and 1970s, about the possible negative effects of modernization or westernization on women. In a monograph published in 1980, Khin Thitsa writes: "The traditional feminine virtues of obedience and self-sacrifice . . . are reactivated today whenever necessary with threats that women will be ostracised not only by their men but by society at large, scorned as 'modern,' 'Westernised' women who have lost sight of all traditional values. Men when they frequent nightclubs, massage parlours and similar places will not be accused of being 'Westernised' as those male activities are in line with traditional ideas of masculine behavior."[7]

The final reason for including an excerpt from this novel involves what may be its most elusive aspect for the reader of the translation: what Krisna called the novel's "Buddhistic" message that desire is the enemy of contentment. As the nursery rhyme plainly says, "Lustful desire has brought [us] here." Krisna is determined to prove that it never stops trying to bring us down, and that we are responsible for responding to this fact of human life with honesty and courage. "We are all, each one of us, in the wrong," Plao tells the assembled cast of characters as the novel closes. "We have created our own troubles. But we refuse to accept the responsibility. We insist on putting the blame on someone or something else—anywhere but the place it belongs, which is on ourselves."

6. In Mattani Rutnin, "The Change in the Role of Women in Contemporary Thai Literature," *East Asian Cultural Studies* 17, no. 1–4 (1978): 103–4. Readers might recall that during the same era (the 1970s), quite a few women in the United States were enthusiastically buying books such as *The Total Woman*, the message of which was virtually identical.
7. Khin Thitsa, op. cit., 19. (See introduction, note 55.)

This, to Krisna, is the novel's core and purpose. It is easy to be lulled by the comic figures, especially Giaw and the dreadful Saay—and, for that matter, Maturot. Krisna excels in the creation of would-be society matrons such as Maturot, a monster of snobbery and ambition who starves her family and her servants (literally and figuratively) in order to compete with her wealthier friends. But, as everyone knows, evil deeds will be paid for sooner or later, if not in this life, then in the next—and in Krisna's novels, karmic retribution may well occur in this life.[8] *This Human Vessel* has an official heroine, Maturot's long-suffering, good-hearted, and far less interesting niece, Nitima. A contemporary version of the ideal woman, Nitima works full-time, manages her aunt's household, never loses her temper, is lovely in a demure way, and is destined for marriage to a handsome, wealthy, exceedingly honorable young man. Nevertheless, as often happens in Krisna's novels, it is the wonderfully awful people who steal the show.

The character of Giaw is particularly interesting in terms of the cultural perception of a fourteen-year-old girl who enters into a sexual relationship with a middle-aged man. Is she a victim? Unquestionably, she is—in the sense of her low status in society and her consequent dearth of honorable opportunities to rise in the world. But streetwise Giaw is more than a match for the comparatively innocent Plao, whose quite willing acceptance of her attentions sets in motion a series of tragicomic events that bring his and Maturot's world crashing down. One senses, on the novel's last page, that Giaw will always find a way.

One thing Krisna Asoksin has in common with Suwanee Sukhontha is a sense of humor that seems to sharpen itself on disaster. Both women have written about the lives of middle-class urban Thais; but Krisna's tales take us into a different neighborhood. In Suwanee's fictional neighborhood, the reader may meet women who live the artistic life, who are concerned with cheating lovers, and how they're go-

8. On the most superficial and immediate level, after the pregnant Giaw drops Pimrot's baby, causing everyone to fear head injury (needlessly, as it turns out), Giaw herself gives birth to a baby with hydrocephaly (an enlarged head due to edema). When first admitted to the hospital, Giaw contemptuously ridicules other women suffering in labor, telling them to shut up and stop annoying her; however, before her own child is born, she suffers greatly, carrying on tremendously and cursing everyone, especially Plao. This display of suffering is one more proof of her base character; a good woman suffers in silence.

ing to pay the rent next month, women who daydream about running off to Rome. The women one is likely to meet in Krisna's neighborhood are concerned with the unsatisfactoriness of husbands, and how to pay the mortgage, women who dream about the day they will be able to make the down payment on the Mercedes or finally buy the big diamond ring with perfect color.

In this anthology, the friends appear under one cover, their neighborhoods not so far apart—two writers who, between them, have shared with readers a wealth of contemporary Thai women's experiences, aspirations, opinions, and responses to the problems and the opportunities that have abounded in late twentieth-century Thailand.

3

DAUGHTERS

The Dancing Girl

Ussiri Dhammachoti

This nostalgic story is about a young man's first
love and the surprising decisions that determine
the course of his beloved's life.

She left her home by the sea when she was very young. She also left
an ocean of sadness in the hearts of a multitude of young fishermen
when they learned that she had become the star of a famous *ramwong*[1]
dance troupe. The most beautiful girl in our town had been transformed into a dancing girl, adored by a mob of admirers who hung
around the dance floor and begged her to wear the garlands of flowers they vied to bestow on her. We hated it.

The depth of our bitterness and disappointment was reflected in
the viciousness with which we soothed our wounded feelings.

"Once, she even asked me for my picture!" one of the boys admitted. "By now, she's probably thrown it in the toilet." He was particularly wounded, since he had given her not only his picture but also
the sea horse he had used to make a key ring.

"Is there any difference between a ramwong dancer and a whore?"
another boldly asked. We were stunned. "Well, you tell me! Dancing
around with men for money, and—you know how those girls act."

We had no idea.

"Forget her?" rejoined the one who had opined that ramwong
dancing was basic whoredom. "Forgetting is too good for her."

Originally published in the collection *Mŭan thalee jà mii jâw khɔ̌ɔng* (approximately, "as
if the sea could be owned") (Bangkok: Kam Kaew Press, 1981). Another, somewhat con-
densed version of this translation appears in Mary Ann Caws and Christopher Prendergast, eds., *The HarperCollins World Reader: The Modern World* (New York: Harper-
Collins, 1994).

1. The ramwong is a stylized folk dance with gestures that evoke Thai classical
dancing. In the post–World War II era, troupes of dancers and musicians developed a
corrupted form of ramwong dancing; men paid to dance with "ramwong girls" at temple fairs and other festive occasions.

Our crowd—that is, my friends from grammar school days, who worked with their fathers on the boats, and I, mysteriously still a student[2]—engaged in long, intimate conversations on the nature of love and friendship, during which we inevitably turned to the subject of our dancing girl and her perfidy. She had been at school with us, she was our age, she had been one of *us*.

Before she had become a dancing girl, she had been nothing more than a girl who cleaned fish at the docks. No—that is unfair. Ever since we were children, she had been the prettiest girl in our town. And when she was grown, even the smell of the fish and the wet, salty air, both of which clung to her, took nothing away from her looks.

Every morning when the boats reached shore and the boys had done their chores, they would casually amble down the dock to the brine house where she worked. They flattered her and showed off, each trying to get the largest share of her attention.

She scraped and washed and gutted fish, then steamed them and sold them in the high-roofed brine house while I had but one desire: to be near the one who was loveliest of all, loveliest in every part. Even her teeth were lovely, as white and as regular as the whitecaps in the bay on a breezy day. Such was the extent of my madness.

But pursuing her was more difficult for me than for the others, for I did not go out fishing with my father; therefore, I had no honest excuse for hanging around the brine house. I solved this problem by developing a passionate, obscure love for the sea. Early each morning, I would wander down to the shore to stare thoughtfully at the waves, to gaze raptly at the horizon, where the sun would soon emerge again. When I thought I had stared and gazed long enough (five or ten minutes), I would casually saunter into the brine house.

If she was leaving to go somewhere, I would discover where she was going. I would follow that graceful, gliding, maddening walk of hers at a careful distance, then run ahead and happen to run into her at her destination.

Perhaps I was a little madder than the rest.

It was a bitter thing to realize that a man had come from a ramwong troupe, had talked her into an audition, had led her away to her new life, and not one of us had known a thing about it until the

2. Several of Ussiri's short stories touch upon the theme of the young man who leaves the village to be educated in Bangkok, as Ussiri has done.

day we went to the brine house and learned, from others who in no way felt about her as we did, the reason for her absence. She had not confided in a single one of us or asked our opinion or even mentioned the matter. It was then that we understood what we were and had always been to her. Nothing.

When we thought of a dancer in a ramwong troupe, the picture in our minds was of a girl in a skirt so short that when she twirled around, you could actually see her *cheeks*. Ordinarily, a girl dancing the ramwong would have the grace of a sandpiper, smartly dipping and bobbing. But this was not the ordinary kind of ramwong, the kind everyone danced in our town on holidays. This was the ramwong of the girls in the professional troupes. It was their job to entice and stir up the men, who paid well to dance with them.

We thought of the girl we had known, the girl whose only scent had been the pure, honest smell of fish. How could she *do* this? How could our own angel of the brine house move the way those girls did in public, in front of a crowd of sleazy men whom we knew perfectly well would all be trying to get at her? How could she sway provocatively between colored paper rainbows and flashing lights, up on a stage, showing parts of the body that shouldn't be seen in public, with red makeup on her face, her lips, her fingernails?

Eventually, we stopped talking about her and even thinking about her. Life went on, we grew up. Several years passed. And then, one day, our dancing girl came home.

It was a day when flocks of birds floated on the bay, their pale, sand-colored wings reflecting the soft afternoon sun. She had come home with the fresh, salty winds we called kite winds, the winds of the southwest monsoon.

There she sat, looking quite composed on the bench of a pedicab. When its brakes squealed to a stop, people turned to look.

"I can't believe it!" one of my friends whispered. "Oh, look—she's got a *kid!*"

We watched her casually, from a distance, as she smiled at the pedicab man and climbed down carefully, holding her baby firmly under one arm.

The friend who stood beside me on that afternoon had a baby son of his own. Almost all of my old crowd had married young and now had wives and children. Everyone was married except for me, whose mysterious, never-ending education did not allow it.

I was the only one who greeted her, and I even dared to start a conversation.

She had changed greatly, but if she had been living the kind of wild life we had imagined, it didn't show. In fact, she looked even cleaner, softer, paler, and better than in the old days. Her clothes were fashionable and up-to-date. Definitely, she looked like a stranger; there was nothing about her to suggest our town.

She had married a guitar player. When he was shot in a fight (over her), she had simply packed up her baby, come home, and left the occupation of ramwong dancer forever. Her plan, she told me, was to work with her father on his fishing boat.

When I told my friends, they laughed themselves sick.

"Yeah, with red nail polish," one scoffed.

Several of them suggested that perhaps her plan was to *lure* the fish into the nets—by standing up in the boat and dancing. Others were sure that she had come home for another reason.

"Isn't it obvious? She needs a new husband to support the guitar player's kid."

That seemed reasonable, but most of us thought that she wouldn't last long enough for that to happen.

"In a couple of weeks, she'll be back in the ramwong. Work out in a boat? Come on . . . can you see her pulling nets in the rain?"

We all agreed on one thing: somehow, the dancing girl had run out of alternatives and had realized that she had no choice but to come home to the old folks.

Her father's boat was small. He brought his catch home to his wife, who hawked the fish on the streets. Everyone had felt sorry for both of them when their daughter went off to begin her ramwong dancing career, caring nothing about their fate.

Years had passed since she left us. Like the sand and the waves, like the current and the voice of the wind, we and our town might look as though nothing about us could ever change. But, in fact, many things had changed.

Surely, our injured feelings had healed long ago, but in their stead were suspicion and mistrust. We knew her, yet we didn't know her at all; so we felt justified in our mistrust, our suspicion, and our contempt.

I could scarcely remember how I had once felt about her. I was quite sure, now, that the girl had never had the slightest notion of our madness. What right had any of us to hold a grudge? For that was what our suspicion and mistrust were grounded in: an old grudge. We had loved her, and she hadn't spared a thought for us.

I decided that I, at least, was above old grudges, yet I must admit that when I told the others about her intention of going out with her father in the little fishing boat and they all laughed, I laughed along with them. The first day the dancing girl went to sea, the sound of laughter reached far, far out over the Gulf of Thailand.

o   o   o   o

My editor frowned.

"What are you talking about? *Why not?* This is a perfect story for you. Why can't you fly down there for a couple of days? Here is this woman, all by herself, going out to sea every day, bringing in her catch—just like a man! It's incredible! I heard about her while I was down there on vacation. I can't believe you didn't think of this story yourself."

I said nothing.

"Come on, you *must* know her—she's from your town, she's your age. The fishermen down there call her Meh Yaa Nang, 'the guardian spirit of the fleet.' It's like something out of a novel. Here she is, a widow with a kid, living with her old mother. She was gorgeous when she was young. She was a ramwong dancer in one of those traveling troupes, the star, so what does she do? Her husband gets shot, she quits, she goes home to a fishing village and goes out to sea with her father.

"Look, I *want* this story, you understand? You go down there, talk to her, get the details. Ask her everything. How does she feel when she's out there in the middle of the night. Is she cold? Is she lonely? Has she ever been really scared? People will want to know what inspired her to take up her father's work, that kind of thing. How much money she makes. What she does for fun. Does she go to the movies? Go to watch the *likay*?[3] What does she think about small-boat fishing as an occupation? And women's rights—whatever you do, don't for-

---

3.   The likay, or traveling folk theater, once popular in rural areas and also in Bangkok, still exists but is much diminished.

get to ask what she thinks about women's rights. Why didn't she re-marry? Ask her about sex—and get the name of that boat."

o   o   o   o

When her father died, everyone thought that would be the end of the fishing. No woman went out alone in a small boat, fighting the sea and the wind. And there had never been a new husband. Alone, she cared for her little girl and for her old mother. When people asked whether it was a hard life, she said that she could endure. And en-dure she did. She was tough and as brave as any man; and she was the only woman on the Gulf of Thailand who went out alone, every night, into the wind, darkness, loneliness, and uncertainty of the sea.

I saw it right away. The words *The Dancing Girl* had been shakily painted in red letters on the bowsprit of the shabby boat.

Each evening, when the wind came off the shore, she would start her engine and aim that small boat out into the darkness, standing with one hand on the helm, her loose fisherman's clothes snapping in the wind, her hair streaming behind her.

I did not expect to see any trace of the girl in the brine house or of the ramwong star, and I did not find any. Her skin was dark and coarse. The palms of her hands were hard and flecked with scars. From head to foot, she was dirty, and she didn't smell good. Her manner was straightforward. She looked strong. There wasn't much about her that was—well, how else can I say it?—that was like a woman.

Too embarrassed to tell her what I was doing there, I said that I had come to visit the old crowd and asked her how things were going.

"Oh, fine," she said, with what seemed to me a measuring look. "And what do you do now?"

"I, uh, write . . . I write things and—and I get paid for it." I figured there was no way I could work the next item into the conversation gracefully, so I just blurted it out. "Would you mind if I took your picture?"

"My picture?" She laughed, and her hand flew to her hair; and in that moment, she seemed shy. "Ooy! Waste your film for nothing."

She glanced away, wiped her hands on her pants, and said, "You know, I still have that picture you gave me."

Yes, it was I who had sent her the picture and the sea-horse key ring. Finally, she let me take her picture.

My old friends had become the fishermen who called her Meh Yaa Nang. Now they told me that they were ashamed to remember their unkindness to her when she had first come home. Now they spoke of her as if she were some miraculous treasure they had been proud to discover. She was theirs. She belonged to them, to the whole town.

It was not an easy visit for me. For several years, I had lived far from my friends and far from their lives. I was a stranger, a foreigner, and worse. The palms of my hands were soft and pale. A little salt water made them peel. Watching the waves offshore made me feel dizzy, and the wind stung my eyes. A few hours in the sun gave me a headache, and I worried about malaria. I was too soft for this place. I thought about how my old friends endured the heat and cold and rain; how they contended with huge waves and frightening winds to earn a living. And so did this woman, at whom we all had laughed when she climbed into a boat with her father on a morning long ago.

Like the sand and the waves, like the current and the voice of the wind, the old town looked pretty much the same, but in fact everything had changed. My friends had changed, I had changed, and she, like everything and everyone else, had changed. She was a different dancing girl.

But I saw in her a kind of beauty I had never seen before, the quality and permanence of which was so much greater than the pretty face I had remembered. She was like a star far above the dark bay or a tern floating on the wind, like the color of the sky or a cloud—all the things that, taken together, made the little town by the sea, which is very beautiful, more beautiful still.

O   O   USSIRI DHAMMACHOTI AND
           "THE DANCING GIRL"

Ussiri Dhammachoti, who writes under his own name, is perhaps the most admired male short story writer in Thailand today. He was born

in Prachuap Khiri Khan Province in 1947, and began writing short stories while he was a university student. With the publication of his first
collection of short stories, Ussiri was immediately hailed by leaders
of the literary community as an important new writer. As of this writing, nine collections of his short stories, three novels, and three books
for young people have been published. He is now the editor of *Siam
Rath*, Bangkok's leading newspaper.

The most political of Ussiri's short stories revolve around the
theme of the individual's responsibility to take moral action, when
necessary at the cost of the traditional Thai virtue of obeying one's
superior. The most famous such short story is "And the Grass Is Trampled," a tale of best friends, Nak and Hern, each of whom works as a
bodyguard to a criminal. When the criminals cease to be friends, each
bodyguard is ordered to kill the other. At the end of a brutal knife fight
just before dawn, as one man lies dead and the other lies dying, the
survivor regrets his act. The theme of this story, written when mili-
tary-political oppressors held the Thai value of loyalty over the heads
of political dissidents and labeled all protest "communist," could
scarcely be missed: "Nak feels the ultimate obligation that has ruled
his life begin to loosen and fall away. He will soon be free of all bonds,
free of the great pledge of his life. There will be nothing, from this moment forward, no one to control Nak or Hern. No bosses."[1]

Admittedly on the basis of conversations alone, I believe that,
among Thai readers, men are more interested in Ussiri's political stories than are women, who have told me that they find them ("And the
Grass Is Trampled," particularly) melodramatic and "the sort of thing
men like." But not all of Ussiri's stories are either violent or tragic. On
the contrary, the sense of humor evident in "The Dancing Girl" is
present in much of his work. While many of his stories portray the
lives of disadvantaged Thais, some of them are disadvantaged simply by dint of their own moral shortcomings, bad habits, and self-
indulgence—characteristics that are often freely confessed and sometimes even celebrated. Typical of these stories is "A Beggar, a Cat, and
a Drunk," a hilarious first-person tale that ends with a crowd of men

---

1.   From my unpublished translation. This story appears in Thai, with an English
translation by Chamnongsri L. Rutnin, in *Kuntong, You Will Return at Dawn*, 3d ed.
(Bangkok: Kaw Kai Press, 1987). The first edition of this collection (only in Thai) was
awarded the SEAWrite award in 1981.

drinking in a squalid shop beside a reeking canal, plying a beggar with coins until he leaps into the canal to retrieve a drowning cat. The theme in stories of this kind (of which the author has written quite a few) seems limited to "you would think a person could do better with his life than this." They suggest that a man's high ideals may be balanced by a discouraging lack of performance in real life: "My best friends and I were discussing our usual favorite subjects. . . . We cursed national politics, we criticized the government. When we tired of the government, we turned to sports, culture, the probable activities of rich and famous people. . . . Ours is not a narrow world. Our interests are numerous and diverse, our conversations enlivened by the power of our imagination, the radiance of our dreams, our natural high humor, and the flow of liquor down our throats."[2]

"The Dancing Girl" is included in this anthology because it is the story of a most intriguing and mysterious woman—*as perceived by a male narrator*—who, in turn, was created by a male author. When I asked Thais to suggest stories about women for this anthology, this story was often mentioned (especially by men). No one pointed out that the woman who presumably is the focus of the story remains entirely unknown to the reader.

This is a woman seen entirely through the male gaze. First, she is an object of adoration; in the early part of the story she is given no lines, nor does she need any. Talking could scarcely add to her appeal. Her appearance is more than enough: her "graceful, gliding, maddening walk," her hands that remain lovely even when gutting fish. Still, the narrator and his friends are outraged when she goes off with the ramwong troupe, not having "confided in a single one of us or asked our opinion or even mentioned the matter. It was then that we understood what we were and had always been to her. Nothing."

She only speaks, and then says very little, when she is beyond desirability: "Her skin was dark and coarse. The palms of her hands were hard and flecked with scars. From head to foot, she was dirty, and she didn't smell good. Her manner was straightforward. She looked strong. There wasn't much about her that was—well, how else can I say it?—that was like a woman."

---

2.   From my unpublished translation. This is the title story of a collection of Ussiri's work published by Kaw Kai Press, Bangkok, in 1988.

In an endearingly self-denigrating passage (very typical of Ussiri's work), the narrator compares himself with the sturdy fishermen: "The palms of my hands were soft and pale. A little salt water made them peel. Watching the waves offshore made me feel dizzy, and the wind stung my eyes. A few hours in the sun gave me a headache, and I worried about malaria."

In the one exchange of conversation between the man and the woman, the former dancing girl chides the narrator for wanting to take her photograph: "'My picture?' She laughed, and her hand flew to her hair; and in that moment, she seemed shy. 'Ooy! Waste your film for nothing.'" These words curiously echo those of the antiheroine of Suwanee Sukhontha's "Snakes Weep, Flowers Smile": "Once I had stood in the midst of [a patch of blooming coreopsis], looking perky while he took my picture. 'Don't waste the film,' I had protested. 'I'm not pretty.' Don't think I said it so that he would contradict me; I meant it. He was stubborn, trusting his hand with the camera."

Although there is nothing about her that is "like a woman," the dancing girl is in a sense beatified by "a kind of beauty I had never seen before." She is "like a star far above the dark bay or a tern floating on the wind, like the color of the sky or a cloud." Beyond desiring, beyond gender. To this extent, this woman is the embodiment of a Buddhist ideal, from two distinct perspectives: She herself is beyond desires (as far as we know), doing her job, supporting her family, fearless, egoless. Moreover, she inspires no tainting lust in the men who once desired and now admire her: "My old friends . . . told me that they were ashamed to remember their unkindness to her when she had first come home. Now, they spoke of her as if she were some miraculous treasure they had been proud to discover."

"Look, I *want* this story," the young reporter's editor demands. "You go down there, talk to her, get the details. Ask her everything. . . . And women's rights—whatever you do, don't forget to ask what she thinks about women's rights." But the readers of Ussiri's story framing a story will never know the answers to those questions, for they are never asked in the glimpse we are provided of the interview. The editor's final demand is that the reporter "get the name of that boat," which he does.

It is a charming story that is not really about a woman but about a man's feelings regarding a woman. First, he imagines her as his adolescent ideal; finally, he imagines her as a composite symbol of sea, sky, and the working poor. We learn the name of the boat, an intriguing clue that is left to the reader to puzzle over, but we never learn the woman's name. She is woman, as sand on the beach is sand, which may be wrought into any number of images in the hands of a skillful artist, only to dissolve with the next rising tide.

Greenie

Manop Thanomsri

This is a sad tale of an orphaned village girl.

Dry straw had littered the ground since the rice harvest. The little girl knelt and reached beneath it, rubbing her palm quickly over the dirt. Smiling, she grasped a tuft of green grass that hugged the dry earth, and pulled.

"Eat!" she said, extending her arm. "This is delicious grass, Aye-Too, not just old straw. Come on, *eat* now. I picked it for you."

She reached up to pat his cheek tenderly, and the old water buffalo blinked three times: *brip, brip, brip.* He exhaled loudly, patiently, then slowly craned his great neck upward and stuck out his tongue. He took the grass, then lowered his head and resumed pushing at the ground with his nose.

"You're still not full?" She put her hand on her hips and frowned. "Oh, Aye-Too! You eat a lot. I don't know what I am going to do with you."

The girl looked woefully into Aye-Too's eyes, shaking her head and making little *jik-jik* noises so that he would know she was quite put out with him.

"You stay here now. There's plenty of green grass under this straw. I'll find more for you. Don't go wandering off."

She gave orders to the buffalo, sounding like a busy mother. Then she turned and knelt again, scrabbling beneath the straw for tufts of new grass.

Originally entitled "Ii làa nɔ́ɔy" (approximately, "little one"), this story appeared in a collection of Manop Thanomsri's short stories entitled *Thaang sǎay rúng* (The way of the rainbow), published by Kradaad Saa, Bangkok, 1984.

•   •   •

Greenie is too small and too thin. Certainly, she looks younger than other children her age in the village. The villagers call her Greenie[1] because her skin is so dark that she makes them think of a black water beetle, so black and iridescent, so oily greenish black that it is blacker than black itself. And when she lifts her great round eyes and peers upward, the whites of her eyes, even though they are not very white or clear,[2] even so, they make her skin look still darker by contrast. "Greenie" is a better name for her than "Pin," the name her father gave her.

Greenie's father left her with his sister when she was very young, declaring that he would go to Bangkok to find work, and that as soon as he had done so, he would send money to pay for school and to meet the other expenses involved in adding a child to the family. No one has heard from him since.

As soon as she was old enough, Greenie was given the job of tending her aunt's sizable herd of water buffalo, gentle animals that could be looked after by even the smallest of children. Every morning, it was Greenie's job to drive the herd out into the fields, stay with it until evening, then drive the animals home again. Greenie and Aye-Too, the oldest buffalo in the herd, hit it off immediately. He was so old that he had not worked in the fields for two years, but Greenie felt that except for his wonderful horns, which curved down nearly to the ground, there was nothing about Aye-Too that would make you think him older than the others.

Every day, when she went to the fields, Greenie rode on Aye-Too's back and stayed with him until the sky began to grow dark. She would slap his side with her small hand, and as Aye-Too loped off, away from the herd, Greenie would laugh with delight and excitement, bouncing and swaying and clutching his shaggy neck. The faster he ran, the farther from the herd, the happier Greenie was.

When Aye-Too galloped across the fields, Greenie could believe that he was carrying her swiftly away, far from Auntie's house, far beyond the whole village, all the way to some other world. Perhaps to a world where her mother and father were waiting for her. For these reasons,

---

1.   Ee-Kiaw, or *ii khĭaw.*
2.   A common result of malnutrition, poor general health, and especially frequent untreated infections.

Greenie scarcely paid attention to the other buffaloes in the herd, which wandered off everywhere. Auntie had scolded her until she was too disgusted to scold her anymore, and after a while Greenie's only task was to care for Aye-Too, the old and useless buffalo with horns that curved to the ground.

The cock crowed beneath the house. Greenie awoke and crept down the stairs into the yard where Aye-Too stood waiting. He had come to meet her, as he always did. She climbed onto his back, and as the pale light of morning began to rise in the east, Aye-Too carried Greenie away. Much later, they stood beneath the full sun of morning, surrounded by the vastness of the dry fields.

Pulling at the grass with his strong teeth and ambling about at will, Aye-Too was forbidden nothing—except the company of the herds. Greenie kept him away from all of them, for the herds were tended by village children, who yelled, "There's Crazy Ghost! Yah, yah, Crazy Ghost!"[3] whenever they saw her. If they noticed her talking to Aye-Too, they would pursue her and ridicule her all the more. Then they would go home and tell their parents and everyone else in the village about Greenie talking to Aye-Too. The villagers whispered about her, recalling things her father had told the aunt about the circumstances of her birth, things that had not seemed unusual at the time but now made them wonder. However, the child's birth was nothing compared with the mysterious and alarming death of the mother— and it was the latter recollections that continued to feed the rumors about Greenie.

Some said that Greenie was quite mad, exactly like her mother. Some said that the girl herself was not mad but possessed by a demon that had put madness into her. A few dared to say that it was this girl herself, this Greenie, who had caused the terrible death of her own mother.

Greenie knew about the rumors and thought about them. The older she grew, the more thoughtful and quiet she became. She shrank from people and was unwilling to speak to anyone. Not the village children nor their parents nor even her own aunt. When anyone spoke

---

3. "Crazy ghost" (*phĭi bâa*) is a strong insult in Thai.

to her, her face would take on a look of queer stillness that no one could fathom, and she would slip away without saying a word. Like a ghost.

But she talked to Aye-Too all day long.

Greenie squatted again to explore a new spot in her search for tufts of fresh green grass. "When will you ever be filled up, Aye-Too? I've worn out all my fingers pulling grass for you—look!" She held her hands beneath his nose. "I said *look*, Aye-Too—see how red they are now?"

Aye-Too stared at the little hands. His ears twitched as a fly buzzed above his head, and his lower jaw continued its patient shifting of Greenie's latest offering.

"Someday they'll all be sorry. 'Crazy Ghost'—*bah!* When I'm big, Aye-Too, no one will call me a crazy ghost, because I won't let them."

Aye-Too blinked and slowly turned his head.

"It's time to go to the mound now." Greenie sniffed loudly and wiped her nose and upper lip with the back of one hand, a habit that effected no change in the small nose's permanent soreness and wetness, or in the rough, chapped skin of her upper lip. Deftly, she pleated the thin, worn fabric of her *pasin*,[4] retucking it at her waist. "Kneel!" she ordered. Aye-Too continued to stand, staring off across the field, twitching his ears and chewing grass. Greenie slapped him smartly on the side three times. "Didn't I tell you to kneel? Sometimes I think you don't even listen."

Aye-Too slowly craned his neck, turned his head to look at her, switching his tail at a bothering fly; then, very slowly, he bent his front legs and knelt beside her. Greenie's eyes flashed as she crawled onto his back. "Do you know that you are a very stubborn, bad buffalo? I should tell Auntie to sell you. Do you know what that means? Sell you to the slaughterhouse, where they would cut off your hands and feet, and cut your throat; and then you would get fried up."

Aye-Too plodded forward, wrinkling his nose and making *f-f-f-t, f-f-f-t* noises at the flies.

"I wouldn't do it, really, but you have to listen better. I'm hungry, too. You're not the only one. But don't think that I want to eat Aun-

4. A simple skirt fashioned from a length of cloth.

tie's rice, because I don't. She is not our mother and father.[5] The ones who love us are our mother and father, that's all. But our father, I don't know . . . where is Bangkok, Aye-Too? Our father went to Bangkok."

Greenie was quiet for a while, staring out over the fields.

"Aye-Too, you were born before us. Did you ever see our mother? We cannot remember what our mother's face looked like. She was beautiful, though. Not black, like us."

Greenie smiled proudly, thinking of her beautiful mother. She bounced and swayed in harmony with Aye-Too's loping stride, then bent forward and laid her face against his neck, wrapped her arms around it as best she could, gently rubbed his stiff, shaggy hide with her fingertips.

"Do you ever get lonely?" she whispered. "We are very lonely." Greenie's large, round, dreaming eyes spilled over with tears. "We think about our father and wonder when he will come and take us to live with him. Auntie has a good heart—but her children have *black* hearts.[6] They never let us get enough to eat. We never, ever get enough to eat."

Greenie let her tears soak into Aye-Too's hair and at last pulled up the hem of her pasin and wiped her face. "I wish I could eat grass, like you," she said, "because then I wouldn't be so hungry." She closed her eyes and fell asleep, and as she slept, Aye-Too carried her toward a cluster of trees on a distant rise of ground, the place to which they returned each day. When he stopped, she awoke. He knelt to let the child down, then wandered off to graze nearby. Greenie sat down and began to play with the old cup and dish she had once found buried here.

"I'm late today, Mama. I had to find so much grass for Aye-Too, poor thing. He has to shove his old nose into the hard dirt to get something to eat, and it hurts him. Are you hungry yet, Mama? I'm making your food now. Don't worry, it won't take long."

She set down the cup and dish, and plucked a withering flower and some dry leaves from a small bush. She scraped a little sandy earth with the cup, carefully poured it over the flower and the leaf, in the dish, and mixed everything together with her fingers.

"Now you eat, Mama. But I'll tell you right now, it isn't very good.

---

5. First-person plural is used in the Thai version in this part of the story. The reference to "rice" suggests food in general.

6. *Jay dam.*

Just some old leaves and a flower." She rose and wiped her hands on her pasin. "You eat, and I'll climb up into the tree and get some tamarind pods."

Greenie pulled herself onto the lowest branch of the tamarind tree that cast its meager shadow over the mound. She reached up, picked a pod, peeled it open, and began to chew on the seed inside. "Ee—ee! Too sour, you old tamarind—you make my tongue numb." But she continued to chew. The tamarind seeds, sticky and sweet-sour, were her morning and noon food every day.

"Aye-Too, shall I sing a song?" She spat a seed, then gravely raised one hand to her ear, as if listening carefully for a faraway, faint sound. It was a gesture she had learned from watching the men who came to the village with the singing shows. Her pure, light voice rang out from the tamarind tree.

> Sleep, my little one . . .
> close your eyes, quickly, quickly now,
> for Mama has gone to the fields.
> Mama, where are you?
> You never return . . .
> Mama . . . in the fields . . .
> time to come home,
> come home, take your baby
> on your hip, walk through the village
> while your baby . . . drinks your milk . . .

"That's all." Greenie jumped down from the tree. "Did you like my song?" She picked up the cup and dish, and tossed their contents aside. "Full now, Mama? You have to eat a lot, so you'll get better. I want to see your face. I want to live with you again, so you have to get better."

She lay on her back, one arm beneath her head. With her free hand, she gently patted the earth beside her. The air had become very still; the quiet had deepened after her song; and she gazed solemnly upward through the tamarind leaves that glittered in the noon sun. Once again, the bad dream started.

Greenie's mother had become ill a few days after the little boy was born. Her symptoms were frightening. She spoke wildly, and no one could understand her. Sometimes she shouted, sometimes she laughed, and sometimes she cried out that she was cold, but her body was hot as fire. She pulled cruelly at her own skin and hair, but didn't seem to feel any pain.

Greenie's father and the other villagers viewed these symptoms with alarm and fear. There was no one who knew how to help her. The baby died. When Greenie's mother had been ill for three days, everyone was sure that she must be possessed by an evil spirit. She became violent, and when she snatched a piece of red-hot charcoal from the fire and stuffed it into her mouth and even chewed on it before they could get it out, Greenie's father had to agree that his wife was possessed by an evil spirit. He went to a nearby village and fetched a monk who was renowned as an exorcist. If she could be cured, his neighbors told him, this monk alone had the power to do it.

The monk came. He was very old. Slowly, he climbed the stairs into their house. Greenie lay curled up in a corner. No one paid any attention to her. Her mother lay on the floor in the center of the room. When the monk looked into her face, he startled the curious villagers who had shuffled into the house behind him by pointing his finger at her and laughing loudly. "Where did you come from, you evil thing?"

The delirious woman tried to get up. She began screaming at the monk, but her words were meaningless. He turned to Greenie's father and said, "Yes, it is true. A strong spirit has possessed your wife. I think that you have waited too long, but I will try to defeat it."

He directed Greenie's father, and the others too, to bring buckets of water. Everyone rushed off, returning with a full bucket in hand. The monk knelt beside her, closed his eyes, and began to pray. As he prayed, the villagers filed by him with their buckets, over which he held a burning candle. When some of the tallow had dripped into each of the buckets, and he had finished praying, he called for a dipper. When he dashed the first dipperful of water into Greenie's mother's face, she shrieked and writhed on the floor and screamed curses at him.

"Ha! It is a very strong spirit," the old monk said. When he splashed another dipperful of water into her face, she only groaned and trembled and then lay still.

"It is gone now," the monk said to Greenie's father. "It was a very terrible spirit from the Pone Tong Forest. But my words also were strong and prevailed over that spirit." He handed the dipper to the man. "Prayer and holy water have done this deed. The Buddha and the Scriptures are all very well, but in such a matter, it is the monk upon whom you must depend."[7] Greenie's father took the dipper from the monk reverently, dipped it into a full bucket, and poured it over his wife's body. And one by one, the villagers followed him, each one lowering the dipper into a bucket and emptying it over Greenie's mother. She did not scream curses anymore or wail or shriek with terrifying laughter or shiver with imagined cold. She looked peaceful.

The monk smiled, slung his bag over his shoulder, and prepared to leave. "Do not let her do any work. She must rest for a few days. From this strong and evil spirit, her body has lost its strength." He turned and looked once more at the woman who lay soaked with holy water on the floor of her house.

The villagers left, talking among themselves in low tones about the fearful symptoms of the possessed woman and the amazing skill of the monk. Soon, the little family was alone again.

When Greenie awoke the next morning, her father was sitting beside her mother, weeping. Her mother lay still, looking just the same as she had the night before. After a while, neighbors came into the house and laid her mother on a cloth and wrapped the ends of the cloth around two poles, and four men bore her away on their shoulders and took her, so they told Greenie, to the rise of land where the tamarind tree grew. Greenie waited and waited for the people to bring her back, but after a while she lost hope; and at last she could not remember her mother's face, only that she was beautiful.

The sun has begun to sink in the west, and the light is soft. Greenie leads Aye-Too into the bog and washes him, then climbs onto his back again. When they reach Auntie's house, the sun is almost touching the earth. A big truck is parked in front of the house, and many villagers have gathered around it. Greenie looks at it with suspicion. The presence of a truck in the village is a matter of great excitement. Very seldom does such a thing occur. When it does, there is a special reason.

Greenie jumps down from Aye-Too's back and approaches the

---

7. In this scene, the monk's tone is rather defensive. The author is illustrating the divergence between true Buddhist practice and the superstitious, ignorant practices of some poorly educated, usually rural monks.

truck. Why has it come here? And why is it parked in front of Auntie's house? Suddenly, she hears a commotion, turns and sees Aye-Too running, a crowd of shouting men close behind him. A smart rap on the back of her head nearly makes her fall forward.

It is Auntie. "Greenie! Make Aye-Too get into the truck!" She looks angry and is gasping for breath. Greenie is pushed forward, struck again. She runs awkwardly, with a searing pain in her chest, knowing what she has refused to know, that she is going to lose all that she holds dear in this life. She stumbles, stops, Auntie shouts at her again, Greenie goes on. The villagers stop their milling about; the men no longer chase Aye-Too. They all are watching Greenie. She walks toward the water buffalo, who is now standing still, breathing mightily, his eyes bulging with terror. Greenie speaks to him; and when he lowers himself, she climbs onto his back and guides him forward. He moves obediently, slowly but without hesitation, across the yard, up the ramp, and into the truck. At once, the villagers leap forward, slamming the gate at the back of the truck, tossing ropes about Aye-Too's neck, securing him.

Greenie slides from his back, jumps to the ground without help. She turns, sees Aye-Too twisting frantically against the ropes, runs to the side of the truck so that he can see her. Auntie takes money from the truck driver, stands counting it while he climbs up into the cab and starts the engine. The truck lurches forward and roars off down the bumpy road in a thick cloud of dust.

The pain in her chest and throat is unbearable. Greenie struggles with all her might not to let the tears escape her eyes. Although the cloud of dust is thick, she can see Aye-Too, fighting, bellowing, struggling against the ropes that bind him.

The villagers stand about for a while, talking about the event. None of them notices that Greenie has lost her great struggle, that her cheeks are drenched with tears that drip steadily onto the ground before her. Soon, they turn to go home. It is over.

What is there to say, after all, about an old water buffalo being driven off to town?

O O   MANOP THANOMSRI AND "GREENIE"

Manop Thanomsri writes short stories and novels under his own name. He was born in Bangkok in 1948, and published his first short story in

1969; thus, he is of the same generation as Ussiri Dhammachoti. Like Ussiri, he is concerned with moral issues. Much of his work focuses on the lives of the very poor, particularly children and prostitutes. Five collections of his stories have been published to date, one of which received a PEN-Thailand award. Manop also has published six novels and one book for young people. Currently, he is an editor with a Bangkok publishing firm.

"Greenie" was chosen for this anthology because it is such a convincing, painful portrayal of the life of a poor, rural girl, and because Manop's graphic depiction of some of the villagers' beliefs and behaviors will be of particular interest to those readers who are not very knowledgeable about Thailand. But there is another, more compelling reason for its inclusion: this is probably the angriest selection in the anthology and the strongest indictment of Thai society.

Even a story as graphic in its description of an ill-used woman as "A Pot That Scouring Will Not Save" does not really take issue with traditional Thai values (except for the implicit message that a woman ought not to have to sacrifice her very life in trying to be a "good wife"). In that story, an evil man takes advantage of a woman who is trying to achieve the feminine ideal. But in Manop's story, some beliefs and behaviors that are quintessentially Thai are treated with contempt: for example, the belief in ghosts of all kinds, a belief that allows the children and adults in Greenie's village to treat her with great cruelty. Just prior to her death, Greenie's mother became delirious, shrieking with laughter while attempting to stuff live coals into her mouth. Her relatives and neighbors interpreted this terrifying and repulsive behavior as possession by evil spirits, and Greenie is suspected of having inherited a propensity for madness.

This is, obviously, a particularly negative view of rural Thai life. The world of this story is one in which people have little interest in each other and no apparent pity. It is a far cry, indeed, from the world we encounter in Kampoon Boontawee's *Child of the Northeast:* a loving extended family. In fact, even the following story, Preechapoul Boonchuay's "Mote of Dust on the Face of the Earth," about a rural girl who becomes an urban prostitute, puts a better face on family life in an impoverished village. There is no suggestion that the village in Manop's story was once kinder or a better place to live. Unlike many other short stories about poor rural folk, this one lays no blame on the influence of outside forces, such as foreigners (including exploitative

Thai "foreigners" from Bangkok). The message is unmistakable: there are aspects of Thai society that could stand improvement. No child ought to live under such conditions: hungry, unloved, uneducated, and completely unaware of what happiness, much less justice, might be. Greenie's only comforts are the fading memory of her mother and the companionship of an old animal. At the story's end, even Aye-Too has been taken from her, not out of spite, but as the result of complete indifference. The role of society in caring for such expendable children is conspicuous by its absence.

A Buddhist monk is portrayed as an ignorant man who defends incantations and rituals that have no real basis in Buddhism: "It was a very terrible spirit from the Pone Tong Forest. But my words also were strong and prevailed over that spirit. . . . Prayer and holy water have done this deed. The Buddha and the Scriptures are all very well, but in such a matter, it is the monk upon whom you must depend." Stupidity, selfishness, and superstition are the villains in this story; and even the monkhood is shown no quarter, an unusual decision in Thai fiction. (Several critically praised works of fiction have failed to win literary prizes over the past two decades, because the author touched the subject of corruption among the ranks of Buddhist monks.)

There are numerous contemporary short stories about sad, poor children, but none of them paints so indelible and unforgettable a picture of life on the margins of survival as this one. And none of them attains its sheer poetry, for example, Greenie's song to her lost mother, who becomes, with each lonely day, an ever more distant and precious memory of a time when someone loved her: "Mama . . . in the fields . . . / time to come home, / come home, take your baby / on your hip, walk through the village / while your baby . . . drinks your milk."

The child has within her a great capacity for love and loyalty; and she is amazingly sensitive, even to an old water buffalo. Therefore, it is obvious that the society is capable of producing loving, loyal, sensitive people. Unlike many of his peers, Manop completely avoids a didactic approach to writing about poverty. He simply tells the story and asks one question: "What is there to say, after all, about an old water buffalo being driven off to town?" The reader is left to think about that.

A Mote of Dust
on the Face of the Earth

Preechapoul Boonchuay

This story is about one girl's journey
from rural poverty to urban prostitution.

Heaven

Malisa was born on a morning when the wind was numbing cold. It
was the kind of cold that cracks the skin, exactly as the sun cracks the
earth in the dry season, cold that invades the body and freezes a person's very bones. Because she was born in such weather, the old people said that she would be unlucky.

But she survived. She grew to know pain and illness and hunger;
she learned to struggle for life like every other child in the village. In
one important respect she differed from many of them. She lived.

Malisa laughed and cried and played between the village houses
with the other children who had been chosen, by natural means, to
survive. Was she so unlucky then?

Although they had named her Malisa, she was called simply Saa.
She was given love by her father and mother, as much as they gave
to her older brother and younger sister. They scolded her when she
was stubborn and comforted her when she felt sad or disappointed.

When she was old enough, she went to school but not every day.
Some days, she had to stay home to help catch small frogs or lizards,
whatever was easiest to find; for Saa and her friends could do without school but not without food.

We all know the feeling of hunger. But the hunger that Saa and
her family so often felt had nothing to do with the pangs that remind
us that we have forgotten to eat breakfast or the growling stomach
that tells us it is time for lunch. This was the hunger that flashes and

This story appears under the title "Thulii pradàp din" (*thulii*, "a mote or particle of
dust"; *pradàp*, "to decorate"; *din*, "dirt; earth") in the anthology *Phét nám ngaam* (approximately, "sparkling jewels"), ed. Suchat Sawatsri (Bangkok: Duang Kamol, 1980;
produced by *Lôok nǎngsǔ* [World of books]).

tears, hunger that twists the gut, that makes one almost forget to breathe.

When Saa was ten years old, one day at dusk when the torches were about to be lit, a stranger came. The stranger was pretty, from her hair all the way down to her shoes. She sat on the porch of the little girl's house, a house so frail that it leaned. When it would collapse altogether, no one could say. Yet Saa heard the pretty lady say that the house was nice, a nice place to live. The air is so clean here, the lady said. It is so nice and quiet.

Even though she spoke the same dialect as the villagers, her speech had the sound of a person from Bangkok. She even talked pretty! But the little girl could not keep from laughing to herself when the lady said that she wished she could live just like Saa and her family.

Saa understood that the pretty lady had once lived in their village. She had gone to Bangkok many years ago when she was very young, and she had done well—not that you would wonder about that if you took one look at her. Yet, she said, she had never forgotten the place of her birth.

Now, she was looking for a little girl, one very much like *this* little girl, in fact—she smiled down at Saa and patted her head—to take to Bangkok and to help her find a job, so that she would have a chance to make something of herself, too. In fact, she knew of a job that Saa could get right now—as a waitress in a restaurant! And that would be only the start.

If the lady should take her! . . . but never mind, she would never, never go to Bangkok with that lady. Even to be a waitress in a restaurant. She would never want to be away from her father and mother, her big brother and her little sister. In this place, she was happy. All her friends were here. It was her place, her home.

The grown-ups talked for a long time. Her mother kept turning, looking at Saa. Her father sat and smoked his cigarette. What was he thinking? Finally, he sent her off to sleep. The grown-up people had things to talk about, he said. Saa did not know how late the lady stayed, because she fell asleep while they were still murmuring in the light from the torches.

Now it was morning, and Saa heard the sound she heard every day: her brother shouting to the water buffalo, which he would soon drive

So young but already has jobs has

to the fields. She hurried to light a fire and set the rice to cook. Her parents had got up before her, as always, but she was surprised to see that they were not preparing to go off to their field. Her mother looked unhappy, and her father looked angry. Something had happened, was still happening, something that she knew had to do with her.

Her mother knelt and deftly fanned the fire; smoke filled the room, and tears spilled from her eyes. *(hiding pain, but she could be crying any ways.*

"Mama! Let me do it. Look at what you did now, you made yourself cry."

But her mother would not give up the little fan. Her eyes were red; her flat nose was redder than usual. The girl sat still and looked thoughtfully into her mother's face for a long time.

"I have to go away with that lady, don't I?"

Now the mother's hurt and bitterness would not be contained; she covered her face with her hands and wept openly. The child went straight into her arms, and in sorrow and fear, they clung to each other, the woman's rough hand caressing her child.

Similar to other story, the woman allows all her sadness to show.

The afternoon sun began to wane. It was time for Saa to begin to prepare for the journey. On the next morning, she would leave.

Why had her father and mother chosen her? She didn't understand and was afraid to ask. Was she the one they didn't want? But that question didn't make any sense, because all day her mother had wept. She knew that her mother loved her. She lay awake most of the night, wondering and afraid.

On the following morning, she woke earlier than usual and slipped quietly from under the shabby mosquito net. She saw her father, sitting and smoking in the doorway, in the half-light. He had been there when she went to sleep. Had he been there all night?

His deep but quiet love for her, his answerless way — there is nothing he can do to save her.

"Saa—come here, child."

Saa tiptoed across the floor and knelt before him. The house was so quiet that she could hear the faint, rhythmic squeaking of her small footsteps on the ancient boards. Beneath the house, the water buffalo had just begun to stir and to breathe their deep, contented early morning sighs.

He drew her to him, put an arm around her, and bent his head to hers until his nose touched her hair. She nestled there, grateful for his strength and warmth, even though she knew this embrace for what it was: the embrace of parting. She felt his every breath, the deep inhalations and the low, steady exhalations.

"I love my Saa," he said in a soft voice. "And Mother loves Saa. But Saa knows how very poor our family is. Yet to know is not to understand, and I know you cannot understand now. So I must simply tell you. People cannot live without money; that is a fact. If you go to Bangkok with the lady, you will have pretty clothes and money to buy things with. You will be able to buy anything you want. At the least, you will be better off than you are now. You will have a job in a restaurant. That is a fine thing. But if you stay here with us? You know how it is. Some days we barely have enough to eat.

"But it isn't only that, Saa. I swore that I would never sell one of my children to go and work in Bangkok, as other people in the village have done, but today we are desperate for a certain sum of money. If we cannot get it somehow, in a few days we will not have even this house. My poor Saa, you are not old enough to understand. But you are old enough to work . . ."

He pushed her gently from him then, and his dark, sad eyes studied her carefully, as if he were looking straight into her heart.

"I know that you wonder why you must be the one to go. It is because your elder brother must help me, and your little sister is too young. You are the only one who is able to help us all, Saa. Perhaps you will not be too angry with me . . ." Her father swallowed hard. He then began to speak rapidly, striving to control his voice.

"Every one of you children is part of your father's heart. I don't know how I will live when my Saa goes away. But sometimes people have to sell life to have life. That is a hard thing, the hardest thing I know. But someday, Saa, I know that you will understand. Not now, not for a long time, but someday."

Saa nodded dumbly. A child of ten. What could she know, beyond love, anger, hunger, and happiness?

She studied her father's face carefully. His face was rough and dark from sun and weather, and heavily lined. His hair was stiff and dry, streaked with gray. Her father looked old. She had asked him not long before how old he was. He was thirty.

She heard the lady's voice below. Suddenly, her mother was beside her, weeping again, kissing her, one arm around Saa's shoulders as they descended the rickety stairs and crossed the hard, dusty earth to the road. In her other hand, she carried the worn-out bag that Saa would take with her to Bangkok.

Her father walked toward them.

"Lady," he said, "I give Ee-Saa[1] into your keeping to care for. I trust that she will be as a daughter to you, as one of your own family."

The lady laughed, raised a hand, and said, "Ooy, don't you worry! When she goes with me, you have nothing to worry about." She smiled at Saa. "We are already like elder and younger sister."

She gave Saa a little push. "Go on, then, *nuu*,"[2] she said.

All the world grew silent then.

Only Saa's little sister saw the journey to come as a step into a wholly better world, and she called out merrily, "Don't forget to buy a piece of pretty cloth, Saa, and send it to me! Promise you will!"

Saa trudged off beside the lady. She felt dizzy, and stopped and turned for a moment. She had to blink hard to bring them into focus: her little sister, jumping up and down and waving; her father standing, smoking his cigarette, his eyes half closed, his expression hard; and finally her mother, extravagant in her misery, as if Saa were not walking toward the road but being carried there on her funeral bier. Her brother was nowhere to be seen.

Saa felt a soft tug on her arm. "That's enough now, nuu," the lady said, not unkindly. As they went off down the road, she chattered amiably about the money that Saa would soon earn, of all that she would see and do, and of all that she would have in Bangkok.

When they reached the edge of the fields, where the woods began, Saa felt that someone was watching her from a hidden place. She knew that it was her brother, who had refused even to speak of her going. She knew that he was there, behind the trees, watching.

Later, when she thought of that day, the last clear picture in her

---

1. *Ee*, or *ii*, is a feminine name prefix that is commonly used within the rural family. Later in the story, when it is used by Saa's employers at the restaurant in Bangkok, it will have a derogatory connotation, emphasizing her low status.

2. Or *nŭu*, literally, "mouse." It is used as a first-person pronoun by female children; it is also used by women in situations where they wish to show deference or respect (as when talking to parents, teachers, and so on); and it is used as a second-person pronoun when speaking to a female child. The use of this word usually does not necessarily imply condescension. (Its use in calling a waitress, in a restaurant, is the equivalent of calling a waiter using the term *boy*. Although not respectful, it is certainly not contemptuous in the cultural context of the situation.)

mind was not of her weeping mother or her father's stern face or of her little sister waving good-bye, but of those trees hiding her brother.

Hell

"Ee-*Saa!* Don't stand there with your ugly mouth open, gaping at nothing. People are waiting to order food, so go! Hurry up, you idiot!"

The first thing Bangkok gave to Saa was a new language: the language of abuse.

The pretty lady had long since disappeared from Saa's world. In fact, she had disappeared immediately, once she had completed her task: the purchase of Saa from her mother and father, and her delivery to the people at the restaurant. Instead of the gold mine the woman had described to Saa's parents—the future of plenty for Saa that had been their only consolation in their grief and guilt—Saa found herself in one version of hell.

The gold mine turned out to be a small Chinese restaurant in downtown Bangkok. The owner required cheap labor, and nothing could be cheaper than the onetime cost of a young girl from an up-country village. Her only pay was room and board: she ate what leftovers there were and slept in a filthy alleyway next to the kitchen. Saa tried to cover herself with the cast-off scraps that served as bedding, but there was no way she could escape the rats and cockroaches. Day after day, she endured in this place—days, weeks, and months of a life beyond bearing.

She could never return to her parents; they could never call her back. She would never again be cherished or indulged, comforted for the disappointments and hurts of childhood. A child of ten, too small, too thin, she did every job that her employers did not want to do. She washed and ironed clothes, scrubbed floors, waited on tables, set up tables and chairs early in the morning, and finished her last tasks long after dark.

She was ten years old . . . then eleven . . .

In place of comfort, Saa received indifference, meanness, and, occasionally, murderous rage. Not a day passed that the child did not absorb coarseness and vulgarity, did not digest humiliation, disgust, bitterness, and pain. Not a night passed that Saa did not store these things in her heart, where they stayed. Although she was usually hungry, there were things that Saa wished for more than food. First: one whole day of rest. After that, the sound of laughter, the kind of laughter that she remembered from the days when she had played with other children in the paths between the village houses. After that, sweet words. And, finally, a little pity.

Of these wishes, not one was granted.

o   o   o   o

(*from See again*)   success me

I want to tell you about my Bangkok: it is a splendid city. I have been here for a long time. Of course, it is not the city my parents believed in, the gold mine that held nothing but prosperity, nothing but money. Not that it doesn't have those things. It has them—but not for people like my mother and father, or for the child I was. My Bangkok is a prosperous, glittering city and a lonely one. But don't think that I feel sorry for myself, because I don't.

Don't call me Ee-Saa—that miserable little creature who worked in the Chinese restaurant. No one has called me that for a long time. Or nuu—you can be sure that nobody calls me nuu . . .

Several years have passed since I learned how to take care of myself, to make something of myself, to—and this is much more important—to deal with all the people who hurt me, in such a way that they remain angry for a long, long time.   (?) *is she talking about* Pretty lady / vulgar Bangkok or family?

When I finally left the Chinese restaurant, a lot of money left with me, thanks to my friends. It didn't take me long to learn that I was not alone. There were a lot of us here. It was after I discovered them that my life changed. We went to the homes of the rich, posing as honest, stupid peasants from poor villages, eager to earn a pittance in Bangkok. We knew how they expected us to behave. It was easy. We let them knock us about for as long as it took to learn where everything of value was kept, and then we disappeared, taking it all with us.

I had hard teachers: cruelty and contempt and people without mercy. And I was a good student. I have always wished that I could tell my mother and father that, finally, I did find the gold mine.

During the first few years, there were many things that I could not control. My girlhood—such as it had been—vanished. I became a young woman, which is to say that I became the prey of the urban beast. The first of these was the "gentleman" in whose house I was working, doing my usual job. Or my usual two jobs, I should say. Washing clothes and also scrubbing floors. The place looked promising, for my friends and my ultimate purpose, and it had been, as usual, no problem to get a job there for a pittance. They were always so eager to hire us.

The man I politely called sir, the man before whom I crouched as he passed by so that my head would never be above his, turned on me without warning one day, trapped me, hurt me, destroyed the virginity I barely knew I possessed. I was hurt and angry, but eventually I let him do as he wished, whenever he wished, and at the end, I even felt a certain loyalty toward him. After all, he was the first.

But, then, there was his wife.

"Slut! What did you think? That you would become the 'lady of the house'? You? Hah! You will walk over my corpse first, you upcountry whore!" And so on and on.

I ask you—was this fair? He rapes me, and then she throws me out. And all the time, while she's screeching away, he sits there, pale as death. And all the promises he made—before, during, and after—are forgotten.

The next night, my friends and I stole everything that could be moved, but that wasn't the important thing. The important thing was that I had discovered my blooming body, and what could be done with it. If I had nothing to keep it for, I might as well use it, and enticing the "sirs" was the easiest thing in the world. Besides, it made the job of removing things from their households even less dangerous.

In the life I lived, there was always more to learn. I even learned a foreign language.

"Hey, GI. My name Lisa. Fi' hundred baht one time . . . ten hundred baht all night . . . wery good serwis!"

I do well for myself, and I suppose that I will go on doing so if I can stay out of jail. My hope is that someday I will have saved enough money to return to Nong Bua[3]—that's my village—and find my father and mother and my brother and sister. It has been so long. So long that I feel as though I have been here all my life . . . and yet. You will find this hard to believe, but I still miss those people. I can

---

3.   "Nong Bua," or *nɔ̌ɔng bua*, means "lotus pond." It seems likely that the author chose this name because the lotus can grow in the foulest swamp or ditch, sending up a stalk from which a perfectly white blossom will open. Thus, it is a symbol of purity. (It is also a symbol for the Buddha.)

scarcely remember them . . . and yet! If I have forgotten their faces, I have not forgotten the warmth and love that they, and only they, ever gave to me. I still remember how it felt, that little heaven of my childhood, even though we had nothing to eat and a house falling down on our heads. My little heaven of warmth and love, my home in Nong Bua.

You know, I never wanted a dazzling life or to shine like a star in the heavens. I would have been content to live like a mote of dust on the face of the earth, amidst the clods of dirt and grains of sand. It is what I was born for.

One day, I will go home. But I won't go back poor. I'll have made enough money, so that I will never have to return to Bangkok. And if I have a child, that child will run and play happily in the fields. My child will not be a slave.

Now I understand my father's words. Sometimes we must sell our life to give life.

But, tell me . . . what is it that makes one person's life valuable and another's worthless? Can you explain to me why some people are so rich that they can buy even another human being? Please, tell me why others are so poor that they must sell the lives of their children. Or sell themselves. Is it karma? I don't think so. Because if it is karma—why, what great sinners many of the people in this country must have been in their past lives! Never mind. Probably, you don't understand the riddle either.

I can't talk anymore. Here comes one of my best customers. See him? He pays very well. Don't tell anyone I said that, though, because he's mine! Remember what I said about going home. Because I'm going to do it. I don't know how, not yet—but someday, Malisa is going back to Nong Bua.

Heaven

"Don't be afraid, child. Miss Malisa is going to take you to Bangkok and help you to get a good job. Think of it! You will have lots of money and pretty clothes to wear. Good food to eat every day.

"Why? Because Miss Malisa was once a little girl just like you. She wants to help you, just the way someone once helped her."

O   O   PREECHAPOUL BOONCHUAY AND
"A MOTE OF DUST ON THE FACE
OF THE EARTH"

During the early 1970s, Preechapoul Boonchuay was a member of the group of writers whose work focused on social inequities and the lives of the poor. He was a photographer before he was a writer, and today is the owner of a photography business in Songkhla, in southern Thailand. Preechapoul has not written fiction for several years.

"A Mote of Dust on the Face of the Earth" was chosen for the anthology because it is a good example, and in some ways a typical one, of stories about girls and young women who find themselves on a path that leads inexorably from poverty to prostitution. If there are villains in this story, they are represented by faceless members of the middle and upper classes who not only knowingly allow and contribute to social and economic inequities in Thai society but also take cruel advantage of the poor.[1]

The subject matter dates this story, which is nearly twenty years old. Generally speaking, prostitution is *less* represented in literature since the dimensions of the AIDS epidemic have become impossible to ignore—and since the prostitution industry has become a national embarrassment. In fact, none of the prize-winning books and stories of the last few years has dealt directly with this serious problem or its causes.

But Preechapoul's story remains current by what it reveals, directly and indirectly, about the circumstances that have made this unfolding tragedy possible.

On her last day at home, after her parents have decided to sell her, Ee-Saa's father holds her close, tells her that he loves her: "He pushed her gently from him then, and his dark, sad eyes studied her carefully, as if he were looking straight into her heart.

"'I know that you wonder why you must be the one to go. It is because your elder brother must help me, and your little sister is too young. You are the only one who is able to help us all, Saa. Perhaps

---

1.   At the end of the story, Malisa is clearly consorting with American soldiers, a feature of the era during which this story was written. Although prostitution did thrive when American and other soldiers were stationed in Thailand, it was during the 1980s, with the boom in sex tourism, financed and promoted largely by indigenous businessmen in the sex industry, that the numbers of both female and male Thai prostitutes grew into the hundreds of thousands.

you will not be too angry with me . . .' Her father swallowed hard. He then began to speak rapidly, striving to control his voice."

This passage displays two common themes in novels and stories about women. First, the theme of the father who neglects, gives away, or simply absolves himself of responsibility for a daughter who never, ever blames him: from Ploy in M. R. Kukrit Pramoj's *Four Reigns* to Khunying Kirati in *Behind the Painting* to Wimon in *People of Quality* to Saa in this story. In these works, a father dearly wishes that he could save his beloved daughter from suffering, but he cannot —through no fault of his own. Second, the theme of the last resort, the family sacrificing a daughter so that the rest of the family can survive. "[S]omeday," Saa's father says, "you will understand." And she does, more or less: "Now I understand my father's words. Sometimes we must sell our life to give life." The latter theme has been challenged during the past two decades by well-documented evidence that an increasing number of families sell their children, mostly girls, into prostitution, not to "give life," but to get television sets, VCRs, and motorcycles.

This anthology is not the place for an extended essay on Thai prostitution or the AIDS epidemic, but these issues are so important to the very survival of hundreds of thousands of Thai women (that number represents only the most direct victims, the prostitutes, not to mention other women and children infected by men infected by prostitutes) that I feel some mention of available, relevant books and articles is appropriate.[2] Marjorie Muecke's 1992 article "Mother Sold Food, Daughter Sells Her Body: The Cultural Continuity of Prostitution" contains a wealth of carefully documented information on the current status of Thai prostitution and also on its roots, from the fifteenth century through the twentieth. Muecke writes:

2.   Books that are partially or largely concerned with these subjects, and that have not already been cited, include: Cynthia Enloe, *Bananas, Beaches and Bases: Making Feminist Sense of International Politics* (Berkeley: University of California Press), 1990; Suzanne Thorbek, *Voices from the City: Women of Bangkok* (London and Atlantic Highlands, New Jersey: Zed Books, 1987); Sanitsuda Ekachai, *Behind the Smile: Voices of Thailand* (Bangkok: Thai Development Support Committee and Post Publishing, 1991); and Cleo Odzer, *Patpong Sisters: An American Woman's View of the Bangkok Sex World* (New York: Arcade Publishing, Blue Moon Books, 1994). Odzer's book, which is written for the general reader but contains a considerable amount of reliable data, is based upon the research for her Ph.D. dissertation in anthropology, the subject of which is "the Bangkok economy of sex."

Current estimates are that in the Thai population of 55 million, there are 80,000 . . . to one million women working as prostitutes . . . plus perhaps some 20,000 girls under the age of 15. . . . An unknown number of Thai women work abroad as prostitutes; estimates for Japan alone are some 10,000. A decade ago, it was estimated that, on a per capita basis, twice as many women were prostitutes as men were monks. For Thai Buddhists, this ratio starkly juxtaposes daughters and sons as moral opposites, daughters being of the flesh and "this-worldly," and sons, detached from corporeal desire, so closer to the Buddhist ideal of "otherworldliness."[3]

Obviously, the fact that such tremendous numbers of Thai girls and women have become prostitutes during the past decade does not constitute a tragedy only for them.[4] Because of the current, critical extent of the HIV/AIDS crisis, girls like Saa have an impact on the life of society at large that prostitutes never had before. Despite the enormous figures cited in relation to both prostitution and the AIDS epidemic, prostitution remains illegal in Thailand. As of this writing, the potential positive and negative aspects of legalization are the subject of widespread debate.

At the beginning of Preechapoul's story, Saa is a frightened child who is forced to leave her weeping mother's arms, and who is taken to Bangkok, not to work as a prostitute, but, in the words of "the lady" who has paid the girl's sorrowing and indebted father for her, to "make her fortune." She will help Saa to find a job, and Saa will then be able to send money home to her family every month. The woman does not take Saa to a brothel but to a busy restaurant where she is put to work as a slave (no more accurate word is possible). This experience is more typical of the 1970s, when the story was written, than

3. Marjorie Muecke, "Mother Sold Food, Daughter Sells Her Body: The Cultural Continuity of Prostitution," *Social Science Medicine* 35, no. 7 (1992): 892. Not surprisingly, estimates of the number of prostitutes are the subject of intense debate; the consensus appears to fall around the 700,000 mark.

4. There is also a sizable male prostitution industry, in which many young boys are involved. Indeed, child prostitution has greatly increased since the onset of the AIDS epidemic, because many men believe that they will not get AIDS from children, especially young, sexually inexperienced children. In Bangkok, places of refuge for these boys and girls include the Human Development Centre at the Klong Toey slum, where for twenty-five years Father Joseph H. Maier has worked to provide over twenty kindergartens city wide, food, and medical care for children. In 1995, a new addition will be built: a hospice for AIDS victims, including child prostitutes, some of whom were students at the kindergartens a very few years before. (The word "refuge," above, must be qualified by the fact that no one at the Human Development Centre has the authority to keep children at the center, or to prevent their exploitation by their own parents.)

of the 1990s, when the journey from home to brothel is likely to be more direct. Saa works in the restaurant from before dawn until late at night, when she falls asleep covered with rags in a rat-infested alley. Prostitution comes later. The product of her lengthy education in survival is Lisa, her own creation, the woman who once was the girl named Saa. If Saa is dead, Lisa survives very well indeed. She is fashionable and has even learned to speak English ("Fi' hundred baht, very good serwis"). Lisa is always a few steps ahead of the game and the law. She is no flower of womanhood; she is, without question, a true lioness in her urban jungle.

In telling this tale, Saa/Lisa reveals quite a few of the circumstances and attitudes that have been essential to the growth of the prostitution industry, among them, "[t]he important thing was that I had discovered my blooming body, and what could be done with it. If I had nothing to keep it for, I might as well use it, and enticing the 'sirs' was the easiest thing in the world." Virginity is a commodity; once a young woman has lost this critical component of her value (willingly or otherwise), once her body is no longer "pure" (and therefore desirable), "[she] might as well use it." Saa's remark is reminiscent of Boonrawd's angry, resentful words to her mother in the excerpt from Botan's *That Woman's Name Is Boonrawd*: "Face the facts, Ma. What are my prospects? No Thai man wants a woman who's been used. . . . Any Thai man who would marry me would know he could walk out any time, and nobody would think worse of him, because I was spoiled when he got me." Although it may seem an unimaginable leap, from the loss of virginity before marriage to the decision that prostitution now represents a logical choice, in fact this happens. There is little reason for a woman to give up prostitution if she is not only already "ruined" but also lacks the education or the skills to get any kind of employment that would pay even a fraction of what she earns in the sex trade.[5]

Saa tells herself that someday she will return to her village: "One day, I will go home. But I won't go back poor. I'll have made enough money so that I will never have to return to Bangkok." This is a con-

---

5. Father Maier told me that it is "all but impossible to convince a woman to leave the trade when she has no self-esteem and really doesn't care if she dies. There is often a strong element of suicidal intent—or just anger, which leads to the same conclusion—in the attitude of many prostitutes I talk with" (telephone conversation with author, August 10, 1991).

stant refrain heard by people who work with prostitutes; but of the relatively few women who do return to rural villages, even those who buy land or start a business, the most commonly expressed dreams, most apparently return to the trade within a year or two, and the life— the friends and contacts—that they know best. Their village neigh-bors' perceptions of them and behavior toward them are rarely a fac-tor in this decision. Prostitutes who go home are not treated badly; on the contrary, they are respected for their wealth and for the fact that they have helped to support their families. (Coming home sick with AIDS, however, is quite another matter.)

In the last few years, some scholars have suggested another view of prostitution. Reynolds writes:

> while feminist scholarship in the West during the 1960s and early 1970s . . . portrayed women as victims of patriarchal structures and values, there has been a shift towards studies of difference, the social and cultural construction of gender, and woman's agency that has eclipsed the "woman as victim" paradigm. Research now emphasizes that in some respects sex work for women is of the same order as working in the fields or in the market-place, namely, it is in keep-ing with an ideal of woman as mother to serve and enhance the well-being of the family. . . . Remitting income from sex work to parents expresses filial piety and the Buddhist value of *metta* (loving-kindness). The circumstances in which the debt bondage is arranged problemetizes [sic] but does not negate woman's agency.[6]

I find it difficult to imagine a prostitute taking comfort from the knowl-edge that she has agency when she also has AIDS.

"A Mote of Dust on the Face of the Earth" was written before this plague came to Thailand. It is no secret that the Thai government was slow to respond in an organized way to the rapid spread of the HIV virus, and that during the first, critical years of the epidemic, HIV/AIDS was considered almost exclusively a disease of foreigners and homo-sexuals (a response that has by no means been limited to Thailand). However, there is now a widespread network of people representing the medical community, relevant government agencies, various non-governmental and foreign-based organizations, and some influential monks who have provided hospice or other services to people with AIDS; and there is royal patronage of some aspects of this effort.

6.   Reynolds, op. cit., 79. (See introduction, note 5.)

Whether it will amount to too little, too late, as some Thai physicians have been predicting for a decade, remains to be seen.

The Thai government is increasingly exasperated by such incidents as the publication in Japan, in 1995, of a *Handbook for Prostitution in Thailand*, which sold out its first printing of fifteen thousand copies almost overnight. The Thai Foreign Minister Thaksin Shinawatra protested that "[s]uch a book is very damaging to Thailand. We welcome tourists, but not the sex tourists. They are not constructive."[7]

Yet sex tourists were quite welcome throughout the 1980s and continue to represent a considerable percentage of tourism overall. A 1983 pamphlet from the Women's Information Center in Bangkok gives the following figures on the increase in tourism in Thailand from the 1960s to the 1980s (table 1):

Table 1   Tourism in Thailand (in thousands)

	1965	1976	1979	1980
Number of tourists	250	1,100	1,600	2,200

SOURCE: Cleo Odzer, *Patpong Sisters: An American Woman's View of the Bangkok Sex World* (New York: Arcade Publishing, Blue Moon Books, 1994), 23.

Even the government does not pretend that these numbers represent foreign families touring Thailand's temples, museums, and beaches. This problem has been increasing exponentially for over a decade and will not be solved without the determination, at all levels of society and especially at the highest levels of government, to take strong, public actions against this hugely profitable industry, against the sex tours and the corruption that not only allows but encourages the sex trade, with its wholesale sexual exploitation and destruction, through disease, of ever-increasing numbers of Thais, most of whom are women.

7.   "Handbook Irks Thais," *San Francisco Examiner*, January 22, 1995, A-6.

Appendix

The following list is based upon information in David K. Wyatt, *Thailand: A Short History* (New Haven: Yale University Press, 1984), 313. Designations of the kings as "Rama I, Rama II," and so on date from the reign of King Vachiravudh (1910–25). They are all so designated here, retroactively in the case of the first five kings, in accordance with current usage. All inclusive dates denote the reigns of these monarchs.

Rama I   Prabatsomdej Phra Phutthayotfachulalok (1782–1809)

Rama II   Phrabatsomdej Phra Phutthalertlanaphalai (1809–24)

Rama III   Phrabatsomdej Phra Nangklaochaoyuhua (1824–51)

Rama IV   King Mongkut (1851–68)

Rama V   King Chulalongkorn (1868–1910)

Rama VI   King Vachiravudh (1910–25)

Rama VII   King Prachatipok (1925–35)

Rama VIII   King Ananda (1935–46)

Rama IX   King Phumipol Adulyadej (1946–)

Bibliography

WORKS IN ENGLISH

Anderson, Benedict R. O'G., and Ruchira Mendiones, eds. and trans. *In the Mirror: Literature and Politics in Siam in the Modern Era*. Bangkok: Editions Duang Kamol, 1985.

Batson, Benjamin A. *The End of the Absolute Monarchy in Siam*. Singapore: Oxford University Press, 1984.

Boontawee. *See* Kampoon.

Botan. *Letters from Thailand*. Translated by Susan Fulop [Kepner]. Bangkok: Duang Kamol, 1977. Originally published as *Jòt mǎay jàak muang thay* (จดหมายจากเมืองไทย), (Bangkok: Duang Kamol, 1969).

Bowie, Katherine A., ed. and trans. *Voices from the Thai Countryside: The Short Stories of Samruam Singh*. Madison: Center for Southeast Asian Studies, University of Wisconsin, 1991.

Chatsumarn Kabilsingh. *Thai Women in Buddhism*. Berkeley: Parallax Press, 1991.

Chetana Nagavajara. "Literature in Thai Life: Reflections of a Native." Paper presented at the Fifth International Conference on Thai Studies, School of Oriental and African Studies, University of London, July 1993.

———. "Unsex Me Here: An Oriental's Plea for Gender Reconciliation." *Literary Studies, East and West / Gender and Culture in Literature and Film, East and West: Issues of Perception and Interpretation*, vol. 9 (1994).

Chitkasem. *See* Manas.

Cholasueks. *See* Sukanya.

Darunee Tantiwiramanondh, and Shashi Pandey. "The Status and Roles of Thai Women in the Pre-Modern Period: A Historical and Cultural Perspective." *Sojourn*, vol. 2, no. 1 (February 1987).

Dhammachoti. *See* Ussiri.

The Dhammapada. Translated by Irving Babbitt. New York: New Directions, 1965.

Dok Mai Sot. *A Secret Past*. Translated by Ted Strehlow. Ithaca, N.Y.: Southeast Asia Publications, Cornell University, 1992.

Ekachai. *See* Sanitsuda.

Enloe, Cynthia. *Bananas, Beaches and Bases: Making Feminist Sense of International Politics*. Berkeley: University of California Press, 1990.

Gross, Rita M. *Buddhism after Patriarchy*. Albany, N.Y.: State University of New York Press, 1993.

"Handbook Irks Thais." *San Francisco Examiner,* January 22, 1995.

Kabilsingh. *See* Chatsumarn.

Kampoon Boontawee. *A Child of the Northeast.* Translated by Susan Fulop Kepner. Bangkok: Duang Kamol, 1987. Originally published as *Lûuk iisǎan* (ลูก อีสาน), (Bangkok: Duang Kamol, 1969).

Karamcheti, Indira. "Cover Stories." *The Women's Review of Books,* vol. 11, no. 4 (January 1994).

Keyes, Charles F. "Mother or Mistress but Never a Monk: Buddhist Notions of Female Gender in Thailand." *American Ethnologist,* vol. 11, no. 2 (1984).

Keyes, Charles F., Laurel Kendall, and Helen Hardacre. *Asian Visions of Authority: Religion and the Modern States of East and Southeast Asia.* Honolulu: University of Hawaii Press, 1994.

Khin Thitsa. *Providence and Prostitution: Image and Reality for Women in Buddhist Thailand.* London: CHANGE International Reports: Women and Society, 1980.

Manas Chitkasem. "The Development of Political and Social Consciousness in Thai Short Stories." In *The Short Story in South East Asia: Aspects of a Genre,* edited by Jeremy H. C. S. Davidson and Helen Cordell. Collected Papers in Oriental and African Studies. London: School of Oriental and African Studies, University of London, 1982.

Masavisut. *See* Nitaya.

Mattani Rutnin. "The Change in the Role of Women in Contemporary Thai Literature." *East Asian Cultural Studies,* vol. 17, no. 1–4 (1978).

———. *Modern Thai Literature: The Process of Modernization and the Transformation of Values.* Bangkok: Thammasat University Press, 1988.

Morell, David, and Chai-anan Samudavanija. *Political Conflict in Thailand: Reform, Reaction, Revolution.* Cambridge, Mass.: Oegelschlager, Gunn and Hain, 1981.

Muecke, Marjorie. "Mother Sold Food, Daughter Sells Her Body: The Cultural Continuity of Prostitution." *Social Science Medicine,* vol. 35, no. 7 (1992).

Nagavajara. *See* Chetana.

National Identity Board. *Women in Literature: Book 1.* Bangkok: Office of the Prime Minister, 1987.

Nitaya Masavisut, and Kwandee Attavavutichai. "The Development of the Thai Novel." Paper written during the 1980s under the auspices of P.E.N. International Thailand Centre.

Nithinand Yorsaengrat. "Sriburapha: A Time for Revision." *Focus* (Bangkok), June 15, 1994.

Odzer, Cleo. *Patpong Sisters: An American Woman's View of the Bangkok Sex World.* New York: Arcade Publishing, Blue Moon Books, 1994.

Phillips, Herbert P. *Modern Thai Literature: An Ethnographic Interpretation.* Honolulu: University of Hawaii Press, 1987.

Rahula, Walpole. *What the Buddha Taught.* 2d enlarged ed. New York: Grove Press, 1974. Reprint, New York: Grove Weidenfeld, n.d.

Reynolds, Craig J. "Predicaments of Modern Thai History." *South East Asian Research*, vol. 2, no. 1. (March 1994).

Rutnin. *See* Mattani.

Sanitsuda Ekachai. *Behind the Smile: Voices of Thailand.* Bangkok: Thai Development Support Committee and Post Publishing, 1991.

Siburapha [Sri Burapha]. *Behind the Painting and Other Stories.* Translated by David Smyth. Singapore: Oxford University Press, 1990.

Sidaoru'ang [Sri Dao Ruang]. *A Drop of Glass and Other Stories.* Translated by Rachel Harrison. Bangkok: Duang Kamol, 1994.

Sivarak. *See* Sulak.

Sri Burapha. *See* Siburapha.

Sri Dao Ruang. "The Letter You Never Received." Translated by Susan Fulop Kepner. *two lines: The Stanford Journal of Translation* (fall 1995): 135–42. Originally published as "Jòt mǎay thǔng phûu thîi mây ráp" (จดหมายถึงผู้ที่ไม่รับ).

Sukanya Cholasueks [Krisna Asoksin, pseud.]. "On Being a Novelist in Thailand." *Tenggara*, vol. 19 (1986). An excerpt of her novel *Rʉa manút* is included in this work under the title *This Human Vessel.*

Sukhontha. *See* Suwanee.

Sulak Sivarak. *Siamese Resurgence.* Bangkok: Asian Cultural Forum on Development, 1985.

Surangkanang, K. *The Prostitute.* Translated by David Smyth. Singapore: Oxford University Press, 1994.

Suwanee Sukhontha. "On a Cloudy Morning." Translated by Susan Fulop Kepner. *Tenggara*, vol. 29 (1990). Originally published as "Wan thîi dèɛd sǔay" (วันที่แดดดสวย).

Tantiwiramanondh. *See* Darunee.

Thai Women. Bangkok: National Commission on Women's Affairs, Office of the Prime Minister, 1993.

Thongchai Winichakul. *Siam Mapped: A History of the Geo-Body of a Nation.* Honolulu: University of Hawaii Press, 1994.

Thorbek, Suzanne. *Voices from the City: Women of Bangkok.* London and Atlantic Highlands, New Jersey: Zed Books, 1987.

Ussiri Dhammachoti. "The Dancing Girl." Translated by Susan Fulop Kepner. In *The HarperCollins World Reader: The Modern World,* edited by Mary Ann Caws and Christopher Prendergast. New York: HarperCollins, 1994.

———. *Kuntong, You Will Return at Dawn.* 3d ed. Thai with English translations by Chamnongsri L. Rutnin. Bangkok: Kaw Kai Press, 1987.

Vella, Walter F. *Chaiyo! King Vachiravudh and the Development of Thai Nationalism.* Honolulu: University of Hawaii Press, 1978.

Wenk, Klaus. *Thai Literature: An Introduction.* Bangkok: White Lotus, 1995.

Winichakul. *See* Thongchai.

Yorsaengrat. *See* Nithinand.

WORKS IN THAI

A complete bibliographic entry in Thai follows each item in English.

Anchan. "Mɔ̂ɔ thîi khùt mây ɔ̀ɔk" (included in this work under the title "A Pot That Scouring Will Not Save"). In *Anmanii hὲεŋ chiiwít*. Bangkok: Khom Bang Press, 1990. อัญชัน "หม้อที่ขูดไม่ออก" ใน รวมเรื่องสั้น *อัญมณีแห่งชีวิต* คม บาง กรุงเทพ ฯ 2533

Ankhan Kalyanapongse. *Baaŋkɔ̀ɔk kὲεw kam sŭan rŭu nírâat Nakhɔn Sĭi Thamarâat.* Bangkok: Sathian Koset Foundation, 1978. อังคาร กัลยาณพงศ์ บางกอกแก้วกำศรวล หรือ นิราศนครศรีธรรมราช กรุงเทพ ฯ มูลนิธิเสฐียรโกเศศ 2521

Asoksin. *See* Krisna.

Boonchuay. *See* Preechapoul.

Boonlua. *Thútìyá wísèt.* Bangkok: Prae Pittaya, 1968. บุญเหลือ *ทุติยะวิเศษ* กรุงเทพ ฯ แพร่ พิทยา 2511

Botan. *Phûu yĭŋ khon nán chŭu Bunrɔ̀ɔt* (excerpt included in this work under the title *That Woman's Name Is Boonrawd*). Bangkok: Chomromdek, [1980s]. โบตั๋น *ผู้หญิงคนนั้นชื่อบุญรอด* ชมรมเด็ก กรุงเทพ [1980s]

Corelli, Marie. *Khwaam phayaabàat: chabàp sŏmbuun.* Translated by V. Vinc-chayakul with an introduction. Bangkok: Dok Yaa, 1987. มารี คอเรลลี *ความพยาบาท* ว. วินิจฉัยกุล แปล และ เรียบ เรียง กรุงเทพ ฯ ดอกหญ้า 2530

Devakul. *See* Subha.

Dhammachoti. *See* Ussiri.

Dok Mai Sot. *Phûu dii* (excerpt included in this work under the title *People of Quality*). Bangkok: Prae Pittaya, 1970. ดอก ไม้ สด *ผู้ดี* กรุงเทพ ฯ 2513

Jantaraprasut. *See* Naren.

Jiranan Pitpreecha. *Bay máy thîi hăay pay.* Bangkok: Saeng Daw, 1990. จิระนันท์ พิตรปรีชา *ใบไม้ที่หายไป* กวีนิพนธ์แห่งชีวิต กรุงเทพ ฯ แสงดาว 2533

Kalyanapongse. *See* Ankhan.

Krisna Asoksin. *Rŭa manút* (excerpt included in this work under the title *This Human Vessel*). Bangkok: Chokechai Thewet, 1970. กฤษณา อโศกสิน *เรือ มนุษย์* กรุงเทพฯ โชกชัย เทเวศร์ 2513

Manop Thanomsri. "Ii làa nɔ́ɔy" (included in this work under the title "Greenie"). In *Thaaŋ săay rúŋ.* Bangkok: Kradaad Saa, 1984. มานพ ถนอมศรี "อีหล่าน้อย" ใน รวม เรื่อง สั้น สายรุ้ง กรุงเทพ ฯ กระดาษสา 2527

Naren Jantaraprasut. *Wípâak rŭaŋ sân raaŋwan siiraay pii 2533 ... "Anmanii hὲεŋ chiiwít" / Katǎw plùak tua aksɔ̌n khɔ̌ɔŋ ... Anchan* (this work crit-icizes the short story "A Pot That Scouring Will Not Save," which is in-cluded in this work). Bangkok: Klum Saayleen Wannakaam Suksaa, 1990. เนรนทร์ จันทรประสูตร *วิพากษ์เรื่องสั้นรางวัลซีไรท์ปี 2533 ... อัญมณีแห่ง ชีวิต กะเทาะเปลือกตัวอักษรของ... อัญชัน* กลุ่ม ไสเลน วรรณกรรมศึกษา 2533

Phûuyĭŋ bon nâa kradàat. Bangkok: N.p., n.d. *ผู้หญิงบนหน้ากระดาษ.* This special publication was distributed at a conference in February 1991, in recogni-tion of the one hundredth anniversary of Thai women's magazines. It in-cludes essays by leading Thai writers and journalists. No editor is given. For further information, contact the author.

Pitpreecha. *See* Jiranan.

Prabhassorn Sevikul. *Sim bây.* Bangkok: Wannakaam Thai, 1984. ประภัสสร
เสวิกุล *ซิ่มใบ้* วรรกรรมไทย กรุงเทพ ฯ 2527

Preechapoul Boonchuay. "Thulii pradàp din" (included in this work under
the title "A Mote of Dust on the Face of the Earth"). In *Phét nám ngaam,*
edited by Suchat Sawatsri. Bangkok: Duang Kamol, 1980; produced by *Lôok
nǎngsɯ̌ɯ.* ปรีชาพล บุญช่วย "ธุลีประดับดิน" ใน *เพชรน้ำงาม* สุชาติ สวัสดิ์ศรี บรรณาธิการ
โลกหนังสือ/ดวงกมล กรุงเทพ 2523

Sevikul. *See* Prabhassorn.

Sri Burapha. *Khâang lǎng phâap.* Bangkok: Baankit, [1930s]. See Works in English, "Siburapha," above for information on the English translation by
David Smyth. ศรี บูรพา *ข้างหลังภาพ* กรุงเทพ ฯ บรรณกิจ [1930s]

Sri Dao Ruang. *Bàt prachaachon.* Bangkok: Met Sai, 1984. ศรีดาวเรือง *บัตรประชาชน*
กรุงเทพ ฯ เม็ดทราย 2527

————. *Matsii.* Bangkok: Love and Live Press, 1990. ศรีดาวเรือง มัทรี กรุงเทพ ฯ
ลีฟ แอนด์ เลอฟ 2533

————. "Nay wannii khɔ̌ɔng Sǐi Daaw Ruang." Interview by Wan Pen. *Prɛɛw,*
vol. 14, no. 335 (August 1993). วันเพ็ญ "ในวันนี้ของ ศรีดาวเรือง" ใน *แพรว* 14: 335
(เดือนสิงหาคม 2536)

Subha Devakul. "Mɯ̂a təə pen mia lǔang" (included in this work under
the title "When She Was a Major Wife"). In *Nay Baang sùan khɔ̌ɔng
hǔa jay.* Bangkok: Praphansan, 1978. สุภาว์ เทวกุล "เมื่อเธอเป็นเมียหลวง" ใน
ในบางส่วนของหัว ใจ กรุงเทพ ฯ ประพันธ์สาร์น 2521

Sukhontha. *See* Suwanee.

Suwanee Sukhontha. "Nguu rɔ́ɔng hây dɔ̀ɔk máy yím" (included in this work
under the title "Snakes Weep, Flowers Smile"). In *Nǎaw khâw pay thǔng
hǔa jay.* Bangkok: Praphansan, 1974. สุวรรณี สุคนธา "งูร้องให้ดอกไม้ยิ้ม" ใน
หนาวเข้าไปถึงหัวใจ ประพันธ์สาร์น กรุงเทพ ฯ 2517

Thanomsri. *See* Manop.

Ussiri Dhammachoti. "Naang ram" (included in this work under the title "The
Dancing Girl"). In *Mɯ̌an thalee jà mii jâw khɔ̌ɔng.* Bangkok: Kam Kaew Press,
1981. อัศศิริ ธรรมโชติ "นางรำ" ใน *เหมือนทะเลจะมีเจ้า* ของ กรุงเทพ ฯ กำแก้ว 2524

Wat Wanlayangkul. *Nakhon haeng duang daw* (or, Nakhon hɛ̀ɛng duang daaw)
(City of Stars). Bangkok: Khon Wannakam, 1984. วัตน์ วรรลยางกูร นครแห่งดวงดาว
กรุงเทพ ฯ คนวรรณกรรม 2527

Suggested Reading

Chatr Kobjitti. *The Judgement*. Translated by Laurie Maund. Bangkok: Laurie Maund, 1983; distributed in Thailand by Thammasat University Book Store.

Chetana Nagavajara. "Parody as Translation: The Case of Phaibun Wongthed." *Crossroads*, vol. 6, no. 2 (1991).

———. "A Persistence of Music Drama: Reflections on Modern Thai Theater." *Tenggara*, vol. 23 (1989).

Chitkasem. *See* Manas.

Darunee Tantiwiramanondh, and Shashi Ranjan Pandey. *By Women, for Women: A Study of Women's Organizations in Thailand*. Singapore: Institute of Southeast Asian Studies, 1991.

Draskau, Jennifer, ed. and trans. *Taw and Other Stories*. Hong Kong and Singapore: Heinemann Educational Books (Asia), 1975.

Khammaan Khonkhai. *The Teachers of Mad Dog Swamp*. Translated by Gehan Wijeyewardene. Santa Lucia, Queensland: University of Queensland Press, 1982.

Khamsing Srinawk. *The Politician and Other Stories*. 2d ed. Translated by Domnern Garden. Singapore: Oxford University Press, 1991; distributed in Thailand by Duang Kamol.

Khonkhai. *See* Khamman.

Kobjitti. *See* Chatr.

Kriengkraipetch, Suvanna, and Larry E. Smith. *Value Conflicts in Thai Society: Agonies of Change Seen in Short Stories*. Bangkok: Social Research Institute, Chulalongkorn University in cooperation with the East West Center, University of Hawaii, 1992.

M. R. Kukrit Pramoj. *Four Reigns*. Translated by Tulachandra. Bangkok: Duang Kamol, 1981.

Limpichard. *See* Maitree.

Maitree Limpichard. *Thai Short Stories: The Pinches*. Translated by Lamoon Rattakorn and edited by Saul Pollack. Bangkok: Norn, n.d.

Manas Chitkasem, and Andrew Turton, eds. *Thai Constructions of Knowledge*. London: School of Oriental and African Studies, University of London, 1991.

Masavisut. *See* Nitaya.

Moore, Cornelia N., and Lucy Lower, eds. *Translation, East and West: A Cross-Cultural Approach*. Honolulu: College of Languages, Linguistics and Literature, and the East West Center, University of Hawaii, 1992.

Nagavajara. *See* Chetana.

National Identity Board. *Treasury of Thai Literature: The Modern Period.* Bangkok: Office of the Prime Minister, 1988.

Nitaya Masavisut. "The Translation of Literary Works and Cross-Cultural Understanding." In *International Workshop on Translation.* Bangkok: Foundation for the Promotion of Social Sciences and Humanities Textbook Project, n.d.

Nitaya Masavisut, George Simson, and Larry E. Smith, eds. *Gender and Culture in Literature and Film, East and West: Issues of Perception and Interpretation.* Honolulu: College of Languages, Linguistics and Literature, and the East West Center, University of Hawaii, 1994.

Pira Sudham. *Monsoon Country.* Bangkok: Shire Books, 1988.

———. *People of Esarn.* Bangkok: Shire Books, 1988.

———. *Siamese Drama and Other Stories from Thailand.* Bangkok: Siam Media International Books, 1983.

Pramoj. *See* Kukrit, M. R.

Reynolds, Craig J. *Thai Radical Discourse: The Real Face of Thai Feudalism Today.* Ithaca, N.Y.: Southeast Asian Program, Cornell University, 1987.

Ruentruethai Sajaphan. "The Thai Women in the Novels of Women Novelists." Translated by Suchitra Chongsatitvatana. *Tenggara,* vol. 25 (1990).

Sajaphan. *See* Ruentruthai.

Senanan. *See* Wibha.

Srinawk. *See* Khamsing.

Sudham. *See* Pira.

Tantiwiramanondh. *See* Darunee.

Thai P.E.N. Anthology: Short Stories and Poems of Social Consciousness. Bangkok: P.E.N. International Thailand Centre, 1984.

Ussiri Dhammachoti. "Under the Bridge." Translated by Susan Fulop Kepner. *Tenggara,* vol. 31 (1993).

Wibha Senanan. *The Genesis of the Thai Novel.* Bangkok: Thai Watana Panich, 1975.

Sources of Publications

Sources of Thai books are given, if known. Books printed more than three or four years ago may be out of print and difficult to locate. Some may be found in libraries at universities that have collections of Thai books; these include Cornell University, Northern Illinois University, the University of Michigan, the University of Washington, the University of Wisconsin, or the University of California, Berkeley.

Books published in Thailand may be ordered from the following stores:

Duang Kamol
GPO 427
Bangkok 10501
Thailand
Telephone: (662) 231-6335
Fax: (662) 247-1033

Suriwong Book Centre, Ltd.
54 / 15 Sri-Donchai Road
Chiang Mai 50000
Thailand
Telephone: (665) 328-1052
Fax: (665) 327-1902

Thammasat University Bookstore
Thammasat University
Tha Phra Jun
Bangkok
Thailand

Tenggara, a journal of Southeast Asian literature, may be ordered by writing to the following address:

Tenggara
Yayasan Penataran Ilmu
Tingkat Tiga
Wisma Mirama
50460 Kuala Lumpur
Malaysia

The addresses of some of the publishers that appear in the bibliography and suggested reading are as follows:

CHANGE International Reports
Parnell House
25 Wilton Road
London SW 1
United Kingdom

Chomromdek
323 Moo 1
Soi Theerapat
Pracha Uthit Road
Bangkok 10140
Thailand

The Foundation for the Promotion of Social Sciences and Humanities Textbook Project
413 / 38 Arun Amarin Road
Bangkok 10700
Thailand

Institute of Southeast Asian Studies
Heng Mui Keng Terrace
Pasir Panjang
Singapore 0511

Laurie Maund
221 / 10 Soi Lang Withyalai Kroo Petchburi
Petchburi Road
Bangkok 10400
Thailand

Klum Saayleen Wannakaam Suksaa
656 / 679 Soi 32
Muubaan Khae Ha Nakhorn 3
Thanon Phattanakan Khwaeng Suan Luang
Phrakhanong
Bangkok 10250
Thailand

Norn
910 Soi Song Peenong
Tambol Samrong
Samutprakarn

Bangkok
Thailand

Shire Books
GPO Box 1534
Bangkok 10501
Thailand

Books by Ankhan Kalyanapongse are available from:

Suksit Siam
303 / 7 Soi Soi Santhipap
Naret Road
Bangkok 10500
Thailand

Index

Compositor:	Integrated Composition Systems
Text:	10/13 Palatino
Display:	Palatino
Printer and Binder:	BookCrafters, Inc.